UPSHUR,
HARD JUSTICE

OTIS MORPHEW

Order this book online at www.trafford.com
or email orders@trafford.com

Most Trafford titles are also available at major online book retailers.

Printed in the United States of America.

ISBN: 978-1-4907-5288-4 (sc)
ISBN: 978-1-4907-5287-7 (e)

Trafford rev. 12/18/2014

www.trafford.com
North America & international
toll-free: 1 888 232 4444 (USA & Canada)
fax: 812 355 4082

PROLOGUE

It was not to have taken more than a month to escort three escapees from Shreveport, Louisiana to Fort Smith, Arkansas, a routine, yet tiring job for Billy Upshur and Rodney Taylor. But in 1880 nothing was ever, just routine, and this job had been no different. They did, however, deliver their cargo, as well as three extra confederates to Isaac Parker, even stayed for the hanging before taking the stage back to Paris, Texas.

It had been a memorable trip for them both, as Rodney had almost been killed in a fall, which left him with an un-repairable shoulder injury, further adding to his reason for tending his resignation as a United States Marshal, a decision he had made before ever finishing the job at hand.

Billy Upshur, well, he did what he had always done, sided his friend in a job that he'd had a gut-feeling about from the start,…and that feeling had turned out to be right! Once again, he was to use his prowess with a gun to bring about the end result.

Both were relieved, and thankful that Rodney's last assignment as Peace Officer was over, especially after what they had been through,…and even though the stage coach was overly cramped at times, it did, however, beat thirty grueling days in the saddle,…and they both looked forward to being home with their families again.

But once again, nothing is ever just routine in the 1880's, and their homecoming was not to be the expected reunion they were looking forward to. Instead, it would be a nightmare, one that would plunge Upshur into the role of gunfighter again. Because to Upshur, and the rules he lived by, justice must be served!

CHAPTER ONE

The jolting of the stage as it slowed in the heavily rutted street jarred Rodney awake with a yelp of pain in his injured shoulder. Grabbing his arm, he looked across at Billy to find him watching him.

"You okay, Rod?"

"What th' hell did we hit?" He replied, gasping for breath.

"Just th' main street a Clarksville, be home in a few hours."

"None too soon for me!" He grimaced again and gripped at his shoulder.

"Shoulder hurt bad?"

"Hurts like hell!" He said, looking down at his tightly bound arm. "Thought I was fallin' again, tried to move my arm,…bad idea!" He reached the vial of laudanum from his vest's inside pocket and took a swallow, grimacing again from the taste. "Be okay in a minute."

They heard the driver's audible, "Whoaaa, team, whoaaaaa", and the coach came to a shuddering stop with them both looking out at the busy street of Clarksville, Texas, with it's many glass-fronted stores and shops. Unlike Paris, which was only now rebuilding it's downtown area with rock and brick, Clarksville had utilized such material in it's infancy. Some were two, and three storied structures. The Courthouse, which could be seen a block off the square, was made of rock,…obviously carted in from somewhere along the Red River, and Indian Territory. But all in all, Clarksville was a fairly clean, and well laid out business district.

Most all the boardwalks were of wood planking, with covered awnings of the same material. The street was not crowded, but had a few wagons and teams, either leaving town, or coming in. However, the walkways were fairly busy with pedestrian traffic,…and the shops were enjoying business. The hitch-rails, of course, were crowded with saddled horses, all slapping at flies with long tails, and all stood with drooping heads.

"Not a bad little town." Said Rodney, looking back at Billy.

The stage Agent opened the door at that moment. "Hi ya, Gents." He said matter-of-factly. "Ya got time to stretch your legs, if ya want,…outhouse outside th' station's rear door." He nodded and turned to take the mail pouch from the driver as he was climbing down from the seat.

"Fifteen minutes, Marshal." Said the driver, nodding at them before following the agent inside.

"Marshal!" Grinned Rodney as he slid across the seat to the door. "Might never get used to this, Billy," He said as he waited for him to get out.

"Yeah, ya will!" He grinned, turning around to help him out. "Besides, Peter's gonna need some sizeable help with his new job."

"Yeah, well,…that thought alone makes me feel better!" He grunted as he stepped down. "Thanks, Billy….Damn it's hot!...I believe it's hotter'n it was in Arkansas." He said, and looked up at the cloudless sky. "Too hot for th' birds, even!"

"Won't get any cooler standin' out here."

"I know that's right!...Where'd he say that outhouse was?"

They came back inside as the driver was collecting the mail pouch. "You men ready, Marshal?" He asked as they came closer.

"You don't have to call me Marshal anymore, Clayton." Grinned Rodney. "I resigned my post recently."

"Yeah?...Why, what happened?"

"This, for one thing." He said, reaching up to pat his shoulder. "I am officially out a commission!"

"Well I'm sorry to hear that,…Jonas there said they could a used your help, you'd a come through yesterday!"

"Why, what happened yesterday?"

"Sheriff Nooney was shot, and th' killer got away."

"Fucker tried to rob th' bank, he did!" Said the Agent. "Nooney caught 'im red handed, had 'im covered dead to rights, he did!...Man drew and shot Nooney before he could shoot, slickest gunplay I ever did see,…never saw 'im draw!"

"Is Nooney dead?" Asked Rodney.

"They don't expect 'im to live!"

"Sorry to hear it, he's a good man!" Nodded Rodney gloomily.

"Load up, Gents, time to go!" Said the driver as he left.

"Come on, Rod, we couldn't help Nooney anyway."

"Who shot 'im, Jonas, they know who he was?"

"Heard say, his name was Hatcher, I think."

Rodney looked at Billy and shook his head before allowing himself to be ushered back out to the stage.

"You know this, Hatcher, don't ya, Rod?" He asked as he boosted Rodney back inside.

Rodney watched Billy get settled on the opposite seat and close the door before speaking. "No, I don't know 'im, Billy, only from a poster I got in just before we left,…Saw it again after th' hanging, when we went back to th' judge's office."

"You worried about 'im?"

"No, not worried, but he's a bad one, a gunslinger. There's a ten thousand dollar reward on 'im!...I just hope he didn't go to Paris, that's all."

"Likely not." Sighed Billy. "Likely got a posse on his tail!"

"Well he's got nine notches on his gun, ten, if Nooney dies!...Anyway, that's not exactly why I hoped he didn't go to Paris."

"Then why?"

Rodney stared out of the window at the pedestrians along the boardwalk. "No particular reason, Billy."

"You brought it up, Rod, now spit it out!"

"From all I've heard about Wes Hatcher," He said looking back at Billy. "He just could be, the one!...You know?"

Billy frowned at him. "Come on, Rod, you still got that on your mind?"

"Yeah, I do!...Billy, I don't think there's a man alive that can beat you!...I just don't want a take th' chance, that's all!"

"That makes two of us." He replied. "But if it's slated to happen, it will happen, Rod, we can't stop it!"

"We don't have to help it, neither!"

Shaking his head, Billy turned to watch the pedestrian traffic as the coach lumbered forward again.

"I know you're right, Billy,…I am obsessed with the idea of you bein' killed someday. I know it's crazy, too!...But if he's there, you'll fight 'im, I am sure of that!"

"If he's there, he's Stockwell's problem, not mine,…and not yours anymore, neither!"

"That's where you're wrong, I think,…if Hatcher's there, he'll damn sure kill Jim!…Jim ain't any part of a gunfighter!"

Billy looked at him for a moment and sighed deeply before answering. "You're right,…I guess that would sort a make it a problem, or our problem!…Neither of us could let that go."

"Damn right, we couldn't!…Jim's one a th' few allies we have in Paris, on th' side a th' law anyway,…and he'd damn sure try to take Hatcher down, if he saw 'im!"

"Yeah, he would." Grinned Billy. "He's a good man,…but, what say we cross that bridge when we get to it?…Stockwell knew about this ten minutes after it happened, and Hatcher would know that."

"Yeah, you're right, I guess!…He's on th' run now, he'll by-pass Paris for sure."

"There ya go!" Billy shrugged then, and swatted at the pesky gnats that had somehow took up residence in the coach. "Besides, there's a thousand Hatchers in this country, Rod, another thousand would be's, or want a be's!…They'll still be here a hundred years from now, too, different, but they'll be here,…and their weapons'll be a lot deadlier!"

"How?"

"You're th' one always readin' newspapers, Rod, it's already happening!…You saw 'em advertise that fancy automatic pistol,…from Belgium, or somewhere. You even had a rifle that came from there!"

"You're right, I did read about that, shoots sixteen times fast as you can pull th' trigger.…Smith, Wesson's already got a similar gun in production.…I get your point, Billy! It's just hard to believe it could get any worse, though."

"Well, believe it, it will!…But we won't be here to see the worst of it."

Rodney shook his head and looked out as they were passing the last few houses inside Clarksville's city limits. "But we know who will be here, don't we?" He said, looking back at Billy.

"They might not see th' worst of it, neither, Rod.…Nobody's ever prepared for th' worst of anything, it'll be so gradual, they won't even know it's happening."

"It's a never-ending thing, ain't it, Billy,...damned if ya do, and damned if ya don't!"

"Th' way it's always been!" He nodded. "We'll just have to deal with it now, let somebody else deal with it, then!...Mister Hatcher, way I see it, is now, and is not our problem, unless we come face to face with 'im!...It's men like you, Jim, and even Gose,...and especially Judge Parker that'll keep the odds even."

"And you, Billy, don't forget that!"

"Yeah, and me, I guess....But it's th' thought a bein' caught and hung, that keeps a lot a killings from happenin',...law keeps 'em thinkin'!"

"You're becoming a philosopher, Billy, longest speech you ever made!" He laughed then. "Anyway, most of 'em ain't afraid a th' law, you know that!"

"Seems that way sometimes." He nodded and looked out of the window at the wooded pastureland. "But," He said, looking back at him. "They all eventually wind up dead, shot, or from hangin'"

"Yeah, I hate that word, made me sick to my stomach to watch it!"

"Robs a man of his dignity, that's for sure." Nodded Billy.

"Only one that didn't piss his pants, when they dropped, was Childers!... Was he as fast as he said he was?"

"I'll just say, he was better than th' others." He shrugged then. "None of 'em had th' confidence they needed to kill me!"

"Couldn't a beat you, if they had!...You should a seen th' Judge's face when you brought 'em all in!"

Billy watched him for a moment, and then grinned. "And you did, I guess!"

"Well, no!" He grinned then also. "That Deputy Marshal told me about it,...said he'd never seen th' Judge in such disbelief before....Wish I had, though!" He sighed then and shifted his body on the seat's thin, worn cushion. "Must a been somethin' to see."

"You give me too much credit, Rod!...You could a done it yourself, a lot a men could."

"Only one in a hundred can pull as fast as you, Billy,...and hit what they want a hit....I doubt seriously, there's even one in a thousand!"

"Rod, how many times have I told you that I ain't no hero?...I'm just lucky when it comes to guns, that's all, and it ain't my fault. I told you what Doc said likely happened to me!"

"I know, but that's neither yea, nor nay, Billy. Not even Doc knows that for sure. But I know that you're th' best there ever was!...I just keep rememberin' what you said once,...that no man is ever th' very best, that there's always someone, somewhere that is better."

"That's th' truth of it, Rod!"

"Yeah, and Hatcher could be that one!...Have you thought a that?"

"I have,...but I ain't gonna let it worry me." He watched as Rodney repositioned himself on the seat again. "What's th' matter, got ants in your jeans?"

"No, but it wouldn't hurt if this coach was bigger." He grunted. "Softer seats wouldn't hurt, neither!"

"Still wouldn't keep your arm from hurtin'!"

"I know,...I'm just bitchy today!...Wouldn't hurt if I could get some sleep, I shut my eyes, and I fall off that bluff again!...Thought sure, I was a goner, never so scared in my life!"

"Makes two of us!...But ain't you stretchin' it a bit? I seem to recall a twenty-foot tall lizard that made you piss your pants."

"Yeah." He laughed. "But it didn't try to pull my arm off!"

They both chuckled at that, and Billy turned to stare out at the heavily wooded landscape again. "Be home in a few hours, Rod." He said, looking back at him. "Can't wait to see Connie and th' kids, it's like we been gone a year, instead of a month!...Besides, Bed rest'll do us both some good!"

"Amen to that!" They both fell silent then, their bodies moving with the swaying, bumping motion of the coach on the wide, well-traveled Clarksville road.

*   *   *

The next, almost three hours passed slowly in the dusty, gnat infested summer heat, and it was even hotter inside the coach, except for the periodic breeze that found its way through the open windows. Billy pulled the bandana from his neck and wiped his face then removed the eyeglasses and finished the job.

"Won't be long now, Rod!" He said, replacing the glasses.

The sound of his voice caused Rodney to open his eyes and look around. "Where are we?"

"Just passed th' Jonesboro road."

"None too soon for me!" He yawned mightily then. "Man, that laudanum is potent stuff, puts a man to sleep."

"I hear that Opium tends to do that."

"Kills hell out a th' pain, though." He peered out through the window then. "Don't care if I never ride another stage coach,...damn near jarred my teeth loose!"

"Would ya rather be on a horse?"

"I can't even imagine how that would hurt!" He looked back at Billy then. "Think they know we're comin'?"

"We wired Jim, I'm sure he told 'em,...unless th' wire's down somewhere. I seen a crew a men workin' on th' poles back a ways."

"That wouldn't be no surprise!...Sure be glad when they get them new-fangled telephones installed. Sure be nice to hear Lisa's voice."

"That ain't gonna be any time soon!...Hard to figure how anything like that'd work anyhow?"

"You thought th' same thing about electric lights, Remember?...Weren't you th' one told me about them at that hotel in Denver?"

"Yeah, guess I was....It remains to be seen, anyway."

"You will, all they have to do, is string wires on them existing poles out there, works th' same as th' telegraph, except you can talk to th' person you call."

"It would be a good thing, Rod, I'll give ya that."

"I know that's right!...Can't wait to see my ladies, Billy. Seems like we been gone forever."

"I'm sure they'll be waitin' on us."

"I hope so, Lisa was pretty worried when we left, I never knew she felt that way about my job."

"It weren't th' job, Rod, it was th' danger part of it that scared her."

"I know that now!......She's not like Connie, she's used to your gallivanting ways., Lisa's not!...She'll be so relieved."

"Gallivantin'?...Rod, you're generally with me on trips like this, when you ain't, she is!...Don't forget, we all heard Lisa's complaint!"

"I didn't mean it like that, Billy,...point taken!" He grinned. "Gallivanting weren't th' right word to use, just the only one I could think of at th' moment….I meant to say, Connie's stronger than Lisa. I expect they'll all be relieved to see us."

"You expect right!"

"Know what else, Billy,…you can forget about us takin' th' family to Shreveport,…place is a pig-sty!"

"Agreed." He nodded.

"Knew ya would." He turned then to stare out at the houses they were passing, and waving at the kids playing in the yards.

The homes along both sides of the road, here, were not as close together as those closer to town, giving these families plenty of room for their gardens, and for the kids to play. However, some minutes later, that all changed as they began passing crossroads, all leading to even more housing behind those along the road.,…and even more behind those! Paris was continuously growing.

A half hour later, the stage was entering the business end of Paris itself where the houses had suddenly changed to business places. Most of these were newly finished, while others were still under construction.

"Must be quittin' time already." Said Rodney. "Nobody's workin'."

"It's five-thirty, Rod."

"Guess it's quittin' time….Ya know,…At times, when I look at th' town, I think they've come a long way since th' fire, but other times, I think maybe they haven't gone very far at all."

"Everything burned, Rod,…it's only gonna be three years, come August!…Be another couple a years before they're done!"

"Looks good, though, don't it?…Square looks better than it used to."

They were both at the window as the coach entered, and crossed the busy square to finally stop in front of the new Peterson Hotel.

"Well, if they knew we were comin', I sure don't see 'em, Billy." Remarked Rodney, watching the pedestrians along the walkway, as well as those in the hotel's open doorway. "Where are they?"

"Don't know." Sighed Billy as he opened the door and stepped down. "They ain't here, Rod." He said, seeing Jim Stockwell come out onto the boardwalk. He turned to help Rodney down. "Somethin' ain't right here, Rod." He said in a low voice, and looked back at Stockwell to notice the worried look on his face. He stepped up onto the walkway to meet the Marshal, quickly followed by Rodney.

"Hey, Jim." He nodded, his face a mask of unanswered questions. "You always meet th' stage like this,…you tell th' families we was comin?"

"Yeah, Jim." Burst out Rodney. "Where's everybody at?"

"They're all okay, Marshal." Nodded Stockwell quickly. "Your daughter's at th' ranch, your kids, too, Billy." He looked down at his boots then.

"What's wrong, Jim?" Asked Billy shakily. "Is Connie sick, she hurt?"

"Oh, no, nothin' like that, Billy, she's fine, both are at th' hospital."

"Hospital?…Spit it out, man!" Said Billy, almost beside himself. "What th' hell happened?"

"Doc was shot, Billy, I'm so sorry."

"What?…When, how, God damn it, who did it?…Is he dead?"

"No,…listen, Billy, calm down!…Doc's alive, ya hear me?…But just barely."

"What about Mama?"

"She's shook up real bad, and scared to death. But she's okay. She's at th' hospital, too. Doc Snyder has her sedated. Don't worry, they're watchin' her." He swallowed hard then.

"What happened, Jim?" Asked Rodney, placing a hand on Billy's shoulder.

"Connie said th' man told 'em his name was Hatcher.…Said he busted in on 'em at noon today, held everybody at gunpoint while he ate the food they were sitting down to. He took what few dollars Doc had, then said he was borrowin' a horse and saddle." He swallowed again, and looked up at the sky.

"Anyway,…Doc followed 'im outside to th' barn, and at that point, I guess, tried to stop 'im!…They were all watchin' through th' window when he shot Doc.…I don't think anything would a happened, but he was takin' Doc's pet horse."

"He took Freckles!" Nodded Billy. "That would set 'im off all right!"

"I brought my buckboard, men, let's load your gear, I'll take you to th' hospital."

*   *   *

Sheriff Gose was at the nurse's station when they entered, and quickly rushed to meet them. "Damn good to see you men!" He said, quickly pumping their hands.

"Where's Doc, John," Asked Billy tightly. "And my wife?"

"Doc Snyder's in with Doc, Billy, won't let anyone in to see 'im yet!... Your womenfolk are in with ms. Bailey....Come on, I'll take you to her room." He led the way down the hall and opened the door for them.

"Billy!!!" Shrieked Connie, and ran sobbing into his arms. "Doc's been shot, honey, my God!"

"I know, honey,...are you okay?"

"Nooooo!" She wailed, and buried her face in his chest. "I'm so afraid for him, mama Bailey, too!"

Melissa had been half asleep, sitting beside the older woman's bed, her head down on folded arms, when she heard Connie's frantic wail, and quickly raised up to see Rodney. Crying loudly, she got to her feet and ran into his one good arm. "Oh, God, Rodney!"

"There, there, honey." He soothed. "It's all right, I'm home."

"Wha,...what happened to your arm, baby?" She asked.

"I fell, honey, hurt my shoulder!...Now dry up, okay?...How's Mattie?"

"She's been asleep all afternoon!" Sniffed Connie as she pulled away from Billy's sweat drenched shirt, and walked to the bed. "Poor soul, we thought she was going to have a stroke, or worse!"

Billy, tears running down his cheeks, moved in to take his adopted mother's limp hand. "It's gonna be okay, mama." He choked. "I'm here now, don't you worry none, ya hear?...Doc's gonna be okay, you both are. I'll take care of it, ya hear me?...I'm gonna take care of it!"

Rodney had been watching Billy's face, had seen the set of his jaw, and knowing what was coming, ushered Melissa to the other side of the bed. "When we leavin', Billy?" He asked with determination.

Billy looked across at him before nodding. "Tomorrow!" He sniffed. "Only you ain't goin' on this one!"

"Th' hell, I ain't!"

"You're out a commission, Rod, you'd slow me down!...You ain't goin'!"

"They're my family, too, Billy!"

"I know that,...that's why you're gonna stay here and take care of 'em!... Connie and th' kids are in your hands....You know I'm right!"

Nodding finally, Rodney wiped at his eyes. "Don't worry about that, Billy."

"I don't!" He looked at Connie then, and hugged her against him. "I'm going after Mister Hatcher, honey,…will you try to stop me?"

"No,…not if you promise to kill him!…I hate him for what he did."

He stared at her in surprise for a minute before wrapping her tightly in his arms. "Right now, honey, I can't think of anything that can stop that! He hurt my family!" He kissed her then, before letting her go to turn back toward the two lawmen.

"Did you go after 'im, Jim?"

"No, not yet, Billy.…By th' time Connie got Doc and Mattie to town, he was too long gone.…I sent wires to all the towns west a here, gave descriptions of him, and Doc's horse. By th' time I got a posse together, th' stage was due in,…someone had to meet you, tell ya what happened."

"I appreciate it, Jim.…But I'll need somethin' else from ya, now."

"Name it!"

"I need Morgan Storm's black horse, if that's okay?"

"You got it!…Anything you need.…I've got a dozen men ready to ride with ya, too!"

"Don't need 'em, Jim!…What I do need is supplies, just what I can stuff in a cotton bag, extra cartridges, too, forty-four caliber."

"It'll all be ready at first light."

"Thanks, Jim." He nodded. "And you, too, John, for stayin' here with 'em." He turned back to Connie then.

"I want to hear everything Hatcher said, and did!…Everything."

She nodded, and they all listened intently as she retold the story. It took her a while, as she had to relate the circumstances between sobs,…and when she was through, Billy lowered his head.

"That's how it happened, Honey." She sniffed. "Everything!"

"He didn't hurt you, or th' kids?"

"No, not really.…He pushed Willy against the wall when he tried to hit him, but he wasn't hurt.…You look so tired, Billy, are you sure you want to do this?"

"Damn right!…You changin' your mind about wantin' 'im dead?"

"Of course not!…It's just,…when he drew that gun, it reminded me of you!…It was so quick."

He looked at Rodney's concerned face then, and knew what he was thinking. "But it weren't me!" He said, looking back at her. "Now, I'm gonna wait long enough to find out how Doc is, then I'm goin' after 'im!...No man hurts my family, and gets away with it!" He looked back at Gose and Stockwell then.

"John, that okay with you, and Jim?"

"If you kill 'im?" Asked Stockwell, and then shrugged. "I wouldn't do any less, Billy."4

"Makes two of us, Billy." Added Gose.

"Thanks." He nodded. "How long since you sent them wires, Jim?"

"Round three, this afternoon."

"If you hear anything back tonight, let me know quick,...that horse will be easy to spot."

"You can count on it, Billy....I'll get your gear together tonight, too."

"Good,...first light, okay?"

"Yes, sir,...first light!"

*   *   *

Both Billy, and Rodney were sprawled in the room's extra chairs, both in a deep, stressful sleep. Connie and Melissa sat on either side of Mattie's bed, each holding one of the old lady's hands as Doctor Snyder opened the door and came in. They got to their feet as he stopped to look Billy and Rodney over, and then smiled and came on to the bed.

"I see they made it back." He said, reaching to pick up Mattie's hand to check her pulse rate, and then listen to her heart.

"This lady has a strong will to live." He said with a smile. "Almost as strong as Doc's!"

"How is Doc?" Asked Connie urgently.

"Well, I got the bullet out, it just took a while. It was lodged less than a millimeter from his heart." He breathed deeply then. "He's lost a lot of blood, too, and that's what worries me right now....I'm running a test now to see what blood type he is, then I'm going to need a donor for a transfusion."

"How will you know the donor?"

"More tests." He nodded.

"How long will that take?" Sobbed Melissa.

"Well,...once I know his blood type, not too long, I'll know what to look for....Doc's pretty strong, for his advanced age, but I think he'll be okay until we can give him some blood. That will be sometime before noon,…this morning, I would think. A nurse is already taking blood from the hospital staff."

"You can check ours, too!" Said Connie quickly.

"Good,…I'll send a nurse in shortly."

"Rodney and Billy can be tested, too." Sniffed Melissa.

"If we need to." He nodded, looking back at them. "I wouldn't wake them yet, they look exhausted."

"When can we see Doc?" Asked Connie, wiping at her eyes.

"I'll let you know….He's in a clean room right now, as germ-free as possible. If I can keep him from contracting pneumonia, I think he'll be home free….Don't worry, ladies, and tell them not to!…I'll keep you posted."

CHAPTER TWO

Mattie was awake, and spooning broth into her mouth when Billy groaned loudly and sat up in the chair. He saw her then, and got up to come to the bed.

"Your hands are shakin', Mama, want me to do that for you?"

"I'm so very glad you're home, son." She said, putting down the spoon to raise his hand and kiss it….No, honey, I can feed myself." She took another spoonful and swallowed it, all the while watching as Connie came up behind Billy to put her hands on his shoulders.

"You have a precious gem for a wife, William,…don't know what we'd have done without her."

"I know, I do, Mama."

"How are you feeling, Mama Bailey?" Asked Connie.

"Oh, fiddle,…I'm fine, honey." She said, dropping the spoon into the bowl. "I'd be a lot better, if they knew how to make a decent bowl of broth around here!"

They were all laughing, as Rodney came to put his arm around Melissa. "They don't use salt in hospitals, Mattie,…it ain't healthy!"

"Well, I didn't come here to die!" She scoffed. "And what's this, I hear about you falling off a mountain,…will you be okay, Rodney?"

"It tore th' ligaments in my shoulder, Mattie." He sighed then. "It'll be okay, I just won't be able to use my arm th' way I used to, that's all."

"Well, you need to be more careful, the both of you!…What with the job you've got, I'm surprised you both are still in one piece."

"He doesn't have that job anymore, Mattie." Smiled Melissa. "He resigned."

"Praise the Lord!…That makes me so happy."

"Thanks, Mattie." Replied Rodney.

"But I'm still not happy with this so-called, broth!...And why haven't we heard from the Doctor yet,...I'm worried about Walter?"

"Yeah, me, too!" Said Billy, turning his head to look at Connie. "Has he been in at all?"

"He came in about midnight, to check on Mama Bailey." She replied.

"What about Doc?"

"He said he was doing fine,...said it took a long while to get the bullet out, it being so close to his heart. Other than that, he's real weak from the loss of blood, and he's worried that he might take pneumonia."

"They're going to give him blood this morning." Added Melissa.

"Yes," Agreed Connie. "They tested us, to see what type we were last night."

"What type?...What do ya mean by type?"

"Not everyone's blood is the same, honey." Said Connie. "They have to find someone with the same type as Doc's."

"Well that was last night!" Argued Mattie. "My Lord,...they don't know how to take care of Walter, I do!" She smiled at Billy then. "I'm sorry, honey, I'm just letting off steam. Walter's a tough old coot, twenty years ago, he'd have beat hell out of that sorry Peckerwood!"

"I know he would, Mama." Grinned Billy. They all looked toward the door then as Doctor Snyder came in.

He paused to stare at their expectant faces for a moment, and then came on to shake Rodney's hand then reached across the bed to shake Billy's. "You two look much better than you did last night, sleep will do it every time. Good to see you." He looked at all of them again.

"Why so glum, folks?...You'll be glad to know, I found a blood donor, she's prepping for the procedure right now." They all seemed to wilt before his eyes then, causing him to smile. He chuckled then, and placed a hand on Mattie's forehead, then picked up her hand to check her pulse.

"You seem to be a lot better than you were yesterday, Mattie, how do you feel?"

"I'm fine," She scoffed. "I want to know about Walter?"

"I just told you, he's doing fine....He's breathing good, no rattle in his lungs so far, and he's sleeping like a baby....All of that is very good news, Dear Lady, and a transfusion of new blood will put him right back on his feet again."

"Thank you so much!" Said Mattie, and wiped at her eyes with a kerchief. "I've been so worried!"

"I know you have,...but the worst is over, my dear....He's not out of the woods yet, you understand."

"I know,...when can I see him?"

"Maybe tonight, Mattie, or early tomorrow morning. We have to consider his age, his ability to produce blood on his own is far less than a younger man's would be. That's why we have to give him blood....He's going to be fine!"

"Oh, I know that!"

"Thanks, Doc." Grinned Billy. "That's a load off our minds." He pulled his watch then. "Almost time for me to go, Mama." He said, and picked up her hand to kiss it.

"I know, William." She sighed. "But, somehow, I wish you'd let it go, Walter's alive, and we'll be okay now you're home."

"I know, Mama....But it just ain't in me to let it go. You're my folks now, and I will not have you molested....I just can't allow that!"

"From what I have heard about you, Mister Upshur." Began Snyder. "I would not want to be that man, when you find him!...That is what you intend to do, right?"

"Exaggerated rumors, Doc, believe me,...but yes, I'm goin' after 'im!"

"Well, there are plenty of those floating rumors around, too. But I'll wish you good luck anyway."

"Excuse me, Doctor." Interrupted Melissa. "When you have time, will you check my husband's shoulder, he hurt it in a fall?"

"Of course, I will."

"Can you tell us who the blood donor is?" Asked Mattie. "I'd love to know, so I can thank her."

"Mary Beth Rhodes,...she eagerly volunteered, too!"

"My goodness!" Smiled Mattie. "She hasn't even moved in yet, and she already saved Walter's life....She's a darling!"

"And you'll need her more than ever now." Said Connie.

"Okay." Said Snyder, moving away from the bed. "If you all will excuse me, they should be about ready for the transfusion....I will keep you informed, Mattie."

"Thanks, Doc." Nodded Billy.

"My pleasure, Mister Upshur." He looked at Connie and Melissa then. "You two should get some sleep, as well." He nodded at them and turned to open the door just as Stockwell opened it and came in.

"Oh,…sorry, Doc,…good mornin'"

"Good morning, Marshal." He left the room, and Stockwell removed his hat and came on toward the bed.

"Mornin' all, Ms. Bailey, glad to see you feelin' better."

"Thank you, Marshal."

Hat in hand, he came on to stand beside Connie and Billy. "It's comin' on to five o'clock, Billy, got your gear, and th' black outside."

"Thanks, Jim, I won't forget it!" He got up to settle his hat on his head. "Did he go West, Mama?"

"Yes, William, on Bonham road….Won't you reconsider, son, I'm afraid for you?"

"I'm afraid for myself, Mama, my heart's not made a rock….But it will keep me aware of things around me….Don't worry, Mama, you, and that wonderful old man in there fightin' for his life, are th' only parents I've known since I was ten! I love you dearly,…but I have to do this….I will not allow any man to lay hands on what I love, or harm what I love, and Mister Hatcher has done both!…He has to pay for that!" He leaned over and kissed her on the forehead before standing to look at Rodney.

"Take care a my family, Rod."

"With my life, Billy."

"I know that!"

"Oh, William!" Sobbed Mattie, holding out her arms to him.

He leaned down again to wrap her in a hug then put his arm around Connie and ushered her out of the room behind Stockwell.

"Billy?" She sobbed as they stepped out onto the long porch.

"I know, baby." He interrupted, stopping her on the steps to kiss her long, and hard. "I love you more than you know. Kiss th' kids for me, tell 'em I love 'em very much!…And tell Willy that I'm very proud of him for trying to stop Hatcher, no father could ask for more in a son." He looked down the steps at Stockwell, then back at her.

"Don't worry, honey, no man can keep me from comin' home to you,…I will be back!" He looked back then as Rodney stepped onto the porch, took his hand, and pulled him into a bearhug.

"Wish you was goin' with me, old son."

"Not as much as I do, Billy, it's hard not to!"

"I know it is,...but I'm depending on you, you hear me?" He went down the steps and took the tall black horse's reins from Stockwell.

"This is some kind a horse, Jim,...I've always admired it! Thanks man."

"Let me go with ya, Billy?" He asked in earnest. "It's my job, anyway."

"You're th' town Marshal, Jim, your job's right here!...Besides, I won't have time to watch your back, and I don't want you on my conscience if somethin' happens,...but I do thank ya, man." He shook Stockwell's hand, and then watched Connie cry as he raised the stirrup to check the cinches.

"I'll be back, honey, that's a promise!" He lowered the stirrup and mounted the sidestepping horse to watch as Stockwell mounted his.

"You need an extra gun, Billy?" He asked.

"Got one, Jim." He looked back at Connie then, and smiled. "I'll be back!" He spurred the horse into a run back toward town, with Stockwell spurring his horse in an effort to keep up. Some minutes later, he waved at the Marshal when he stopped at the hitch-rail, and was soon across the square and on the Bonham road, galloping west in pursuit of Wes Hatcher.

*   *   *

The entire length of Bonham street, from just off the square, to Doc and Mattie's home was still under some kind of construction. Homes were being built, streets being cut and graded in order for even more housing, and these houses were being erected almost as fast as lumber, or brick could be delivered. Paris, Texas was growing at an even pace. More business places, manufacturing companies. More and more farmlands were being cleared for planting cotton, corn, and other commodities.

But Billy did not see any of this as he rode by, all that was on his mind, was Wes Hatcher, and what he had done to his family. He rode with a determination he had never felt before. His eyes were on the wide, rutted road ahead of him, and only slowing the tall black horse to a fast trot as he reined it around freight wagons, and workers crossing the road in front of him, to finally slow to a walk as he came abreast of Doc's house. Tears formed in his eyes as he looked at it, and thought again of them both, one fighting for his life, the other for her sanity.

With lips drawn into a tight, thin line across his teeth, he forced himself to look away, and urged the big black to a gallop again along the dusty, rutted road, and watching the powerful animal's bobbing head while his thoughts fought with his remorse.

What would he do if Doc were to die, he wondered? He also knew that if he did, Mama would surely follow him. Her heart, as big as it was, would never stand the strain! He could lose them both! However, he knew that it was inevitable, that he would lose them one day, anyway. But not this way, he thought bitterly! Not at the hands of a killer.

He was sure of only one thing, he would have to depend on Doctor Snyder to pull Doc through. He was a good Doctor, and an even better surgeon,...if anyone could do it, he could. He had to, too many people depended on him to save the man who helped settle, and build the town of Paris. The man who gave medical care to the surveyors that laid out the town's plot, and delivered many dozens of newborns into the population through the years. Doc had to live, he thought, he just had to!

Either way, he vowed, Mister Hatcher was going to pay dearly for what he done! Shaking the thoughts from his mind, he finally settled himself in the saddle and relaxed, allowing his body movements to match those of the galloping horse and for the next few hours, rode in deep determination that was strongly mixed with a foreboding anxiety. He paid no mind at all to the miles of plowed grounds, the forests of trees, or the barbed wire fences separating the borders of each ranch, or farm. He rode with only one thought in his frantic mind, a fear that he might never catch Wes Hatcher at all! For if he were to change horses somewhere along the way, he might never be spotted, or recognized!...No, he thought, Freckles was a good, strong horse, Doc had hand-fed, and raised him from a colt, had never had a hand raised against him in abuse. If he didn't catch Hatcher, and bring that horse home, Doc would be devastated!...If he lived?

It was close to mid-morning when he passed the area of the shootout three years earlier, and for the next half hour, relived the episode that ended with Morgan Storm's death. He had been sort of disappointed when he learned that the man was an assassin, because he liked him. Shaking his head to clear it, he reached down to pat the black's neck.

"He had an eye for good horseflesh, didn't he, black boy?" he said aloud. But, no sooner had he put the episode behind him, that he found himself thinking of the hospital again, and of Doc's fight for life. As it stands now, he thought angrily, Hatcher was a good eighteen hours ahead of him.

'He has got to stop sometime', he thought then. 'And when he does, I'll gain some time on him'!....But it would help if he had some idea where he was going? He decided to slow the horse to a fast trot for a while to cool him down and it was then, that he began eying the barns, and farm houses on either side of the road hoping to catch sight of Doc's horse near one of them,…but he knew it was just wishful thinking.

It was just past noon when he began meeting traffic on the road. Several large wagons, loaded with freight, and one or two that was stacked full with milled lumber, some of which was hanging out the end of the wagons to almost drag the ground. He met several spring-wagons, some with families, and all were headed toward Honey Grove. These he passed at a gallop, raising a hand in greeting as he did.

Mid afternoon found him tying up at the hitch-rail in front of the sheriff's office. He stepped up to the boardwalk, after a look up and down the long street, and as he opened the door, stopped again to peer at the horses along the hitch-rails, and satisfied that Doc's horse was not among them, sighed and stepped inside the sparsely furnished office. A paper-strewn desk was to the right of the door, three chairs next to it. On the left, along the wall, was a gun case filled with rifles and handguns. A coat-rack was to the left of the door he noticed as he moved inside and closed it behind him. That's when he saw Morgan Storm's gun rig hanging from a peg on the wall behind the coat-rack.

Shaking his head with a smile, he walked on across the floor to touch the pot-bellied stove, and found it cold. Turning, he scanned the room again quickly then saw the open cellblock door.

"Charlie Daniels!" He called out loudly. "Hey, Charley, you back there?"

"Yeah!" Came the muffled yell, and as he came through the door. "Who wants me?" He stopped to stare at Billy for a moment, looking him up and down, and then grinned.

"Upshur, ain't it?"

"Bill Upshur!" Nodded Billy, and shook his hand.

"What brings you to this pint-sized city?"

"Wes Hatcher!"

Daniels frowned at him for a moment before nodding. "I got th' wire from Stockwell yesterday....Hatcher's a bad one, Bill! I read the flyer on 'im after I got th' wire....But we haven't seen, nor heard of any new faces in town, and the only gray horse in town belongs to Jared Womack, over at th' saddlery." He studied Billy's stolid face for another moment.

"You bein' here means you're goin' after 'im, don't it?"

"That's right!...He shot my adopted father yesterday, and stole his horse."

"Sorry to hear it, man...He kill 'im?"

"Came close, but no, he's in th' hospital....I need some idea where he might be headed."

"Let's take a look at th' poster." He went to his desk, shuffled through the papers to finally come up with it. "Says here, he's from New Mexico territory, got nine known killings to his credit." He gave Billy the poster as he spoke.

"Think he'll go back there, Charlie?"

"Hard to tell, he might not!...Killed his first man there seven years ago....I wired Sheriff Kelso in Amarillo today at Jim's request, also at Wichita Falls. Kelso wired me a description on 'im, five, ten, hundred and eighty pounds, long blond hair."

"What age a man is he?"

"He was twelve seven years ago,...make 'im nineteen or so."

"Quite a reputation for a kid!" Nodded Billy. "In a short time, too."

"About like that of Bill Bonney." Returned Daniels. "Twenty one men, and not much older than this Hatcher."

"Who's this Bill Bonney?"

"You never heard a Billy th' kid?...He's from New Mexico, too."

"I might a heard th' name before, Charlie!...But do me a favor, will ya?...You get any better news on Hatcher, wire Jim with it, and every town you can think of between here and this Amarillo town. I'll get th' word eventually."

"I'll do it Bill,...And I sure don't envy you goin' after a man like that!"

"Don't like it much myself!...Thanks, Charlie, be a seein' ya!" He turned and quickly left, mounted the black and galloped out of town, with Sheriff Daniels standing on the boardwalk watching.

*   *   *

They were, all three walking Mattie up and down the wide, polished hallway, stopping every few feet to admire, and appraise the large paintings along each side and commenting on each, when they saw Doctor Snyder coming toward them.

"Oh, Doctor!" Cried Mattie. "Is Walter all right?"

"Doc's fine, Mattie, I finished the transfusion at ten this morning, and we have monitored him most of the day. His heart and pulse rate has been improving ever since. He's going to be fine."

"Thank God in Heaven!" She cried, shedding tears of joy and pent-up frustration as Connie held on to her.

"When can we see him, Doctor?" Asked Rodney.

"I thought you would never ask!" He chuckled. "He's awake right now."

"Praise the Lord!" She cried. "Can I see him?"

"Of course you can, follow me."

They followed him down the long hallway until they reached a room marked, "Recovery-Clean room," where he stopped them.

"One of you can go in with Ms. Bailey, one at a time after that." He gave Mattie and Connie a cloth mask to put around their mouth and nose.

"He's still in a crucial period right now, the mask will help prevent the spread of bacteria....Come on." He placed his own mask in place and led them into the room.

"Jesus, what a relief!" Sighed Rodney. "Wish there was some way to get word to Billy."

"Talk to Jim, maybe he knows a way, the telegraph, maybe?...Wonder where he is by now?

"Don't know where he might be, honey?" Said Rodney with a frown. "It's got a be close to five o'clock....I figure, somewhere the other side a Honey Grove. Was me in his place, I'd contact th' law in every town for any information I could get,...and that's what I think he'll do!...You're right, I'll ask Jim to wire th' news ahead of 'im somewhere, and then hope he gets it!"

"Maybe it'll change his mind, and he'll come home!"

Rodney looked at her worriedly, and then shook his head. "You know, that's wishful thinkin',...Hatcher had better find a very deep hole somewhere and jump in it!...It ain't in Billy to let somethin' like this go,...just ain't his way,..mine, neither!"

"He might, if he could see how it effects Connie when he's gone like this,…she hardly talks to me at all. Just mopes around all day!"

"Like you do when I'm gone, right?"

"Yes, just like me!...But it hurts me to see her that way."

"I know, honey, I've seen it, too….But he's like a whole different person when he's been wronged, nothin' can stop 'im!" He sighed heavily then. "He'll get justice for Doc!"

"I know." She nodded. "Rodney, you need to go home tonight and check on the kids, tell mom and dad that Doc's all right."

"You're right about that, too." He nodded. "But I don't have a horse,…If Jim doesn't come back today, I'll walk to town and borrow one….I'll get 'im to send those wires, too."

*   *   *

Bonham, Texas was one of the oldest towns in Texas, and fairly large in the way it was laid out. Built along the main road through town, with a dozen cross streets running north and South. A town square that like Paris, was surrounded by storefronts of all descriptions.

The tall, two storied, Fort English stood about a mile East of the square. An all log structure, Fort English was still occupied by a few dozen army recruits. But at one time, had been an important center for the war effort. Fort English had been the headquarters of General Henry McCullough, who was Commander of the Northern Sub-district of Texas.

It was a Confederate Commissary during the war, supplying clothing, blankets, harness, saddles and food to the many Confederate brigades in North Texas. But now, if not for the recruits, Fort English would eventually fall in disarray.

Billy sat the saddle for a minute to stare at the huge structure surrounding the Fort and parade ground, the wide gates lit up appropriately by the two, tall Kerosene pole lamps on either side, and then at the Union Flag on a much taller pole. The flag, of which lay immobile in the hot, breezeless night.

After a couple of minutes, he sighed and pulled his Sam Colt pocket watch. 'Midnight', he thought as he put it away and looked up the partially pole-lighted main street. All the storefronts were dark except for one, and he knew that would be the saloon. Breathing deeply again, he urged the horse on up the street at a walk, seeing the two uniformed policemen as they walked the walkways and checked for unlocked doors along the way. They stopped to watch as he came abreast of them, only to step down into the street when he reined the black toward them.

"I heard there was a police department here." He said, removing his hat, and then the bandana to wipe sweat from his face and neck. "Don't think I ever seen uniforms like that before,...some different than th' army's."

"They're hot as hell, too!" Returned the bigger of the two.

"You just passin' through, Mister,...ah, who are you, anyway?" Inquired the second man.

"Name's Upshur, from down Paris way,...Deputy Marshal." He took the badge from his shirt and showed it to them.

"How come you ain't wearin' it?" Quizzed the bigger man.

"Might make a target for th' man I'm after." He grinned and put it away.

"You got business in Bonham, do ya?" Inquired the second man. "You think he might be here?"

"Don't know." He said, looking up the street again. "He could be anywhere,...all I know is that he was headed west on this road....He's a killer, name a Hatcher. Be ridin' a dappled gray horse,...seen anybody like that?"

"It wouldn't be us, we work nights. Ain't seen no horse like that tonight."

"Got a Sheriff's office in town?"

"Yes'ir, up on th' square yonder....But he ain't there, be home in bed, I expect."

"How about a telegraph?"

"Same thing, on th' square."

"They a Deputy up there?"

"Nope,...jail's closed at night....Locked up tight, we checked it an hour ago."

"You plannin' to stay over?" Asked the bigger man.

"Thought I might." He nodded.

"Got a hotel just off th' square, couple a roomin' houses a few blocks up....Or you can wait on th' bench in front a th' Sheriff's office, be in by seven."

"Much obliged." He nodded at them and retied the bandana around his neck before reining the big horse on up the street. He turned for a look back at them for a moment then sighed and began watching the dark doorways until he came to the wide, open square and there, he stopped to scan the dark buildings until he saw the sheriff's office, and reined the black toward it.

"Well!" He breathed, and once again observed the empty expanse of the town square. "Guess they don't have any criminal element in Bonham, Texas." He dismounted with a grunt, and had not realized how tired he really was. Even the saddle, he thought as he heard the groaning of old leather. He stretched, and once again looked over the empty square.

"Where th' hell are you, Hatcher?" He said aloud. "You quit for th' night, too, huh?...You camped out under th' stars in a peaceful sleep, are ya?" He shook his head in anger and disgust then spotted the armchair and bench against the wall. Making a decision, He lifted the horse's stirrup and loosened the cinches before leading it to the trough for water, a dozen feet away.

A few minutes later he was sprawled in the straight-backed armchair, and tilting it back against the wall....He was instantly asleep.

*   *   *

Rodney opened the glass-paned door to the telegraph office and had to grin widely at the scene before him. Both, Jim Stockwell, and the telegrapher were in their chair, both snoring loudly,...and he chose that time to close the door, quite loudly. The sudden noise caused Stockwell to fall out of his chair and stare up at him.

"Wh,...what's wrong, Marshal, Doc okay?"

"Doc's okay, Jim." He laughed. "I just couldn't resist th' temptation!... He's been awake all day, and still awake when I left."

"Then,...what's up, why are you here?...How'd you get here?"

"I walked, th' moon's up, and it's quite nice out,...and cooler!"

Stockwell got to his feet, straightened the chair up and sat back down. "But,...why?"

"Why walk?...I waited all day for you to show up!" He walked over to sit down in one of the extra chairs. "When ya didn't, I walked in....I thought you, or at least Ben would have come to check on us....But that's all right, walk done me good. What I need is th' loan of a horse, Jim, Lisa wants me to go to th' ranch and check on things."

"Well, sure, Marshal, mine's right outside, take it!...How'd you know where to find me anyway?"

"I stopped at your office, Ben told me.....I would a borrowed his, but I thought I'd see if you heard anything yet?"

"Well," Said the telegrapher. "We only had one positive wire come in, and that was around four o'clock yesterday."

"What do ya mean, positive,...was it about Billy?"

"No, sir....it was about this Hatcher fellow."

"He killed another man, Marshal." Said Stockwell. "In Oak Ridge, place just east a Gainsville, Texas."

"Who?"

"Local Gunnie, I think. In a saloon there....I was gonna bring everything to the hospitol in th' mornin'....Think Billy got that far yet?"

"Don't know....I figure if he saves horseflesh, like he always does,...he ought a be close to forty, fifty miles out, maybe."

"Be almost in Sherman, Bonham, anyway, if he stopped to sleep!" Volunteered the telegrapher.

"That's likely right!" Nodded Rodney. "He'll need sleep, too,...so will Hatcher,...How far is Oak Ridge from Bonham?"

"Well,...Sherman's around thirty miles west a Bonham, Oak Ridge, another fifteen or so after that."

"So, Billy's still a good fifty miles behind that Bastard!"

"At least!" Nodded the agent.

"I sure don't envy 'im none, Marshal." Said Stockwell.

"I'm not a Marshal anymore, Jim....I quit, remember?"

"I know,...hard to break old habits, Ma,...Rodney!"

"How well, I know!" He sighed, and then looked at the Agent. "Cyrus,...I'd like you to send a wire to all the larger towns west of, say Sherman. I need to let Billy know that Doc's out a danger now, he's gonna make it!...Send it to Sherman, too!"

"Yes sir!" He grinned. "That is good news!" He moved his chair closer to the desk, and began sending.

"Can Billy beat Hatcher, Rodney?...Don't get me wrong here, Billy's th' fastest I ever seen, but I ain't seen that many!...It's said this Hatcher is God awful fast!"

"Not a man alive can beat Billy, Jim, and I have seen a few!...Mister Hatcher will pay th' price for shootin' Doc."

"All he's got a do is catch 'im!" Sighed Stockwell

"He'll catch 'im, too....He won't quit!" Said Rodney with feeling. "I should have his nerve and ability!...What are you doin' here, anyway,...you stayin' up all night?"

Stockwell leaned forward to rest his arms on his knees before nodding. "If that's what it takes....I'm gonna stay on top of this thing, Rodney, I have to!" He sat back up in the chair and reached for the makings. I need to be th' one goin' after Hatcher, anyway." He said, pouring tobacco into the paper and rolling it.

"You really think you'd have a better chance a catchin' 'im?"

"Hell, no!...But it's my job, not Billy's!" He lit the smoke. "If I didn't catch 'im, leastwise, I'd know I tried."

"Don't beat yourself up over it, Jim. You did th' right thing by waitin', believe me!" He turned to watch the Agent for a second before looking around the dimly lit room.

"Know what I think, Rodney?...I think you're beatin' yourself up over this, even more than me!"

"You think right!" He nodded. "I'm officially not a lawman anymore, but I still have my badge....I should be with Billy right now!"

"No, Billy was right, I think....Your arm like it is, and all."

"Yeah!...I appreciate what you're doin', Jim, it means a lot!....But you need your sleep, too, why don't you go on home, man!"

"I can't, Rodney,...not till I have to!...I will in th' mornin', though, John Gose will be here."

"All I can say then, is thanks, Jim,...and thank John for me, it means a lot!"

"No need for that."

Rodney got to his feet. "Cyrus, appreciate th' help, man." The Agent nodded at him, and he looked back at Stockwell. "I'll get your horse back to ya tomorrow, and thanks again, Jim!"

"My pleasure, Rodney....I'll have all the return wires for ya then."

Nodding, he turned and left, mounted, and reined the animal back toward the hospital.

*   *   *

Billy woke with a start when he felt the hand on his shoulder.

"You lost, Cowboy?" Asked the well-trimmed man with the star on his vest. "Or just sleeping one off?"

"Neither." He said with a mighty yawn, allowing his eyes to take in the older man's appearance. He was graying at the temples, narrow of face, and sported a thick mustache along his upper lip. He wore a white shirt beneath a black leather vest, creased, black trousers, with boots of the same elegance, as well as a black hat,...noticing that as his eyes met the lawman's.

"Name's Bill Upshur." He said, pushing the chair away from the wall. "Deputy Marshal from Paris."

"Oh, yes!" He replied with a smile. "I got the wire from your Marshal, Stockwell....Come on inside, I'll put some coffee on."

Groaning from the pain of stiffened muscles, He got to his feet, and after a look at the, now, busy square, followed the Sheriff inside to sit down again while the coffee was dipped into a blackened pot and placed on the stove.

"Your man, Hatcher has not been seen in, or near here, Mister Upshur." He said as he put wood in the old pot-bellied stove to start the fire. "I've had men watching for that horse." He blew out the match and closed the grate. "That yellow-haired gunman would a been easy to spot, too." He went to his desk, reached into a drawer, and took out the paper.

"However, according to this wire from yesterday, Mister Hatcher killed a man in the saloon at Oak Ridge."

"Where's that?"

"A hole in the wall, some eighteen miles west of Sherman....It's just off the westbound stage route, you'll see the marker."

"They say when it happened?"

"No,...wire came in around four o'clock....I have a flyer on this, Hatcher, too, he's a bad one!...And forgive me for saying this, but you don't look like a gunfighter to me!...That's what it's going to take to get him, you know!"

"What's a gunfighter look like, Sheriff?"

"I have learned to spot a gunman in my twenty years as lawman,…and I meant no offense, Marshal."

"None taken." Said Billy, watching as he went to stoke the fire. "If you don't mind, Sheriff, I'll skip th' coffee and be on my way. Got a telegraph office here?"

"Got the office, but nobody to run it!...Telegrapher's home in bed with influenza."

"Good enough….Thanks, Sheriff." He got to his feet. "How far is this, Sherman, it on this road, too?"

"Thirty miles,…you ought a make it by nightfall." He straightened and closed the grate again. "You know that puts him some forty-odd miles ahead of you, not very good odds!"

"He was that far ahead a me when I left Paris, Sheriff,…I'll catch up!"

"Name's Westmoreland, Mister Upshur,…George Westmoreland." He came to shake Billy's hand. "I want to wish you the best of luck, too."

Billy nodded then turned and left, tightened the black's cinches, mounted, and rode out of Bonham at a gallop.

He didn't even notice the rest of the town, just kept the big black horse at a steady gallop. He realized there were dozens of people stopping to stare at his passing, but all he could think about, was that Hatcher was close to fifty miles ahead of him,…and if he didn't somehow close the gap between them, he might not catch the gunman at all.

*   *   *

Bells, Texas, not a place one would call a town, or even a village. What it was, was mostly a stage stop, and trade center for travelers, but also served the area farmers. It did have a post office with the name above the door. Several business places adorned the semi-wide street, which was also the main road. There was a saddle shop, and a Blacksmith just outside the rear of the Post Office. A hardware store, feed and grain, and a saloon were on the street's opposite side.

A couple dozen small wood houses dotted around the area of what could only be called a Community. But what usually caught the traveler's eye was the Trading Post. It was huge, several dozen feet long, and several feet wide, with living quarters upstairs, as well as rooms to let.

It was just past mid-day when Billy slowed the black horse to a walk along the street. Most of the storefronts were dark, with exception to the saloon, and trade center, and he thought that a bit strange. He stared at the horses tied up along the hitch-rails in passing, and seeing nothing that remotely resembled Doc's dappled gray, decided to stop at the trading post and ask his questions.

Dismounting tiredly, he tied the horse, stepped up to the deserted boardwalk and pushed open the heavy door. Before he could take in the conglomerate of merchandise, the sound of a cocking hammer caused him to freeze,...and with his right hand at his side, used his thumb to work the leather tie-down from the Colt's hammer.

"Who are ye?" Came a gruff voice from somewhere in front of him. "What do ya want?"

"Name's Upshur,...And with a reception like this, I don't want a damn thing!"

A balding, heavy-set, man came around the end of the long overloaded display rack in front of him with a sawed-off shotgun to confront him.

"What's th' gun for?" Asked Billy, his fingers slightly spreading, and within an inch of the holstered pistol.

"Protection!" Said the man, the gun never wavering from Billy's midsection. "What do ya want, supplies?"

"Some answers." He replied, his muscles tensing for what he thought could be the inevitable.

"Answers to what?" Came the gruff voice.

"Man on a gray horse!"

After what seemed to take several seconds. "What's he to you?"

"A killer!"

The man lowered the gun and came forward in the half light of the room to look at him. "You th' law?"

"Deputy Marshal." He nodded. "From Paris, Texas....You see anybody like that?"

"Damn right, I did!...Son of a Bitch robbed me!...Took money and supplies,...but he weren't ridin' no gray horse, it was a paint!"

"When?" Breathed Billy with disappointment.

"About this time yesterday!...Took all the supplies he could tote, about a week's worth....Said he had a long way to go!" He raised the gun slightly then. "Can I see your badge?"

He reached in his shirt and retrieved the badge, holding it out in the palm of his hand. "Which way did he ride out?"

"Didn't,...walked his horse out a town without a care in th' world, th' Bastard!...Went west, toward Sherman....He th' one you're after?"

"No, my man's on a gray horse, but I will watch out for 'im....Much obliged." He turned and walked out and off the walkway, mounted, and galloped away.

'I don't even know if I'm on the right trail any more', He thought angrily. He urged the horse to a gallop again on the uneven road, taking care to keep it on the road's outer edge, as deep ruts have been known to cripple a running horse,...and that was one thing he could not afford to have happen!

'This same time yesterday', he repeated in his thoughts. 'If that had been Hatcher, he would have been twenty-four hours ahead of him, not the eighteen he first thought, and according to Westmoreland, even that was wrong! If it was Hatcher, he had already traded horses, and that thought alone gave him a depressing, mental attitude, and he wondered if he would ever catch him? 'Anyway', he thought wryly. 'Hatcher would have to stop sooner or later, at least to sleep! He was a killer, but he was human, of which, at this moment would not be what he would call him!...Grimly, he settled in the saddle, keeping the horse at a steady gallop, only slowing at intervals to cool it down, and kept it up for the rest of the day, stopping just long enough for water at intervals during the hottest part of the day.

He slowed the horse again just before full dark, and after walking the animal for several minutes, stopped in the road and dismounted, took the canteen from his saddle, removed his hat and poured water into it before holding it to the black's mouth to drink.

Sighing, he put on his hat, took a long drink of the warm water, and mounted again. Sighing once more, he urged the horse to a fast walk, and looked up at the brilliant, star-studded sky to briefly think of the moving light they all had seen in the night sky, some years before, and that brought thoughts of the tribe of ghost Indians, and of White Buffalo.

He shook the thoughts from his head, and wondered when the moon might come up enough to light up the road? Because right now, he had to almost guess at the lane's condition. If the black horse were to be injured now, Mister Hatcher would surely get away with it!...And he could not let that happen!

He was almost sure Hatcher was traveling off the road itself, not wanting to be too obvious about who, or what he was,…someone would remember seeing him!...But then again, he thought angrily, 'the son of a Bitch might just be arrogant enough not to care! He hoped that was not the case because if he was riding across country, it would slow him down. However, there was always the chance that at some point, if he was staying clear of the road,…he just might eventually get ahead of him, the road being so much faster?

No, he decided. Hatcher had already proven that he was not concerned with being seen. His arrogance was such that he believed no one could stop him! That thought alone made him mad!

"You're wrong, Mister Hatcher!" He yelled suddenly, and was almost thrown from the big black's back, having to quickly calm it down to prevent it from bolting. "Whoa, boy!" He soothed. "It's okay." He said, reaching down to pat the animal's neck to reassure it.

"You are a son of a Bitch, Hatcher!" He said aloud. "You shot th' wrong man this time!" He sighed deeply then, and thought of his foster father, fighting for his life in a hospital bed, while his would be killer was out there somewhere enjoying his freedom.

"I'll get 'im, Doc!" He said, and patted the horse's neck again. "No man harms my family!" He looked off into the darkness again. "You hear that, Hatcher? Watch your back trail, you Bastard, cause I'm comin'!"

He patted the animal's neck again and laughed. "Think I'm crazy, don't ya?...Well you ain't far from wrong! But we'll both have to live with it." He strained his tired eyes at the dark road, not able to see anything but darkness, and shadows. But the tall grass on either side appeared lighter, and kept him on the road,…and although urgency had his mind in it's grasp, and his heart as well, he forced himself to keep the horse at a fast walk while waiting for the moon to rise.

*   *   *

Sherman, Texas was named after General Sydney Sherman, a hero of the Texas revolution. The town was designated County Seat, thus creating

Grayson County in 1846. In 1846, a post office began operation, and by 1850, had become an incorporated town under Texas law. It had also become a stop on the Butterfield Overland Mail route through Texas, and by '52, a log Courthouse, and several businesses, a District Clerk's office, and a Church along the east side of the square had been erected. From that point onward, Sherman had grown rapidly, even participating in the regional politics. In '61, Sherman had its first flour mill. During, and after the Civil War, north Texas outlaw bands led by Jesse James and William Quantrill were seen there,…and it was said that years later, Jesse James spent his honeymoon there, where he was photographed on horseback.

Today, the city was a sprawling conglomerate of business, the downtown area spread out for a mile or more. Business and housing within the city's limits went on for a mile or more.

Billy stopped the horse on a hill in the road, able to see the large, dark expanse of Sherman in the distance, and pulled his watch to check the time.

One, thirty, he thought as he put it away, and that must be Sherman, Texas. About time, too, he thought tiredly. He knew that if it had not been dark, he could have made better time!

"Come on, Blackie!" He said, kicking the horse in the flanks. "Let's see what's goin' on in Sherman, Texas." The moon was high enough to light up the road, so he urged the horse to a trot, still keeping it along the unused side of the rutted lane as much as possible,…and an hour later, he was passing houses on both sides of the road as he entered the city's limits.

It was a bigger town than Bonham, he noticed, already passing a wagon yard on his right, and a brick yard on his left. He passed more houses after that, before coming to a cotton gin, and a boiler plant. He tried watching it all in passing, but as tired as he was, figured there was no point in it,… and urged the black horse to a lope as he entered the business district, only slowing down when he reached the large square, checking the dark buildings as he slowly walked the black across.

'Well', he thought, when he saw the Sheriff's office, and the dim light in the window. 'Appears they're open for business here', and reined the animal toward the hitch-rail where he stopped and sat the saddle for a minute to peer through the dirty window then sighing, dismounted with a grunt, and tied the reins.

Still peering at the lighted window, he stepped up to the boardwalk and moved closer to the window, seeing two men, one leaning against the wall beside the desk, and one seated at the desk.

Turning for a look back at the empty square, he moved to the door and knocked then waited until he heard footsteps inside, and the door was opened.

He stood there while the deputy looked him over, his unwavering stare never leaving the lawman's face.

"Well." Asked the deputy curtly. "State your business, Mister!"

"Let 'im in, Lem, who is it, anyway?" interrupted the other man.

"I don't know 'im, Mister Cartwright,…drifter, I guess." He moved aside enough for Billy to come inside.

The Sheriff got up and came around the desk. "Sheriff Cartwright." He said, holding out his hand.

"Bill Upshur." He responded, and shook the man's hand. "Deputy Marshal from Paris."

"Of course, Mister Upshur, do come in and sit down, man….I'm sorry for the way Lem acted, he's had a long night."

"Makes two of us." He replied, nodding at the deputy. "I like a man that does his job, Lem." He sat down then. "You likely know why I'm here, Sheriff, have you seen th' man I'm lookin' for?"

"Wes Hatcher?…No, We haven't seen 'im….Lem, there has been watching the square all day, with no luck, sorry to say."

"Yeah, I'm sorry, too."

"Lem, go in back, get the Marshal some coffee." He watched the deputy go into the cellblock then looked back at Billy. "I hear tell, this Hatcher is bad news, Bill, he killed a gunslinger over in Oak Ridge, day before yesterday."

"I know,…Sheriff in Bonham told me….Did you check it out?"

"Right after we got the wire, yeah, been gone an hour when we got there, though."

"You give chase?"

"No, I had two deputies with me, and hardly anybody was sure which direction he went!" Lem came back with the hot cup of coffee then, and gave it to Billy.

"Thanks, I can sure use this, Lem." He took a swallow of the strong liquid, and felt the scalding heat all the way down.

"You're welcome to a bunk in one a my cells, Marshal, if you want a sack out for a while."

"Many thanks, Sheriff, but I can't afford the time….Way it's shapin' up, Hatcher's still a day ahead a me,…I got a make up some time somehow."

"Well, a gunslinger has to sleep sometime, too." Returned Cartwright. "Chances are, that's what he's doin' right now!"

"I hope you're right,…but if I can make up a few hours on th' son of a Bitch, I'm gonna do it!"

"I understand….Well, I can't help you a lot, but I can sack up some cold sausage and biscuits for ya."

That would help, Yeah….Thanks."

"Lem," He said, and jerked his head toward the cellblock. At that moment, the door opened, causing them both to look as the smaller man came in.

"What's th' rush, Elmo?" Grinned Cartwright.

"Found this wire on my desk a while ago, Reno must a took it sometime yesterday and forgot to tell me about it. Anyway, I seen your light on, and thought I'd bring it over. Sorry about the mess-up." He gave Cartwright the paper and left.

"Appears this is for you, Marshal." He gave Billy the paper. "Sounds like good news."

"Yes, sir, it is, damn good news!" He drained the cup of strong coffee then, and got to his feet.

"Hatcher shoot this, Doctor?" Asked Cartwright.

"Yeah, stole his pet horse, too!...Doc's my father, Sheriff." He held up the wire. "This news is gonna make th' manhunt a little more pleasin'!"

"Here ya go, Marshal." Said the Deputy, giving him the cloth sack. "Lem Harold's th' name, mighty glad to meet ya."

"Likewise, Lem, keep up th' good work." He shook Lem's hand, nodded at the Sheriff. "Thanks for your time, Sheriff, and th' grub." He mounted the black, and with a wave, sent it down the street at a gallop.

Late yesterday, he thought wearily, that would put Hatcher the twenty-four hours or more ahead of him. If he does stop to rest at night, 'I got a be gaining on him a little bit'!...He was sure that the time involved in all of this was far from being accurate,…but at least, now, he could go after him with one less worry on his mind,…which brought up yet another question, was

Hatcher even trying to kill Doc, or purposely wound him to get away? Not that it made a damn, he thought angrily!...Hatcher's a killer, he has to be stopped!

It was daylight when he spotted the sign post, showing the way to Oak Ridge, but there was no reason to go there, so he allowed the black horse free rein to gallop, keeping it at that pace until mid-morning before slowing to a trot again to avoid a wagon, and a team of mules, urging it off the road completely to allow it to pass, and then yelling at the farmer as he did....He also had to grin, because he had seen the four year old boy grab the lines and turn the team toward him.

The farmer stopped the team, and got to his knees on the seat to chastise the youngster, and was about to do it severely.

"Hey, man!" Yelled Billy, and urged the horse back beside the wagon to lean on the saddle-horn. "Boy didn't mean that much harm, did he, I'm still in one piece?"

The man turned back around and sat down again. "Awww, Mister, he does that all th' God damn time! Can't seem to break 'im from it....I try to watch 'im, but he's smart enough to wait till th' right time, when I ain't lookin'!"

"We're awfully glad you ain't hurt, Mister." Said the woman beside him. "We've tried to break 'im from it!"

"Stand th' boy up for me, I want a show 'im somethin'." He waited for him to make the boy stand up then reached the badge from his shirt and pinned it on.

"Do you know what this is, boy?" And when the child nodded. "Do you know what I am?" He nodded again. "What am I?"

"You're a sheriff?"

"A United States Marshal!" He said, and tapped the badge. "Sheriffs work for me!...Do you know what can happen to you for playin' a game like that?" The boy's eyes grew wide, and he shook his head. "I can take you away from your mama and papa, and put you in jail, is that what you want?" The boy began crying then, and shook his head.

"Okay, I'll give you one more chance....If you don't start listenin' to your folks, and I hear you done this again, I'll come back,...and I'll take you away! Now sit down and behave yourself!" He grinned as the boy quickly sat down out of sight.

"Thanks, Marshal,…name's Waterfield,…this is my wife, Sissy." He said just as another wagon and team was passing.

"Hey, Corey," Called out the driver.. "He do it again?" He laughed loudly and slapped the lines on the team's backs, urging them on down the road.

"My neighbor!" Nodded Waterfield. "He's an ass hole."

Billy grinned then. "No harm done, folks, but a word a warnin',…there's bad people on these roads sometimes, don't let 'im do that to the wrong one!" He tipped his hat to the woman, and rode out behind the wagon at a gallop.

The road had now become busier, as he was meeting more and more wagons, some with freight, others with families. But it was coming on to mid-day and to him, was understandable.

He then began stopping a few at random, especially those men on horseback, to ask about the dappled gray horse and rider. None had seen them, but a couple told him of the Oak Ridge killing. He kept the black at a steady gallop, slowing periodically to cool it down. It was well past noon when he saw the second marker showing the road to Oak Ridge. Two roads in, and out, he thought. That eased his mind some, as Hatcher would have to come out on this very road again, however, the question was still the same, and since no one so far had admitted seeing the gray horse,…did he stay on the road, or just cross it?

He had convinced himself that he had crossed the road and was riding cross-country, when he heard the gunfire. Three fairly loud retorts echoed toward him from farther up the road, and he urged the horse to a hard gallop again. Trees were thick along both sides of the wide lane with wild Pecan, Cottonwood, and some Burr oak. The brush, fallen limbs, briars and vines were thick beneath the heavy, spreading limbs, preventing passage through the foliage. So he stayed on the dusty road.

As he rode, he unpinned the badge from his shirt, returning it to his shirt pocket then reached down and removed the tie-down from the Colt pistol's hammer as the black horse ate up the last hundred yards to a blind bend in the road.

Hearing the loud voices, he stopped and walked the horse around the bend, and that's when he saw the source of the gunfire. Two men, bandanas in place over nose and mouth, were holding guns on the stage driver, and as the driver threw down the money box, one of the men saw him, and yelled."

He quickly raised both hands, and continued walking the horse toward them, all the while assessing the situation. He saw the body of the shotgun guard then slumped over the driver's box. He was within forty feet of the team of horses with guns pointed at him, when one of the mounted men called out.

"That's close enough, Pilgrim!" Snapped the man closer to him. "You got three choices here!...Drop them hands and die, sit that horse till we're gone, or turn around and run like hell!"

"My hands are up, man!...Why'd you have to kill that man?"

"He had a gun in his hand, now shut up!...Luke," He said, without looking at him. "Grab that strongbox."

"Leave it!" Said Billy, and wondered why he had so brazenly spoke up? "What I mean is,...you already killed a man here, aint that enough?"

Both men chuckled. "Will be, when we got that money!...What are you, cowboy, some kind a hero?...No, it ain't enough, so why don't you reach down and unbuckle that gun-belt before you're next, funny man?"

"Okay, man," He nodded. "Don't get excited, I hear ya." He started to lower his arm then.

"Left hand, Pilgrim!"

He lowered his left arm, and as both men's eyes were focused on it, dropped his right hand, drew and fired, all in one eye-blinking motion. Horses reared and squealed at the sudden thunderous explosions as he fired twice. Both men were thrown from their saddles as their horses bolted past him and the prancing black in a hard run around the bend in the road.

He urged the horse in closer to the first man, who was just trying to sit up in the road, and was almost crying as he clutched at the wound in his upper shoulder area.

"Get up!" Ordered Billy.

"There's two more behind us, Mister!" Yelled the driver, and he urged the horse around the men to look for them, but saw nothing and came back.

"I said, get up!"

"I can't, God damn it!"

"Then crawl, move over beside your ass hole buddy....Do it!" He moved the snorting black even closer to him, it's hooves threatening to step on the man, causing him to yell and painfully scoot himself toward his fallen companion beside the coach.

The driver climbed on down as Billy dismounted, and removed his hat. "What just happened here?" He blurted, looking down at the badly wounded men. "They had you dead to rights!" He said, looking back at Billy. "I was watchin' you, never saw you draw, never seen nothin' like it in my life!...Whoever you are, many thanks, friend." He reached and shook Billy's hand.

"I was lucky." Grinned Billy then nodded at the coach. "You carryin' any passengers?"

"Three women, they're cowerin' down inside."

Hearing the voices of several running men, Billy looked back to see men coming toward the coach, it was then that he saw the wagons that had been stopped there.

"There was four of 'em." Said the driver then. "Two back there to stop traffic, two here to rob us....Them other two must a ran like scared rabbits when these two went down." He quickly went to intercept the teamsters and stop them, and then they all came walking back toward the coach to stop while the driver came on to talk with Billy.

"That man up there,...is he dead?"

"Never had a chance." Returned the driver. "Never even saw 'em."

Nodding, he took out the badge, and held it up for all to see. "Name's Upshur, deputy Marshal....I need some a you men to tend these two, bandage 'em up enough to stop th' bleedin'." As they came forward, he got the driver's attention.

"When they're done, tie 'em up on top a th' stage, turn 'em over to Sheriff Cartwright in Sherman....Pick up th' guns, too,...tell Cartwright what took place here." He looked back at the wagons again.

"You came out a th' town back yonder, what is it?"

"Place called Southmayd, we didn't stop there, all it is, is a tradin' post. Past that is Whitesboro, we stayed th' night there....Why you askin'?"

I'm chasin' a man on a dappled gray horse, thought ya might a seen 'im?"

"Sorry, friend, wish I had....We come all th' way from Gainsville, didn't see nothin' like that!...Left there at noon, yesterday, took on a woman at Muenster's Tradin' post, stayed th' night at Whitesboro,...and here we are."

"Didn't hurt to ask." Nodded Billy then turned to take up the black's trailing reins.. He mounted and looked down at them. "I wouldn't waste too much time getting' to Sherman, that man up there'll get ripe pretty fast in this heat."

"You're sure right about that, thanks again for th' help."

He nodded, and turned the horse around before kicking it into a fast trot past the men and coach. Looking back, he watched them as they tended to the outlaws, thinking that it was damn bold of them, robbing a stage coach at mid day, on a heavily traveled main road. He grinned then, as he stared at the several loaded wagons, and worked the black around them, only to see even more oncoming traffic as he cleared the last wagon and urged the black to a gallop again.

He thought back at what he had done then, and knew that what he did was damn bold of him as well,...pulling on two men with drawn, and cocked forty-five caliber handguns.

"That was a dumb thing to do, Bud!" He said, reaching down to pat the big black's sweating neck. "Let that be a lesson, there's luck, and then there's dumb luck!...And what I done was pure dumb, luck!"

He knew that, at the time, he'd had no intention of pulling on them, the thought never crossed his mind! In fact, he was sure that he would have shucked the gun belt like they wanted. But he also knew that, when he saw them both watching his left hand, his reflexes took over. That's the way it must have been, he thought.

Unless it was possible that his mind was thinking on it's own, at least part of his mind. One part complying with the armed men's orders, the other part waiting for an opening. He remembered what Doc had told him once, about how the blow to his head, when his folks were murdered, had somehow altered his motor-skills. He hadn't thought much about it at the time, mostly because he didn't know what it all meant, or what he was even talking about....'I still don't', he thought, but now wondered if it could be true?...He only knew that something had made him chance being killed, to stop a robbery.

'Beats hell out a me', he thought, and then shook his head to push it from his mind. Hatcher had to be somewhere on the other side of that Gainsville town, if he was still heading west, because he had passed dozens of crossroads, and cutoffs to at least that many small towns along the way. He could have taken any one of them, he thought, but he didn't, he went to Oak Ridge!... That, he thought wryly, was the only way he knew he was still on his trail.

He saw the buildings then as he slowed the black to a trot again, four or five small houses along the road, and a few more behind a larger building. 'Must be Southmayd, he thought, and that has to be the trading post, the driver told him about. He eyed the several horses at the hitch-rails in front, as well as the three or four unkempt men in front of the building talking. The men stared at him as he went by, and staring back at them until he passed the store, he urged the black horse to a gallop again.

Maybe he should have stopped, and asked his questions, he thought then, but again, decided against it. Hatcher had a week's worth of supplies, he would not have stopped this side of a bigger town!...'Hell, he might not even be on the road anymore', he thought, remembering that he had not been seen by anyone. 'Comes right down to it, I've got no idea where the Son of a Bitch is'!

CHAPTER THREE

Gainsville, Texas, originally laid out on 40 acres of tree-covered flat land that was surrounded by prairie, was now a large, sprawling city. This was cattle country, in every sense of the word, with ranch buildings, barbed-wire fences, and cattle-populated acreage in all directions. Acreage that stretched North toward the Red River, encompassing the growing community of Sivells, one of the areas where Ranches were being devastated by rustlers.

Coming in on the Sherman road, one would see frame houses that were erected no more than fifty feet apart, each separated by wood fences. The dwellings literally covered both sides of the wide, dusty thoroughfare. In the distance, further west, rose the reddish, brick buildings of downtown Gainsville. Buildings, that appeared to spread for miles along the skyline. A sleeping city, totally dark at night, except for the many kerosene lamp posts lighting part of the road into town. This same lighting was used every fifty feet or so around the square.

Today, acting Sheriff, J. W. Hicks sat at his desk, his two deputies lolled in chairs against the rear wall, and all were listening respectfully as the owner of the Latham Ranch voiced his opinions, and accusations.

"Now, just a minute, Lamar!" Said Hicks as Latham shouted. "Lamar!" He shouted again, stopping the rancher's ranting.

"What, God damn it?" Shouted Latham.

"Calm down, Lamar!" The anger in his voice caused Latham to grow silent.

"That's better, man!" He said, getting to his feet to pour more coffee in his cup. "Lamar," He said, replacing the pot on his desk then turning back to face him.

"First off, I know you're losing cattle, about all th' ranchers are!...But you haven't lost a single steer since Sheriff Quin was killed, leastwise that's what I hear from the other cattlemen,...have you lost any?"

"No, and I can't afford to!...But we both know that Quin's dying sent them into hiding. Be just a matter of time till they hit us again. We need to do a full-scale search of the County, flush 'em out!"

"I'm not a duly elected lawman, Lamar, you know that!...Hell, I'm not a lawman at all, don't know the first thing about being one,...I'm just holding down the position until one can be found."

"God damn it, J. W., I know all that! But ain't now th' time to be trackin' these bastards down?...They're close, man, I can feel it! They could hit us again anytime! A bunch like that has got to be noticed by somebody, J. W.....Something's got a be done here, or they're gonna start up again, bigger'n hell!"

"They are also a dangerous bunch, Lamar!...Every job they've pulled was well planed out, I can't even imagine where to start?"

"Sheriff Quin found 'em," Stated one of the deputies. "And he was killed for it."

"Sure he was!" Said Latham, in response. "But he was doing his job, too!...I'm as sorry as any of you that he's dead, his deputies, too." He bowed his head then. "He saved the majority of my dwindling herd, though....My wranglers hadn't heard the shooting, and tried to help?...Well, they scared the bunch off,...but,...they were too late to help Quin."

"We realize that, Lamar." Sighed Hicks, and drained his cup. "All right!...Since you feel so strongly about this,...maybe they are still somewhere in th' County, I don't know!...But I'll deputize some men and ride out to your place in th' mornin'. Maybe you can spare a few men to show us where all this happened?...Because, frankly,' Lamar,...me, and these deputies here are new at this."

"I will do that, J. W. !...I'll even go with you."

"Good!...We ought a be there before noon."

"Lookin' forward to it!" Said Latham, and abruptly turned and left the office.

"Whoever's stealin' them cows won't be easy to catch, if we do find 'em, Mister Hicks."

"Sheriff, Mister Meeker!...Call me Sheriff." He corrected. "Maybe I'll start believing it!" He went to pour himself more coffee.

"But that ain't no shit, neither!...Don't know th' first thing about finding that bunch." He turned back to look at them then. "Both of you were Quin's deputies, and I'm lookin' to you two to teach me how a manhunt works."

"Us?" Said Meeker. "We was jailors, Sheriff,...we patrolled downtown here, but that's all!...Sheriff Quin never took us on any manhunt. He always took Gentry, and Sloan with 'im, left us in th' office."

"You must a heard 'em talking, making plans,...surely you got some idea to what went on?"

"Yes, sir." He replied. "Some, I guess....We'll do our best, Sheriff."

"I know ya will,...so will I!" He took a swallow of the hot coffee. "I just don't understand how a gang of cow thieves could steal so many cows, and nobody sees anything?"

"Sheriff Quin knew!" Returned Meeker.

"Took 'im six months to figure it all out!" Said the other deputy.

"We don't have that long." Sighed Hicks. "But we need to end it, and quick,...make sure they don't come back!"

"How?" Questioned Meeker.

Hicks shrugged. "By catching them!...Lamar might be right, they could be just laid back somewhere till it all cools down,...till everyone stops lookin' for 'em....How many men can you round up?"

"Dozen, maybe, Me and Ralph here can go see them that Sheriff Quin always used....Tell ya one thing, though,...we find where they're hid out, I'll get men from every ranch in th' county to help take 'em down!"

"Might need 'em, too!...Okay, you two go do your recruiting, we leave at sun-up!"

*   *   *

Billy woke with a jerk when the black snorted loudly, and yawned mightily as he stared at the lighted windows of the, otherwise darkened houses on both sides of the road.

"This is Gainsville, I guess." He muttered tiredly, and reached down to pat the black's sweaty neck. "Welcome to Gainsville, Texas, Blackie!" He laughed aloud then continued to watch the fenced-in yards, with their barking dogs,…and listening to his stomach growl when the aroma of strong coffee, and frying bacon filled his nostrils.

An hour later, he was crossing the tracks of the Katy railroad, and entering a large town that was only now in the process of waking up to a new day,…and was just showing some life as he entered the large, open square, with it's many pole lamps illuminating the dark storefronts.

At that point, he saw the group of mounted men in front of what he was sure had to be the sheriff's office. 'That', he thought, 'has got to be a posse,' as he reined the horse toward them,…only to stop at the hitch-rail in front of the open, lighted doorway. Twisting in the saddle, he eyed the silent group of not so happy men, unable to see their faces, but very capable of reading their body languages,…and all of them were speaking that same language.

"You men a posse?" He asked, still eying them.

"Who wants to know?" Came a voice from the doorway, causing him to turn and look at the source.

"Name's Upshur." He responded, and then dismounted tiredly. "Bill Upshur,…you be th' Sheriff?"

"The acting Sheriff, yes!"…What's your business here, Mister Upshur?"

He stepped up to the boardwalk. "Trackin' a man, name a Wes Hatcher, ever hear of 'im?"

"I have, got a poster on him." Returned Hicks. "Would you be a lawman?"

"Deputy Marshal,…he'd be ridin' a dapple gray horse,…that jar your memory any?"

"I'm afraid not,…but I am damn glad to see you, Marshal! Come inside, please, I need to talk with you."

Curious, he took another look at the posse member's sullen faces against the pale dawn sky, and followed Hicks inside the large office. Six chairs were positioned side by side along one wall, and beneath large pictures of both, Lincoln, and Robert E. Lee. A large picture of Grant was on the wall behind the desk. But the desk was what caught his eye, It was clean, everything in order, and, he had to admit,…the first one he'd ever seen in that condition. The wall, next to the cellblock door was adorned with a large gun-rack consisting of four repeating rifles, two shotguns, and a hunting rifle, scope and all.

He watched as Hicks brought one of the chairs to the desk then went into the cellblock, to return shortly with the coffee pot and two cups.

"What's th' posse for, Sheriff?" He asked, walking over to sit down beside the desk. "Bank robbed, or somethin'?"

"Rustlers!" Said Hicks as he poured the coffee and sat down, he placed a cup in front of Billy. "Up until three weeks ago, the four largest ranches in the County were losing cattle to 'em, have been for nearly six months."

Billy took a swallow of the coffee, his eyes on the Sheriff's face, and as he swallowed, shook his head. "The answer's no, Sheriff, I'm sorry!...I'm after a killer, and he's somewhere ahead a me."

Hicks swallowed his coffee and then placed the cup down with a sigh. "Look, Marshal,...I'm a storekeeper, not a lawman....Three weeks ago, come tomorrow now, Sheriff Quin, and two of his deputies died at the hands of these Bastards!...They were murdered!...I do not know how to run a manhunt, or where to start one, or even where to look for men like these!...I need you!"

"I ain't your man, Sheriff,...sorry." He said this, also with a sigh, and gave back the empty cup. "Man I'm after killed two good men on th' way here, one was a lawman!...That brings his total up to twelve men.....My job's to stop 'im!"

"But, you're a Marshal, you have legal jurisdiction, let alone being your duty!"

Billy sighed heavily, finding it very hard to say no to a man he felt believed in justice as much as he did. He also knew there was no way that he could help him, he was no lawman, either!...He had no experience as one, he couldn't even track his own horse! He had done his share of tracking down men like these, but had always had Peter Birdsong to do the tracking for him,...otherwise it was ninety percent luck when he succeeded.

He looked around at the immaculate office again, the large clock on the wall, the gun-rack, display of handguns beside the picture of Grant, and finally back to meet Hicks' pleading eyes. "Say this has been goin' on for six months?"

"About that." He nodded. "Until Sheriff Quin was killed, no one had ever been able to see them do it.....Quin figured it all out, and was waiting for them, he didn't confide in anyone, other than his two deputies.....He was on to something, that's for sure, and he was right!...He caught 'em red handed!" He sighed then. "They never even got off a shot when they were killed.....Only good thing to come of it, was they didn't get any cows that night. Latham's hands heard the shooting, and went to help." He sighed again, and continued to stare at Billy.

"I need you, Marshal."

"Look, Sheriff, from what you told me, th' rustlin' stopped when this Quin was killed….Why take out a posse now, they're likely gone for good, now they were caught?"

"That's what I think, too!...But that ain't good enough for Lamar Latham. He really thinks they're hid out somewhere, just waiting for things to cool down before starting up again!...He insists that we search th' County for 'em, and that's what I have to do!...He didn't say it, but if we don't do something, he'll go to th' Governor for help. Things won't be so good after that."

"I don't envy ya none, Sheriff, sounds like you need somebody,…but it ain't me, I'm sorry!" He got to his feet as he spoke. "From what you told me, it appears this bunch knows when, and where to steal these cows….And that tells me, they might be getting' a head's up on th' when, and where! Almost like they get that information ahead a time, ain't it?...Ya know, Sheriff, was me, I think I'd pay a call on each a these ranchers, and have a talk,…see how many new hands they got, say, one that's been there for six months, or more."

"What are you telling me, Marshal,…that one of these rustlers actually works on one of these ranches?"

"Or on all of 'em….Somebody's supplying th' information."

"I'll be damned, a spy workin' on the spreads they're stealing cows from….Wouldn't that be a little far-fetched?"

"Maybe,…but till your Sheriff was killed, nobody had a lead on 'em. Got a be a reason why?" He walked to the door then looked back. "They only been seen that one time, Sheriff.…Stands to reason, they knew your Sheriff Quin was gonna be there, and turned th' tables on 'im!...They was waitin' for him! How would they know that?...From what I've heard here, that Sheriff Quin was a seasoned lawman, smart one, too!...Would he of walked into a trap like that, if he didn't think he would surprise th' bunch?... No, he wouldn't, good lawmen wouldn't do that!"

"Good God!" Said Hicks, getting to his feet, and shaking his head. "Meeker!" He yelled then came around his desk. "Meeker!...Come in here for a minute!" He came on to shake Billy's hand. "Thank you, Marshal." He turned, and went back to his desk.

Nodding, Billy waited until the deputy entered then walked out across the boardwalk, jerked the reins loose, mounted, and then sat and watched the lighted doorway for a minute before looking at the rider closest to him.

"Mind pointing me to your telegraph office, friend?"

"Across the square, behind us there, Marshal." He replied, turning to point at another open doorway.

"Much obliged." He reined the horse back away from the hitch-rail, and then around the group to cross the half-empty square, watching as a man was going from one lamp post to another, step-ladder in hand, to snuff out each of the flames. Smiling, he dismounted at the hitch-rail and looked back at the posse again.

He would like to help them, he thought sadly, but he just didn't know how? He had chosen not to tell Hicks, he was not a lawman at all,…that he knew Hicks' frustration. But he was not a tracker either, and he didn't know the first thing about finding rustlers, or anyone else. He continued to watch as the Sheriff and deputy came out, spoke to the men, and then mounted. Three of the men rode back east then turned north on the next street, while the rest rode out the west road.

"Guess he took me seriously." He thought aloud, and shaking his head, crossed the boardwalk and through the open door.

*   *   *

"Have you heard from William yet?" Asked Doc, searching their faces. "Anything at all?"

"No, Walter," Said Mattie, from her chair beside the bed. "Not since Rodney wired him about your recovery….We're worried about him, too!"

"Why?" He asked. "All three of you darlins know he's come through worse than this,…you forget how he brought our grandson home, all by his lonesome?…Don't worry about William, that boy's the very best there is!"

"We know that, too, Walter!…but we're still worried."

"I know you are." He made a feeble attempt at a chuckle, grimacing in pain as he placed a hand on her's. "William will not get into anything, that he can't get out of, all four of you know that, especially Rodney there!… Nobody on God's green earth can outshoot that boy!"

"No, sir!" Said Rodney, from the foot of the bed. "I believe that, too.... But I should be with 'im,...and I know that, too!"

"And do what, son?...He gets in trouble, the kind you're scared of, one arm won't help 'im much!...He'll be okay, likely ain't somewhere that's got a telegraph right now....He'll be okay, he'll bring Hatcher back, too!...Or kill 'im!...And that'll be just dandy with me!"

"Don't get yourself in a snit, Walter!" Smiled Mattie. "We all have faith in William. Besides, all this talk is only upsetting our daughter in law."

"You're right, old Darlin'." He replied then reached to take Connie's hand. "I am sorry, daughter....Just don't you worry none about that husband of yours,...he'll be all right."

"Oh, I know that, Doc." She sniffed. "It's just that, he was so mad, like nothing I've ever seen before....He tried to hide it, but I know! I'm afraid he might get careless like that."

"He does have a way about 'im!" Sighed Rodney. "Gets to a certain point, he won't listen, takes things real personal."

"What do you mean, Rodney?" Asked Connie.

"I mean, that he takes family matters personal."

"No, no, you said he has a way about him?"

"I don't know exactly, Connie....It's like,...he won't have his family or friends laid a hand on,...They harm you, they pay for it!...I don't know!...This last trip was th' first time I ever heard 'im say anything like that,...I never knew about it!...Something else, too,...he said he never wanted to kill again, and that's what worries me!"

"Why, Rodney?" Asked Connie.

Rodney shrugged, I,...don't really know that either. Except,...well, he might try to wound Hatcher, and not kill 'im when they meet."

"Would that be a bad thing, honey?" Inquired Melissa, speaking up for the first time. "Would it?"

"No. baby, it wouldn't, except,...and I'm sorry, Connie....Hatcher might be as fast as he is. Even Connie said, he reminded her of Billy!...Forgive me, Connie, I'm just worried too."

"I know, Rodney. But I'd feel better just hearing from him."

"We all would." Agreed Melissa.

"Well," Grunted Doc. "You all just dry your eyes, and stop all this worrying, William will get the job done in no time!...Be home soon, he will!"

"Well, I wish he hadn't gone at all." Sighed Mattie. "That man was the devil himself, Walter,...heartless!"

"Well, that devil shot me, old darlin',...took Freckles, too!...You heard Rodney, William couldn't let that stand, and neither can I....What better man, to bring that devil to justice, than William?...None, that's what!"

"I do believe that horse meant more to you than your own life, the way you talk!...Don't you know you almost died, you old coot?"

"Now don't get your feathers ruffled, Matilda." He grinned. "I'm a sick man, you might upset me to the point of remission....Besides, it all comes down to principals!"

"Principals?...Keep on, I'll make you think principals." She burst out laughing then, and looked at all of them. "He's going to be fine, he's complaining." That made them all laugh.

"I am not complaining!" He retorted. "That horse was like one of our kids, old Darlin', you said so, yourself!"

"Am I interrupting something?" Asked Stockwell, as he stuck his head inside the door. "Not throwing things, are ya?"

"It ain't reached that point, Jim!" Said Rodney. "Come on in, Doc's just feelin' his oats."

"Have you heard from Billy?" Asked Connie quickly.

"That's why I'm here." He said, coming in and closing the door behind him. He grinned, and came on to the bed, giving her the paper to read. "That came in about five this mornin', I rushed it right over here."

"What does it say, Connie?" Urged Melissa.

"Okay,...Am in Gainsville, Texas....great to hear Doc okay, give him my love....Hatcher still ahead of me somewhere....will keep going....tell kids, Doc, Mama, all of you, I love you all....home soon....I love you.... Billy"

"Short, but sweet!" Chuckled Rodney. "Never was too much for words."

"But he's okay!" Smiled Doc. "Told you that!"

"Yes, but I'm still worried about 'im." Nodded Mattie.

"Makes two of us, Mama Bailey." Smiled Connie. "Thank you, Jim." She said, putting the paper in her pocket.

"My pleasure, Connie,…Well, I'll be going folks." They all thanked him profoundly as he left.

"At least, we know he's all right!" Said Melissa.

"Amen to that!" Breathed Rodney. "Gainsville, Texas is every bit of a hundred miles away….A hundred miles in, what, four days, in heat like this, too!…Hatcher must be traveling pretty fast."

"He's killing my horse, is what he's doing!" Muttered Doc. "Damn his soul!…That horse ain't never known anything but kindness!"

"It's just a horse, Walter, my Lord!" Cried Mattie. "I love Freckles, too,…but that horse almost got you killed, you old fool!"

He grabbed her hand and squeezed it. "I admit, that was a damn fool thing for me to do, old Darlin'. But when he took hold of Freckles, I didn't know what I was doing! It just stuck in my craw, that's all!"

"Shush now, Walter, what's done, is done, and you're not well yet!…Keep it up, you'll aggravate that wound."

"Awww, I'm all right, why don't you go on home and rest some, you're wore to a frazzle, you all are!…Need to feed the animals anyway, milk the cow, udder's likely dragging the ground by now, been four days!"

"Lord, God, I'm tired just thinking of all that!"

"Then we'll all go, Mama Bailey!" Laughed Rodney. "We'll do the chores, you get some rest….We'll stay the night, come back in the mornin'"

"We can do that!" Smiled Connie. "We've got the buggy outside."

"I'll get it ready." Said Rodney, taking Melissa's arm. "Come on, Baby, I need a couple extra hands."

*   *   *

Billy pulled his watch to check the time before turning back to look at the telegrapher. "It's been more'n an hour, think they got it?…It's past six o'clock." He put the watch away as he spoke.

"Unless th' wire's down somewhere, they did!…Sometimes, they just forget to send confirmation of delivery….Besides, every wire we send is heard by more'n a dozen telegraphers. Any one of 'em could be at fault, if they intercepted it somehow….As good as the telegraph is, damn thing ain't perfect sometimes. Usually no problem with it, we all got a code we use." He picked up a paper. "Got all the towns we cater to from here, see, here is,

Gains, for gainsville, Paris would be, Par, or just Paris. Wire comes through, we see where it's going, and pay no mind to it."

"It's important, I know they got it."

"I know it is, Marshal, I'll request one again for ya." He turned back to the desk and sent the wire.

Billy watched him for a second then shook his head in disgust. He was wasting time, he did not have, and was already feeling the urgency in his gut,...or could it be hunger, he thought? But Connie needed to know he was okay, they all did! He needed to know that they did. He was also beginning to think like Mattie, that he should not have come after Hatcher at all....But he also knew that it just was not in him to quit!

"Got it this time!" Laughed the telegrapher. "They forgot to send it, went to breakfast instead."

"Much obliged." He said quickly, and started to leave.

"Wait a minute, Marshal!" Said the agent quickly. "Saw you coming from the Sheriff's office a while ago. Was gonna deliver this wire when I saw him ride out, anyway, you being a lawman, and all, you might want to read this wire for the Sheriff, maybe you can give it to 'im."

"I doubt it, what's in it?"

"Robbery and killing over at Slidell yesterday morning. Seems somebody broke into the tradin' Post, and got caught doin' it!...Anyway, the store keep was pistol whipped." He chuckled. "Man's wife fired a greener at 'im, shot the window out!...Constable heard it, and came runnin',...he was killed for his trouble, man got away....Anyway, they're asking for the law to take care of it."

"They know who did it?"

"Nope, got away on a gray horse, is all it says."

His heart skipped a beat then. No wonder he couldn't find anybody that saw him, he was going cross country, if it was him at all?...But his gut told him it was Hatcher.

"Where is this Slidell?"

"Wise County, little southwest a here, you gonna take care of it?"

"Yeah, I am! What's th' fastest way there?"

"Decatur road, take you in a mile of Slidell....Ain't nothin' there but that store, saloon, and a few rundown shacks." He came past Billy then out onto the boardwalk.

"Take that street yonder, and go south." He pointed. "Beside the bank there. You'll see the sign post about a mile out."

"Thanks,...Do me a favor." He said, digging a coin out of his pocket. "Send another wire to Jim Stockwell in Paris, tell 'im where I'm goin', tell 'im I got a lead on Hatcher." He gave him the coin, crossed the boardwalk, mounted and galloped along the row of shops, past the bank, as well as a few early risers, and sent the black at a run down the deserted street.

Gainsville, he noticed, was laid out with hundreds of streets, side streets, alleyways and congested stores and housing. He galloped the black horse along the southbound street for, what seemed to him, a long time before ever reaching the city's town limits. But once he did, and saw the old weather-beaten marker for Decatur, he reined the horse onto the somewhat overgrown, rutted thoroughfare.

If it was Hatcher, he thought, and the robbery happened sometime yesterday morning,...it would mean that he had somehow cut the distance between them considerably, not the two days, originally thought. 'And that', he thought again, would mean that going across country had slowed Hatcher down. That, or he was taking the time to sleep at night. Maybe he was becoming less sure of himself, or so sure of himself that he thought no one would be following him. Because if they did, he might realize that leaving dead men in his wake, just could raise his odds for survival.

But, he thought grimly, as it stands right now, those odds were at most fifty-fifty against it already! He was pushing his luck to the limit,...'and if I catch the son of a bitch, it'll be zero'! But as the black horse ate up the miles, he was still worried, he might not find the killer....He had to find him, he thought with determination, he could not, and would not let Doc down,... and the only way he could do that, was by bringing both, Hatcher, and Freckles back alive and well!...If he could fight back the urge to kill him?"

Knowing that it was time, he slowed the horse to a trot to cool him down, and at the same time, wondering when he had decided to bring the killer back alive, when he had vowed to kill him for what he did? All he could think of was putting a bullet in him for what he done! But four days without sleep, and hard riding had made him remember his dislike for killing and now, all he wanted was to bring him back alive. That would satisfy Doc anyway, he thought, he would have the satisfaction of seeing Hatcher hang! But then, in the back of his mind, there lurked the possibility of Rodney's being right,…that Hatcher could be the man to finally best him,…and that worried him, too.

He was not so confident as not to know that as long as he wore a gun, he would one day meet his match, every man did! There was always someone faster, or luckier somewhere in a country this big.

'Well', he thought grimly. What will be, will be! But he will die, too, if he is!…He sighed and began watching the endless miles of barbed wire, and grazing cattle in the pastures. He passed farmers behind plows driving the mules in fields, as they plowed under the remnants of last season's crops,… and for the next two hours of frequent rest periods for the horse, he finally came to the marker for Slidell, and reined the black onto the side road.

"That Agent was right!" He said aloud, on entering the small community. The several wood-sided houses were very time worn, but inhabitable. At the house, farthest out, he could see that it housed a black family, and a minute later, he was dismounting in front of the Slidell General. He climbed the steps and walked to the closed double doors, tried the knob, but found it locked. Walking back to the edge of the long porch, he looked across the narrow, weed and grass grown street, and noticed that the saloon was also closed, and sighing, turned back to knock on the door.

It took several loud knocks before he heard the woman's muffled voice. "Go away, we're closed!"

"I'm a lawman, ma'am!" He shouted back. "I need to talk with ya." He looked at the boarded up window for a second then heard the bar being lifted from the door, and as the heavy door swung inward, found himself face to face with a haggard-eyed, slender woman with graying hair. He removed his sweat stained hat, and smiled at her through his week's worth of beard and grime.

"You don't look like no law, I ever seen!" She said sternly. "Show me your badge!"

He took the badge from his shirt pocket and held it up for her. "I was in Gainsville when th' wire came in about th' trouble here,…how's your husband doing?"

"Bastard near-bout killed 'im, that's how he's doin'! She said angrily. "Might die anyways,…what do ya want a know?"

"First off,," He said, looking back across the street. "Place looks empty, where's everybody?"

"Hill behind th' store here. They be buryin' Constable Blaine."

"I heard he was killed,…you get a look at his killer?"

"Same som'bitch that broke in here, that's who it was!"

"What'd he look like?"

"He was young, tall as you, yella beard, long yella hair."

"I'm huntin' a killer, Ma'am, been on his trail a week now. He'd be ridin' a dappled gray horse,…you happen to notice that?"

"He'd be th' one you're after, I reckon."

"Many thanks, Ma'am." He said, and put on his hat. "I'm real sorry about your husband, but I'll be a goin' now."

"You find that Bastard, you kill 'im, ya hear?"

"Yes Ma'am….which way did he ride out?"

"Way you rode in, most likely went to Decatur, likely stay a while, too,…Sheriff there ain't got no balls!…you kill 'im!"

"Yes'um, I'll do my best." He went down the steps and mounted, tipped his hat to her, took another look at the boarded window, and then rode out of town at a gallop.

*   *   *

Decatur, Texas was not a large town, compared to that of Gainsville, but in the days before the Katy railroad came, was a stopover for drovers from cattle drives on the Chisholm trail. Until Quanah Parker's surrender in seventy-five, the town had periodically been plagued by marauding Comanche, and though more frequently in years prior, had survived and continued to prosper.

Now, save an occasional robbery, assault or rare killing, Decatur, Texas was a clean-looking, mostly law abiding community. The town was built mostly of logs and milled lumber. It had one main street through the center of town with a dozen more cross streets, and even more alleyways. In the sixties, the town had built four different Courthouses, each one larger than the last. It was a growing town of prominence.

John Wilkins Hogg, Sheriff elect, had been in office since seventy-eight. A square-jawed lawman who was tough as nails when it came to keeping the peace in Wise County. But he was also an aging man, married, and had grown children,…and was at a point in life where his desires were now on retirement, not on risking his life! Today, however, J. W. Hogg was a worried man as he reread the wire from Slidell. He dropped the paper on the desk then sighed as he looked up at the young deputy.

"I don't know, Oren,...it could be Hatcher, I guess,...the poster just don't give enough details about his description to be sure."

"It says, he's a yellow haired killer, J. W.,...you know it's him!...I know, I do!"

"You watch your tongue, Oren, remember who you're talkin' to!"

"I'm sorry, Sheriff, but you got a know he's Hatcher!...Everybody in that saloon's afraid of 'im, it's got a be him!...He's been here for two days now, people in that saloon's been there since last night!...You know it's Hatcher!" He frowned then as he looked at his boss, and with a sigh, leaned down to place both hands on the desk and stare at him.

"What's wrong, J. W.,...You've changed in th' past few months,...what's come over you?"

"Oren,...I'm gonna retire, come next election, and I want to be alive to enjoy it!...Man in that saloon is a gunfighter, a killer!...I just ain't anxious to even talk to 'im, let alone go against 'im!... You're right, Though, I ain't th' same man!" He breathed deeply then, and looked up at Oren.

"I ain't goin' up against a gunman like Hatcher, Oren, and I ain't about to let you, or Joe go up against 'im!...Joe still watchin' 'im?"

"At th' bar, yeah, he's been there since last night, too, Hatcher won't let anybody leave!...But I'll tell ya this, J. W., and you know I'm right!...Joe's hard put, just to stand by and do nothin', it's just a matter a time before he cracks, and takes 'im on.....Hatcher's got everybody in that saloon buffaloed, Son of a Bitch is drinkin' whiskey, and playin' cards like he owns th' place!"

"He's winning, I guess." Sighed Hogg.

"Them he's playin with are too scared to win, and he won't let 'em quit!... We got a do somethin'!"

"I know, Oren." He sighed. "I know....But he ain't shot anybody yet, and maybe he won't!...That bein' th' case, I'm of a mind to wait 'im out, give 'im some time, he'll get tired and be on his way,...and we'll still be alive!"

"I can't believe this, J. W., he's a wanted man, a killer!...We just gonna let 'im leave?"

Hogg cursed, and got up from the desk. "That's what I want a do, Oren!...But no, we're not!" He came around the desk then. "But we are gonna wait till he leaves th' saloon, catch 'im outside,...maybe we won't have any locals getting' hurt."

"Yeah, well I'd be okay with that, J. W., but Joe might not see it that way, you know he fancies himself a fast draw....He's hot headed enough to try it, too!"

"I know that." Nodded Hogg. "Think you can get Joe out a there without somebody getting shot?"

"Don't know, but I doubt it!...So far, Hatcher ain't lettin' nobody leave!... Everybody in there is afraid of 'im."

"How many people are in there?"

"Don't know that, either. I looked through th' window a time or two,... but all I saw was th' three men at th' table with Hatcher....Three girls on th' floor, four or five men at tables, another four or five at th' bar, countin' Joe, and th' bartender....Sixteen, or seventeen people."

"God damn it!...Why'd he have to get thirsty in Decatur?"

"Think Joe might take 'im, J. W.,...I mean, if he did start somethin'?"

"Why, hell no!...Hatcher pulls that gun like a devil, I've been readin' about 'im from Colorado, to Texas....Only way to stop a man like him, is from ambush,...and that's what we'll do when he leaves that saloon!

"You know that'll put Joe in th' middle."

"Maybe not!...He comes out, Joe'll be behind 'im, us in th' front....Joe will be on his own, just like we will....I just hope he does the right thing, and not start any shooting."

"Don't count on it!"

"Well, let's hope he don't....Now, you go on out there and recruit some help, get everybody away from that saloon outside, tell 'em to go in the stores, down th' street, whatever,...just get 'em out a sight!...Then you position yourself on th' saddle shop's roof, and wait....Take plenty of water, could be a long wait....Go on, Oren."

*   *   *

It was mid-afternoon when he slowed the black to a walk along the old rutted road, and when he finally intersected with the main stage route to Decatur, he urged it to a fast trot, and was soon passing the outlying older houses, with their barking dogs, and playing children in the yards.

The town, he thought as he entered the business district, was totally different than that of Gainsville, as most all the buildings were of aging lumber, but all were painted either an off-white, or a tan color. He also noticed that a lot of people were moving toward his end of town, both, on the boardwalks along both sides, and in the street. Men on horseback, wagon and teams,...and all doing their best to find room enough to whip the animals into a run. Wondering about it, and thinking it odd, he turned the black around, grabbed the reins of a cowboy's horse and hauled it to a stop.

"Hey!" Yelled the man angrily. "What th' hell are you doin'?"

"Settle down, Friend!" He yelled back. "What's all th' rush, somethin' goin' on?"

"Don't know, don't give a shit!...Th' law said to leave, and I'm leavin'! He pulled the reins from Billy's hand, and spurred the animal into a lope as he weaved around pedestrians and wagons.

'Hatcher', he thought!...He felt the excitement building, and it was at that moment, that he heard the gunfire, and spurred the black to a hard run, scattering pedestrians, and forcing horse and wagons alike to move out of his way as he headed toward the center of town. People were everywhere on the street, and boardwalks. Men were yelling, and ducking behind wagons, and into open doorways, women screaming as they were ushered out of danger from flying bullets,...yet all were curious enough to partially impede the black's progress toward the continuing gunfire.

He reined the horse through, and around the on-lookers, yelling at them to give way as he thundered by them. Most of the shooting had stopped by the time he finally slid the black to a stop, he saw the bodies of two men in the street, and another, with a badge on his vest bending over one of them.

"What happened here, Sheriff?" He asked, leaning from the saddle to be heard over the noise of the now, crowded street.

Hogg looked up at him with obvious pain in his eyes. "Who are you?"

Deputy Marshal, who did this?"

"Wes Hatcher!" He said loudly.

"Where'd he go?"

"Nowhere yet!" He said, looking toward the west end of town. "He's right yonder." He said. "Son of a bitch is darin' us, gloatin' over it!"

Billy looked over the heads of the curiosity seekers, and saw him. Hatcher was sitting on Freckles at the end of the street. He couldn't see it, but he was sure of the gloating smile on the gunman's face.

"Heee-yaa!" He yelled suddenly, and spurred the black horse to a jumping start then to a dead run, seeing Hatcher turn the gray and gallop out of town ahead of him. Both animals were running all out as they raced up the dusty road, with the black gaining on the gray horse with every stride.

For the next twenty minutes, the chase continued, the distance between them only two hundred or so yards, too far for an accurate pistol shot. But then he saw the gunman veer onto a side road ahead of him.

Running the black onto the partially overgrown, and tree-lined road, he slowed to a trot and pulled the Colt Pistol. Hatcher was nowhere to be seen, and not hearing the sounds of a running horse, he knew that he had either stopped, or was walking his horse as well. He continued up the winding roadway, and the trees were so thick along one side, that he could not see the road ahead where it turned.

The hair was standing up on the back of his neck, as the warning signals took over, and he knew that the gunman was waiting for him to show himself. He strained his eyes at the dark shadows in the trees, but saw nothing, and continued to walk the animal. Every nerve in his body was on edge as he neared the bend in the road, but then stopped to look at the gated archway, and then up at the carved headboard over it that read, J – M Ranch.

He was just about to move forward again when the sudden, unexpected impact of the bullet struck his left shoulder with such force, that he was lifted from the saddle and thrown backward off the horse to fall on his back and side on the road's hard, dry surface. The breath was forced from his lungs with a gush as he hit, and then there was nothing.

CHAPTER FOUR

Connie gasped loudly as her eyes opened wide. "Billy!" She said loudly, jarring the dregs of sleep from her frightened mind as she quickly got out of bed, She looked around wildly as awareness slowly took her back to normalcy.

"My Lord honey, what's wrong?" Asked Mattie, as she also woke up. "You have a nightmare, sweetie?"

"God, Mama Bailey. I hope so!" She looked worriedly at the older woman, as Mattie got out of bed. "Billy's hurt, Mama, I felt it happen!"

"Oh honey, surely not!...It was just a bad dream....You're worried, that's all!"

She sat down on the bed to rest her head in her hands. "I don't think it was a dream, Mama,...he was shot, I felt the bullet!"

"What happened?" Shouted Melissa, as she rushed into the room ahead of Rodney. "You all right?"

"She's okay, kids, she just had a very bad nightmare!"

"It was not a nightmare, Mama!" Insisted Connie. "I felt it happen!"

"Felt what happen?" Asked Rodney urgently.

"She thinks William is hurt." Said Mattie, and then sat down on the bed beside her. "Tell us what you felt, sweetheart."

"I don't know what I felt?" She responded, shaking her head. "It was just,...pain, it seemed to go plumb through me,...a searing pain, all over!"

"Lord, honey!" She sighed, and then looked at Rodney and Melissa as they moved to stand in front of them. "I don't know if it's possible to feel another person's pain when he hurts,...but I pray that you're wrong!" She looked up at Rodney then, and the gun in his hand. "You going to shoot someone, dear?"

He looked at the pistol then grinned and stuck the gun in his belt. "Never can tell, Mama Bailey."

"Especially in this day and age." Added Melissa.

"So true." She said, looking back at Connie.

"I need to know, Mama,…I have to know he's okay?"

"He was okay this morning, Baby, what on earth could have happened?"

"I don't know!…But something did,…he was shot!"

"Well, I'll tell ya what." Said Rodney. "We've already done th' chores, it's goin' on four o'clock. What say we lock up and go back to the hospital? We'll stop on th' way to see if there's any news?"

"Oh yes, Rodney, thank you!" Sniffed Connie.

He took Melissa's arm and ushered her back to the other bedroom.

"What if she's right, Rodney?" Asked Melissa. "He could be badly hurt!"

"I don't know, baby, but I've learned to pay attention to gut-feelings! I've been afraid a this ever since he left.…Didn't nothing make sense, or feel right about it!" He buckled on the gun-belt and put the gun in it before tying the holster down.

"Come on, honey, let's ready th' buggy."

*   *   *

"How is he Doctor?" Asked the slender, auburn-haired woman urgently.

"Lucky to be alive, is what he is, Jaclyn!" He cleared his throat as he secured the bandage. "Bullet went through cleanly, did not miss his heart by much,…any idea who he is?"

"Only this," She said, giving him the badge.

"Lawman." He sighed and gave it back to her. "Must have been chasing the man that shot up Decatur this afternoon.…You say you heard the shot?"

"We all did!…Hank, and couple of hands went to check it out. According to Hank, a man riding a gray horse did the shooting. He took off when he saw them coming,…will he be all right?"

"I think so,…if he can be still long enough to heal!…You'll need to keep the wound clean." He backed away from the bed then. "Must have been chasing that man for a while, too, got a week's worth of sweat and grime on him,…and might I add, smells to high heaven!"

"I'll bathe, and shave him, Doctor,…I'll take care of him."

"I have no doubt about that, Jaclyn, you're like a mother hen when it comes to animals and sick men." He grinned, and picked up his bag.

"I'll be back tomorrow to check on him,…right now, Oren Campbell is still in a touch and go battle for his own life!"

"Isn't he Sheriff Hogg's deputy?"

"That, he is,…Same man shot both Deputies before getting away.…Poor Joe kingsley didn't make it!"

"My God!" She said with a gasp. "I'm so sorry!…Thank you, Doctor."

"It's a pleasure, my dear,…I'll see you soon." He went into the lavishly furnished parlor, crossed the room and was about to open the door, when it opened to admit Sheriff Hogg. "Well, Sheriff, you startled me!"

"Me, too, Doc, pardon me,…I just wanted to inquire about th' Marshal?"

"He'll be fine, J. W.,…All he needs is rest."

"Of course, Doc, I won't bother 'im none. I need to ask Ms. Garnette about what happened, is all!"

"Do come in, Sheriff!" Called out Jaclyn Garnette, as she came into the room.

"Well," Said Doctor Rickers. "I'll be going.…See you tomorrow, Jaclyn, J. W." He left, closing the door behind him.

Hogg removed his hat and looked around the large sitting room. "I sure do admire this room, Ms. Garnette, whole house, actually."

"Thank you, Sheriff, it's quite comfortable."

"I know it is,…Maxwell had great taste, I'll say that!"

"Can I get you anything, Sheriff,…water, coffee?"

"Oh, no, Ma'am,…I would like to know what happened, though?"

She motioned him to a hand-tooled, decorative armchair before sitting down on the cushioned settee across from him. "Well, Sheriff,…I don't know who or what,…but, along about two, thirty today, Myself, Hank, and two other hands were on the front porch, Hank was giving them some last minute instructions. Anyway, we heard the shot, and I sent them to check it out!…According to Hank, a man was about to dismount at the gate, but saw them and rode away.…That's when they found the Marshal."

"Th' man they saw,…was he ridin' a gray horse?"

"I believe Hank did say he rode a gray horse."

"Hatcher ambushed him!" He said angrily.

"Hatcher?" She asked. "Who's he?"

"Wes Hatcher." He nodded. "He's a gunfighter, and outright killer,... killed one a my deputies,...the other one might die."

"I'm so sorry, Sheriff."

"Thank you, Ma'am, so am I." He looked back toward the road then. "Ain't that the old Rush Creek road?"

"Yes it is,...and I'd like to talk to you about Rush Creek."

He looked at her for a second. "What about it,...can't be nothin' left over there, place was deserted years ago!"

"You just have not been there in years." She replied. "Have you been there lately?"

"Why, no, Ma'am,...got no reason to....Prob'ly been twenty years."

"Well, there's still buildings there, Sheriff, a saloon, post office, the old school, houses,...there's folks still living there, too....Anyway, there's been a lot of extra activity there of late,...And I think you should see about it!"

"What kind of activity?"

"Well, as you know, or might not, my property borders Rush Creek to within a few hundred yards, and several of my hands reported seeing horses in a corral behind that saloon, and smoke coming from it at times.... Someone, besides the local residents are living there in that saloon, or, according to my foreman, hiding out there!...I know for a fact, that it has not been open in a long time."

"He say how many horses there was in that corral?"

"Only that it appeared to be a dozen or so."

"A dozen." He repeated, reaching to rub his chin. "Ain't nobody reported any rustling activity hereabouts, wonder who it could be?...You lost any cows lately?"

"One or two,...I'm not saying they didn't just get out and wander away somewhere, and my hands have found no broken fences anywhere.... So, unless they jumped my five wire fence and ran away on their own, something else has happened."

He looked at her for a moment. "Could those residents have reopened th' saloon,...what's your thoughts on it?"

"Mine?...On what, my cows?...I think they were butchered and toted away, maybe by whoever is populating Rush Creek now."

"Don't guess your hands have checked th' place out?"

"I will not send my hands into possible danger, Sheriff, that's your job!... But it should be checked out."

He nodded and got to his feet. "Tell me, was that th' direction Hatcher was goin' when he left?"

"Yes, it was."

"That's bad news, I think." He sighed heavily then. "I'm a couple deputies short right now, Ms. Garnette,…but as soon as I can put some good men together, I will check out Rush Creek!...Oh," He said, reaching the eyeglasses from his shirt pocket.

"Last I saw th' Marshal, he was wearin' spectacles. I found these on th' road, might be his." He gave them to her.

"Thank you," She said, and took them. "Is that all you wanted to see me about?"

"Yes'um, for now.….But if any a your hands see more activity at Rush Creek, or somebody usin' th' road out there that you don't recognize, I'd like to know about it."

"You will see about it then?"

"Oh, yes, Ma'am.….But I got a tell ya,…if Wes Hatcher is there with 'em, I'll need some serious help when I do!...I ain't about to tackle it alone,… and it'll take time to put a posse together, especially after the whole town saw what Hatcher could do yesterday."

"Thank you for coming, Sheriff."

"Yes'um." He nodded, and walked to the door, and after another look at the room, left and closed the door behind him.

"Typical, good for nothing man!" She said aloud, then sighed and went about heating water for the task of bathing her patient.

*   *   *

"Hey, Marsh,…I mean Rodney!" Exclaimed Jim Stockwell as he came to shake his hand. I was about to go home, anything wrong, Doc okay?"

"I guess so, Jim, me and th' girls just got back from Doc's house, they dropped me off here.….I need a favor, Jim."

"Anything for you, man, what can I do?"

"Come with me to th' telegraph office, I need you to find out if Billy's okay?"

"I don't understand, Rodney, he sent that wire this morning?"

"I don't understand either, Jim....Connie woke up from her nap this afternoon all upset,...said Billy had been shot, swears she felt th' bullet that hit 'im!"

"Man!...That's a mite far out, ain't it?...I mean, it had to be a bad dream or somethin',...don't ya think?"

"Jim, was a time, I'd agree with ya." He sighed then. "But over the past eight years, I've seen, and done things that would boggle any man's imagination!...So, who am I to say somethin' like this ain't possible?"

"Things, like what?"

"Someday, I might just tell ya, Jim." He said with a smile. "But you won't believe it then, either!...Come on, let's send them wires."

"Let's go!" Stockwell grabbed his hat, told Ben he was leaving, and followed Rodney out, and across the square to the telegraph office.

*   *   *

"Daughter!" Said Doc, as he reached to pat her on the hand. "Something like you just told me, is a documented phenomenon....I read about it in the medical news, I get every month. It's rare, but not uncommon!...Maybe Rodney will bring us some news.....Other than that, I wish there was something to say that would ease your mind."

"Don't worry yourself about it, Doc." She smiled weakly at him. "I'm just making you worse by fretting like this,...I wish Mama hadn't told you."

"Poppy-cock!...You have a right to worry, and so do we....We'll wait for Rodney, he'll ease all our minds, you'll see!"

"Well, I pray he does!" Said Mattie gloomily. "Anyway, I believe her, Walter. I knew William was coming home, remember?...I felt that, too!"

"I remember, old Darlin', very well!"

"I didn't want him to go at all, He was so mad....But I knew we couldn't stop him....Now let's all shush about it, Walter, before you have a relapse! Connie's right, you shouldn't worry about anything."

"I'm not worried, old Darlin',...I'm okay! And I'll tell you why?... William is the best there is at what he has to do, and the best we can do, is keep the faith!"

"Amen, Doc!" Breathed Melissa.

"Is Rodney going to walk back from town?" Asked Doc.

"Yes, he said he was." Said Connie. "Don't know how long it'll take him."

"Well, let's see." Began Doc. "You gals have been here a half hour, took you ten minutes to get here….Give him another hour, hour and a half to get here. You all get the chores done all right?" He chuckled then. "Bet Bossie was glad to see ya!"

"I'll say!" Replied Melissa. "She was standing in the barn bawling her head off, got almost two pails of milk."

"You put it in the well to cool?"

"Yes, Walter!" Said Mattie. "We fed the chickens as well." They heard the knock at the door then and looked, as Rodney came into the room.

He stopped at the door to stare at them, their faces all mirroring their anxiety. "Well," He sighed, still searching their faces. "We sent the wires,… Telegrapher said we wouldn't likely get a reply back before morning. Jim will bring us word."

"How did you get here so fast?" Asked Melissa. "We didn't expect you for an hour yet."

"Oh,…I brought Ben's horse, Jim'll take it back in the mornin'."

"Well," Said Doc, and cleared his throat. "Makes me wish that new-fangled telephone, I've heard so much about, was here already!…Damn telegraph gives a man ulcers waiting on it!"

"Yes'ir." Agreed Rodney, as he came and put his arm around Melissa's waist. "It would make a difference, all right….That'll be in th' next ten years or so, I'm sure."

"If then!" Sighed Doc. "Take another ten to make it work!"

"Well, it's getting late, Walter, you need to rest!" Sighed Mattie, and then looked across at Connie. "And so do you, Daughter, you hadn't been asleep ten minutes, before you had that infernal dream!" They all heard the knock then, and looked toward the door.

"Now, who can that be?" Said Rodney as he went to open it. "Heyyy, there,…Come in ms. Rhodes. "He smiled and stepped aside to let her pass.

"Am I intruding?" She asked, and smiled warmly at all of them.

"Oh, honey," Cried Mattie. "You could never do that, come in, dear."

"By all means!" Grinned Doc. "Appears we're related now,…blood relatives, so to speak!…I want to thank you, sweet lady, Doctor Snyder said, you helped save my worthless old hide."

"It was my pleasure." She smiled, and looked at all of them again. "The reason I came in, is that I was talking to the Doctor earlier,…and he said it would be acceptable for me to sit with Doc tonight, give you all a chance to get some needed rest.…He had three more beds moved into my room.…It's a little crowded, but it's big enough for all four of you."

"You didn't have to do that, honey." Replied Mattie. "We're all just fine."

"I wanted to,…that is, if it's all right with all of you?"

"Oh, yes!" Said Connie. "I've had a headache for hours!"

"Well, okay, Mary Beth." Sighed Mattie. "I am a little worn out."

"Sounds good to us, too." Said Melissa.

"Good!…Now go, why don't you, all of ya, Doc will be fine."

*   *   *

The explosive crack of a rifle caused his eyes to fly open, and in a panic, tried to sit up, his hand searching for the Colt pistol. But all he found, was naked skin where the gun should be and confused, tried again to sit up, but the pain in his left side and shoulder was so intense that he fell back onto the pillow in exhaustion.

It slowly came back to him then, the bullet's impact, the instant numbness in his upper body, and the bone-jarring impact of the hard ground as he fell. He felt of his arm, and then his shoulder, which made him gasp with pain. He realized then that he had not been dreaming, he had been shot!…Breathing deeply a time or two, he squinted at his surroundings, but saw nothing of any detail. The room was large, he saw pictures on the wall, and furniture, able to make out a couple of chairs, a vanity dresser, a tall cabinet with glass doors, and several smaller tables with doilies.

"Where th' hell, am I?" He muttered, raising his right hand up to touch his clean-shaven face, and then to look back at the walls of the room which, without the glasses, appeared as splotches of blues and lavenders. He moved his hand beneath the quilt again to feel his naked skin, and was in a panic all over again.

"Hello?" He yelled loudly. "Anybody there?" He heard the footsteps then, and watched the door expectantly. When it opened, he watched the woman enter and come to the side of the bed.

"Well," She said, in a voice that was almost musical,...and though she appeared a little blurred, the voice seemed to come from a face that was almost angelic. She had long auburn hair, too, which to him, was stunning. "Welcome back to the world of the living."

"Wha,...Who?" He stammered. "How'd I get here?"

"You were shot yesterday, don't you remember?"

"I was reminded a that, when I tried to get up!...How'd I get here?" He asked again.

"We heard the shot, my hands went to see about it,...they brought you here."

Nodding, he raised the quilt and looked at himself. "They put me to bed?"

"Yes, they did,...Then I sent a man for the Doctor."

"Thank 'em for me,...and thank you, very much!...I thought I'd bought th' farm."

"What farm?"

"Oh, no, Ma'am, that's just....I thought I was dead!"

"Oh, I see, yes, I'm sorry, I should have known what you meant." She watched his face for a moment, and then. "Who are you?"

"Bill Upshur." He grinned. "Most call me, Billy."

"Well. It's very nice to meet you, Billy,...I'm Jaclyn Garnette, I own this ranch, and you are in my bedroom."

"Your what?...I'm sorry, Ma'am." He tried to raise himself up again, but the pain caused him to fall back.

"You have to be careful, you'll open that wound again." She leaned over him to check the bandage then, and the aroma of lavender, and fresh, clean skin made his head swim. "Good!" She said. "It's not bleeding, now please, just lie still." She went to the dressing table and came back with the eyeglasses.

"Are these yours?...Sheriff Hogg found them where you fell?"

"Yes, Ma'am, they are, thank ya kindly."

She leaned and helped him fit them over his eyes and ears, and he was taken aback, as the full scope of her beauty came into focus. But it was her eyes that held him mesmerized, seeing something in their softness, something that frustrated him, something that made him feel a strong stirring in his loins. What he saw, he thought, was lonliness, and a need that was almost akin to love. He stared at her until at last she smiled.

"What?" She asked, her face flushing a little.

"Oh, sorry, Ma'am. I didn't mean to stare....Uh,...my night clothes seem to be gone." He said, lifting the cover again. "It's sort a embarrassing."

"Yes, I know,...your clothes were filthy, so I washed them last night, they're on the line drying." She smiled again, even wider. "You were filthy, too,...so I bathed and shaved you."

He reached to touch his face again, and then his mustache.

"It's still there." She smiled. "Looks good on you."

"Ma'am,...You,...you gave me a bath?"

"Hot, soapy water, and a washcloth, yes I did." She smiled again, at his flushed face. "Would you feel better if I said, I closed my eyes?"

"Yes, Ma'am,...no, Ma'am, I don't know!...Ahh, did your hands see who shot me?" He asked, to change the subject.

No, not exactly,...just a man on a gray horse. Of course, Sheriff Hogg said the man's name was Hatcher, I think....He rode off when he saw them coming....Was he the man you were chasing?"

"He's a killer, yes, Ma'am!...Been on his trail for a week now."

"Well, he came to within an inch of killing you."

"How well, I know!...I owe you my life, Ma'am."

"Oh, no!...You can thank my hands, if you want, they ran him off. You don't owe me a thing!...You're welcome here, Billy." She looked down at the bed then.

"Are you married?" She asked, without looking up.

"You have a family?"

"Yes, Ma'am." He responded curiously. "I have three kids." He was watching her intently as he spoke, seeing her shoulders slump some with his answer. Somehow, he knew it was not what she wanted to hear, and suddenly wished he had not told her. "What about you, you married?"

She sighed again, and looked up at him. "I was,...Maxwell died over a year ago."

"Sorry to hear it."

Nodding, she turned, and went to the chest of drawers,...and he once again felt the uneasiness in his lower extremities as he watched her graceful, almost provocative swaying walk. She was beautiful, he thought, still watching as she took an item of clothing from a drawer.

He suddenly felt ashamed for what he was thinking, and those thoughts felt like a betrayal. He loved his wife with all his heart, so what was he suddenly feeling for a woman he had only met a few minutes ago?...What was it that made her so desirable to him? He was still watching as she turned around to come back.

"Is something wrong, Billy?" She asked with a smile.

"What?" He stammered, quickly meeting her eyes. "Oh, no, Ma'am, nothin' at all!"

"Good!" She said, and came on to the bed. "I found a pair of my husband's Union bottoms, they're yours now. Come, I'll help you put them on." She began pulling the quilt and sheet up over his feet and legs.

"No, Ma'am, wait!" He said, quickly pulling his legs up, and then gasping with pain from the sudden movement.

"You don't want them?" She asked skeptically. "You said you wanted clothes."

"Yes, Ma'am, but....I'm naked!"

"Billy." She breathed. "I have already seen everything you have, what's the problem?"

"Well, I didn't know it!"

She smiled then. "Okay, Mister Modest,...tell you what,...put your legs back down, I'll slide them on your feet and legs, you can pull them on beneath the covers, while I go get you a bowl of potato, and chicken soup.... You are hungry, aren't you?"

"Starving, yes, Ma'am!"

"Then straighten your legs out!" She worked the long-john bottoms over his feet and up to his thighs then stood back with her hands on her hips. "There, think you can manage the rest?"

"Yes, Ma'am,...maybe."

"And my name is not, Ma'am, I don't like, Ma'am!...My name is Jaclyn!...I'll go get your food now." She turned and went to the door. "You can't handle it, call out!"

He watched her leave the room, glad that she had not lifted the covers any higher, as he was very conscious as to what she would have seen. Grunting from the movement, he reached down and finally hooked his fingers in the waistband of the underwear, and after several attempts, and a lot of pain, managed to work them up over his hips.

He was breathing hard, and grunting with pain when she returned with his soup, the aroma of which just added fuel to that pain.

"I hope modesty was worth the pain." She said, placing the wooden serving tray across his upper body, and placing the steaming bowl of soup on it. "Want me to feed you?"

"No, Ma,…Jaclyn, I can do that, thanks." He took the spoon, ladled a spoonful, blew on it to cool it, and then ate ravenously of the strength-giving broth.

"My," She smiled. "Guess you were hungry."

"Yes'um." He nodded, swallowing hungrily. "Been a couple a days."

She pulled a chair to the bed, and sat down to watch him eat, her eyes studying the profile of his rugged face.

"How long have you been a Marshal, Billy?"

"A week." He replied between bites. "This time."

"What do you mean?"

He looked at her then, and her eyes seemed to melt him again. "Wes Hatcher shot my father a week ago." He looked away from her mesmerizing stare, and cleared his throat. "It's a complicated story, Jaclyn….Let's just say, th' Marshal was in no shape to come after 'im, so, he deputized me….Which he does from time to time."

"What's your wife's name?"

"Connie." He said, looking at her again. "Her name's Connie."

"Pretty name,…and the children?"

"William, he's th' oldest. Then there's Angela, and Christopher."

"Where are they?"

"Paris."

"Never heard of it." She replied. "Is it far?"

"Week's ride,…somethin' over a hundred miles….Why all th' questions, Jaclyn?"

"No reason." She sighed then. "I just like to know my guests."

"I won't be a guest for long, Jaclyn,…I got a killer to catch."

"I know that,…I guess I'm worried that the next time, he'll kill you."

He looked at her eyes again, and became weak, still not understanding what he saw there, but definitely felt the pressure in his loins.

"Why?"

"Why, what?"

"Why would you worry about me?"

"I don't know, really,…it's just that, when I look at you, I feel like I've known you for years!…It feels like we were more than just friends."

"I definitely would a remembered that, Jaclyn,…because, I sort a feel th' same way,…only,…I ain't never been to this part a Texas before now."

"I know, I would have remembered, too."

He pulled his eyes away from hers and uneasy, began eating again.

"Well." She said, standing up. "I have to meet my foreman and pass out today's work schedule. The Doctor is coming later today to check your wound.…I'll be back for the tray in a bit." She nodded, but before she left, their eyes locked again.

He could see the loneliness there, and something else, something that made his heart beat faster, and his mind somewhat bewildered. He had only seen that look in the eyes of one other woman.

*   *   *

Rodney had just moved away from the nurse's station with a tray and four cups of coffee when he saw Stockwell enter the hospital and come quickly down the hallway. Placing the coffee on the counter again as the lawman approached, he shook his hand then noticed the worried look on his face.

"What's th' news, Jim?"

"Bad, I'm afraid, and good, too, I guess!…Billy was shot yesterday afternoon."

"What?" He exclaimed, his heart close to stopping. "How,…what happened, was it Hatcher?"

"Yeah, It was Hatcher,…but Billy's okay, Rodney, he's at a ranch outside a Decatur, Texas."

Rodney turned to lean on the counter for a minute, while he calmed his nerves. "In a stand-up fight?" He asked, looking back at Stockwell.

"No, it was an ambush, rifle shot!…I knew you'd want a know right away. How are you gonna tell Ms. Upshur that she was right?"

"I don't know, Jim, th' truth, I guess."

"I'm damn sorry, Rodney." He said, giving him the paper.

"When did this come in?"

"Twenty minutes ago….Sheriff Hogg wired Gainsville last night, trying to find out who Billy was, telegrapher there knew 'im and got th' information from Hogg, and then wired me!...That's all I know….That wire came in last night, Cyrus told John, and he came to get me. I had Cyrus wire Decatur for more information, it's on th' back a that paper there, it came in this mornin'."

Rodney opened the paper again, and turned it over. "J, and M, Ranch!...Well, he's alive, that's th' best news!...But now, I need a favor, Jim."

"I thought ya might,…I brought a horse and saddle with me."

"Oh, no, I wont need a horse!...How well do you know Jasper Long?"

"At th' stage office, well enough, I guess, why?"

"Well enough to commandeer a stage coach, with driver?"

"That, I don't know, Rodney,…but I'll try. What else do ya need?"

"A dozen, thin King Edward cigars, enough beef jerky for a week, box a forty-four shells, and a slicker. All I'm takin' is my saddle bags and rifle….I'll pick up a horse somewhere, if I need it." He reached in his pocket for some money and gave it to him.

"This means, you're goin' after 'im, right?"

"Damn right, I am!...Jim, if Mister Long won't give us a stage, I'll need th' regular schedule."

"What about your shoulder?"

"I shoot with my right hand, Jim….Got another favor now!...I need you to keep watch over things here, if you will, th' gals are gonna worry, so is Doc?"

"I'll do my best, Rodney, you know that!...I'll go gather up your supplies now. When you're ready, ride my spare horse back to town….When do you want a go, anyhow?"

"I'll be ready in an hour, Jim, we'll go from there."

"Good enough!" Said Stockwell.

He watched the lawman leave and sighing, picked up the tray to walk slowly back to Doc's room where he took a deep breath, opened the door with a grin on his face, and went in. "Coffee is served!"

"Oh, good!" Chimed Connie, and Melissa, both coming to take a cup from him.

He went on toward the bed and gave Mattie hers. "Sorry, Doc,...Nurse said you couldn't have any just yet." He picked up his cup, and put the tray down,...and then watched the women sip theirs a few times before speaking.

"I have some bad news, Connie." He hesitated then, seeing the terrified look come into her eyes. "I'm sorry Connie,...it's not good news, but it ain't real bad either."

"Well, what is it, boy?" Asked Doc urgently. "Is William all right?"

"He's alive, Doc." He looked back at Connie then. "Your dream was for real, he was shot yesterday."

"Oh, God, nooo!" She wailed, and both her and Mattie had to sit down to keep from falling.

"What happened, Rodney?" Asked Doc shakily.

"Well, it seems he found Hatcher,...and he was chasin' 'im down, I guess, when Hatcher ambushed 'im."

"He is okay, though?" Asked Connie. "You're not lying to me?"

"I would never lie to you about somethin' like this."

"Spell it out for us, Rodney." Insisted Doc.

"That's all Jim told me, Doc. He din't say how bad it was, just said he was alive."

"Thank God!" Whispered Mattie. "Praise the Lord!"

"What else is there, son?" Asked Doc.

"I'm goin' after 'im, Doc!...That's what else!"

"No, Rodney!" Gasped Melissa. "You can't, he'll shoot you, too!"

"I'm goin', honey,...I will not allow one man to destroy my family!"

"But, Rodney!"

"I'm sorry, baby, but I'm leaving in an hour, I have to! Please understand."

"He'll be okay, Lisa," Said Doc. "William needs him now."Thank you, Rodney."

"No need, he's my brother!" He wrapped Melissa in his arms then. "Billy's hurt, Honey,...If Hatcher finds out he's still alive, he could go back to finish th' job!...I'll be okay, honey, try not to worry."

CHAPTER FIVE

Rush Creek, Texas, once a thriving community in just five years past. Now had only six families living there. The school was still in use, when they could get a teacher, and the Post Office, which also served as the General Store. The saloon, however, had been closed for a while, until Haskell Oring, and gang came to town and took it over. It did not take long to scare the few residents into submission, keeping them well away from that part of town.

The saloon was not a large building, only one big room, with the bar running along the west wall. The floor was still littered with a few broken, or smashed tables and chairs, but there were a few that were still intact,… and these were occupied by a dozen of the dirtiest, bearded men of the worst kind. They were all of a single category, killer, thief, rustler and, or bank robber,…and all part of a gang of rustlers led by Haskell Oring, himself a notorious killer!

Off to one side of the room, four men were drinking, and playing cards, and three of those were constantly cursing, and grumbling as they continuously lost hand, after hand to the blond headed man.

Haskell Oring stood against the rickety bar with a bottle in his hand, and watching the gaming table. Finally, he watched one man get up and come to stand beside him. "Somethin' on your mind, Amos?"

"Hatcher's on my mind!…How come you let 'im move in on us like this?"

Oring turned and placed his elbows on the bar. "Amos, that yellow haired man is likely th' fastest man with a gun, you'll ever see!…If I can persuade 'im to throw in with us, he'll be an asset."

"He'll be trouble, Boss, that's what he'll be."

"Maybe, maybe not….But you don't want a cross 'im!"

"You afraid of 'im, Boss?"

"I fear no man, amos!…He'd kill me, but come down to it, I'd fight 'im….Just stay away from 'im, Amos, and tell th' others."

"When we gonna steal some more cows, anyway?…We all got money we can't spend from th' last bunch." He looked over toward Hatcher then. "If he stays, he'll have it all!"

"Is he cheatin'?"

"If he is, I ain't caught 'im at it!…But I know he is."

"Ya can't brace a man without hard proof, Amos, and you don't want a be th' one to do it!" He turned back around to watch the game. "He's a boy with no morals, and he's fast with a gun,…he don't mind killin' a man, probably likes it!…Be a couple weeks yet, before we hit them Gainsville herds again. So, next week, you can go make contact with th' boys up there. I'm figurin' on about five hundred head next time, maybe more!"

"Five hundred head?…we'll damn sure be noticed with that many, Haskell!"

"Yeah, I know,…But we'll be takin' cattle from all four spreads this time, take us, maybe,…at most, three nights in a row….We'll drive em across th' Red to Atoka, ship 'em from there….Call it quits, after that."

"Quit?…And do what, Haskell, punch cows for a livin'?"

"Quittin' this area, Amos, yeah!,…killin' that Sheriff was a bad deal!"

"Why Gainsville, then,…hell, there's got a be a thousand head on that ranch, right over there, why not take them?"

"You would do that, wouldn't ya?…Use your head a little, Amos….We take them cows, Th' Sheriff'd have a posse after us in half a day, and once he used that telegraph, every lawman between here and th' border would be waitin' for us!"

"Yeah, okay, boss!…I'd just feel a lot better if Hatcher was gone, that's all."

"I'll talk with 'im tonight,…just remember what I said!"

"Yeah, I'll remember!…But stayin' cooped up here for a month, ain't helpin' any!,,,We need to go to town, somewhere there's people, women! I can't remember th' last time I had a woman."

"Ain't a woman anywhere, would even look at us, Amos!…You boys go to a town, th' way you stink, women would run from ya!…Look at us, our clothes are filthy, sweat caked on 'em, us, too….And with a runnin' creek out back, at that! You need a bath, all of ya, me included,…a shave wouldn't hurt either!…In fact, I think I'll go do that very thing." He went to the end of the bar, took a well-used bar of lye-soap from his saddlebag, and left the saloon.

Amos turned and leaned on the bar, watching him leave, and shaking his head, and at the same time, knowing that he was right.

"Hey, Amos!" Called one of the men, from across the room. "Where's Haskell goin?"

"Take a bath!" He replied, turning back to look at the man. "Crik out back!"

"No shit,…a bath?…God damn!" He laughed aloud, causing the others to laugh.

"Hey, Amos!" Yelled one of the men at the card table. "We need some fresh money over here, come take a hand."

"Not me!" He said, hatefully looking Hatcher over. "I don't play with card sharps!"

Hatcher stared at the cards he was holding for a long few seconds then smiling, pushed his chair back, and stood up. "Amos,…that your name?" He asked the question in a nasty sort of way.

"It is,…why?"

"Amos," He repeated. "You old boys been mighty hospitable, lettin' me ride in and stay, this way."…He looked around at the bearded men in the room. "I even decided to stay for a while, in spite of th' fact, you all smell like a hog-wallow." He eyed their hard faces as he spoke then looked back at Amos.

"So, I'm gonna ask you,…which one of us here, are you callin' a card sharp?…Because, if it's me, I have to tell ya….I do not like being called a card sharp, that's th' same as bein' called a cheat!…Well, which one of us are you referring to?"

"Let's just forget it, Hatcher!"

"Be glad to, Amos, but first," He said moving away from the table to walk toward him. "I'm gonna have to ask you to apologize, say you made a mistake,…That,…or prove it!"

Remembering what Haskell had said about Hatcher's gun speed, he was suddenly afraid for his life, but even more afraid of showing yellow in from of the men who took orders from him. He nervously moved away from the bar, his eyes flitting from the other men, to the smiling face of the gunman.

"Go on, Amos," Nodded Hatcher, as he stopped beside the bar. "Unlatch th' tie-down on your pistol, can't pull it like that!"

"Stand down, Hatcher." He said nervously. "Haskell don't want any gunplay here!"

"Then apologize!" He looked around at the room then. "I thought this was a tough outfit,…I'd hate to think I was wrong, you bein' Oring's second in command, and all!...Am I wrong, Amos?"

"Come on, Wes!" Said the man at the card table. "He meant nothin' about it!...He's right, Haskell don't want any shootin' here."

"Won't be none, if he apologizes, Abner." He nodded at Amos then. "What'll it be, man?"

"You're pushin' me, Hatcher!"

"Yes, sir, I am,…you called me a cheat, and I want satisfaction.…Go on, man, I'll let you draw first!...Or, you can tell every man in this room, you're a cowardly pussy!"

"Th' hell I will!" His hand jerked toward the gun, and had just wrapped his hand around the grip, when he found himself staring down the muzzle of Hatcher's drawn Peacemaker. He froze then, his eyes large and disbelieving, and then slowly dropped the gun back into the holster.

"Okay." He said, holding both hands out in front of him. "I was wrong, I apologize!...That enough?"

"No!" He said hatefully, and still smiling, he pulled the trigger. The explosion was deafening in the almost dark room, as the slug's impact seemed to lift Amos, driving the wind from his lungs as he was thrown back along the bar, to fall in the open doorway.

As soon as he fired, Hatcher had turned the gun to cover the room, as the other ten men had gotten to their feet, and were reaching for weapons.

"I would not do that, boys!" He said quickly, causing them to stop and glare at him. "He had his chance!...Now, what you got a decide, is which five of you will die next?...You'll get me, but I'll get th' first five to draw them guns."

"What th' fuck's goin' on here?" Yelled Oring as he burst into the room in nothing but soaked clothes, and a gun in his hand.

Almost tripping over Amos's body, he stared down at him then glared hatefully at Hatcher.

"Lower you gun, Oring." He ordered, pistol pointing at the leader's midsection.

Oring lowered the gun. "Why'd you have to do that, Hatcher,...gun's still in his holster,...why shoot 'im?"

"He tried to pull on me, Oring!" He smiled even wider then. "Most men do."

"You had 'im beat, why kill 'im?...He was my best man, for Christ sake, and also my friend!"

"Come on, Oring, men like you ain't got no friends, you're a meal-ticket, that's all!" He swung the gun around to point at the other men. "Theirs, too,...they follow you because you make 'em money....Now, do you want a know why I killed old Amos?"

Oring placed the gun on the bar, grabbed the bottle and drank from it before looking down at Amos again. "Put your gun away, Hatcher,...he was a good man, but he was also a hothead!" He looked back at Hatcher then.

"I'm a man short now, because of you,...you want th' job?"

"Don't know, describe th' job!...I don't like robbin' banks, if that's it."

"Neither do we,...we steal cattle."

"Rustlers?" He shook his head and holstered the pistol.

"Relax, men!" Said Oring, and watched as they sat down again. "You want in?" He asked, looking back at him.

"That depends on where this rustling takes place, and if there's any good money in it?"

"It takes place ninety miles from here, two weeks from now....It'll be easy, I got men in place....They'll tell us when, and where to steal th' cattle."

"Normally, I'd say no, Mister Oring....But right now, I've got th' law on my ass, I shot one of 'em on th' way here!...You got a buyer for them cows?"

"In Kansas, yeah, two bits a pound, on th' hoof, for five hundred head!"

"Average steer, six to eight hundred pounds." Mused Hatcher. "Five hundred head,...that's close to fifteen hundred apiece."

"In Kansas, yeah....Take two to four days to round 'em all up,...we swim 'em across th' Red River, drive 'em to Atoka stockyards, and ship 'em by rail to Abilene, Kansas."

"Sounds pretty scary to me!"

"Why, because it's so easy?...I got a man workin' on each a th' four largest outfits in Cook County!...They tell me where the cattle are, and where th' hands won't be,...we take th' cattle and drive 'em away."

"Kansas, huh?...That just might be a good place to lay low for a while." He nodded then. "Tell ya what, Oring,...you guarantee me fifteen hundred dollars, I'm in."

"You got it!,...man that handles a gun like you do, could come in handy."

"Good, but just so we understand each other" Said Hatcher, pulling his gun to replace the spent cartridge. "Any attempt, by any of you at revenge, will result in your death,...and that is not a threat, sir....You need an extra gun and right now, I need th' safety in numbers."

"Safety in numbers?"

"Yeah, th' more of us, th' safer we all are!...That lawman I shot, was on my tail for days. Man's got a rest sometime."

"Well, you got two weeks to catch up on that!...No man here will raise a hand against you....And th' law won't come here."

*   *   *

Billy rolled onto his right side, and with some grunting effort, swung his legs off the bed and sat up, and immediately found him self breathing hard from the exertion.

"What in the world?" Gasped Jaclyn Garnette as she opened the door and saw him, and then quickly rushed to his side. "You're not strong enough yet to sit up, Billy, you'll reopen that wound!"

"I'm okay!" He said, lifting a hand to stop her. "Just need a minute to catch my breath."

"But you don't realize how close you came to dying, you need to rest!... You lost a lot of blood, you know!"

"Yes'um, I know!" He looked at the concern in her eyes then. "Look,... Jaclyn, I ain't got th' time to just,...lay here and do nothin',...th' man I'm after's a good three days ahead a me now,...I have to get 'im, it's important to me."

"Well, it's important to me that you get well first!...I mean, you can't hope to catch him in this condition!"

He stared at the dampness that had suddenly appeared in her half-closed eyes, and once again felt the stirring in his loins and suddenly frustrated, stared down at the floor.

"Why?" He asked suddenly.

"What?"" She sniffed.

"Why so important?"

"I,…no,…it's just,…I don't know!" She threw up her hand. "Fine,…do what you want, I,…I'll get your clothes, and make you something to eat." She quickly left the room, leaving him more frustrated than ever.

"I have got to get out a here!" He said aloud, and was instantly worried at what he felt when she was near him. It was something he had not felt since he laid eyes on Connie for the first time,…and he was suddenly afraid, because, other than Connie, no woman had ever made him feel that way. He was also afraid that, if he didn't leave, he might betray the woman he loved so dearly.

She came back then with his pants and shirt and not looking at him, shook out the pants and knelt before him to work them up over his feet and legs.

"Think you can manage the rest?…No, of course not! Come on." She put her arm around his good shoulder, and helped him to stand, somewhat unsteadily, then helped him work the pants up over his hips and buttoned them for him.

"Now, the belt." She sniffed., taking it and working it through the belt loops and buckling it. She grabbed the shirt then and helped him pull it on, working his right arm into the sleeve, and pulling it over his injured shoulder and arm.

"You are a stubborn man, Billy Upshur." She said while buttoning it.

"I can't argue that none." He said, and grinned weakly. "Thank you, Jaclyn, I mean that!"

"Oh, I know that!…I can see it in your eyes.…Now, I want you to get up and sit in my armchair, and rest, and I mean rest,…while I fix you a meal."

"Wouldn't have a steak, would you, I'm just not a soup man?"

"A steak, it is." She nodded. "And since you're dressed, you might as well sit at the table to eat.…Now, come on!" She helped him to her armchair and eased him down on the soft cushion. "I'll be back for you." She left the room then and closed the door, to stop there and lean back against it.

Taking a kerchief from her pocket, she wiped her eyes before starting across the sitting room to the kitchen, and was almost across when the door opened. She stopped as her foreman entered, hat in hand.

"Is there a problem, Hank?"

"I knocked, but when you didn't answer, I opened the door, Sorry."

"That's okay, Hank,...you wanted to see me?"

"Yes'um,...well no,...actually, I was just checkin' on you,...and our patient, of course."

"Well, we're both doing fine, Hank. He's up and dressed today. I was about to fix some lunch."

"That is good news, Miss Jaclyn, means he'll be leavin' soon."

She frowned at him then. Why would that concern you, Hank?"

"No reason, I guess....I just, well, I don't feel right, him bein' alone with you in th' house,...that's all."

"What could possibly be wrong with that?"

"Nothin' at all, Miss Jaclyn....It's just what th' hands might think, is all."

"And you're worried about my reputation, is that it?"

"I guess so, yes, Ma'am....It's just that, well, I care about you, that's all."

"Why, thank you, Hank." She smiled. But I am fine, and don't worry about my reputation, because I'm not!...Is everything else all right?"

"Oh, yes, Ma'am, but,...well Jeff just got back from town, said you could expect some company later today."

"Company?"

"Women from that temperance outfit, you know."

"Oh yes, I know!...He bring the supplies?"

"Sure did,...um, you need me to do anything while I'm here?"

"No, Hank, and thank you." She watched him leave and close the door behind him then stared at the doors for a moment, because she knew why he had come, and it was not about her reputation. He had shown jealousy before, and felt sorry for him because of it. Sighing, she looked back at the bedroom door then went on into the kitchen.

*   *   *

Rodney had spent most of the hot afternoon being jostled about in the fast moving coach, and plagued by the pain in his shoulder. He took the flask from his shirt pocket and took a swallow of the pain-killing laudanum. As he put it away, his thoughts turned to the news of Billy being shot, and wished he knew for sure he was okay. Between that, and the look on Melissa's tear-stained face when he left, was almost more than he could handle.

He had to come though, would never have lived with himself if he had not. Billy was hurt, maybe near death, and he intended to be there for him,...like he had for so many years. To top it off, he could not get the thought out of his mind that Hatcher might be the man Billy was sure he would meet someday,...the one that would beat him to the draw. The fact that Hatcher had bushwhacked him had not dulled that fear one iota,...he could still be the one.

He thought of lighting one of his cigars, but didn't think that smoke would make the dust any better to breathe. Billy should not have made him stay home, Jim would have watched over things,...and it was not as if a hurting shoulder would have stopped Hatcher from shooting him, but he might have prevented it!

'A bit late to worry about it'! He thought angrily. He was going to be there for him now, and if Billy dies from his wound, he would make Wes Hatcher his life's work!

"Comin' in to Honey Grove, Marshal!" Yelled down the driver, leaning down close to the open window. "Be changin' horses here, take about twenty minutes."

He began watching the houses in passing, seeing the pale lights in the windows then sighing, pulled his watch and struck a match. It was after nine o'clock, he thought wearily. If it had not taken so long to ready him a coach, he might be half way to Gainsville. Still faster than having to stop and cool down a saddle horse all the time....But he knew that patience was impossible right now and like it or not, was something he would have to bear. He also knew that it would likely be morning before reaching Sherman. At least, he thought, he could send Jim a wire, and ease Lisa's mind a bit. He felt the coach slowing down, and watched out the window at the lighted windows of Honey Grove, as well as the few pedestrians along the boardwalks. He could see Charley Daniels behind his desk at the jail through the open door, thinking he might pay him a visit, but then dismissing it as the coach turned into the wagon yard.

He had made good time considering, he thought, it being six o'clock when he left Paris. He couldn't believe there would not be a stage out to

Sherman or Gainsville until tomorrow morning. He'd had no choice but to wait, that, or ride a horse, and he was not quite ready for that right now. The coach came to a stop, and once the driver climbed down, he opened the door and got out, went behind the coach and relieved himself.

*   *   *

Hank, and another hand finished lighting the wall mounted, coal-oil porch lamps, and went down the steps toward the bunkhouse. Arm's folded, Jaclyn Garnette watched them leave then opened the screened door, and stepped out onto the long, wrap-around front porch to watch the road in. It was not long before she saw the buggy's swinging lamps as it turned into the road.

She liked the two women, in spite of their politics. Sharon Houston's periodic bouts with paranoia, the belief she had that everyone was after the fortune her late husband had left her, and Sandra Baylor, the more carefree of the two, who was just willing to enjoy life to the fullest,...and let others worry about the politics. But they were both involved in something worthwhile, women's rights! She knew, too, what this after dark visit was all about,,,,the strange man in her house. Oh well, she thought, they were her best, and only friends in Decatur. She watched as the driver pulled up at the front steps and watched the two women. But they can be self-richeous at times, she thought with a grin.

"Hello, Sharon, Sandra,...what brings you two out after dark, it's not like you?

"Please," Said Jaclyn. "Sit anywhere, I'll pour the teas."

"Thank you, Sam." Said Sharon as the Coachman helped her down, and then Sandra, and looking up at Jaclyn, "We came to visit a sister in arms, Jaclyn, that's all!...We haven't seen you in ages."

"Yes." Said Sandra. "We haven't seen you at our meetings, nor at Church on Sundays....We were concerned!" She came up the steps to hug Jaclyn. "So good to see you, dear."

"You as well, Sandra." She smiled sincerely then both looked back down at Sharon as she talked with the driver. "We won't be too long, Sam." She said, and climbed the steps to also hug Jaclyn, and then to step back and look at her in the porch lamp's poor light.

"Jaclyn, I swear, my dear, don't you ever wear a dress anymore?...A woman in man's trousers looks so,...vulgar!"

"Nice to see you, too, Sharon!" She smiled and reached to open the screen door. "Come in, Ladies, I have hot tea, and tea cakes."

"Oh, how nice!" Exclaimed Sharon. "You are a doll, Jaclyn." She entered the house, missing completely, the wide-eyed smile Sandra and Jaclyn gave each other before following her in.

"Please," Said Jaclyn. "Sit anywhere, I'll pour the tea."

"Thank you, dear." Sighed Sharon as they both sat down, each smoothing the wrinkles from their dresses.

Jaclyn poured the tea, and lifted the cloth from the platter of treats. "So," She smiled, as she sat down across from them. "What really brought you out here in the dark to see me?"

"Like I said, honey." Replied Sandra hurriedly. "We missed you at Church, the last two Sundays."

"Well, as you know, I have a very large ranch to run, and it takes all seven days sometimes to do that."

"Well, it can't be all that hard, Jaclyn." Commented Sharon as she ate.

"Sometimes it is, Sharon, and I'm sure the Lord understands that!....So tell me, how are the children these days?"

"Bleeding me dry!...I swear, Jaclyn, every time I turn around, one of them has an emergency that ends up costing me a pretty penny!...You just don't know!"

"No, it's you that don't know how to say no!...But I'm sure it's not that bad, you have lovely children."

"Thank you, Dear,…but what about you, how are things with you?…I mean, is everything okay out here, you're all alone here among a mob of ruffians?"

"Those ruffians all work for me, Sharon, and I might say, necessary to run a ranch of this size!…You know we've been through all this before, Sharon!"

"I know,…but what about the wounded Marshal that's staying here?… Everyone is talking about him in town. The ladies at the club are all worried about you being alone with a stranger in the house."

"So, that is why you came to see me!…Why don't you just say what you mean, and not beat around the bush?"

"Well, yes, mostly, that's why we came." Said Sharon. "You know how some people start rumors, dear!"

"Oh, yes I do!…And you can go back, and inform those ladies at the club, that my guest is a gentleman, and I'm sure he'll be leaving soon to catch the man he's after.…His name is Billy Upshur, by the way."

"Well." Sighed Sharon, placing her cup on the table. "We didn't mean to pry, my dear.…We just love you, and don't want to see you hurt. The ladies at Church were worried about you, too, is all,"

"I'm fine, you can tell them not to worry."

"We will do that very thing." Said Sandra. "In fact, I already have!"

"I've told them not to worry, too, Sandra!" Scolded Sharon, and then looked at Jaclyn. "We're just worried, dear, after all, you are a beautiful, very wealthy widow.…Any man in the County would want to marry you!"

"There's not a man in the County that I would have, Sharon!"

"I know that's right!" Smiled Sandra.

"Well you do plan to remarry someday, don't you?" Asked Sharon.

"Someday,…maybe, if another Maxwell should come along."

"Well!" Said Sharon. "That will never happen, I'm sure!…You just be careful, that's all!" She finished her teacake, and drained her cup before getting to her feet. "We really must be going, dear." Said Sharon, smoothing her dress again, it'll be well past our bedtime, by the time we get back!…It's so good to see you, my dear.…Come Sandra, it's getting late!"

She watched them leave before going to the door to watch the driver help them into the buggy. Waving from the open doorway, she watched for another moment then closed it and went to check on her patient.

*   *   *

"Well," Began Doctor Long, taking the stethoscope from his ears and placing it in his bag. "Nothing wrong with your heart, or lungs, Mister Upshur….Most folks with a wound like yours come down with Pneumonia, but, aside from you're being out of bed a week too soon, your wound seems to be healing quite nicely….How do you feel?"

"Anxious, like I need to get after th' man that shot me!…He'd be a week ahead a me again by now."

"That's about what I thought you'd say. So now, I'll tell you what I know for a fact!…One, you're about as stubborn as that jug-head nag, I got pulling my buggy and two, you get on that horse of yours before you're able,…you won't last a mile! Takes a while to build back the blood you lost, worst case scenario being,…you could start bleeding on the inside, which could be fatal, being that close to your heart."

"How long, Doc, how many days before I can safely ride?…I know you said two weeks, but I won't wait that long!"

"You need a week, anyway,…plenty of red meat and vegetables. That's what replenishes your blood….You need to heal from the inside out, then you'll get your strength back enough to let that man shoot you again."

"That's one thing that won't happen again!"

"I hope you're right,…but in the meantime, don't be in any hurry. Take a few more days, you have a wonderful nurse, and a comfortable bed to heal in….But, of course, the end result is all up to you!" He closed his bag, and picked it up.

"What do I owe ya, Doc?"

"Do my ears deceive me?" He asked, turning back to grin at him. "Those are wonderful words, Mister Upshur!…Well now, let me see. Two trips out here, away from a busy schedule, not counting my medical expertise, and good advice….Would ten dollars be too much?"

Grinning weakly, he took the wallet from the bedside table and took money from it. "Twenty dollars wouldn't be too much!'" He said, giving him the money.

"Mister Upshur, you have just changed my entire opinion of you. Twenty dollars is much appreciated,…Thank you, sir!…You know, I noticed the scar of another wound there on your side, must have been a nasty one…. Mini ball?"

"Yes," He nodded. "And it was nasty, got it in sixty five, just after th' war."

"Well," He nodded. "Thank you again sir."

"A small price for savin' my life, Doc!"

"My pleasure, son….But I'm quite serious about what I said, or it'll all be for naught.!"

"Okay Doc, you convinced me."

"Good, I'll be back before then." He nodded at Jaclyn. "Good bye my dear."

"Good bye, Doctor,…thank you." They watched him leave the room, and she looked at him with her dreamy-eyed expression that never failed to unsettle him. "You need to lie back now and rest, Billy….Lunch will be ready soon."

"I'll never be able to repay you, Jaclyn….I sure am sorry to put you through this."

"You're no trouble to me, Billy,…and yes, I know you can never repay me….But that's okay, I'll live with it!…Lie down now, I'll go fix lunch." She gave him another heart-wrenching look then that made him weak all over, and then she left the room.

"It had been slow in coming, but as he watched her walk away, he suddenly realized, or thought he did, that she was in love with him. That had to be what he saw in her eyes, he thought,…and then wished that he had never been brought here. Because now, he knew he was not the only one that was hurting. It would be so easy to love her back, too, he thought sadly, but if he did, he would never be able to forgive himself, or look Connie in the eyes again. What was he going to do?…He couldn't leave yet, and he could not give in to what he was also feeling. Sighing, he lay back on the bed to stare at the ceiling for a time, and then closed his eyes.

CHAPTER SIX

Rodney yelped in pain, as he was thrown hard against the inside wall of the coach, jerking him awake from a heat imposed nap. Groaning, as he was once again jostled roughly when the stage tilted sharply on one side, and then came to a grinding halt in the middle of the wide, rutted road.

Grunting, and with the aid of the seat, he righted himself enough to know that the coach had lost a wheel, as it was leaning almost on it's side. Putting an arm out of the door's open window, he turned the latch, and fell to the ground when the door flew open.

Cursing mildly, he sat up on the hot, sun-scorched road, and grunting from the pain in his shoulder, reached for the flask of Laudanum in his shirt. Taking a swallow of the drug, he recapped it and put it away again before looking out over the waist-high grass alongside the road. There was nothing but thick timber to be seen and sighing, he looked down the side of the coach at the buried axle-shaft and behind it, the long plowed out rut it had made before it could stop.

The wheel's iron rim lay bent alongside the road, with what was left of the splintered wheel and spokes, and they littered the road for several yards behind them. He sighed gloomily, and fished a thin cigar from his vest and lit it.

"You all right, Marshal?" Asked the driver, squatting down in front of him. "Hurt your arm again?"

"Yes, on both counts, Pat. Appears we lost a wheel, though." He grinned at him then. "That was quite a jolt, I'm here to tell ya!...You do have a spare wheel,...Don't ya?"

"That was th' spare wheel, Marshal....Link's unhitching one of the horses now, gonna ride back to Bells for another one."

"Bells, where's Bells?"

"Mile or so back down th' road,...Be back before dark, I think....Sure sorry about this, Marshal Stockwell told us how important it was to get you to Gainsville. There just weren't time to get another wheel, took all day to repair th' coach,...this is one they were retiring."

"Ain't your fault, Pat, what'll make me feel bad, is if we don't stay ahead a th' regular coach!"

"Not a problem." He laughed. "Won't leave before noon tomorrow.... Anything I can do to make ya comfortable,...Help ya back into th' coach, anything?"

"No, Pat,...I think I'll just sit here in th' shade, maybe I'll catch a breeze."

"Then while you rest, I'll clean th' road up a bit, cut a pole to jack this thing up with while Link's gone." They both looked up then, as the relief driver trotted the horse past the coach then galloped back the way they had come.

"How far to Gainsville from here, Pat?"

"About twenty-odd miles to Sherman from here,...another thirty, forty miles to Gainsville. We'll make it by late tomorrow afternoon, save another busted wheel!"

"That bein' th' case, take your time,...I ain't goin' anywhere." He watched the driver get up and go to pull an axe from the coach's rear boot, leaning it up against the rear of the stage while he set about picking up the debris in the roadway.

His thoughts turned to Billy then, and they were flooded with all kinds of possibilities. If Hatcher even thought he might be alive, he could try to finish the job. If that happened, Billy would not be able to defend himself,... and Hatcher would kill everyone at that ranch if they interfered! He also knew Billy well enough to know that as soon as he could stand up and hold a gun, he would go after him again,...and he would not be in the shape needed to fight the man, he'd be too weak!

"If he couldn't get there in time to help him, he thought grimly, he could die anyway!...He threw the partially-smoked cigar into the road with another mild curse. If Billy dies, he thought, he would hunt down Hatcher himself,…and he would kill the son of a bitch! He reached down then and unlatched the Colt pistol to pull it from the holster, flipped open the loading gate,…and with the fingers of his secured hand, held it while he spun the loaded cylinder.…Yeah, He vowed silently, 'I will kill him'!

He holstered the gun and gloomily leaned back against the open doorway's iron step used to enter the listing coach, and reread the wire he had sent to Stockwell from Bonham. They expected him to be in Gainsville by tonight, he thought, and there was no way he could tell them otherwise,…until he gets to Sherman. Then again, as much time as they were losing now, Pat would likely go right on through Sherman,…and that would be the best thing to do. He sighed heavily then, he had never seen Lisa so scared before. It was the hardest thing he had ever done, leaving her again so soon after he had come home.…But, He thought gravely, Billy needs him now, and he knew she understood that,…she was just scared for him.

He was not just doing this for himself, though it was the biggest part of it,…he was doing it for all of them, too. They were family, and without Billy, it just would not be the same. He couldn't let them down,…he wouldn't let them down!

*   *   *

"Billy?" Asked Jaclyn, in her musical voice as she opened the door and looked toward the bed. "Did the lamp go out?"

"I blew it out!" He said from the darkness. "I think better in th' dark."

"I see,…well it's a little late, but supper is ready, shall I help you up?"

"Oh, no, Jaclyn, I'll manage it, be right out."

"Okay then, don't tarry." She left the door open, and went back to the kitchen.

Sighing, he mustered his strength, rolled over, and with his good arm, pushed himself up on the side of the bed, and after breathing hard a few times he got to his feet, and with his hand, smoothed down his hair before following after her.

"Sit down." She smiled as she poured his coffee. "Are you still feeling weak?" She asked as she sat down,

"No, not as much.…Shoulder's a mite sore, is all." He grinned at her, causing her to smile even wider.

"You have a wonderful smile." She said, and then seemed to flush a little.

"Wouldn't know about that, Jaclyn,…but yours is beautiful."

"Well,…thank you very much!" They began eating then in silence until he finally looked up at her.

"Would you ask that foreman a yours to saddle my horse in th' mornin'?"

"What?…Billy, you heard what Doctor Long said, you could….."

"Bleed to death!" He interrupted. "I know what he said, Jaclyn,…but I have to go,…if I don't,…well,…th' man I'm after is halfway to New Mexico by now! That's where he hails from….If he makes it, I might never catch 'im!"

"What did you start to say, before you told me that?"

"Nothing,…it was nothin',…will ya do it?"

She looked at him with moisture forming in her eyes then sighing, she shook her head. "No," She said softly. "I don't think so."

"Why, I won't drop dead out there?"

"That's not what I meant."

"Then, what?"

She wiped her mouth with a napkin. "That road out there dead ends about twenty miles from here, at a place called Rush Creek….That's where your Mister Hatcher went."

"I don't understand, Jaclyn,…are you sure?"

"Fairly sure, yes. There used to be a thriving community where it dead-ends. It's a dying community now….It still has an old saloon, Church and school, even a post office and general store….There's also four or five families living there. Anyway, my riders say there's men staying at that saloon, they've seen horses in the corral there."

"And that means, what?"

"Timber and brush is so thick between here and there, a horse would have a hard time getting through it. The man that shot you rode off in that direction."

"And you think he's still there?"

"Could be, I've had a hand watching the road since you were shot, and no one has come from there." She looked down at her plate then. "Now eat your supper….Tomorrow, I'll have Hank saddle your horse, he will take you across my range to see for yourself."

"And then?"

"You said he was riding a gray horse,…see if it's in the corral!…At least, you will know for sure, won't you?…If you can stay in the saddle long enough!" She looked up at him then, and shook her head.

"I'm sorry, Billy,…I'm being cynical, and that just isn't fair to you,…nor to me. I shouldn't have spoken so harshly to you."

"I took no offense, Jaclyn, for speaking your mind."

"I know, but I wasn't,…I was speaking from my heart."

He stared at her for a moment, seeing her downcast expression. "Don't worry about me, Jaclyn, please?…I'll stay in th' saddle."

"Oh, I know you will!"

"Then what's wrong?"

"Nothing's wrong!" She looked up at him then with tears in her eyes. "You're just so,…hard headed, that's all!…You should rest, at least another week!…What if?" She shook her head again… "You should rest!"

He placed his knife and fork on the plate, and sighed heavily. "Look, Jaclyn, Hatcher has killed eleven men. He shot and almost killed my father when he came through Paris.…If it's th' last thing I ever do, I'll bring 'im in!…I have to."

"Dead?"

"Not if I can help it,…I hate killing!…But I will get 'im!"

"Why,…because it's personal?…You want revenge?" She wiped at her eyes with a kerchief.

"I guess I do, yeah." He said, in a much softer voice. "My real folks were murdered when I was a kid,…I watched 'em die!…Doc Bailey and his wife took me in. They are th' only folks I've known since I was ten!… Wes Hatcher shot 'im and took his horse! No man harms my family and gets away with it, Jaclyn, it's just th' way I am!" He could only look at her as she wiped tears from her eyes again.

"I'm not a real lawman, neither, Jaclyn, I borrowed this badge from one."

"Then, what are you?"

"I was a farmer,…but now, I run a tradin' post in th' nations, Indian Territory."

"I don't think that's all you are, Billy,…a farmer would not chase after a killer this way, not alone, a storekeeper, either!"

"You're right, Jaclyn." He took a deep breath then. "Guess you could say I'm not much better than Wes Hatcher.…I have killed men, myself!…Still do, when I have to,…but only within th' law. My best friend was a U. S. Marshal, he's watching over th' family while I'm gone."

"If he's th' lawman, why didn't he come after this, Hatcher, why you?"

"He was hurt,…and I'm better with a gun!"

"You're a gunfighter!" She said, nodding her head.

"I guess you could say that, yeah."

"Well, I still don't want you,…killed!"

There was a lump in his throat at this point, and he quickly tried swallowing it down as he watched her. He knew she was silently crying inside, and she was so beautiful, he thought, as he watched her. It was at that point also, that he knew she was in love with him. But for the life of him, couldn't understand why?

"Jaclyn," He said suddenly, causing her to raise her head and look at him. "I have never met a woman as beautiful as you are, my wife, yes, but never since,…and I ain't blind! I can see what's in your eyes when you look at me. I could never say I understand it, but I see it!...If I weren;t a married man?…I feel th' same for you, Jaclyn, that's why I got a go, and right now!

"I know." She sniffed, and then got up from the table. "I'm so sorry, Billy!"

"No, Jaclyn,…I'm th' one that's sorry!...You are so special to me, I can't even explain it,…please understand, that it can't happen?"

"I do." She sniffed. "Really, I do! Now, if you'll excuse me, I'll go talk with Hank about getting your horse ready." She turned and walked down the hallway, leaving him to feel sorry for her, and for himself. Because at that moment, he felt as though he had lost something very special, something he would never forget!

*   *   *

"You have a nice nap, Marshal?" Asked the driver as he shook him awake. "Link's back with a new wheel,…and I'm gonna need your help liftin' this contraption, think you're able?"

"What?...Oh, yeah, I'll do what I can." He got to his feet and looked around. "It's dark, Pat, what time is it?"

"After nine, in th' P M, Marshal, we'll be on th' road again in a few minutes now....Come on, I've got th' jack in place. We'll hold it up while Link sets th' wheel."

"You got it!" He followed Pat to the heavy pole. One end was wedged beneath the coach's axel, the rest was laid across a large rock, with the length majority at a 45 degree angle from the ground.

"Ready, Marshal?" And when Rodney said yes. "Get th' wheel ready, Link, and make it quick when we lift it!"

Rodney jumped and wrapped his good arm around the pole, as did the driver and together, applied their weight to leverage the coach up high enough for Link to slide the wheel onto the axle, apply more grease, and then screw on the heavy nut to secure it.

They released the pry-pole, and Rodney stood by panting from pain while Pat pulled the pole free to toss it in the grass alongside the road. Link helped him roll the heavy rock off the road.

Rodney took another pull at the laudanum flask, and returned it to his shirt pocket.

"What happened to that arm, anyway?" Asked the driver.

"Doctor said I tore up th' ligaments in th' shoulder."

"How'd ya do that?"

"Took a dive off a cliff, couple a weeks back....Be pretty much useless from now on, I guess."

"Too bad." He said then went to help Link hitch up the team again.

The horses were hitched up in short order, and Pat came back to stop at the front wheel. "Get aboard, Marshal." He climbed up to the seat, as did Link as Rodney climbed back into the coach and closed the door.

"Heeeyaaa!" Yelled the driver, and the coach shuddered into motion again. They kept the coach at a gallop, the swinging lanterns providing enough light to keep the team on the road.

Rodney fished another cigar from his vest and lit it, smoking as he allowed his mind to travel ahead of him to Decatur, Texas, and the ranch Billy was supposed to be recouperating on. He must be hurt pretty bad, he thought nervously, and hoped it was bad enough to keep him in bed, at least until he got there! It was hard to believe that anyone could sneak up on him close enough to put a bullet in him. Billy had always had a sixth sense about such things.

He smoked in silence as he tried to figure out what he would do if he had already gone after Hatcher, because he would not know where to look for him when he got there. The whole trip would be for nothing!

He sighed and smoked while looking up at the brilliant night sky until finally tossing out the cigar onto the road, adjusting himself on the seat, and going to sleep again.

*   *   *

Jaclyn came into the room as Billy was tugging on his boots with one hand, watching in silence as he stood up, grabbed his gun belt, and tried slinging it around his waist. When he could not, she came forward to put it around his waist and buckle it.

"Thank you, Jaclyn." He smiled. "And thanks for binding my arm against my chest this way last night, can't move it at all."

"Won't make a difference if you fall off that horse, the shock will kill you!"

"I'll be careful."

She suddenly grabbed him around the neck and on tiptoes, pulled his head down and kissed him on the mouth, long, and hard, her tongue stabbing into his open mouth with an urgency he had never before experienced. But the result was evident to her, as his manhood made its-self known with pressure at her lower extremities.

When she finally pulled away, he almost lost his balance, having to use her as leverage to catch himself. "I,...I'm sorry, Jaclyn." He said quickly, moving his hat down to cover his desire.

"I'm not!" She said, suddenly reaching behind the hat to grab his manhood and squease it through his jeans. "Just in case,...that's all!" She smiled then as she manipulated him. "I wanted you to know how much I need you,...I am in love with you, you know!"

"Yeah,...Jaclyn, I know." He said, and moved her hand from his privates.

"Don't worry, Billy, it won't happen again....If you're ready, Hank has your horse outside." She went to open a drawer on the Hutch, and took out a pair of binoculars.

"These belonged to my husband." She said, giving them to him. "Maybe they'll help you spot that gray horse of your father's."

"Jaclyn," He began, taking the binoculars from her. "You have no idea how I wish things was different!"

"I know,…I can see things in your eyes as well." She sniffed.. "Wh,… when this is over, I mean,…if things ever do change at home, and you are left alone, Heaven forbid!…But,…if something should happen, you know?…I'll still be here."

"That's th' one thing I will remember, and that's for sure, Jaclyn." He looked into her eyes until he became dizzy again, and then cleared his throat.

"Well,…I'd best not keep Hank waitin'." He walked out ahead of her and crossed the lavishly furnished sitting room and out onto the porch where he stopped. "I forgot about th' Doc comin' today, tell 'im I'm okay, will ya?"

"I'll tell him." She came out onto the porch to watch him shakily descend the steps and walk toward the horse, where he grabbed the mantel, placed his foot in the stirrup and then grabbed the saddle horn to pull himself up, and into the saddle. After a few seconds of hard breathing, he looked across at the stern face of the foreman and stuck out his hand.

"Don't think I thanked you for runnin' off that bushwhacker,…many thanks, friend." He shook Hank's hand then. "Name's Bill Upshur."

"Henry Gates, call me Hank."

"Damn good to meet ya, Hank!"

"Hank," Called out Jaclyn. "Take him the shortest route to Rush Creek,…he wants to see if that gray horse is in the corral there,…and don't be seen, you hear?"

"Yes Ma'am,…be back tonight!" He turned his horse, and headed toward the barn.

Billy looked at her for a minute, then smiled and reined the black around to follow the foreman. Hank had opened the pasture gate, and was waiting for him to come through before closing it again. They urged the horses to a fast walk through the tall grass, scattering the fattening cattle on they're way north.

His shoulder was sore, and aching some, but otherwise, he felt like his old self again. What worried him most, was the overly spirited black horse, and he kept a tight rein on him.

"That's some piece a horseflesh, Marshal." Commented Hank after a while. "He fast?"

"Let's just say, if Hatcher hadn't bushwhacked me, I'd have caught 'im in th' next hundred yards."

"How big a start did he have on ya?"

"Maybe three-quarters of a mile, a little more….And you're right, he is fast, long winded too!"

"That gray horse, he was ridin', what's that to you, you don't mind me askin'?"

"My father's horse, a pet!…Hatcher shot 'im when he stole it."

"Sounds like this Hatcher's a bad one."

"As bad as they come, yeah….Killed eleven men, that I know of."

"Eye to eye?" And when Billy nodded. "Must mean he's fast with a gun."

"Among th' best, so I've heard,…never laid eyes on 'im!"

"If you don't mind my askin',…how fast are you?"

"Among th' best, when I ain't been shot!"

"Then it might not turn out th' way you want."

Billy looked at him, and then nodded. "Every man meets his match, sooner or later."

"And that don't worry you none?"

"Course it does."

"Then why, if there's a chance he might kill ya?"

"He done my family harm, laid hands on my son….No man does that!"

"Ya know, Bill,…that don't sound much like what a lawman would say."

"I ain't a lawman, Hank, I borrowed this badge from th' town Marshal in Paris, Texas….A good friend a mine….He thought it might come in handy."

"Guess it would, at that." Grinned Hank. "Don't worry, I'll keep your secret!"

"Don't matter none, your boss lady already knows….She's got some fine lookin' cattle here, don't she?"

"Best beef cows in this part a Texas!" Turning to look over the sleek white-faced cattle with pride. "Mister Garnette insisted on th' best, all whiteface Herefords."

"Tell me about this Rush Creek, Hank,…how close can we get?"

"Our fence comes within five hundred yards a that old saloon. Damn thing's about to fall in! Me, and another hand was up there, couple a weeks ago, spotted a dozen or so horses in th' saloon's old corral out back….

Somebody's usin' th' old place for a hideout, been livin' off our cattle, too, I think!...We found blood on th' ground there, and we was a cow short a th' number a steers we put there at talley time."

"Eatin' well, too, from th' looks of these cows."

"Mighty well!...Trouble is, blood was all we found, no carcass, no severed feet, no horns, hide, nothin'!"

"Hard to prove anything that way,...you tell th' Sheriff?"

"Jac,...Ms. Garnette did, th' day we brought you in. Lot a good it'll do, Hogg's about as worthless as a cur dog!...She wanted 'im to go there and check th' place out, and he said he would,...as soon as he could hire more deputies....He won't!...It's a shame, too,...when he first took office, he was hell on wheels!...You gonna be leavin' if that gray horse is there?"

"If it's there, yeah, tomorrow mornin',...you sound like that's important to ya,... is it?"

"Yes, it is,...and I don't mind sayin' so!" He looked at Billy then. "Don't tell me you ain't noticed how beautiful she is....I just don't want her hurt!"

Billy grinned slightly. "When are you gonna tell her, Hank?"

He met Billy's stare for a moment. "Tell her what?"

"That you're in love with her."

"Come again?"

"Come on, Hank, you heard me!"

Hank stopped his horse to lean and cross both arms on the saddle horn. "I tried to a couple a times,...she's always so business-like, straight to the point!...Don't leave much room to tell her somethin' like that."

"Hank, you're right!" He said, still studying the foreman. "I did notice how pretty she is, she's about th' prettiest woman I ever laid eyes on, to tell ya th' truth!...But you don't have to worry about me, man,...I'm married, got three great kids at home, and my wife?...She's also one a those women!"

"Well, that wouldn't stop most men!"

"All th' more reason to tell her how you feel.....But I got a say this....She don't appear to me like th' kind a woman to give in to just anybody, she'll have to love him, too!...Somethin' to think about! Now,...if we're gonna get back by dark, don't ya think we ought a get movin'?"

Nodding, Hank urged his horse to a fast walk again, and as Billy pulled alongside. "I'd as soon you didn't say anything to her about this."

"Not my style, Hank." He said, once again looking over the healthy herd of cattle. "Ever had a problem with rustlers?"

"Not in th' ten years I been here, no!"

"Then tell me this, that one steer th' only one that's been lost?"

"Th' second,…some a th' hands reported one gone a couple a weeks before that….Same thing, no carcass, no nothin'!…we lose a few to cougars, wolves or coyotes now and then, but there's always a carcass left, and a lot a animal sign."

"Then I'd say you're right about th' other two."

"I know I am….I'd take th' hands and see about it myself, but Jaclyn strictly forbids it!…Anyway, we'll be shippin' a thousand head to eastern markets come next month."

"How many does she have?"

"Last talley was eight thousand head, give or take!…There's almost twenty thousand acres to this ranch, Bill."

"A lot a land for one so small."

"Yeah, she's little, but she makes up for it in guts. She knows more about th' cattle business than anybody I know,…most as much as Mister Garnette did!"

"She's some kind a woman all right."

"You sure you're not interested in her?"

"Course I am, Hank,…but that's as far as it goes. I'm goin' home in a few days, Lord willing!…Tell ya this, though, if I was of a mind to, I'd a done told her I loved her, no beatin' around th' bush,…you don't somebody else will!"

"I know that, too!" He nodded.

"I know ya do,…how far to this place, anyway?"

"Twenty miles along th' road, half that as th' crow flies….Another four or five miles,…we'll be there by noon."

"Got plenty a water on th' place, I see."

"Thirty seven running creeks, twenty two cow ponds and one two and a half by five and a half mile lake, up on th' northeast section!"

"I'd call that plenty a water!"

"How's th shoulder, Bill, how are you feelin'?"

"Aches some, but no bleedin' yet….I feel pretty good, but th' heat's getting' to me a little,…not much of a breeze here."

"Gonna feel worse tomorrow." Said Hank. "Because, if your man is there, he'll have a dozen men around 'im!...You got any kind of a plan workin'?"

"Nope, not a one."

"You're just gonna ride in and call 'im out, just like that?"

"Hell, no!...I ain't that dumb yet!...What I'm hopin, is that one a your men can go into town for th' Sheriff, and a posse! Preferably men that are good with rifles!...Now, Jaclyn told me there was folks still livin there, is that right?"

"Four or five families, at th west side a town. They raise vegetables, melons and such, haul 'em into town twice a month to sell 'em....Got a schoolhouse, but no teacher, that I know of,...got a Church, but no preacher, a store and post office, save that delipidated old saloon."

"When you was spyin' on 'em, you see anybody out and about, maybe keepin' an eye on th' road?"

"Not a soul....Nobody ever goes there, guess they feel safe."

"Well. They're not!"

"Ya know, Bill,...I use a rifle good as anybody, four or five a my hands do, too! If you was to ask Jaclyn for help, she might agree to let us side you?"

"That's awful white of you, Hank, thanks,...that's what I'll do,..if all else fails! You have a job to do right here, ya know, protectin' that little woman's holdings."

"Don't worry about that none, Bill."

"Don't believe I will....But ya best take my advice, tell that woman ya love her!"

"I'll do that, too, soon's this is over."

"Good man!" He looked up at the cloudless sky then. "Hotter'n hell today, ain't it?...Sweat's pourin' off a me!"

"That's cause you ought a be back in bed, stead a here!" Returned Hank, and pulled his bandana to give him "Wipe your face and neck, we'll move over in th' trees for a spell till you cool down. They reined the animals beneath the spreading limbs of a giant Elm Tree and stopped.

Hank took out his canteen and opened it. "Here, Bill, hold that bandana out, I'll wet it down for ya." He poured water on the bandana for him. "Now, wipe your face again, and keep it around your neck."

"Thanks, Hank." He nodded, and did as he was told. It was not long before he was breathing normal again..

"I got a tell ya, Bill, I think this was a bad idea!...A man can take pneumonia, even in summertime, with a wound like that!"

"I know that!...But I'm okay!...I don't hurt when I breathe."

"Good." Hank gave him the canteen then. "Have some water, too, cool th' insides down."

He drank deeply of the warm water then gave it back. "I'm okay now, thanks, Hank....Sure came on quick."

"Well, just keep that scarf wet, wear it around your neck,...want a turn back?"

"Not a chance, we're almost there,...how much farther?"

"Three, four miles, you gonna be okay, man,...I ain't hankerin' to tell Jaclyn I let ya die out here?"

"I'm okay,...let's go!"

*   *   *

"We're here, Marshal!...Wake up, man."

Rodney's eyes jerked open, and he sat up on the seat to stare bleary-eyed at the driver for a second before recognition finally took over. "Where are we?"

"Gainsville, Texas, we're here."

"What happened to Sherman?"

"You slept through that, too,...you must a really been out of it!"

"Laudanum, Pat!" He sighed, moving across the seat to the door. "Shoulder was hurtin' like hell,...from layin' on that pry-pole, I guess.... Where's th' Sheriff's office?"

"We're right in front of it!"

He looked out through the open door at the pedestrians on the boardwalk, seeing them stop and stare at him before moving on. "What time is it, Pat?"

"Close to three o'clock, Marshal, made a little better time than I thought we would!...You gonna need us anymore?"

"What?...Oh, no, Pat,...I'll get me a horse here, I'm goin' on to Decatur. Thank you, Pat, Link, too, for your time. You didn't have to do it!"

"Forget it, Matshal, we didn't do it just for you, we did it for Doc!...He delivered all three a my boys, and kept Nora alive doin' it!...It's th' least I could do." He started to turn away, but stopped.

"We can take you on to Decatur, Marshal, just say th' word?"

"Thanks, Jim,...no, you've done your part."

"Then we're gonna get some shut-eye before startin' back."

"Who's th' Sheriff here, Pat?"

"J. W, Hicks,...He's just fillin' a spot left by Sheriff Quin, I'm told!...Quin, and his two deputies were ambushed by rustlers, a few weeks back....Well, you change your mind, we'll be at th' hotel."

"Let Jim know I'm okay, and where I'm at. Tell 'im where I'm goin', too! He'll tell th' family."

"You got it, Marshal....Good luck!"

He nodded then climbed out of the coach and stood by as Pat drove the coach away and then sighing, went to step up to the boardwalk and peer through the open door. Seeing no one in the office, he walked on in and looked around before sitting down to watch the half open cellblock door,... and was there when the Sheriff and a deputy came back into the office.

"Who are you?" Asked Hicks, with mild surprise. "Rodney stood up as he spoke.

"Rodney Taylor, U.S. Marshal!...You must be J. W. Hicks?"

"That I am!" Said Hicks. "Good to see you, Marshal. "How can I help you?"

"You got trouble back there, have ya?"

Hicks looked at the cellblock door. "None, what so ever!...Had to quiet down some rustlers back there, is all....What brings you here, Marshal?"

"Billy Upshur, deputy a mine. He was through here a few days ago."

"Yes he was, his advice helped us catch these four men!...I understand he was shot, down Decatur way."

"That's where I'm goin, now, Sheriff,...and I need a horse!"

"Of course,...Meeker," He said, turning to the deputy. "Get the Marshal a good horse, tell the hostler, I want a good one,...and make it quick!" He smiled at Rodney then. "Coffee is luke warm, Marshal,...help yourself, right through that door." He nodded at the cellblock door before going to his desk to sit down.

Sighing, Rodney went through the door to the pot-bellied stove, grabbed a tin cup and poured some coffee before going back in.

"I'm not a duely elected Sheriff, by the way, Marshal." He said when Rodney came back. "I'm just filling in for a while."

"So I heard." He replied, taking a sip of the almost cold liquid. "What about those men in there,...how'd Billy help ya?"

"By suggesting I talk with the ranchers, find out who they hired in the past six months!...Seems they were telling the rustlers when to strike, and where to strike."

"I'm glad it worked out!"

"So am I, believe me!"

"How far is this Decatur from here?" He asked, draining the cup.

"Forty odd miles to the southwest,...you'll make it by nightfall!"

"There been any more news from there?"

"Not since the last one,...one that said a Marshal was shot trying to catch a killer, name of Hatcher!...Seems he killed a deputy there, and wounded another making his escape....You might talk with the telegrapher, if it didn't concern me, he wouldn't necessarily bring me the wire....Are you worried about something?"

"Yeah, I am....He forgot to kill Billy,...he finds out he's still alive, he might try to finish th' job!"

"I see where you're coming from, Marshal!...This Hatcher must be a bad one."

"One a th' worst,...how do I get there?"

"Other side of the square, street beside the bank,...you'll see the marker about a mile out....Be a stage going that way tomorrow morning, you want a wait?"

"I need to go now, thanks anyway."

*   *   *

Stopping just inside the grove of trees, they stopped their horses to sit and look the old buildings over.

"Low building on this end there's th' saloon, Bill." Said Hank. "You can see th' corral pretty good from here."

Billy pulled the binoculars from his saddlebag and peered at the corral. He could see what appeared to be a dozen or so horses milling around, but

Freckles was not there. He sighed, and was about to lower them, when he saw Doc's pet horse come from behind the rear of the old building.

"I see th' horse, Hank, Hatcher's there all right!...That's Freckles, I'm sure of it!...not that many horses with markings like that."

"Freckles?"

"Doc's pet horse. Hatcher took it when he shot 'im."

"Well, who is Doc?"

"My father, Hank, man that raised me when my folks was killed."

Hank stared at him for a minute. "Bill,...are you after this Hatcher as a lawman,...or for revenge?"

"Both!...I'll take 'im back to hang, if I can....But if I can't, I'll kill 'im!... Either way, he's goin' back!" He lowered the glass and put it away. "Does it matter, Hank, one way or th' other?"

"No, I guess not!...Guess I'd feel th' same way, somebody wronged Jaclyn." He looked at Billy then.

"You ain't got me to worry about, Hank, I'm leavin' tomorrow."

"Glad to hear it, Bill!"

"We get back, I'd like you to send in a man for th' Sheriff, can ya do that?"

"If Jaclyn says okay, I will do that!"

"Will you also take some advice?"

"I'll listen, yeah."

"Jaclyn's a woman alone, tryin' to do a man's job and I might add, one that's too big for her!...It'll make her old before her time. What she needs is a man who'll take charge, take some a that responsibility away from her.... She's one a th' handsomest women I ever laid eyes on, a caring woman!... She needs a man to love her, take care of her....A strong man, Hank!...You askin' her permission for everything you do ain't bein' that man!...You're gonna have to prove yourself, take th' bit in your teeth sometimes, and run with it!"

Hank was watching him with a hard expression on his face, but then nodded. "I'll send for th' Sheriff when we get back, Bill,...thanks."

"And all th' men he can muster, we leave at first light."

"That, too,...let's go home."

*   *   *

"I'll send that man to town right now, Bill." Said Hank as they stopped the horses at the large front porch. "You best go in and rest a spell, if we're gonna do this!"

He dismounted when another wrangler came to take the horses. "I'll need 'im first thing in th' mornin'."

"Sure thing!" He said, and led them away toward the barn, with Hank on his heels.

"I was beginning to worry." Said Jaclyn, quickly coming across the porch, and down the steps. "You look exhausted!" She took his arm and helped him up the steps and into the house. She stopped him in the lamplight then reached up to remove his hat and look at him. "You are as pale as a ghost, Billy, you should not have gone out there today!...Doctor Long was very unhappy when he left."

"I figured that!...I'm okay, Jaclyn....I'm just tired.'

"You're hard headed, too!...Go wash your hand, I've been waiting supper on you."

"Yes, Ma'am!" He said quickly, the smell of fresh fried steak and potatoes making him groan as she opened the sitting room door.

Returning in a hurry, he sat down across from her, his eyes devouring the meal on his plate before looking up at her.

"Thanks for cutting up th' meat, Jaclyn,...you been doin' that for days now, and I don't recall thankin' ya for it."

"I wanted to, Billy, besides, you couldn't do it!...Don't let it get cold."

He grinned and began eating, almost ravenously.

"So, tell me," She began, between swallows. "Was your torturous ride in the hot sun worth it?"

"It was, yes." He took a swallow of cool water then. "He's there all right, we saw th' horse!...I'll be goin after 'im at daybreak."

"I thought you might." She sighed then. "Billy,...I want to apologise for this morning....It was very unladylike of me!...I have never purposely groped a man like that before, not even my husband, and I am sorry."

"Jaclyn, I..."

"Let me finish, Billy!...I do not apologise for kissing you....I,...I do not know how, or why it happened. But I am very much in love with you!...I don't believe I ever loved Maxwell this much, nor anyone else,...and I never will again!...When you leave tomorrow, my heart will go with you, I need you to know that!...I also want you to know, that no matter how long it might take, or whatever the circumstances might be, I believe we will find each other again....It is meant to be, Billy, I know that,...and I'll be right here when that time comes!...Now,...don't say anything, please, just eat your supper, and I'll change your bandage before bedtime."

He cleared his throat when he saw the moisture in her eyes. "I'm sorry, Jaclyn, I got a say somethin', too! And truthfully, I don't know how....But you're th' prettiest woman I ever saw, my wife is, too,...but not like you, I think!...I ain't never felt th' things you make me feel before. All I know is that I want you,...and I can't have you. Because I love my wife and family,... and at the same time, I'm in love with you, too!...I don't understand it either, but all I know is this!...I'm leaving tomorrow, and that's a good thing, for both of us!" He looked down at his plate then. "I'm sorry, too, because I won't be back. Nobody knows what's ahead of us, we're not supposed to, I guess. But I won't forget you, or what you said." They both picked at the rest of their food for a time before pushing their plates away.

"Come," She said softly. "I'll change your bandage, then I'm going to bed."

*   *   *

Rodney slowed the heavily breathing horse to a walk once again, and reached for the canteen with his free arm, but stopped to grab his shoulder instead. The pain was not as severe as he thought it might be, but it was enough to retrieve the flask of laudanum from his vest and take a swallow of the drug. If he was not careful, he thought, putting it away, he could become dependant on the stuff. He had been taking it quite often of late....Breathing deeply, he grabbed the canteen and drank from it as well.

'I should be getting close', he thought tiredly and looked up at the setting sun. The question, though, was what to do when he got there? He knew he would have to go to the Sheriff's office, that was not the problem,... the problem was finding Billy, because if he was already on Hatcher's trail again he might not find him at all! Coming after him just might turn out to be foolhardy,...no, he thought, it was the right thing to do, for all the reasons he had ever thought of!

It has to be close to eight o'clock, going by the sun and would be dark in another hour,…and everything in town would likely be closed up for the night and he had no idea where that J and M ranch was? He looked up again, and could already see a few stars in the ever-darkening sky, and urged the horse to a gallop again, wanting to cover as much ground as he could before total darkness set in. Urgency was a living thing inside of him, and he had never felt so alone before. Even when he was doing his job alone, he knew what the purpose was in being there. But here, he thought, he knew nothing, not even if Billy was alive and that, he thought, was his sole purpose for being here now! He picked up the canteen again and drank more of the half-warm water.

He replaced the canteen with some difficulty, as his body was moving with the horse's gait,…but managed it, and at the same time came to a more well traveled, and much wider road,…and a sign post that read Decatur, with an arrow pointing to his left. He continued to let the animal gallop along the better lane,…and an hour later, was passing houses, with lighted windows on his way into town. At this point he slowed the horse to a fast walk again, and was able to hear barking dogs in the fenced in yards as they tried their best to get out. Another half hour found him entering the small square, and seeing the lighted windows of business places lining the boardwalks around it.

He had just urged the horse to a trot again, in search of the Sheriff's office, when the galloping horse and rider entered the square from the opposite side, only to slide it to a stop in front of what he thought must be the Sheriff's office.

He rode up, and dismounted as the man was pounding on the office door.

"What's th' trouble here, friend?" He asked, stepping up to the walkway.

"It's law business, man, none a yours!" He beat on the door again, and that's when they heard the muffled yell from inside.

"Open up Hogg!" Yelled the man, and then stepped back as the door swung inward to reveal the man with a badge on his vest.

"Who th' hell's knockin' on my door, God damn it? I was just about to go to bed!" He peered at the man a minute then reached inside the door for a lantern, holding it up to see both their faces. "You work for th' Garnette spread, don't ya?" He said, looking at the cowboy.

"Name's Henry, Yes'ir, boss sent me in for ya!"

"Hell he did,...who's this with you?"

"Name's Taylor, Sheriff, U. S. Marshal!"

"Th' hell you say!...Well, come on in, th' both of ya!" He stepped back inside to allow them to come in. "Pull up a chair." He said, going to sit down at his desk. "Okay, Mister Henry, you first, what's th' ruckus?"

"Hank said for you to be ready, and at th' ranch come daybreak tomorrow, they're goin to Rush Creek!"

"Rush Creek, what th' hell for?"

"Don't know that, just said bring men with ya, men good with a rifle!"

"Ain't this more in your line a work, Marshal?" He said, looking at him.

"It's also in yours, Sheriff!" He nodded at him then looked at the cowboy. "Is there a wounded lawman at that ranch?"

"Sure is, he's th' one gonna lead th' posse in!"

"Can you take me out there?"

"Not tonight, I can't, I was told to come out with th' Sheriff,...you do got a empty cell back there, don't ya, Hogg?"

"Yeah, yeah, go ahead!" They watched him go into the cellblock before the Sheriff looked at him again.

"I got one deputy dead, another bad hurt, ain't a man in town that'll go up against a gunman like Wes Hatcher!"

"That where Hatcher is, Rush Creek?"

"Must be, Ms. Garnette told me her hands seen horses there in a corral. Hell, ain't nothin' but a few families still livin' there, every buildin' in th' place is in rot!"

"Somebody else is there, too!" Said Rodney. "And if Hatcher is with 'em, it could be a battle....How do I get to that ranch?"

"Can't, not in th' dark, miss th' road for sure."

"Then I'll go with you at daybreak, got another cell?"

"Hell, help yourself, ain't nobody else in 'em!"

"If you know anybody else that might go with us, I suggest you go see 'em right now!"

"Now,...I was just goin' to bed?"

"You are th' Sheriff, ain't ya?...I also suggest that you do your job, and at least try to get us some help!...Billy can't do it alone, so we're gonna help 'im!"

"How ya figure, you ain't got but one arm, and that's all he's got?...How much help you gonna be, because I don't think your Bill Upshur can do it at all, Hatcher most killed 'im already!...Son of a Bitch is a devil, killed my men then sat his horse in th' street, and laughed at us.....Ain't nobody gonna ride with us!"

"Then you and me will do it, Sheriff, if that's what it takes!...At any rate, you are under my jurisdiction, sir, and if you want a keep this job, you go try to raise a posse!"

"All right!...It's gonna get us all killed, but all right!" He angrily grabbed his hat and gun-belt, and left the jail.

*   *   *

Billy's eyes fluttered open as Jaclyn opened the door, and he rolled onto his side and sat up on the side of the bed.

"Good morning, Billy." She said sweetly. "Be daybreak soon." She came on into the room, took his trousers from the back of the chair, and squatted to work his feet and legs into them.

"Mornin', Jaclyn." He responded weakly then stood to help her pull the denims up over his hips so she could button them. "Are you all right?"

She looked up as she buttoned his pants for him. "I'm always all right, Billy, don't worry about me!"

"Thanks, Jaclyn." He said when she finished. "What time is it, anyway?"

"Five o'clock in the morning, and I've got your breakfast ready." She grabbed his boots as he sat down again and helped him put them on, and as he stood up, picked up his gun belt to buckle it around him.

"Now!" She sniffed, backing away to look at him before going to the bureau to take a folded, clean shirt from it.

"This was Maxwell's, I'm sure he would want you to have it!" She worked his right arm into the sleeve then wrapped it around his shoulders and buttoned it up,...and with his help, stuffed the tail of it into his pants.

"There!" She said, stepping back again to look at him. "You're ready to go get yourself killed!"

He suddenly reached out, and pulled her against him, hearing her gasp with surprise as he bent and kissed her open mouth long, and hard. She was breathless when he released her. "I do love you, Jaclyn, a hell of a lot!...I want you to know that I would stay, if I could!...But I can't, I got a killer to catch,...and a family that's waitin' for me to come home....That weren't th' case, I'd never leave you!"

She looked up at him with tears streaming down her cheeks. "I know, my love." She nodded. "I know." She sniffed again then wiped at her eyes. "Come, now, breakfast is ready, you can't fight on an empty stomach." She looked up at him again.

"He'll kill you next time, Billy, you're too weak to stop him."

"No,...Jaclyn, he won't!...And that's a promise....I will take him down! I would never lie to you."

Nodding, she took his hand, and led him through to the dining room.

When the meal was over, she got up, came around the table and kissed him again, her tongue probing his open mouth with an urgency he found heartbreaking.

"That has to last me for the next thirty or forty years." She sniffed. "We will be together one day, Billy Upshur, you can count on it!...I'm not going anywhere."

The knock came at the front door then and she moved away from him, allowing him to get to his feet. "I love you, Billy, never forget that!...Now go, that will be Hank at the door."

Nodding numbly, he grabbed his hat and followed her across the sitting room. She stopped at the door to look at him again. "Take care of my heart, Billy Upshur." She opened the heavy door.

"Mornin', Jaclyn." Said Hank, removing his hat. "You ready, Bill?"

"I'm ready,...Sheriff here yet?"

"Still waitin' on 'im!" He said, looking toward the road in. "If th' cowardly bastard comes at all....Sorry, Jaclyn." He said quickly. "Anyway, I got four men goin' with us."

"Four men?" Gasped Jaclyn. "Can we spare them?"

"Yes'um, be five men, countin' me!...I'm goin', too! We got a stop our beef from bein' slaughtered....But don't worry none, hands all got their orders for th' day, and we'll be back by dark."

"Well, okay, if you say so, Hank."

"I do say so, Jaclyn,...we'll be fine....Here they come, Bill!" He said, looking back down the road. "All three of 'em!...Guess he couldn't raise a posse."

Billy stepped to the edge of the porch, peering at them as they got closer, and was focusing his attention on one man with a dangling shirtsleeve.

"Rodney!" He said in disbelief then went down the steps as the horsemen pulled to a stop by the porch. "What are you doin' here, Rod?" He asked, taking the horse's reins and looking up at him.

"Who's lookin' after things at home?"

"Jim's doin' that, you okay, Billy?"

"I'm okay, Rod,...You shouldn't a come."

"Yeah,...you didn't see Connie's face when she heard you was shot!...I did! I couldn't stay there and do nothin', buddy, not knowin' if you were alive, or dead!...No way!"

Billy reached and gripped his leg. "Thanks, Rod." He looked at the others then as Hank's four men rode in beside them. "Guess we're ready." He went to mount the black then, taking two tries to finally pull himself into the saddle and once seated, looked at Jaclyn on the porch for a minute. He smiled at her and nodded, then reined the black around and galloped down the road with the others in pursuit.

CHAPTER SEVEN

Doctor Snyder finished bandaging Doc's wound and stood up. "Doc, I think it's about time you got up out of this bed some,…sit in a chair, prop your feet up, walk down the hall and back, whatever!…You have plenty of help for support."

"That's exactly what I've been telling these mother hens!" He replied.

"Well, don't get too excited, it won't be that easy at first….Your legs may not want to hold you up the first tme!"

"We'll see he's careful, Doctor." Nodded Mattie.

"Good,…when he get's his strength back, you can take him home."

"Now that's the news I've been waiting on!" Grinned Doc.

"Well, it'll be a couple of days yet,…we'll see how well you do."

"Thank you, Doctor." Said Connie, causing him to look at her and frown.

"Ms. Upshur, if you don't get some rest, and stop this worrying so much, I'm going to have to put you in a bed….You'll make yourself ill in the state you're in, and that goes for this other young lady as well." He said, looking at Melissa. "It's not healthy to cry so much! What you both need is rest and I can help you with that, if you'll promise to take it?"

"What is it?"

"A sleeping pill, but it will help you rest. Will you take it, both of you?…I have a spare room just two doors away with two beds in it?"

"Okay, Doctor," Nodded Connie. "I am very tired."

He looked at Melissa then and saw her nod. "Good!" He took a bottle from his pocket and gave each of them a pill. Take it with water, preferably after you eat something….Room twelve, same side of the hall" He nodded and excused himself, meeting Jim Stockwell on his way out.

Doc?' He said, and then came on in to smile at Mattie and the others. "How you feelin' today, Doc?"

"I'm well, Jim." He returned. "Got any news today?"

"You bet, I do!" He said, and dug the paper out of his shirt pocket. "Came in Yesterday, and Cyrus sends his apology, he fell asleep again right after getting' it and must a knocked it off th' desk....He found it this mornin'." He gave it to Melissa. "It's from Marshal Taylor,"

"What's it say, Lisa?" Asked Connie nervously.

"Am in Gainsville, Texas- am okay- am buying a horse for trip to Decatur- hope to find Billy there- tell all I love them- not to worry." She looked up at them then. "The rest is for me." And she turned toward the window to read it.

"Well, he's likely with William by now." Said Doc, reaching to grip Connie's hand. "Be all right now, nothin' can stop them boys when they're together."

"I hear that, Doc." Nodded Stockwell. "They're a pair to deal with, that's for sure!"

"And they both could be killed, too!" Sobbed Melissa. "You all are acting like it's already over, well, it's not!...They could be killed!"

Mattie quickly put her arms aroubd her. "They didn't mean it like that, my darling, we're just trying to make light of a very dangerous situation.... Jim only meant they have a better chance at staying alive together, than alone!"

"I know that, Mattie!" She sobbed. "I'm just afraid."

"We all are, Lisa." Sniffed Connie. "But I know Billy will come home, he's never broken a promise to me, never!...Rodney made you that same promise, remember?"

"Yes,...he did!" She nodded, and moved away from Mattie. "I'm sorry, Jim, everybody, please forgive me?"

"No need, Ms. Taylor....But there's no need to worry none....Tell ya what I'll do, soon's I get back. I'll send a wire to Decatur, find out if he's there, and if he found Billy. I'll send it to th' Sheriff there."

"I wish you would, Jim." Said Doc. "Before these girls lose their mind!"

"I'll do it right away, Doc!...Well, good day all, I'll let you know."

"All right now." Said Doc. "Seems like we have done all we can,...them boys are after a killer, and my money's on them getting him! So shush now, and help an old man to that soft armchair over there....Doctor's orders,... well, come on!"

*   *   *

Billy raised his hand, stopping them a good quarter of a mile from Rush Creek then looked at both Rodney, and Hank before looking back up the road. "What am I looking at yonder, Hank, that th' saloon?"

"Yeah, part of it, rest a th' town's behind th' trees....How do ya want a do it?"

He looked at the heavily timbered woods on their left for a minute. "Well,...sun's been up a while now, got a be mid-mornin'!...We go chargin' in there as a group, they'll hear us,...be waitin' on us!...Can a man and horse get through that stuff?" He nodded at the trees beside them.

Hank stared at the maze of timber and brush for a second before turning in the saddle and looking at the man behind him. "Can he, Toby?"

The Indian nodded. "Not easy,...but I can do it!" He looked at the trees also. "Tell me what you want?"

Hank looked back at Billy then. "Tell 'im what you want?"

Breathing deeply, he looked back at the end of the saloon. "If we could get a couple men through there, and maybe on th' roof of a one a them empty buildings,...might make a difference."

Hank looked at Toby again. "Pick a man, Toby."

"We'll wait here for a half hour,...that enough tome, Toby?" Asked Billy, also looking back at him.

"Maybe so, I think." He picked his man, and they were soon leaving the road to disappear into the trees.

"That sound okay with you, Rod?"

"I've learned to trust your judgement, Billy!" He said, also staring at the saloon. "You feeling okay?" He asked, looking back at him. "You look a bit pale to me."

"As good as I'm gonna feel!" He returned with a nod.

"Then what's gonna happen, if one of 'em sees us sittin' here in th' sun like this?"

"We go in hell bent for leather!...If they don't,...in thirty minutes, we walk our horses right into town, one at a time."

"Okay," Breathed Hank. "Let's say we make it without bein' seen, then what?"

"Once you all find cover,...I'm gonna ride in and call Wes Hatcher out!"

"Don't be a fool, Bill!...Ask Hogg there how fast that man can pull iron!"

"I never seen none faster, that's for sure!" returned the Sheriff.

"Well, I have!" Nodded Rodney. "And he's sittin' right here beside me!"

"Is that a fact, Bill?" Asked Hank. "I know what you told me yesterday,...but Hatcher ain't been wounded, and you ain't in shape yet?"

"I have to try, Hank." He breathed deeply of the hot air and looked at him. "If I don't,...Rod here will kill 'im!...That's th' fact of it!"

"That's good enough, I think!" He was looking at Rodney's armless sleeve as he spoke. "I hope!" He turned to his wranglers then. "Check your guns, men, Make damn sure they're loaded!"

"Are you sure about this, Billy?" Asked Rodney nervously. "Cause I ain't!"

"Nope!" He said, shaking his head.

"Well,...that makes me feel better!"

"I'm new at this sort a stuff, Bill, so tell me....What if he don't come out,...what's to keep him, or all of 'em from cuttin' you down?"

"Th' challenge, Hank!...A gunfighter can't resist it....He'll come out, he won't let the others shoot me neither!"

"That's th' truth of it." Nodded Rodney. "It's dumb as hell, but true!" He reached in his vest for the laudanum flask then, and took a swallow before holding it out to Billy. "You just might need this!"

Nodding, he took a small swallow of the pain-killing drug, and gave it back. "Hatcher might not have to kill me, Rod, that stuff tastes like shit!" He shook his head, and then urged his horse almost into the treeline to wait. The others followed suit, putting them all out of sight from anyone at the saloon

"Now, we wait!" Said Billy, reaching to pull the Sam Colt pocket watch. "We start in about fifteen minutes. Hank, you'll go first,...stay in close to th' trees. When you get there, tie up somewhere, and find a place to fight from....That goes for all of ya, leave your horse, and find a place for cover!"

"Rod, you'll follow Hank in, don't put yourself too far from that saloon, you can't use a rifle!...Sheriff, you follow Rod in, take your rifle!...The other three men are yours, Hank, tell 'em what to do." He waited for Hank to give his orders.

"Okay,...I'll tell you all when to go, we wait for Toby and his man to get in place first!" He looked down at his watch again, and after a few minutes, nodded.

"Go now, Hank....walk your horse in slow, horses in that corral hear ya, they'll give us away!"

Nodding, Hank pulled his rifle, and urged the horse around them to continue along the treeline.

Billy watched him for a good three minutes. "Go, Rod, keep your head down."

"Always, buddy." He fell in behind Hank, keeping at a safe distance.

"Sheriff, you're next, go ahead." One by one, he watched them all make their way toward Rush Creek before falling in behind the last wrangler.

He couldn't see a trace of any of them as he entered the weed-grown old street and with a look at the dilapidated buildings in passing, he rode to within ten yards of the saloon's open doors and dismounted. He dropped the black's reins and stepped in front of it to stare at the dark, open doors of the saloon. Something was not right, he thought nervously, and then licked his dry lips,

"Wes Hatcher!" He called out loudly. "I'd have a word with you!" He waited, reaching down to unlatch his gun. "What's wrong, Hatcher, you yellow?...Come on, man, it's your chance to finish th' job,...face to face this time!...Are you in there, you son of a bitch, come on out!" At that point, he knew the place was empty, and was suddenly very angry with him self, for not expecting something like this to happen. He pulled his pistol and slowly walked to the open doorway to look inside. It was empty!...Dejected, he walked back into the street to wave the others in, watching as they all showed themselves and walked toward him....All but one of them, he noted.

"They're gone, Rod!" He said, as Rodney stopped in front of him. "Must a left yesterday, or sometime last night!

"What now?"

"Send th' men home. I guess." He looked at them all. "Thanks for th' help, Sheriff, might as well go home." He shook his hand, and watched him walk away. He walked over to shake Hank's hand then.

"You're a good man, Hank, many thanks!"

"Our pleasure, Bill!"

"By th' way, ain't you short a man?"

"He's comin' around th' saloon there, Bill." He said, waiting for him to come in. "What did you find, Toby?"

"Tracks of thirteen shod horses. They crossed that creek back there and headed northeast."

"How long ago?" Asked Billy.

"Ten, twelve hours,…ground's too hard to be sure."

Nodding, Billy turned to Hank. "Ask your men to go see them folks still livin' here,…me and Rod'll need supplies, if we can get 'em?"

"You're goin' after 'em alone?"

"Oh, yeah,…if it takes me a fuckin' year, I'm takin' that man down!"

"If we ever needed Peter, this might be it!" Replied Rodney.

"Hold on." Said Hank. "You tellin' me neither one of you can read sign?"

"Trackers, we ain't!" Admitted Billy.

"I see." He nodded then looked at Toby. "How would like to track those men down for th' Marshal,…take all th' time you need, with full wages?"

"I'd like that fine, Boss!"

"That okay with you, Marshal?"

"More than okay, my friend." Smiled Rodney, and shook both their hands. "Much more,…thanks, Toby."

"Tell me somethin', Marshal." Said Hank, looking at Rodney. "You are for real, ain't you?...A real, for true U. S. Marshal?...No, forget it, I don't really care!...Who is this Peter, fellow?"

"Skinny little Choctaw Indian, he's head of th' Choctaw Police force in th' nations,…and soon to be U. S. Marshal!"

"Well, Toby here is a full blood Yaqui, best tracker in these parts!"

"Just th' man we need." Nodded Billy.

The wranglers were back in a while with vegetables, flour, coffee, coffee pot, frying pan and lard.

"They wanted to give more." Said a wrangler. "But a lot of their vegetables was in rot, and they were out a meat….They were too scared to try and go to Decatur to sell their goods, so they couldn't buy any supplies…. But they're damn glad to be rid a that bunch."

"They tell ya when they left?"

"Sometime after dark.,...kids saw 'em leave."

Billy nodded then looked at Toby. "You any good with wounds, Man?" And when he nodded. "Mind lettin' my arm loose, can't stand it bein' bound to my body this way?"

"Goes for me, too!" Said Rodney. "We'll leave when you're done."

"Okay then." Said Hank. "I'll be takin' th' boys home now, you handle it from here?"

"We'll take it from here, Hank." Nodded Billy, as Toby began helping him off with his wet shirt. "Many thanks, my friend,...and thanks for Toby here, we'll damn sure need 'im!"

"No thanks needed, Bill. Catch 'em or not, they won't be comin' back to Rush Creek!...And I hope there'll be no reason for you to come back?"

"I hope so, too!...Give my thanks to th' Boss Lady, you all saved my bacon."

"I'll do that!...Let's go home boys!"

They watched them go for their horses, and eventually to ride back down the old road.

"No reason to come back?" Repeated Rodney. "Wonder what that meant?"

"Ain't got a clue,...wants no more trouble, I guess."

"Amen to that!" He watched Billy's pained expression as Toby lowered his arm down. "Are you sure you ought a do that?"

"I don't see any blood on th' front here,...Any on my back, Toby?"

"No blood." He said and helped Billy on with his shirt.

"I'll get used to it!" He grimaced. "Got a work th' soreness out....What do you think, Toby?"

"Seems to be healing well." He responded. "Only I would not fall on it, or hit anything."

"I'll keep that in mind, thanks....While he does yours, I'll fetch th' horses, Rod,...yours, too, Toby."

        *   *   *

Haskell Oring stopped the group of men in the shade of a large grouping of trees. "Loosen th' cinches, boys," He said as he dismounted. "We'll cool down here for an hour." He threw the stirrup up over the horn, and loosened the cinches before grabbing the canteen and drinking from it. He then took a slab of sun-dried beef from the saddlebag and gnawed off a bite while watching them.

"Benny!" He called to one of the men, and when he came over. "Eat some jerky, and get a nap,...when we leave, you head on in to that Latham ranch first, then th' rest....Tell th' boys we want six hundred head this time, hundred and fifty from each spread....Tell 'em they'll be comin' with us this time,...we're movin' on!"

"Where'll you be, Haskell?"

"Along th' river, usual place." He watched him leave then saw Hatcher coming toward him. "What's on your mind, Wes?"

"Mostly, why we left ahead a time?" He squatted down to watch as Oring sat down on a fallen limb.

"Yancy saw a couple men on horseback watchin' us around noon, yesterday, saw th' glare on glass....Had to be th' law!...Ain't that what we're all runnin' from?"

"You, maybe!" Smiled Hatcher. "They don't bother me much, if I can see 'em comin'!"

"Yeah, well you're young yet, you'll learn!...Not fearin' th' law don't stop a rifle bullet,...I'm alive today cause I don't take chances. I pay attention to things that don't set right!"

"Okay,...sooner we get to Kansas, th' better, I guess." He stood up then. "It's your show, Mister Oring." He grinned and went to lie down close to his horse.

'Smug Bastard', he thought as he watched the killer roll and light his smoke. 'I ain't forgetting you killed Amos'! He sighed and bit off another bite of meat. At the time, he didn't dare challenge his reason for killing Amos, but he knew it was not a legitimate reason. He also knew that he would not have a chance if he fought him over it, none of them would!...He grinned then, 'But men do die sometimes running beef', and that, he thought grimly, would be his revenge.

He watched Hatcher smoke as he chewed the tough meat, and the more he chewed and swallowed the nutrient, the more he hated the gunman for killing his friend. "And the sooner, th' better!," He muttered aloud...He got to his feet, stretched, and then sat down again. He was sitting on the ground and leaning against the limb when he woke up,...and cursing, began slapping the ants off his hand, and the dried beef. Still cursing, he threw the meat against a nearby tree, got to his feet and walked to where Benny was sleeping and kicked his foot.

"That time already, Boss?"

"Yeah, best get goin', old son!...We're gonna have to move fast on this last job, too many things have gone wrong lately. Tell th' boys to work fast,...you know where we'll be!

"Yeah, sir!" Said Benny, and got up to roll up his blankets and stow them then tightened the cinches, mounted, and galloped out from under the tree.

"Am I part of the things that went wrong, Mister Oring?" Smiled Hatcher.

"You're part of it!" He replied, looking down at him. "Most of it's that lawman seein' us there....Bad luck when things don't go right!...And things just ain't goin' right at th' moment!

"Well in th' first place, that weren't no lawman watchin' us, I killed him!...All your man saw, was ranchhands with a pair of field glasses. Besides, didn't you say the law never came there?"

"Didn't till now!...Trust me, Hatcher, that was th' law!

"Well," He said, getting to his feet. "If it was, means they'll be trackin' us, don't ya think?"

"Not yet,...they'll go back to town first to use th' telegraph. By th' time they raise a posse, we'll be long gone!"

"Where is this hideout of yours, anyway?"

"Old ferry house on th' Red River, we'll be there in two days."

"How do we get th' cows across?"

"We swim 'em across, river's lower than it's been in two years, damn near walk 'em across."

"You do know, that if you know that,...the law will, too!...They could be waitin' on us."

"They ain't lost no cattle in a month now." Said Oring. "No,...they likely think we went elsewhere by now,...ought a be easy pickings."

"Okay, you're th' rustler, man, you ought a know, I guess."

"Damn straight, I do!" He looked around at the sleeping men then. "Let's move out, men!" he said loudly, and went to his own horse, raised the stirrup and tightened the cinches.

*   *   *

"How's th' arm, Billy?" Asked Rodney, who had been quietly watching him slowly work the arm back and forth as they followed Toby's lead.

"Fairly sore, Rod." He replied, turning slightly to look back at him. "Yours?"

"Aches!...But, like th' good doc said, about as good as it's gonna get!... You gonna be able to face that bastard?"

"Guess we'll find out,...got a catch 'im first!"

"They'll have to stop sometime, Billy,...if Hatcher's even with 'em now?"

"My thinkin', too!...Don't make sense him joinin' up with anybody,... gunman like that!"

"He's been swingin' a wide loop, that's for sure!...Seems he's been killin' for th' fun of it!...Was me, I'd be lookin' for company, safety in numbers, and all that!"

"That ain't gonna help 'im, Rod. Comes down to it, he'll meet me face up! It's all in th' challenge!...He's nothin' but an eighteen year old kid, who thinks he's th' best there is!...But he's wrong!"

"What if he is?"

"Then I'll take 'im with me!...I can't let this go, Rod, you know that!... He near bout killed Doc over a horse!...Laid hands on my son, too!...That don't set right!"

"I know, Billy." He sighed, shaking his head.

"I want you to stay out of it, too,...unkess I go down!"

"Well, that could happen, you know!"

"Anything's possible....If it does, look after my fanily."

"That goes without saying!...I've seen you go up against a lot a guns, Billy, never really worrued me,...but this one does, and I don't know why?"

"You tryin' to make me quit and go home, Rod?" He asked, turning to look at him again. "Are ya?"

"Hell, no!...I want 'im as bad as you do!"

"Good!...No man's th' very best at anything, Rod, that includes me!... Jammed gun, misfirin' bullet, any a that can get a gunslinger killed!...Don't always take a gunslinger to kill one, neither."

"Don't Hatcher worry you any?"

"Oh, yeah, Hatcher worries me!...He scares me to death, a kid like that!...But every man I ever faced scared me, too."

"Scares me, too!...Look, Billy, I know all that, I know what you have to do and I agree with ya. But I also know that a man that fights when he's mad, ain't as fast as he could be, if he weren't!...You're mad as hell at this kid, and you're wounded ta-boot!"

"I'm okay, Rod....I'm over bein' mad at th' man." He grinned at him. "Been workin' with you too long, I guess, don't like killin'!...I'm gonna,... Nope, we are gonna take mister Hatcher back to Paris, and hang 'im!... Gonna take Freckles back to Doc, too."

"Don't you know how fast you'll need to be to keep him from killin' you?...Damn it, Billy, you'll have to shoot his gun arm!"

"Guess so!" He looked around at the surrounding trees and thickets then up at the circling birds overhead. "Must be th' heat!" He grinned.

"Sometimes, you worry me, Billy." Said Rodney with futility.

"Sometimes, I worry myself....Too damn hot to worry about it, anyway!...What will be, will be!"

"Rodney nodded. "Guess so....Think they rode all night?"

"No doubt about that, they know where they're goin'!"

"Wish we did!...Don't think I've ever been this hot before!"

"Trees knockin' th' wind off of us!...How's your shoulder?"

"Aches like a son of a bitch!"

"Still got some laudanum?"

"Yes, but I don't want a use too much a that stuff." They grew silent then as they followed the Yaqui Indian, and for the next couple of hours, swatted swarms of gnats and cursed the heat to no avail. They followed Toby in and out of thickets and trees until just before dark when he stopped in the shade of a giant Elm, turned his horse around and waited for them.

"Problem, Toby?" Asked Billy as they stopped beside him.

"They stopped to rest here." He said, looking at the ground.

"For how long?"

"From the looks, no more than an hour."

"Well, they got a be tired!" Sighed Rodney. "I know I am!"

"Toby, can you track in th' dark?" Asked Billy.

"Maybe so, maybe no, ground's real dry."

"Be dark in an hour or so, we gonna ride all night? Asked Rodney.

"I don't think even Peter could track 'em in th' dark, Rod!...Don't know about you, but I'm tired, shoulder hurts, too....They'll be there when we get there, I reckon....We'll stop here, Toby, head out at first light."

"Okay,...but one rider rode northeast, while the rest rode north!...The one man ran his horse, the rest walked."

"What's northeast?"

"Big town called Gainsville, three, four small towns in between."

"Why would he go to Gainsville?" Muttered Rodney.

"Good question, Rod....What's north, Toby?"

"More small towns, ranches, Red River." He shrugged.

"How far's th' river?"

"You think they're goin' to th' Red, Billy,...why would they?"

"Not sure,...Just some trouble Sheriff Hicks was tellin' me about in Gainsville. It's just a hunch, Rod....How far, Toby?"

"Sixty, seventy miles, hard to say, Marshal....Could be more."

Nodding, Billy looked at Rodney. "We keep followin' these tracks, we'll know for sure." He dismounted weakly, having to clutch the saddle-horn with his good arm, and then his hand as he slid his way to the ground.

Toby saw him, and quickly dismounted, as did Rodney, and together helped him under the heavy branches to the fallen tree limb, occupied by Haskell Oring only a few hours before.

"You okay?" Breathed Rodney as they eased him down.

"Yeah,...I'm okay. Thanks, both of ya!...Legs still a mite weak, is all."

"You ought a be in a bed somewhere, Billy."

"If I was, we wouldn't know where they went!"

"Where they might be goin', you mean!" He sat down beside him and looked around the clearing. "Tell me about that hunch a yours,...why do you think they'll go to th' river?"

"Ranches around Gainsville been losin' a lot a cattle last few months. Nobody could figure out why they been getting' away with it,...till th' previous Sheriff figured it out!...He was killed for his efforts, him and two deputies." He winced in pain then.

"Anyway, they knew he was comin, was waitin' for 'em....I told Hicks there was only one way they could a known they'd be there, why they couldn't catch 'em!"

"Rustlers had men workin' on those spreads!" Nodded Rodney.

"That's what I told 'im....Anyway, he was gonna check it out when I left."

"And you're thinkin' these might be th' rustlers, right?"

"Don't know,…rustlin' stopped when th' Sheriff was killed.…They wouldn't hang around with a posse huntin' 'em."

"That makes a lot a sense, Billy,…but why go back now?"

"Well, I think they might a seen me and Hank spyin' on 'em yesterday, and figured it was time to go."

"And you think they're goin' back for one last roundup?"

"Before leavin' th' territory,…might be!" He nodded.

"Why didn't they take th' Garnette Cattle, those were beautiful Hereford cows?"

Toby squatted down in front of them then to listen. "I would like to kow that as well." He said. "All they did was butcher Madam Garnette's beef.… Why did they not cut the fence and take what they wanted?"

"I don't rightly know for sure, Toby,…maybe it was too close to th' hideout. Maybe they figured it would bring th' Sheriff lookin'!…But, I don't think they was ready to leave yet!…Them seein' us forced 'em to leave ahead a time."

"And so," Nodded Toby deep in thought. "The one man that rode northeast will be going to these ranches to set it up,,,,with men that are already there?"

"You catch on quick, Toby!" Grinned Billy. "But I don't know, could be!"

"You're an Indian, Toby," Said Rodney curiously. "How is it, you speak as good a English as we do?"

"I have been working for the Garnettes since I was a boy, Madam Garnette taught me your language."

"Then tell me," Said Billy. "There any place on th' Red River a dozen men could hold up, without bein' seen?"

"Maybe so." He nodded. "About ten years ago, Mister Garnette sent one thousand of his cattle to Abilene with the Goodnight cattle drive. Mister Hank took me along, so I could learn about cattle.…We crossed the Red River at a place called Bulcher, I think!…A ferry barge was there, several buildings, too! The man there said he was quitting, going back where his home was.…If he did so, maybe no one lives there now."

"Could be where they're goin', Billy."

"Could be.…Think we could pick up th' pace a bit tomorrow, Toby?"

"Yes, but,…will that be good for you?"

Billy sighed then, and moved his arm some. "If I need to stop, I'll tell ya."

"Then we will go faster....Right now, I will clear a place for fire, make biscuits to eat with potatoes. Make you stronger."

"And coffee, Toby, please?" Reminded Rodney.

"Yes, working men must have coffee."

"Amen to that!"

*   *   *

Hatcher caught himself before toppling from the saddle and cursing, spurred his horse past Oring to stop in front of him.

"What's wrong now, Wes?" He asked with impatience, and stopped his horse to glare at him.

"I don't know about you old men, Oring,...but I need me a couple hours sleep!...And here is as good a place as any!"

"Well now!" Said Oring with a scowl. "Us, old men are used to goin' without a little sleep....Business we're in requires we get to where we're goin' before we rest!...It's safer that way."

"Business I'm in requires a clear head, I'm safer that way!...I signed up with you for two reasons, you need my gun, and I need to get to Kansas with a little expense money....If you want, we can part company, I won't be any worse off!...otherwise, we stop here and get some sleep!...Hell, it's almost dark already!"

Oring stared at Hatcher's dead-looking eyes for several long seconds before finally nodding. "All right!" He said. "But no more than four hours, you heard me tell Benny three days,...we still got fifty, sixty miles to go!"

"I'll be ready!" He nodded, and reined his horse in under the tree before stopping to look back at him. "I know you're mad at me for ole Amos, Oring, so I'll say this!...Tired or not, I'm a light sleeper!...That's very good information." He dismounted and loosed the gray horse's cinches before spreading his blankets on the ground,

Oring stared at him angrily then turned to look at the other men. "You got four hours to get some sleep, boys, make th' most of it!"

"What's he doin', Haskell?" Asked one of the men as he urged his horse up beside him. "He leavin' us, I hope?"

Oring took his eyes off Hatcher and peered at his underling. "Says he can't go any farther without sleep!"

"Guess he can't, damn near fell off his horse back there!...Let's leave th' son of a bitch, boss, we only got couple a days left to get there?"

"I'm aware a that, Levi,...but we might need 'im before we're done, you seen them two watchin' us yesterday,...it's already brought bad luck down on us!"

"Yes sir!...They was lawmen all right!...Think they're a comin'?"

"My gut says they might be....No, we'll wait! Go on, Levi, get some rest."

"You're th' boss, Haskell!" He reined in under the trees with the others and dismounted, leaving a still fuming Oring to follow suit.

Oring dismounted to raise the stirrup and loosen the cinches on his horse, and untying his bedding, spread it on the ground before taking his last slab of dried beef from the saddlebag,...and looking across at the sleeping form of Hatcher, sat down to eat. He knew that Hatcher had a reason for shooting Amos, and to him, that reason was not what the gunman said it was!...He was sure his reason was to prove his superiority over the rest of them. It worked, too, he thought angrily....'But if I get the chance, I'll do you in, you little shit'!...'Cows are gonna make mincemeat out a your worthless hide'! Getting up again, he returned the beef to the saddlebag,... and with a last hate-filled look at Hatcher, lay down and closed his eyes..

CHAPTER EIGHT

"Well, Doc," Said Doctor Snyder, taking the stethoscope from his ears to hang them around his neck. "I can't find any reason to keep you any longer."

"Praise the Lord!" Laughed Mattie as the two women hugged her broad shoulders. "Thank you, Doctor Snyder."

"Not necessary, dear lady, he did it on his own!" He looked back down at Doc then. "There are some heavy restrictions, however, which means no going out of doors for at least another week. Do your walking indoors, stay in bed as much as possible, and no lifting at all,…and I mean, nothing!…I will send some laudanum home with your wife for pain you might have. And, by the way, Mary Beth Rhodes will be going home with you, she has her things all packed and waiting. I understand she works for you now, anyway!"

"Oh, yes," Said Mattie. She's a darling of a woman."

"Well, can I put my pants on now?" Asked Doc Gruffly, making them all laugh.

"No, Sir,…but these ladies can do it for you!…I'll have a man hitch up your buggy for you."

"Can you also get word to the Marshal, that we're going home,…we're expecting word from Billy, and Rodney?"

"I surely can,…I'll be out to see you in a day or so, Doc." He turned and left.

"Well, get my britches, old Darlin!" He grinned. "I am ready to go home!"

*   *   *

"It will be daybreak soon." Said Toby, gently waking Billy up.

"What?" He grunted. "Oh, yeah, thanks, Toby." He grunted to a sitting position, and reached up to see if his eyeglasses were in place.

"You awake, Rod?"

"The Marshal is pouring the coffee, and the horses are ready. Come, I will help you up." He got Billy to his feet then set about rolling up his bedding.

"You okay this mornin', Billy?" Asked Rodney, giving him his coffee.

"I will be,…I must a been tired!" He took a drink of the hot coffee and swallowed it. "Damn, that's strong!"

"Well, it might need to be." Said Rodney as he poured the rest on the small fire to douse it. "Toby said, he heard at least two riders pass us last night, said they stopped, then moved on! What do you make a that?"

"Whoever they was, they know we're here." He nodded, turning as the Yaqui approached them. "Think they doubled back on us, Toby?"

"No,…them I heard go in the same direction….But we must be ready for them, I think."

"We will be." He finished the coffee, and Rodney took the cup to put it away. "I guess we're ready." He mounted the black, with a boost from Toby then waited for the Indian to lead the way back to the trail they were following.

The sun was slow in rising above the trees, and all three of them were vigilant as they strained their eyes at their surroundings, but as yet saw nothing that might tell them they were being watched, or maybe followed. They saw nothing in the shadows of the darkened trees, and the prairie grass, weeds and sand mounds were so high that a buffalo could have remained hidden.

They kept the horses at a fast walk, and a trot at times, but frequently had to slow due to the jarring pain in Billy's shoulder and arm. But his eyes never left the surroundings.

The one thing that was telling on all of them was the heat, and the sun was almost directly overhead when they saw Toby stop his horse to dismount and lift his horse's foreleg to check the hoof.

Billy pulled alongside and stopped, as did Rodney.

"On our left." Said Toby, just loud enough to be heard. "Movement in a cluster of Buffalo Grass."

Billy looked up at the sky as he unlatched the colt's hammer,…and as he looked back, two men with rifles stood up in the tall grass to lever their rifles. At the first sound of the weapon being levered, Billy twisted in the saddle, drew and fired. The explosion was deafening in the heat of a windless day, as the slug tore through the man's hand and rifle butt, the impact turning him around with a yelp as he was thrown back out of sight in the grass.

Almost as Billy fired, Rodney drew his own pistol, firing just as the man was pointing his gun, the bullet shattering his upper arm between elbow and shoulder. Toby pulled his own gun as the second man fell, and hurriedly climbed up the sandy dune as Rodney dismounted to follow him.

Billy sighed and holstered his gun then pulled the bandana from around his neck to wipe his face. He watched as they steered the wounded men down onto the trail. One was holding his broken arm, and crying loudly, the other was clutching his hand where two of his fingers used to be.

"You Bastard!" He yelled, looking up at Billy. "Look at my God damn hand!"

"Guess you won't be bushwhackin' anybody for a while!" He said. "Ain't so fun on th' wrong end of th' bullet, is it?"

"Fuck you, God Damn it!"

"Both of ya get out a here!" Ordered Rodney. "Be glad you're alive."

"Least get our horses for us, man, we can't!"

"Horses broke and ran with th' shooting." Said Rodney. "You're afoot!"

"Afoot?" Cried one of them. "You can't leave us afoot in this heat, man, we'll bleed to death!"

"Sure we can!" Said Billy. "That's what you had in mind for us, ain't it?" He nodded at Rodney then. "You'd a took th' time to look at that man's vest, there, you'd a seen th' star pinned on it.…Now, get out a here!"

"Best get out a this sun, too!" Said Rodney. "Do your walkin' at night."

"Sons a bitches!" Cursed the man with no fingers, and then they both began walking back down the churned up trail.

"Rod," Said Billy. "Best collect their handguns, and rifles."

"Sure thing!" He went back up the dune and disappeared.

Toby grabbed the saddle-horn and put his foot in the stirrup. "You ain't a lawman, are you?" He saked, mounting his horse to look at Billy.

Billy took the badge from his shirt and held it up. "This says I am, Toby."

"Yes sir, it does....But you are a gunslinger, I think!"

"Any man can use a gun, even you, Toby."

"But not that fast, Marshal....He never got that lever down all the way before you shot him....I ain't complaining now, Marshal, but tell me,...is th' man you hunt that fast?"

"Yeah," Sighed Billy. "He is!"

"No!" Said Rodney quickly as he slid back down the dune. "He ain't!... No man is, Toby." He put the two handguns in his saddlebag, and pushed one rifle through the straps at his bedroll. The second rifle was minus the stock, leaving only splintered, blood spattered remnants, and he held it up to show them before throwing it into the tall grass beneath the trees.

Toby looked up at him again. "Well, I hope not, my friend!...If he is, you might not save my life again!" He mounted, reined his horse back onto the trail and led off at a trot.

"You up to it, Billy?" Asked Rodney as he mounted.

"Let's go!" He urged the black to a gallop until he caught up to the tracker then slowed to a trot again to watch the slender Indian's sweaty back. 'I hope to hell, I am fast enough', he thought wearily.

*   *   *

"Time to move out, boys!" Said Oring, in a loud voice. "Get a move on, Wes, time to go!" He went to his horse and raised the stirrup.

They were all up, and taking dried beef from saddlebags and holding it in their mouths as they tightened cinches and mounted.

They all followed Oring out of the trees at a trot and headed north again and almost immediately, Wes Hatcher rode his horse up beside him.

"What is it, this time, Wes, not enough sleep last night?"

"No, I had plenty a sleep,...Thought I heard gunshots before I fell asleep, you hear anything?"

"Nope,...wouldn't be unusual though, why?"

"No reason, I guess....They were a long way off."

"Ain't no lawman tailin' us, Wes, if that's what your thinkin'. We're out a th' county now!"

"Don't be so sure, Oring, man I shot weren't local, he was trailing me!"

"You killed 'im, didn't ya?"

"You know, Oring,…for a man that claims to be so smart, you don't think all that well, ya know that?"

"What does that mean?"

"Means one a them two men was a ranch hand!"

"Or maybe both!…Come on, Wes, you slept four hours!…I think it's you that ain't too smart! Whoever they are, they went back for a posse, trust me on that!"

"Could be, I guess!" He slowed the horse, to fall in behind Haskell again, and was barely able to distinguish the men behind him in the dark, So he pulled aside to allow the other men to move ahead of him and followed them, his mind still on, what he believed to be gunfire, because they were too close together to be just one man,…unless, he thought, that man was a gunhand? But who's to say a lawman can't be a gunhand?…But what was he shooting at, he wondered? There was something that was not right about it, he knew,…his gut was telling him so!

He grinned then, and reached up to scratch his jaw through the week's worth of blond beard. He also knew that Oring wanted to kill him for shooting his friend,…and he really did not know why he did kill old Amos, he had beaten the man's half attempt to pull his gun, so why shoot him?

But he knew why, he thought, remembering what another older, and seasoned gunhand had told him. "Never pull on a man that's armed, unless you kill him. You beat him to the draw and don't kill him, he can kill you!"…That was why he killed him!…And he knew that Oring would kill him for it,…if he could?

He grinned again. 'But he can't', he thought, and felt the ever present comfort in knowing that he was the best there was with a gun,…had proven it more than ten times already! Oring would try, too, he thought. Question was,…how? Well, he thought then, it didn't matter how, or when? Because he had his own plan to kill Mister Oring, as well as the other men! But he wanted to wait until the cattle were sold and take it all. After all, twenty-one dollars a head, for six hundred head was a tidy sum! Oring had said they could get two bits a pound in Kansas, but he knew he was only telling him that to join him up!…An average steer was six hundred pounds, and beef just was not bringing three hundred dollars on the hoof, pedigreed Bull, maybe, but not a trail herd….Twenty dollars a head was more than seven thousand dollars….'That ought a do me a good long time'!

He turned in the saddle to scan the dark trail behind them, because there was a gnawing in his gut that bothered him, that, and the sounds he had been sure was gunfire. There was still a lawman trailing him, he felt sure of it,…and right now, he was better off with a dozen men around him!

The only other thing that bothered him,…was what he might have been shooting at, because a lawman would also know how gunfire could echo in this stillness. The thought that they would be caught up with didn't worry him, because it was bound to happen….What did worry him, was what Oring might do, because his back would make a good target when he went out to meet this new lawman.

*   *   *

"You okay, Billy?" Asked Rodney, pulling up beside him. "You're leaning a little low in th' saddle here, that shoulder hurting?"

"Yeah, a bit….Sort a twisted it when I drew my gun,…still a bit painful!…I'm okay, Rod! We can't afford to waste any more time."

"Want another swallow of Laudanum?" When he nodded, Rodney gave him the flask.

"How do you stand this stuff?" He grimaced and gave it back to him.

"It kills th' pain!"

"Yeah, it does at that!…Thanks."

Rodney kept his horse in pace with the black as he put the flask away. "How'd you know that man was up there, Billy,…I didn't see 'im till you fired?"

"I knew he was there, you heard Toby warn us!…He breached th' rifle, I drew when I heard it."

"I heard it, too, but it didn't register….You never cease to amaze me!"

"Seems I heard you say that a few times, too!…What's so amazin' about it?"

"I don't know,…the things you do, I guess. You seem to feel th' presence a danger when I can't!…You pull that pistol, like th' devil's after you!…If that ain't amazing nothin' is!" Rodney looked at him then. "Laudanum workin' yet?"

"Seems to be." He said, flexing his left arm. "Guess I turned th' wrong way when I fired.,,,You ain't got much a that stuff left, Rod, best slow down on it!"

"Hell, I ain't usin' it, been savin' it for you!"

"Dumb thing to do!"

"Yeah, well let's hope it ain't!" He dropped back behind him again, and they rode in silence until late afternoon when they saw the Indian stop once again to study the ground. They pulled up beside him as he dismounted to feel the tracks.

"They stopped here." He said then walked in under the trees.

They both dismounted to stretch tired legs while they waited for him to come back. Rodney took one of the last few cigars he had left from his vest, struck a match and lit it to blow blue smoke into the still air.

"They slept here, too!" Said Toby when he came back. "Cold camp." He walked farther up the trail and stooped to check the tracks again before returning.

"We are closer than before, the new tracks are fresher."

"How close?" Insisted Rodney.

"Couple hours, maybe three."

"Still goin' due north." Mused Billy. "I think you're right, Toby."

"How is that, Marshal?" He asked, looking up at him.

"That place on th' river, what was it,…Bulcher?"

"Bulger, Bulcher, something like that."

"Well, I think that's where they're going,…or somewhere close to it! They're avoidin' any place with people, must a passed a dozen farm houses along th' way, few ranch houses, too."

"Couple a towns in th' distance." Added Rodney. "I seen th' buildings."

"They do not want to be seen." Nodded Toby.

"We got no choice but ride tonight." Said Billy. "Maybe we can make up some more lost time…How far ahesd of us, are they, Toby?"

"Maybe nine, ten hours,…but they might not stop again, Marshal."

"That's true,…but we might shorten th' distance even more, if we pick up th' pace."

"What about your wound, Marshal, you could open it again?"

"I ain't got a choice, Toby, you both know it!…Hatcher gets across that river, he's gone for good!…I can't take that chance."

"I don't think so," Said Rodney. "Not if they're waitin' for their man to bring 'em that information….If they want them cows, they'll wait for 'im!"

"You're probably right!...But then again, that whole thing was just a theory a mine, Rod!...They might not even be th' rustlers, they might just be tryin' to get across to Indian Territory."

"Okay,…do you want to take that chance?"

"No way, let's go, Toby!"

The Yaqui swung astride his horse and urged it to a gallop with them on his heels, the animals jumping clusters of tall grass, and cactus plants and at times, dead, fallen tree branches in the wake of the Indian's galloping horse.

Billy flexed his arm several times again, while watching the straight-backed Yaqui Indian in front of them. He knew that the tendons in his left shoulder might be somehow connected to those in his right. Move one arm, it affects movement in the other, and that worried him! 'I just hope it doesn't affect my right, when the time comes', he thought. Because, if it's too bad, Hatcher could kill him for sure,…and he was not all that sure he could beat the younger gunman, anyway!

He was, however, very sure that he would take the little bastard with him. Wes Hatcher has to be stopped! Preferably hung and if not, dead. He likely knows that somebody is after them, he thought, because that gunfire would have echoed for miles. But that could be a good thing, he thought again,…might do Hatcher good to feel a little up-tight. A little anxiety might slow his gun arm some!

It was almost full dark now, and the lighter color of the Indian's white shirt was their only way of knowing he was there, that, and the sounds of his running horse, and that worried Billy some.

"Hold up, Toby!" He yelled, loud enough to slow him down and pull alongside. "Let's cool down th' horses, got some foam formin' on 'em!" Nodding, Toby continued ahead at a walk.

"Can you actually see a trail here, man,…I can barely see you?"

"They are going North, Marshal, and so are we!"

"How do you know that?"

"North star, see, the bright one."

"I do now." Sighed Billy.

"Ever see anything strange up there, Toby?" Asked Rodney from behind them. "Somethin' you wondered about?"

"Many times, Marshal!"

"Like what?" Asked Billy.

"Well,…like shooting stars, lights that move in a straight line, with no tail like the Comet has."

"Have you wondered about those?"

"Not too much.…Indian lore says that the Gods came here from the stars many thousands of years ago.…They taught the Indian many things. The lights with no tail are the Gods watching over us."

"You asked, Rod." Said Billy. "Toby, are you speakin' of Quitzel Coatle?"

"Ahhh, you have heard the story of the Aztec, they are my ancient ancestors."

"The Yaqui are direct descendants of the Aztec, Billy." Said Rodney. "Didn't think of it before."

"How do you know all this, Marshal, you spoke the name of a God, not many know this?"

"If we run into each other again, Toby, I'll tell ya.…You'd be surprised how much we know about it!…Best lead out again, Toby, and keep that star in sight.…Moon'll be up soon!"

Toby gigged the horse to a gallop again, only to slow the animal to a fast trot.

"Come on, Rod, we don't want a lose 'im!" Yelled Billy, and urged the black in pursuit for several yards before also slowing behind the Indian, all three of them keeping the bright star in sight.

They rode like that until the landscape became visible in the pale, yellow light of the moon, becoming even brighter as the large orb rose higher in the night sky and that's when the Yaqui urged his horse to a gallop again on the parched, clay-like ground, only slowing from time to time to rest and water the horses from the canteens. They kept up this off and on pace until well after the moon was setting, and the hint of a coming dawn was making itself known in the East.

Toby chose that time to stop his horse, and wait for them to catch up. "Horses are very tired now, Marshal, breathing is hard. We stop for a few minutes to rest them." They all dismounted and loosened the animsl's cinches.

"No water until we start to leave." He said. "Is bad for them."

"How long till dawn?" Asked Billy.

"One hour, not much more."

"Think we're still on their trail?" Asked Rodney.

"If they go north, we are." Replied Toby.

"Think we ought a take time to eat, wait till it's light to go on?"

"Your decision, Marshal." Replied Toby. "Half hour will not matter that much!"

"Then I say yes." He groaned and sat down on the packed sand beside his horse then looked up at Rodney. "Grab a biscuit out a my saddlebag, will ya, Rod?"

Rodney did as he asked, and squatted to give him one. "You okay?"

"Legs are sore as hell, ass aches, shoulder's sore as hell!...Guess I'm good, for th' shape I'm in."

"Makes two of us!" He said, sitting down beside him. "Sure could use a stiff wind right now!...Shirt's plastered against my back, And that saddle's about to gall my ass!...Your arm's gonna be good as new before long, Billy,... but not before you have to fight Hatcher, so I think you should take more of this laudanum once we find 'em. You'll be a lot better if you ain't hurtin'!"

"Thank's Rod, I might do that....Wish your arm was gonna heal."

"Mine's gonna be around for a spell."

"What is wrong with your arm, Marshal?"

"He fell off a cliff, Toby,...tore th' muscles up in his shoulder."

"It can't be fixed, Toby." Added Rodney. "Doctors don't know how."

"I am sorry to hear that, Marshal....But you must not allow that to win, you must use the arm anyway, and it will heal. Your body has a way to do this!"

"Thanks, Toby,...I will!" He began eating the cold biscuit then.

"Where you from, Toby?" He asked, as he chewed the cold bread.

"I came here from Arizona more than ten years ago....My family, and tribe moved around a lot, sometime New Mexico, sometime Arizona,...until soldiers raided the village....My family was killed there, only I got away."

"Damn, I'm sorry, Toby!" Said Billy with feeling.

"What is done, is done, Marshal,...I have a new life now!"

"I believe you do, and Hank thinks a lot of ya, too!"

"Mister Hank is a good man, he has taught me a lot!" They sat in silence for the remainder of the rest period, and then were in the saddle again, and once more following Oring's trail in the coming dawn.

*   *   *

It was just coming daylight when Oring stopped them, and turning in the saddle, looked them over. "One a you ole boys get down and make some coffee,...we'll rest th horses for a spell." He watched them dismount and go about staking out the horses, all but Hatcher, and he waited for the gunman to ride up beside him.

"What's th' deal, Oring?"

"No deal, Wes....Today is day three, we'll be at th' river by late afternoon, benny'll be waitin' on us."

"Think I'll take a nap." He said, reining his horse around to follow the others.

"Smug Bastard!" He muttered aloud as he watched him. 'Can't wait till I see him dead'!

"Ahhh, well!" He sighed, and dismounted to lead his horse into the trees. "Be there by tonight, boys!" He said, as he loosened his horse's cinches. "Back in business by tomorrow night, if th' boys do their job?"

"Ain't let us down yet, Boss." Said Levi, looking up at him from where he was sitting. "I can't wait neither, don't like this waitin' around!...Besides, I'm near bout broke again!"

"Wouldn't be, you'd quit gamblin', Levi!" Laughed one of the men building the fire.

"You know he's right, Levi." Grinned Oring. "You ain't a gambler!" He looked at all of them then. "This is our last job here, boys,...gonna be a big herd this time, biggest yet. Don't want any slipups this go round neither!... We'll hit them cows quick, and drive 'em off quick! We'll have four more men to help us this time, that way four of you will stay at th hideout to drive th' herds across th' Red when th' rest of us bring 'em in....We'll use that same arroyo to hold 'em in, it ought a hold six hundred head with no trouble!...We're done, we'll drive 'em to Atoka, use th' railroad to ship 'em North. You think on that real strong, now....Don't want any more killings!"

"Weren't our fault that Sheriff found us, Haskell….Besides, it was you ordered th' killin'!"

"I know I ordered it, God damn it!...I had no choice!...Hadn't been for walt's warnin' us, we'd be th' ones dead, or in jail!....Weren't nobody's fault, Woody, but we didn't get any cows that night neither!...I want a payday this time!...Now get that coffee on, man, we ain't there yet."

He sat down by the fire as the coffee was set to boil, and stared across at the gunman, who had already spread his blanket and was fast asleep. He knew that Hatcher was a dangerous man in spite of his age, having heard of his exploits before. But now that he was here, he knew there was much more to him than the fact he was a killer! The man had no feelings, no remorse, he was nothing but a cold-hearted murderer, he thought, remembering that Amos had not even drawn his gun!

Nodding, he looked back at the other men as they ate their dried beef, and waited for the coffee.

"Levi?" He said, getting the rustler's attention. "After you have your coffee, I want you and Grover there to ride on ahead. Check th' place out before we all get there."

"Ain't never been nobody there, boss." Returned Levi.

"Ceptin' us!" Chuckled Grover.

"Ya never know! We ain't been there in a month, better safe than sorry!... If Benny's there already, tell 'im we'll be in before dark."

"And if he ain't?" This, from Levi.

"Then he'll be there later!...Anyway, if things ain't th' way we left it, head on back and tell me, we'll go from there."

"You got it, boss….We don't come back you'll know it's okay, we'll leave soon's we get us some coffee."

No hurry!" He said, walking out from under the trees to look back the way they had come. He knew that Hatcher was right, someone was following them, he had felt them the second day out, but didn't say anything. 'It has to be the law', he thought, and if it was,…he knew that it was Hatcher that led them to him. Damn his soul, he thought, and shook his head. He'd had this rustling operation going for most of a year now with no problems, even had men in key spots for insurance. He had it down to a science, it was perfect!... And then came Wes Hatcher from out of nowhere, to fuck it all up!

At this point, he was not sure they would even get any cattle, because it was too soon yet,...Latham could still be looking for them!...Another couple of weeks was all he needed, and Latham would have let his guard down again. He knew that if Benny made contact all right, they still might have a chance,...a slim one, but a chance!...He had always known that when bad luck sets in, it most always stays for the duration....If that was the case, and Latham was still up in arms, Benny might not show at all,...his men may not even be in place to help him. Between Wes Hatcher, and having to kill those lawmen a few weeks back, bad luck was like a shroud of darkness around him.

"Oh, well!" He muttered, taking his eyes off the trail behind them to look back at the small fire beneath the trees. "Every mistake is fixable." He walked back in to his horse, retrieved the rest of the dreid meat, and went to sit down near the fire.

*   *   *

The moon's light had helped a lot during the night, as they were able to keep the animals at a faster pace over the tree-shrouded prairie. But now, sitting around the small fire, Billy could feel the strength ebbing from his body and lay back. His idea was just to rest his back for a few minutes, but was instantly asleep.

Rodney saw Toby nod toward him and looked, and then grinned. "We'll take an extra thirty minutes, he needs it!"

"Who is he, Marshal?" Asked Toby, setting the pot on the flames to boil.

"Best friend I ever had, Toby,...must a saved my life a dozen times over th' years."

"Don't mean that, Marshal,...who is he?"

Rodney looked at him for a time then nodded. "I'll expect you to keep this between us, Toby....There lays the fastest man with a gun that you'll ever see, let alone meet!...His name is Billy Upshur, course that weren't th' name he went by when I first met 'im!...Anyway, I'll tell you a little about 'im....I was a hotel Clerk in a town called Sycamore when we met, he was a mess to see, too.

Rodney told the Yaqui his story in its shortest form while the coffee boiled, and Toby listened intently, holding on to every word, and when he finished.

"That's about it, man." He sighed. "Not all, by a longshot!...But there was a time we all lost track of 'im, and when he finally came home, we was there waitin' for 'im! He's got three pretty terrific kids now, too.…There ain't a man alive can outshoot 'im, Toby,…he's th' best there is, bar none!"

"I already knew this, Marshal." He nodded, then grabbed his kerchief and poured the coffee before grabbing the skillet and putting lard in it to melt. "This man, Hatcher." He said as he sliced up a potato. "Catching him is important to him, is it not?"

"Yeah," He sighed. "Hatcher shot his adopted Father, and stole his horse."

"I knew this." He nodded. "He is a strong man, an honest man.…I am an Indian, I know these things."

"Billy will track 'im to hell and back, if he has to!"

"He will need a plan, there's a dozen men with him, only three of us!"

"Two of us, Toby, we can't ask you to risk your life."

"No need to ask." He smiled. "I volunteer!...I come from a long line of fighting warriors, the Yaqui have fought for survival for generations."

"I can believe that!...And I agree that we need a plan, too!...If I know Billy, he's going to ride in and call Hatcher out just like before. He won't even think about th' rest of them."

"Then when we get close, I will get some help."

"Where?"

"From the ranches, these men are rustlers. They will want to catch them to protect their herds!"

"That's a hell of an idea, Toby. We'll surround th' place, give Billy a free hand to deal with Hatcher."

"But with more men, he will not have to, Marshal."

"Yeah he does, Toby, it's personal to him. Besides,…Hatcher won't give up without a fight, he don't believe he can be beaten."

"Are you sure Mister Upshur can kill him?"

Rodney sighed and looked at Billy. "Truth, Toby?...I don't know, he's been wounded!...He's weak.…He told me somethin' once,…He said that no man is the very best at anything, th' world's too full of people to even consider that!...He said that somewhere, there will always be somebody better at what he does, than he is!...That has always stuck in my mind. Every fight he has scares the hell out a me!...Scares him, too, because he believes what he said." He looked back at the Indian then.

"Wes Hatcher scares me more than any of the others did....Flyer on 'im said, he was to be considered a brick shy of a full load."

"What does that mean?"

"Means he's half crazy, Toby,...no feelings!...He's a killer that likes to kill."

"I see!" He nodded, and then placed the potatoes in the melted lard to fry.

"How much farther is this Bulger?"

Toby shrugged. "Thirty miles, maybe thirty five. We will be there before daybreak tomorrow....I will go for help tonight!...You will follow the North Star the rest of the way....When you see the river, begin looking for the old buildings....Go east to do this, not west. I will have men there to help before daybreak, if I can!"

"Sounds good to me,...and Toby, surround th' place when you get there!...Thank's man!"

"De nada, Marshal, now wake the Marshal, he wil need to eat."

"Amen to that!...And Toby,...Billy's not to know about what I told you, my friend. He don't like folks knowin' what he was."

*   *   *

Oring stopped the horses on a hill overlooking the rotting buildings on the bank of the Red River, and waited until Hatcher and men stopped alongside.

"That's it, Wes,...we're here!" He said, shifting his weight in the saddle. "Them old buildings is well hidden by trees on three sides, th' river on th' other,...all except for th' way in! Nobody comes here anymore, we been usin' it for several months now, off and on, ain't seen a soul!"

"Why is that?" Asked Hatcher, still looking the place over.

"Man that left it, still owns th' land, never sold it to anybody,...just packed up and left!...Look at that old river there, see how low it is on that far bank?...That's where we'll take th' cattle across. It's a little wide, but we can damn near walk 'em across."

"Nobody comes here, huh,...ain't that what you said about that Rush Creek?"

"This is different."

"It better be, man,...but we still got a get 'em first, Oring!"

"We will,...if Benny's down there, we'll start roundin' 'em up tomorrow night! Three days from then, we take 'rem across, scott free!

"You sound real sure of yourself, I'll give ya that!"

"Why not, I have a system that works?"

"You have a system that used to work, Oring,...but they might be lookin' for you to start up again now....You thought about that?"

"We'll know once we talk with Benny!...You ain't nervous, are ya?" He grinned widely as he looked at him. "I do believe you are, Wes!"

"I'm always nervous, doin' somethin' I never done before!...And you might need to be!"

"You still think they followed us, don't ya?"

"I know they did, Oring!"

"Tell you th' truth, Wes,...I about half believe they did, too!...That's why I'm postin' two men up here with rifles." He looked down the line of men.

"Morgan, you're th' best rifle shot....Stewart, you, Too!...You boys stake out up here somewhere, one of ya sleep, one keep watch, take turns, but stay alert! We got a lot at stake here!...Rest of ya, let's go!" He urged the horse down the grade and was followed closely by the others, all riding at a gallop up to the first of three buildings, only to slide the horses to a halt at the open doorway where they were met by Levi and Grover coming forward to take their horses.

"What about it, Levi?" Asked Oring as he dismounted.

"Same as always, Boss, it's all ours!" They all dismounted then, and Wes gave his horse to Grover who led it into the dark building. The other men dismounted and led their own mounts inside.

"Any sign a Benny, Levi?"

"Nope, ain't here yet!"

"Got four ranches to make contact with, takes time I guess....He'll be here, meantime take care a th' horses, they got sore backs!"

Hatcher listened to the conversation then looked back at the open space in front of the building. Almost fifty yards of open ground, he noted, not liking it much.

"What's th' matter, Wes, see somethin'?"

"No,...but I ain't all that comfortable with th' situation, too much open ground in front here, too many things to hide behind out there....Old wagon there, water tank over there, tool shed yonder!"

"You need to relax, man,...nobody knows we're here. Besides, Stewart and Morgan will let us know if anybody comes lookin'. Come on, we'll get some vittles cooked up while it's still daylight, can't chance a fire at night." He walked off inside the building, and after another minute, Hatcher followed him.

The old building was quite large, and littered with broken furniture, a few rusted pieces of farm eqiopment, some large drum-barrels and harness. The walls had cracks in them between the planks, and the ceiling was open on one end of the structure. Hatcher looked it over distastefully before going to his horse for the bedding, and rifle, found a suitable place, and spread the blankets out before sitting down on them....He did not like this at all!

*   *   *

It was late afternoon when Toby stopped to dismount, and check the ground. He looked up at them as they also dismounted.

"They stopped again here." He said, and pointed toward the trees. "They led the animals beneath the trees." He said, taking his horse's reins and walking it in under the hanging limbs with them on his heels, until he stopped to look around.

"They made coffee." He said, pointing at the fire residue. "Ate some Jerky, too....One man slept here, grass is laid flat!"

"How long ago, Toby?" Asked Billy.

"Eight, maybe ten hours."

"Stayin' well ahead of us, Billy." Breathed Rodney.

"Appears so!...How far to this place now, Toby?"

"Fifteen miles, due north....They are there now!"

"Then let's get started,...don't want a keep 'em waitin'!"

"You will go alone from here!" Said Toby. "A large ranch lies no more that eight miles to the east of here, I will bring help from there."

"If you leave, how will we find 'em?"

"The star, my friend, it is already there!...Follow it north. I have already explained it to the Marshal while you slept."

Billy looked at the sky through the branches. "What day of th' month is it, Rod?"

"Does it matter?...Almost six weeks from th' day we started to Shreveport!"

"That makes it June, twelfth, there abouts!...Shouldn't be this damn hot yet!"

"You'll think hot, we still got July and August to go."

"It will be very hot this summer." Said Toby. "But a hard winter is coming!"

"How do you know that?"

"An Indian knows these things."

"Which means, you don't know." Said Billy grinning, and then he saw the bright star, barely visible in the afternoon sun. "Okay,...Star ought a be easy enough to follow."

"Remember this, Marshal,...if they heard the shooting yesterday, they will be distrusting....They will have a sentry, maybe two men, be aware of this!...If you ride hard tonight, you will be there by daybreak. You must see these men first and quieten them silently, if you are to surprise the man you seek."

"We understand, Toby. Good luck." The Yaqui leaped astride his pony, and urged it eastward at a gallop.

"Up to us now, Billy."

"Better get to it, then."

"Amen to that!" Theyboth mounted up, rode out of the tree's protection, and galloped away to the north.

CHAPTER NINE

Connie kept the buggy at a snail's pace, having to hold back constantly on the lines to keep the horse in check and even then, it was quite difficult having to maneuver the animal into missing the many dips and holes in the dry road.

"How's he doing, Mama Bailey?" She asked nervously.

"Don't ask her, daughter!" Grumbled Doc. "Ask me, I'm doing just fine!...The horse can go faster, you know!"

"No, it can't, Doc." Said Melissa from beside Connie. "Not unless you want your wound to open,...hospital bed is still waiting for you!" She grinned at Connie then.

"Yeah, okay,...you're doing just fine, daughter."

"We think so, too!" Chuckled Mattie. "Right, Mary Beth?"

"Of course, we do."

"Don't know why he kept me an extra day, though."

"You ran a fever after you got dressed, remember?"...He was worried about it!" Replied Mattie. "You'll have to be careful not to over do it, Walter."

"I know, I know!...Be tomorrow night getting' home at this rate!"

"Jim stockwell is riding up behind us." Said Melissa. "Maybe he has word from the boys?"

"Hi ya, folks!" He smiled, riding up beside the buggy. The Doctor sent word you was going home, Doc. Thought I'd go along, check out th' house brfore you go in."

"We appreciate that, Jim." Smiled Mattie.

"If we ever get there." Grumbled Doc. "Any word from the boys, Jim?"

"Not since th' one from Rodney, Doc,…sorry."

"Well, no news is good news, so they say."

"I pray to God, it is!" Sighed Mattie.

"Can you stay a while, Jim?" Asked Doc. "Cow ain't been milked in a day or two, no one to do th' feedin' neither?"

"Consider it done, Doc, it's one a th' reasons I'm here."

"Bless you, Jim!" Smiled Mattie.

"You got it all wrong, Ms. Bailey.…I'm here to check on Ben, he's been here since last night!...Chores are all done already."

"Then, God bless you both!"

"Thank you, Ma'am!" He laughed. "Little extra help never hurts."

"Son," Said Doc then. "You did send that wire, checking on the boys, didn't you?"

"That very afternoon, Doc, bet your life, I did!...Decatur acknowledged our request, but said he would have no news until the Sheriff returned to town. Seems he left town real early that same mornin'. If you recall, he had one deputy killed, and one wounded when Billy got there."

"Please, Jim?" Cried Connie. "We know Billy was hurt, I just need to know that he's all right!"

"Sorry, Ms. Upshur." He said sheepishly. "guess I spoke without thinkin'"

"No, Jim,…I am!...I'm just worried sick, that's all."

"Yes, Ma'am, I know!...Tell ya what, I'll just ride on ahead folks, open up th' house, light th' lamps and such." He galloped on ahead of them then.

"My, God!" Sniffed Connie. "Why did I say that? He was just trying to help!"

"It's okay, Daughter." Said Doc. "I'm sure he understands."

"I hope so." She sniffed. "Think he might leave Ben there for a couple of days, I'd like to go get my children, and I know Lisa needs to see her folks, and daughter?"

"I'm sure he will, Daughter, Besides, Mary Beth will be there."

"That's right," She said cheerfully. "I'm moving in!"

"And we are blessed to have you, my dear." Nodded Mattie.

"No, no, it's me that's blessed, I feel I have a family again."

"You do, dear lady, you and me are now kin, we share the same blood."

*   *   *

Billy stopped his horse on the bluff amid a stand of Pecan Trees to wait as Rodney stopped beside him.

"What now, Rod?" Sighed Billy. "You can see th' river through th' trees there, but no buildings."

"Don't know, unless we missed th' mark a bit,…Toby said, if we come out wrong, go east a ways, and we'd find it."

"Okay, let's go down to level ground, and give it a shot." He urged the black down the crumbling slope and into the tall grass and trees, with Rodney close behind him and together, rode east along the wide river's bank.

"Wonder how long before dawn?" Asked Rodney in a low voice.

"Hour, maybe two,…but it don't matter, I see th' buildings now,… through th' trees there, see 'em?"

"I do now!" he whispered. "And all we got a worry about now, is th' lookouts….Where would they be, ya think?"

"Th' bluff up there, way they came in….Got a be off there in front somewhere, I'd say….Keep your eyes open, we're bound to see one of 'em move up there." It took only a few short minutes before he saw the man stand up. "And there he is!"

"Yeah, I see 'im,…how do we work it?"

"We take 'im down….We'll leave th' horses here, and climb th' bluff this side of 'em. Come on." They dismounted, and using the darkness of the trees, quickly made their way back to, and up the sandy bluff again. Once on top, and in the grass, he told Rodney to make his way farther out into the trees and come in from behind.

"No guns, Rod!" He whispered, and once he moved away, inched his way toward where he had seen the guard stand up.

It seemed like a long time to him, and was just wondering where Rodney was, when he saw him. But at the same time, he saw the sentinal stand up and point his rifle at him. He quickly pulled the hunting knife from his belt, grabbed the blade and threw it hard at the man, seeing him pitch forward with an audible grunt as he fell. He watched then as Rodney came to stand over the man's body, and he was pointing toward a group of rocks.

He moved forward again until he came to the dead man, removed the knife and wiped it clean just as he saw Rodney bring his gun butt down on the head of the second man and then looking around, made his way back to him.

"That was some throw, Billy, thanks, I didn't even see 'im."

"He weren't where I thought he was neither….I'm just lucky I didn't miss, ain't practiced in a while."

"What now, back to the horses, we know they're there?"

"Yeah,…I was hopin' Toby would be here by now."

"Me, too!...What's th' plan?"

"Ain't got one!...We don't know how many men are in there,…at least twelve."

"Nine!" Said Rodney, "Ten, with Hatcher, we got two of 'em….So, what are we gonna do?"

"What they don't expect!...But I think you are gonna belly up behind that,…what th' hell is that down there, water trough?"

"Looks more like th' bed of a wagon, turned upside down."

"Whatever it is, that's where you'll be, take an extra rifle just in case, pistol, too, wouldn't hurt." He leaned to pick up the fallen man's rifle, and pistol then gave them to him. "Best take th' gunbelt, too, might need th' cartridges." As Rodney stripped the corpse of the gunbelt, he looked the dark building over.

"Got it."

"Okay, go on down there from here, Rod….Keep low and out a sight."

"What about you?"

"I'm gonna ride that black horse right up in front a that open door down there!...Then I'm gonna call that bastard out again."

"That's crazy, Billy, they could all open up on you!"

"They might, but it's somethin' I got a do!...Maybe we'll get some help by then."

"You're at least gonna wait till daylight, ain't ya?"

"You know I am, Rod….I want 'im to see me there waitin' on 'im!...Th' challenge, Rod, it's all about th' challenge, don't forget that!...But, if he beats me, and he's still standin', kill 'im!"

"No doubt about that!"…It's you, I'm worried about!"

"Well don't!...This is personal!...I don't plan on killin' 'im, I just want 'im to know he can be beat!"

"If he can be?"

"Go on, Rod, get in place down there, it's getting' lighter." He went back through the trees and tall grass then back down the bluff, leaving a frustrated Rodney to shake his head and make his way down the crumbling bluff, only to stop half way down and look back then to shake his head again in despair.

The sky was getting lighter as he got back to the horses, and with a long look back toward the open yard in front of the building, he saw Rodney raise up to look his way for a moment before ducking down again.

"Showtime!" He said aloud, and placed his boot in the stirrup to pull his self up into the saddle. "Let's go, black boy!" He said, reining the horse around and walking it through the trees and into the open area of hard packed yard in front of the old barn. Changing direction, he went on to stop at the overturned wagon to look down at Rodney. "You ready?"

"Yeah, but you're crazy, Billy, this ain't like you!"

"I know….You see any movement through th' door yonder?"

"No, but there's horses inside, they got a be there, too!…Think about this, Billy, will ya, what about Connie and th' kids?"

"I am, Rod….Stay down, be ready." He urged the black on past the wagon, and turned toward the building's open doorway to stop some forty feet away and sit the saddle while he waited for the sun to appear at his back. Once the heavenly orb rose above the treeline and he felt the warm rays on his back, he sighed then glanced again at Rodney's hiding place before slowly dismounting. He unlatched the Colt's tie-down, lifted the gun slightly to loosen it in the holster and then released it again.

"WES HATCHER!" He yelled, his voice loud in the morning stillness. "YOU HEAR ME, HATCHER?"

The gunman's eyes popped open, and he sat up quickly, gun in hand, cocked and ready. He saw Oring get to his feet, the other men as well.

"Stay away from th' door, Oring,…keep everybody back." He warned, also getting to his feet to check the loads in his gun. "So much for your lookouts, Oring!" He said, glaring at him hatefully.

One of the other men made his way to the wall to peer out through one of the gaps in the planking.

"Who's out there, Mackie?" Asked Oring, also pulling his pistol.

"All I see is one man with a black horse!"

"Nothin' else?"

Mackie moved down the wall, still peering through the gaps at the outside. "He's all by his self, Haskell, far as I can tell!"

"One man ain't no prob…."

"No!' Said Hatcher, interrupting Oring.

"Black horse, you say?" He asked this of Mackie. "Tall, lean man?"

"That's him, all right!…You know 'im?" Blurted Mackie, slowly moving back away from the wall.

"These walls ain't gonna stop no bullets, Boss!" Said Levi nervously. "What we gonna do?"

"You know 'im, Wes?" Asked Oring, his eyes still on the open door, and when Hatcher didn't answer him. "WES!" He said louder. "Do ya know 'im?"

Hatcher grinned then and nodded at Oring. "I think I do, Oring." He said, and holstered the gun.

"Well,…who th' hell is it?"

"WES HATCHER!" Yelled Billy again. "IF YOU'RE IN THERE, GET YOUR ASS OUT HERE, YOU'RE UNDER ARREST!"

"Th' man you said you killed!" Blurted Oring suddenly, and shook his head.

"I must a pulled my shot a little!" He said, grinning at Oring. "That shit happens sometimes,…But that's all right!…This way, I get another shot at 'im!"

"COME ON OUT A THERE, HATCHER!" Yelled Billy again. "OR DO YOU NEED THAT WHOLE BUNCH TO SIDE YA?…COME ON, YOU HALF-BAKED EXCUSE OF A GUNFIGHTER, LOOK ME IN THE EYE THIS TIME!"

"We can take that bastard easy, Wes, he's only one man!" Said Oring. "He'll never know what hit 'im."

"But, I would!" Returned Hatcher. "Man just challenged me to a duel,… and I like it!…Hell, I live for it!…You just stay put, Oring, keep your men in check,…I won't be long."

"I'M WAITING, HATCHER!" Yelled Billy.

"I'M COMING, MARSHAL!" He yelled back. "HERE I COME, NO GUN IN MY HAND!" He smiled again and moved toward the door. "You heard what I said, Oring, stay put!…You shoot 'im, I'll shoot you!" He stepped into view then, to stop and look Billy over before moving forward.

Billy turned his body, giving Hatcher a side view of him, and watched the slender, blond haired, yellow bearded gunman walk out through the open door of the building.

"Still got that fine lookin' black, I see." Said Hatcher, still moving forward. "You'd a caught me, if I hadn't stopped!...Tell me,...how far did I miss you, I must a had an off day?...I don't usually miss an easy shot!"

"Too bad, you didn't stop and wait for me!" Said Billy tightly.

"I was drunk, Marshal, been drinking for two days,...Weren't thinkin' too straight!...But drunk or sober, I always hit what I shoot at....An off day, that's all!"

"You're off day, was bein' born!"

"Could be, you're right, Marshal,...how long you been chasin' me, anyway?"

"Long enough!"

"Okay,...then why was you chasin' me?"

"You shot my father, stole his horse!"

"That old man was your fa...." He laughed then. "Now, that was the old fart's own fault, you know!...Should a stayed in with th' womenfolf. You'll get over it, Marshal!"

"Already have,...you missed him, too....He's alive and well."

"Then why are you here?"

"Hangman's waitin' for ya!"

Hatcher laughed again. "And you're gonna try and take me back?"

"No,...I aim to take you back!...Just wanted you to know that."

"Well, ya better be real fast, Marshal!...Are you fast, Marshal?...I am!...I'm so fast, I'll even let you pull first, how's that?"

"Wouldn't be fair, Hatcher."

"Why not?"

"You figure it out."

"Then, we're going head up, right,...that your choice?"

"Eye to eye, Hatcher!" Said Billy, watching him closely, and then Hatcher blinked, and he drew and fired from the hip, quickly twisting his body as he did. Both shots sounded as one, the duel explosions deafening in the morning stillness, as Hatcher was forceably spun around and thrown backward to fall, screaming on the hard-packed ground, his gun arm shattered, the gun hitting the ground some ten feet away from him.

Still screaming, the gunman got to his knees in obvious pain, his arm dangling limply.

Billy gathered himself, and breathlessly looked at the dark doorway again. "I DON'T KNOW WHO YOU ARE IN THERE, BUT YOU'RE SURROUNDED!...THEM OLD WALLS AIN'T THICK ENOUGH TO HELP YA NONE!...DO YOURSELVES A FAVOR, AND COME ON OUT!" He watched the nine men file outside to spread out in front of him.

"What ya got in mind, men?...If it's a fight, I got a tell ya,...I'll get three, maybe four of ya,...my friend over there will get th' rest. Stand up, Rod!"

Their eyes widened to see the rifle trained on them.

"You're best bet is to throw them guns down, gents!" Said Rodney, with authority. "I'm a United States Marshal, so is he!"

"Do it, boys!" Growled Oring. "Appears we're outgunned this time." He unbuckled his belt to let the holstered pistol drop to the ground.

Billy waited until they all were disarmed then walked forward to squat in front of the sobbing Hatcher.

"Ho, ...how th' fuck did you beat me, you son of a bitch?...You tore my arm half off!"

"I know," He grinned. "Just when things was goin' you're way, too!... What are you, seventeen, eighteen years old?"

"Kiss my ass!"

"That's where you fucked up, ya know,...you're just too young! Too busy bein' a smart aleck kid, that thinks he knows it all!...You hadn't shot my father, and pushed my son around, I wouldn't even be here!...Now you think about that on your way back to Paris, Texas, cause that's where you're gonna hang, young man!" He stood up then, having heard the hard running horses, and turned around to see Toby, and close to twenty armed men circling the yard.

He grinned as Toby, and another man dismounted and came toward him, as did Rodney.

"We got here as fast as we could, Marshal!" Said Toby. "Mister Latham here didn't believe me at first."

"I'm sorry to say, I didn't!" Said Latham. He shook Billy's hand and then Rodney's. "Lamar Latham, he said then, those are my wranglers. He turned then to give orders to gather all the weapons, and bind up Oring and company's hands.

"You two men have singlehandedly caught the rustlers that have been stealing the ranches blind for going on six months now. My hat's off, to you!...We can never thank you enough!"

"Don't thank us, Sir!" Commented Rodney. "That's th' snake we were after." He said, looking down at the still groaning Hatcher. "Rest of 'em's just a bonus."

"This man is the famous Wes Hatcher?" Asked Toby with disbelief, and squatted down in front of him. "He's just a boy with whiskers, almost a baby yet!"

"Fuck you, you stinkin' Indian!" Yelled Hatcher. "Get away from me!"

"A baby Rattler!" Said Billy, reaching up to rub his shoulder. "Fast as one, and just as deadly."

"And you can kiss my ass, you son of a bitch!" yelled Hatcher, causing them all to laugh.

"Was he as fast as you thought?" Asked Toby, looking up at Rodney.

"Too close for comfort, Toby....Too damn close!"

"Yes," Said Latham. "But not quite close enough, I think....We heard the shooting a quarter mile out,...Toby there feared the worst, so we came running!"

"Well, they're all yours now, Mister Latham." Said Billy. "All but this one!...He's got a date with the hangman."

"Go to hell, you whore!" Snapped Hatcher.

"Want me to spank him, Marshal?" Grinned Toby, causing Hatcher to kick at him, then yelp with pain.

"Don't touch me, you fuckin', stinkin' Indian!"

"You can set his arm for 'im, Toby, make it do till we get 'im a doctor."

"I said, you ain't touchin' me!"

Toby suddenly lashed out with a leather-like fist and Hatcher hit the ground, out cold. "Now, I'll set the arm." He said, getting up to hunt for suitable splints.

"You sure those are th' men doin' th' rustlin', Mister Latham?" Asked Rodney, turning to watch them being tied up.

"I will, we got five of them in jail already. They had a man workin' for me, another on the Bar H, Kingman, and Lazy T. Sheriff put us on to them....Got the fifth man when he came asking for that bastard!...yeah, we'll see if they all know each other."

Billy saw them leading the horses out of the building then. "Rod, go bring Freckles over here, will ya, he looks in bad shape?"

"Does, don't he, ribs are showin' a little!...I'll get 'im."

"Freckles?" Asked Latham, watching as Rodney took the reins and led it back to them. "Well, I can see where you got the name, never seen markings like these before, do look like freckles in places."

"My father's pet horse. Mister Hatcher took him after he shot my father."

"Jesus, man, Is your father dead?"

"No, he made it!" Replied Billy.

"That's good to hear." Nodded Latham, and looked back at the horse. "Well, Marshal," He said, looking at Billy again. "From the looks of you, you won't be doing much traveling for a couple of days, give me two days with this horse, I'll bring him into town in good shape for you."

"I'd appreciate that!" He nodded. "The saddle, too, got Doc wrote under th' skirt, if it's th' same one?"

"Sure thing, I'll send him on ahead to the ranch." He called one of his hands over. "This is Jory, best man with horses, I've ever seen!...Jory, take this horse back to the ranch, give it some tender loving care!...And Jory, when you get there, send Opie into town, tell J. W. we're bringing in this bunch.... Take the horse and go ahead on!"

"Yes sir!" He took the reins from Rodney, led Freckles to his own horse, mounted, and left at a trot.

"He's a good man, Marshal, he'll get him in shape for ya."

"That's good, thanks."

Toby came back with several short sticks for splints, squatted back down and began to masterfully set Hatcher's shattered arm as they watched.

"How far is it to town, Mister Latham?" Asked Billy, reaching to grab his shoulder again.

"A good thirty miles, Marshal, take most of the day!...Why don't I send for a wagon, don't look like you can sit a horse for that far, you're looking awfully pale."

"A good idea." Said Rodney. "Hatcher shot 'im a week ago, he ain't healed yet!"

"We're all ready to go, Mister Latham." Said one of his wranglers, coming to join them.

"Not yet, Joe,...send a man after a wagom, on the double. Marshal here needs to rest some and we got to haul that killer back!"

"Got a dead man on that bluff up there." Said Rodney, pointing. "Straight behind that upturned wagon bed there. And if he ain't dead, there'll be another with a sore head."

"You heard him, Joe." Said Latham. "See to it!...Send for that wagon first."

"Let's get you over in that building, Billy." Said Rodney. "Shade will do ya good, come on."

*   *   *

Billy sat down on the wagon's bed, tying the black's reins to an iron ring on the sideboard as Latham's hands carried the rustler's body to the wagon and loaded it then slid it forward to make room.

Rodney pushed the cursing Hatcher to the wagon, and forced him up into the bed on his knees, the splinted arm hanging around his neck in a sling.

"Move up to th' front, Hatcher!" He ordered.

"I will, if you'll kiss my ass, you bastard!"

"You will, anyway, or I'll kick your ass,...now, move it!"

Hatcher opened his mouth to speak, but then moved forward anyway where he sat down to lean back against the sideboard to eye Billy hatefully.

"Don't look at him, man!" Laughed Rodney, causing Billy to turn around. "You got beat today by th' best there is!...Hurt your pride, too, didn't it?"

"Why don't you go screw yourself!" He growled.

"Know what your problem is, Hatcher,...you're a crybaby! Your old man didn't whip your ass enough as a kid."

"Fuck you!"

Laughing, Rodney went to help the pistolwhipped sentry into the wagon, and then went to grab his horse and sit down next to Billy, to tie the reins in place. "How ya feelin', man?"

"Like shit!...I'm damn sure tired."

"You smell like shit, too!" Spat Hatcher. "Horse shit!"

"Hatcher!" Said Rodney angrily. "You want a be hogtied and gagged?" When Hatcher grew silent, he looked back at Blly. "You ought a be tired,... got a spot a red on your shirt there, too....Wound's bleeding."

"I'll see th' Doc in Gainsville."

"Well, Marshal?" Said Toby, stopping his horse in front of them, and dismounting. "I will be going home now." He shook their hands, and then looked at Hatcher. "Sure wish I had seen that fight! Must have been something to see!"

"It was, Toby!" Nodded Rodney. "Close, too!"

"Thanks for th' help, Toby." Grinned Billy.

"Any time." He grinned. "Mister Hank will not believe this when I tell him….So long, Marshal, both of you." He mounted and galloped off toward the bluff.

"A good man." Remarked Rodney, and looked at Billy. "Tell me somethin',…how th' hell did you beat that ass hole?" He asked, just above a whisper. "He was faster'n hell!"

"Guess I was faster, and luckier."

"You always say that, Billy….A man makes his own luck, remember sayin' that to me?...Was he th' best you ever faced?"

"One of 'em, I guess." He nodded.

"Then who was th' best?"

Billy sighed, and then watched the wranglers as they strapped the rustlers to their saddles. "Two men comes to mind. Rod." He said, looking back at him. Lance Ashley, and Joe Christmas."

"Yeah, I clean forgot about that Kiowa, you're right, he near about got ya!"

"An inch is as good as a mile, Rod.,…when ya miss."

"Amen to that!"

"You men ready to move out?" Smiled Latham as he stopped his horse.

"Ready as we're gonna be." Nodded Billy. "What are your men up to?"

"They're burnin' th' place down, it's an eyesore anyway." He waved his arm then. "Move 'em out boys, stay close to the wagon."

They watched as the buildings were torched, and the wranglers responsible as they scrambled to mount their horses afterward to take their place behind the wagon.

"Sure you don't want to ride, Billy?...This thing will jar your teeth out."

"Not today, Rod." He said, turning to return Hatcher's hate-filled stare.

"Who are you?" He asked, still glaring at him.

"Why?...You forgot already?...I'm th' man that ended your glorious career!"

"Why didn't you kill me then, damn you?...Be better than this!"

"I wanted you to hang,...you got eleven men to pay for!"

"Why?"

"Why?...To me, it's simple!...You should a left my family alone."

"That's it,...th' whole reason?"

"That's it!...I won't have me, or my family laid hands on...I won't have them harmed neither!...And you did both!"

"I needed food and a horse, that old fool tried to stop me!...Hell, man, a posse was after me, I had no choice!"

"That old fool was my father, Hatcher,...and you did have a choice!...If you lived to be a hundred, you wouldn't live to be th' man he is!"

"Didn't you have a father?" Asked Rodney.

"Yeah, I had a father, so what?"

"You should a listened when he tried to teach ya somethin'."

"Kiss my ass!"

"You ever see a man hang, Hatcher?" Asked Rodney. They piss their pants just before that trap door opens....We're gonna watch you piss your pants, too, you sadistic little piss ant!"

"You shut your God damn mouth!...I ain't sadistic!"

"Then why do you enjoy killin' folks?"

Hatcher thought about that for a moment. "Because I can, I'm th' best there is!"

"You was th' best!" He nodded toward Billy then. "He's th' best there is!...And that makes you a piss ant, one that just got stepped on!"

"You shut your fuckin' mouth, I ain't crazy!"

"Don't agitate 'im any more than what he is, Rod, I ain't in th' mood!"

"Just havin' some fun, Billy....He deserves every bit of it!"

"He'll be paid in full before long."

"Guess you're right!" He took a thin cigar from his shirt, struck a match, and lit it. "I'm gonna wire Jim as soon as we get to town, folks are likely goin' out a their minds about now."

"I wish you would,...wonder if Doc's home yet?"

"Surely not!...He nearbout died from th' loss a blood!"

"He is okay, though, right?"

"He's out a th' woods, yeah,...he'll be fine!"

"Be hard to go on without 'im."

"You got that to go through one day, you know that!"

"But not this way, Rod!"

"Amen to that!"

As the road became smoother, the driver whipped the team to a faster pace, keeping it up until late afternoon before stopping for food and water.

Billy eased himself off the wagon, as did Rodney, and took the black horse to the fresh water creek where the others were letting their animals drink. While the horses were drinking, they took canteens from the saddles to walk a few yards to a small, cascading wall of fresh water pouring into the creek from the rocks above it.

"Looks like they got plenty a water out here." Said Rodney, as they empted the stale water, and collected the fresh. "Might not be here come the end of August."

"Creek like this is fed from under ground somewhere, Rod,…water's almost cold."

"Good, too!" He said, capping the canteen, to watch Billy drink. "You feeling any better?"

"Shoulder and arm aches, otherwise I'm okay." He started back as Rodney followed, passing several others on their way to water. Taking the horse's reins, they took them back to the wagon and tied them before going to Latham for a share of the jerky.

"You still look a mite pale, my boy, you okay?" Asked Latham, giving them a slab of the dried beef.

"Yes sir!" He nodded. "I'll see th' Doctor In Gainsville, I'll be all right!"

"I certainly hope so, Marshal….You two men saved me from going broke today, you hadn't, they might have rustled me blind, the other ranchers, too!"

"Maybe not, you got th' key men in jail already!"

"But so far, they ain't talking, and we can't be everywhere at once, not enough men….No sir, you boys did us a great deed today,…and I'm deep in your debt for it!…Where'd you find this bunch, anyway?"

"Didn't,…they just happened to be where, Hatcher was, we just followed 'em."

"From where,…we have searched this county over?"

"Decatur." Said Rodney. "They were holed up in a ghost town there, place called Rush Creek."

"Seems I've heard of that place somewhere....That's got a be a far piece from here, no wonder we couldn't find them!"

"We're just glad we could help you out, Mister Latham." Returned Rodney. "We get Hatcher back to Paris, we'll be done!"

"I was through there three years ago, come July,...You all had one hell of a fire after that, didn't you?"

"Whole town burned." Nodded Billy. "Buildin' it back now."

"I can't even imagine a disaster like that!...Heard the bank was robbed, too, is that right?"

"We caught 'em!" Said Rodney.

"I can well imagine that, too!...You boys must be the best they got!"

"Not any more, I'm afraid, tore my shoulder up on th' last assignment....I'm done when this is over!"

"Sorry to hear it,...how about you, Marshal?" He asked of Billy.

"Yeah, me, too, Mister Latham, this is my last job."

"Well, all I can say is,...they will miss you, both of you." He turned then, as a wrangler approached. "What is it Lew?"

"You want a feed that bunch, Mister Latham?" He asked, looking at the captured men.

"Hell, I don't even know their names, Lew, leave 'em be, I'll let J. W. figure 'em out. They ain't gonna die on us between here and town."

"Yes sir!" Lew nodded at them, and walked away.

"Well, boys, shall we get on in to town?"

"Waitin' on you!" Grinned Billy.

"Good, oh,...You got blood on your shirt there, that where you were wounded."

"Yeah," He said. "I've had better days!"

"I can believe that, too!... Toby told me about you being shot." He chuckled then. "I didn't know what to expect when he banged on my door, an Indian like that! Didn't believe him at first, neither, till he mentioned the rustlers, and that old river barge. That's the one place in Cook County we didn't look!...He's quite a fellow, that Toby,...thinks the world of you two men, too!"

"We agree with you." Said Rodney.

"Well, you two get loaded up, I'll send a man on into town ahead of us, make sure that Doctor is waiting for us at the jail.

They thanked him and walked back to the wagon, while Latham rousted the men again.

"How about some water up here?" Said Hatcher.

Rodney uncorked the canteen and gave it to him. "That's enough!" He said, and gave it to the other man to drink. Taking it back, he went to join Billy again, helping him into the wagon before climbing in himself. "God, I can't wait to get home again!" he said tiredly.

"Everybody okay when you left?"

"I already told you they were okay, Billy, didn't you believe me?"

"I think you sugarcoated it a mite!"

Rodney stared at him a second and then grinned. "Guess I did, a little....Yes, physically everyone is okay!...Emotionally, not so good."

"I came close to turnin' back a couple a times,...But I just couldn't bring myself to do it!...I was too mad, hurt, too, I guess....But I just couldn't!"

"I know that, knew it when you left....Connie knows it, too! And she was okay with it,...till she heard you was hurt!...I admit, that bit a news got to me, too!...I couldn't stay away after that and that's why I'm here now."

"I know,...thanks, Rod." He bit off another bite of jerky and chewed it, as did Rodney. "Wonder how far town is?"

"Latham said it would be around nine o'clock tonight."

"You men ready?" Said Latham, riding up beside the wagon. "I took the liberty of telling Lew to register you both at the Sully House hotel on the square."

"Sounds good to us, thanks."

"None needed." He raised his arm then and yelled at the other men to fall in behind the wagon. "Whip 'em up, Jake!...Let's go to town!" The wagon lurched forward then, and they settled in for the duration of the ride.

They both pulled bandanas from their necks to wipe the sweat from their faces and then, as Rodney replaced his, he watched as Billy cleaned his eyeglasses and put them on.

"I don't know how you get by, having to wear them things."

"You would if you couldn't see without 'em! Lots a folks wear 'em, even Doc! Guess most of it comes with age."

"Guess so." Sighed Rodney, turning to look back at the uncommonly quiet, Wes Hatcher, who was still leaning against the wagon's sideboard clutching his upper arm, and staring down at the floor of the wagon. "You shattered that arm pretty good, didn't ya?"

"Got a hurt pretty bad, too." Said Billy, also looking at him. "He'd never use it again, that's for sure."

"I have never seen you shoot from th' hip before," Grinned Rodney. "But you sure did this time,…that was somethin' to see, Billy,…how'd you do that, and still wing 'im?"

"I aimed before I pulled!" He grinned then. "Naww, I guess it was just luck, Rod, I'd rather not talk any more about it!"

"I hear ya, man….That arm looked nasty, though,…bone stickin through th' skin like that,…gave me goosebumps!"

"It wasn't pretty." He agreed, then turned his body around and lay down in the wagon's bed, placing his sweat-soaked hat over his face.

Rodney watched him and grinned then reached a thin cigar from his shirt and lit it.

*   *   *

Mary Beth Rhodes finished setting the table with plates, cups, glasses and silverware, and then came the platter of fried eggs, another of sausage, a platter of biscuits, and a bowl of gravy. She poured the coffee, and milk for the young ones before calling out.

"Breakfast, everyone!"

Willy, and the three younger ones were the first at the table.

"Now, you children sit still till everyone is here." She said, and went to the doorway to watch them all come into the dining room.

"My, would you look at this table?" Smiled Mattie as she helped Doc to sit down. When all were seated, Doc looked around the table and cleared his throat.

"Mary Beth, in this house, family eats together!...Now set yourself a plate and William, go get that extra chair."

"Okay!" He nodded when all were seated, and they all bowed their heads. "Lord, we are humbled to have you in our presence, please bless this food we are about to partake of. Bless this family here with you and Lord, bring our sons home safely….In your holy name, we pray, Amen!...Let's eat!"

They were almost through the noisy meal when Stockwell came through the house and into the kitchen. "Sorry folks, I knocked, but didn't think you heard me."

"Come in, Jim." Smiled Doc. "Had breakfast yet?"

"Well, I'll just have some coffee, Doc, that's all." He took the paper from his shirt pocket and unfolded it. "We finally got th' one you been waitin' for, folks." He came around the table and gave it to Doc. "Go on, Doc, read it!"

"Grinning, Doc quickly picked his eyeglasses from his shirt and put them on. "It says,…To Jim Stockwell, Marshal, Paris, Texas."

"We all know that, Walter, read the wire, for pete-sake!"

He grinned even wider. "Okay,…be advised to inform Judge Bonner- Have Wes Hatcher in custody-Me and Billy in good shape- inform Lisa and Connie of our love- be home in three or four days- inform Doc Freckles with us- your horse, too, Jim-,…It's signed, Rodney Taylor, He sniffed loudly then, and nodded at the rest of them. Didn't I tell you all, that it would be okay?" He watched the women then, as they all were bent over, hands covering their faces and crying. He sniffed again, and looked up at Ms. Rhodes.

"Mary Beth,…set another plate, Jim's having breakfast after all!…Praise the Lord!"

*   *   *

J. W. Hicks was just inside the cellblock door at the pot-bellied stove pouring coffee when he heard Billy and Rodney come into the office, but to be sure, he leaned out to look around the door at them before taking two more cups off the wall and pouring coffee in them as well. He came into the office with the coffee, and bade them sit down before giving it to them.

"I want to thank you men." He said, going to sit at his desk. "Every one of them old boys back there, knew each other,…thought we'd never catch them!…I want to thank you special, Marshal Upshur, didn't get a chance to the other night. You were right about them having men workin' those ranches. I met with the owners, like you said, and it weren't two days till they brought 'em in!"

"Glad it worked out." Said Billy. "Hatcher give you any trouble?"

"That's one sorry little piece of shit, Marshal!...Bastard bitched and cussed for an hour after you left,...till I held his ass down long enough for th' Doctor to pour a double dose of Laudanum down his throat!...He's still asleep in there, been dosing him again, off and on....Some pretty powerful stuff, that laudanum....Ought a be called, Peace Maker, stead a laudanum!"

"You kept 'im asleep for two days?" Asked Rodney.

"Except at mealtime, yes I did!...Got a jail full of dirty, stinking, foul smelling assholes back there, Marshal, and that Hatcher was keeping all of them awake and surly with his cussing, and raising hell!...What would you a done?"

Rodney shrugged. "Same thing, I guess."

"There ya go....I do not envy you having to ride that coach with him all the way back to Paris!"

"Yeah, well I got laudanum, too!" Grinned Rodney.

"You find out about our stage coach, Sheriff?" Asked Billy.

"Yes sir, I did,...be here as soon as it's ready....Had to do a little work on it, being it was ready for the parts pile, but it'll do!...My deputy's bringin' your animals from the livery for ya....Wouldn't want to sell that big black, would ya, that's one fine horse?"

"I agree with ya, but he belongs to a lawman back home."

"I thought not!"

"Did, Mister Latham bring in a gray horse, Sheriff?" Asked Billy. "It belongs to my father."

"He did, last night!...Deputy took it to th livery,...he'll be bringing that one, too." He looked toward the door then, and got up. "Gentlemen, your ride is here, I do believe." They all looked out through the open doorway at the old stage coach."

"Then you'd best get our prisoner, Sheriff." Said Billy, also getting to his feet. "We're sort a in a hurry to get home."

"Amen to that!" Laughed Rodney. "Feels like we've been gone a year!"

"Well then," Said Hicks, moving toward the cellblock door, and taking the cell keys off a peg, "One of you come with me, I'll let 'im out for ya." And when Rodney got up to go with him, he stopped him at the door.

"I don't aim to put a crimp in your plans, boys, as good as you're feelin' now, but there's a couple of bounty hunters in town,...been askin' questions about your, Mister Hatcher."

"Bounty hunters?" Asked Rodney, casting a sharp look at Billy. "You know that's what they are?"

"Oh, I know!...Hard-eyed gents, trail-worn, their guns tied to their legs,...strangers, too!...I'd be ready for trouble, if I were you."

"Bounty on Hatcher still ten thousand?" Asked Billy.

"Dead or alive." Nodded Hicks. "Could be more than just those two out there!"

"How you reckon they found out so quick?" Asked Rodney in disbelief.

"You must be joking, Marshal!...That was a hell of a thing, bringing in those rustlers,...especially one of the most wanted men in three states! That sort of news travels like a wildfire! Besides," He said, going into the cellblock to insert the key in Hatcher's cell door. "The Daily Hesperian ran a full page story on it, even to how many steers have been stolen by these old boys. Even came in here to take pictures." He opened the door and went inside, with Rodney on his heels.

"But old Hatcher here," He continued. "Got full treatment,...a cell to look at the sleeping gunslinger in, and a half page history, calling him the fastest gun in Texas! Anyhow, the paper's story was mailed to more than fifteen hundred subscribers, in half that many towns....Likely picked up by a dozen newspapers besides."

"Could be a problem, at that!" Breathed Billy, staying outside the cell while they woke Hatcher up.

"Come on Hatcher!" He said Loudly, and shook the gunman awake.

"What th' hell do you want now?" He spat, quickly rubbing his eyes with his left hand, and groaning painfully when he tried to use his right. "Son of a Bitch!" He moaned and then spotted Rodney there beside Hicks.

"You get th' fuck away from me!" He rasped then saw Billy standing outside the cell. "Arrest that man, Sheriff, he shot me in th' back, th' son of a Bitch!"

Rodney reached and grabbed his good arm, heaving the gunman to his feet,

"Where th' fuck we going?"

"Get a move on Hatcher!" Said Hicks. "You're leaving us."

"You crazy?" He yelled, menacingly. "I can't sit no horse with this arm!"

"Come on!" Said Rodney, grabbing his shirt and pulling him toward the door. "You're takin' th' stage, now move it!"

"Don't you fuckin' touch me!" He yelled, slapping Rodney's hand away. "See that man out there, Sheriff, Who th' fuck is he,…he's a gunslinger, you gonna arrest him, too?"

"He's the law, now move out!" He pushed him toward Rodney again, and he grabbed the left arm in a tight grip, pushing him out past Billy and into the outer office.

"Hold on, Rod!" Said Billy, coming past him. "I'll go out first, just in case." He went out onto the boardwalk to stop and look around.

"Th' Doctor didn't set my arm, Sheriff!" Yelled Hatcher, "He gonna set my God dman arm first, it's killing me?"

"Hatcher!" Said Hicks, looking at Rodney. "The bone in your arm can't be set, it's shattered!…Here, take another swig of this." He produced the half-pint bottle of laudanum and gave it to him.

Hatcher took the bottle and stared at it. "This th' same shit that knocked me out last night?"

"Didn't have any pain, did ya?"

"No!" He snapped, and took a swallow.

Hicks took the bottle from him before he could drink too much, capped it, and gave it to Rodney. "You might need this." He said, and pushed the gunman across the room and out onto the boardwalk.

A couple of dozen onlookers had gathered, both in the street, and on the walkway as Hatcher was forced into the waiting coach,…leaving Billy and Rodney to watch the crowd of people, and to study their expressionless faces for signs of trouble. Billy was about to step off the boardwalk, when Rodney gripped his arm to get his attention.

"Two men back there at the corner, Billy, behind th' two men and woman."

"Bounty hunters." He nodded as he studied them. "Hicks described them real good, didn't he?"

"Pretty hard to miss, all right!…Think they'll try somethin' here?"

"I sort a hope they do!…But no, they'll wait and hit us on th' road somewhere, …too many people in town."

"Damn it!" He muttered. "I was hopin' to enjoy our trip home."

"They might not try anything at all, Rod,…raise too many questions about where they got 'im, somethin' like that could put them behind bars as well."

"Not if they take 'im to Kansas, Billy....Newspapers didn't go that far north."

"I wouldn't bet on it!...Ten thousand dollars is a lot a money!"

"Yeah, and if they bring 'im in dead, who's to know how they came across 'im?...Course, they'd have to kill us all to get away with it!"

"There ya go!...They look th' sort, too!" He stepped off the walkway then, and as Rodney followed, made their way to the stage.

Hicks finished securing Hatcher inside the coach and stepped down again to also spot the two men. "Like wolves waiting to pounce." He said, looking at Billy. "You see 'em?"

"Two of 'em." He nodded. "Could be a third one somewhere."

"I hope you two are ready for it!...Guess I could arrest them for something, give you a head start, what do you think?"

"Law's on their side till they break it, Sheriff." Sighed Rodney. "No law against looking."

"There is against loitering."

"You'd have to arrest everybody here." Said Rodney.

"Well,...I told you I was not a lawman."

"Fill th' drivers in on this, Sheriff." Said Billy. "Tell 'em what to expect,...we'll watch for 'em."

Hicks shook both their hands. "All right then,...but I'm going to bring them in anyway, see what they're up to....It is th' Sheriff's job to question strangers in town,...ain't it?"

"I believe it is." Grinned Rodney. "Thanks, Sheriff."

"Somethin' I'd like to talk to you about, Sheriff." Said Billy, moving him to one side. "Hatcher's got a reward on his head,...how would you go about collecting it?"

"Well, I don't rightly know, Marshal....I could talk to the Federal Judge here about it, what did you have in mind?"

"I'd like to take eight thousand of it and divide it between th' four ranchers that lost cattle. I'd like two thousand of it to go to a Yaqui Indian, name a Toby....He works for th' J and M Ranch in Decatur, Texas.... Wouldn't a caught Mister Hatcher, or any of 'em without 'im!"

"I'll check into it, glad to do it, too! Now get aboard, I'll talk with Harold, and Jim up there."

They climbed into the coach, after first checking to see that the two horses were secured, and sat down across from the gunman.

"Who the fuck, are you, man?" Blurted Hatcher. "I know you shot me,…but, who are ya?"

"Name's Bill Upshur,…like I told ya."

"Who was you before that, God damn it?…You had to have a reputation! I got a fuckin' right to know, don't I?…damn right, I do!"

"Have you noticed," Said Rodney, with a look at the gunman. "That every man you ever faced, thinks he has to use vulgarity to prove how bad he is?"

"Yeah, I have,…but ya know, Rod,…I think he does have a right to know me."

"You ain't gonna tell 'im, are ya?"

"Shut up, you!" Said Hatcher angrily. "Come on, man, tell me?"

"Calico Kid!" He said. "That make you feel any better?"

"I knew you had a reputation,…you're just like me, ain't ya?"

"Oh, no, kid,…I was never like you, I lived by th' code!"

"What th' hell are you talkin' about, code,…there ain't no fuckin' code!"

"Oh, yeah," Nodded Billy. "The gunfighter's unspoken code,…and you do not live by it, you did, you wouldn't go around killin' people that mean you no harm! Now shut up!" He hid his smile long enough, but then grinned at Rodney, and looked out of the window.

"I don't believe you!" Snapped Hatcher.

"Then I really hate to disappoint ya!" He shifted his weight on the seat. "Truth is, we're both just ordinary store keepers,…and you should a steered around Paris, Texas."

"If ya had, you wouldn't be here now!" Added Rodney.

Hatcher looked out of the window for a minute. "You ain't got me there yet, ya know." He looked back at them and nodded. "You'll have to fight to keep me!" He smiled then. "Yeah, I heard you talking out there.…They look pretty able to me, both of 'em."

"Won't make it any easier for you." Said Rodney. "You'll pay for your crimes, either way!"

"That bein' true, why won't you tell me who you really are?…And don't tell you're that Calico kid, I know a lie when I hear it!"

"That's somethin' you'll never know, Mister Hatcher!" Breathed Billy. "And you might as well shut up about it, we got a long way to go!"

"No," Said Rodney. "I'd like to know what made you turn out this way?"

"You would, would ya?...Well that's somethin' you'll never know!"

Just then, the coach jerked into motion as the driver slapped the lines on the horses backs, and the lumbering coach headed off down the town's main street, they stared out at the two bounty men in passing, watching as Hicks, and his two deputies stopped the two as they went for their horses.

"That ought a buy us at least an hour." Said Rodney, leaning back in his seat.

"That ain't much time, Rod, seeing as how we're towing two horses, driver's keeping th' team at a trot all th' way."

"We'll manage, Billy."

"Yeah," Grinned Hatcher. "This won't be no face to face shoot out, Mister Gunslinger,...They're gonna shoot this fuckin' stage up real good, them slugs is gonna rip through this thing like paper, and ya know what?... They'll kill us all!"

"Won't matter to you!" Said Billy.

"You're right about that!...Beats hell out a hangin', though!"

"You ain't getting' out that easy." Said Rodney. "I aim to see you piss your pants when that trap door opens!"

"Why don't you just kiss my ass!" He snapped. "Give me another swallow of that pan killer, will ya, my arm hurts bad?"

Rodney gave him the bottle, and watched as he drank a generous swallow before taking the bottle from his hand, and capping it. They watched as Hatcher made himself comfortable,...and was surprised when he spoke again.

"I killed my father." He said with closed eyes. "That's what made me like I am....Been doin' it ever since." He dropped off to sleep then.

"What makes a boy kill his old man, Billy?"

"I wouldn't know, Rod....Abusive, I guess."

"Well, I'm damn glad he met you right now, no tellin' how many he might a killed before somebody stopped him!"

"Everything all right down there, Marshal?" Yelled the guard as he leaned down out of the driver's seat.

"We're okay, yeah!" Returned Rodney.

'One thing, though," Said Billy,... "Keep an eye out behind us!"

"Been doin' that, Marshal, no sign of anybody yet!"

"Don't think ya will, least for another hour or so!...That happens, stop th' coach, and take cover on th' ground. We can't outrun 'em anyway!"

"What about you in there?"

"We'll do th' same!...Take care of yourselves. Tell th' driver!"

"You got it, Marshal, be out a town in a few ninutes."

"So,...you do think they'll bushwhack us?"

"It's what I'd do,...if I wanted Hatcher bad enough!...Hatcher might be a kid, but he's trail wise enough to know how a gunman thinks."

"I'll agree with that. But why would you do that, and not just ride out in front to stop us?"

"Think about it, Rod!" He grinned at him then. "What would you do,... you're a bounty man, you want that bounty,...but you saw us put 'im on th' stage, and you know that we brought 'im in!...You also know that for any man to bring in Wes Hatcher, he would need t....."

"He would need to be better than Hatcher is with a gun!" He interrupted. "I get your point....I wouldn't want to chance just stopping th' stage either!"

"There ya go!"

"Okay, while we're on the subject,...when you drew on him, you turned your body side ways,...why,...I never saw you do that before?"

"That was your fault!"

"My fault?...How?"

"You keep harpin' at me about maybe he's th' one that kills me,...made me wonder about it my self!"

"But, why did you turn that way?"

"I gave 'im a smaller target to shoot at!"

Rodney nodded, and looked across at the sleeping Hatcher. "Didn't do it to scare ya, Billy, I was just worried."

"I'm worried about every fight, Rod, scared to death!...You know that, I've told you a hundred times....This was no different."

"Well, I'm sorry, Billy, I won't mention that anymore, you can count on it."

"I do wish you wouldn't."

"How long we been gone now?"

"Not very long,…ain't even out of th' town limits yet….Hicks still got 'em inside talkin', I think,…likely keep 'em an hour or so!"

"Damn, I hope so!...I'm tired, Billy! Shoulder aches, arm's sore as hell!"

"Makes two of us, Rod….Take you some a that laudanum to ease th' pain."

"Believe I will!" He uncorked the flask and took a swallow before looking at Billy. "Want a shot?"

"Not me, ole son!...Stuff tastes like shit to me."

"You told that guard what we would do in th' ambush,…what's th' plan?"

"Plan is not to be a sittin' target!...Th' shootin' starts on one side, we're out th' door on the other."

"If th' driver stops th' stage!"

"Either way!...It'll stop though, they don't want a be targets any more than we do."

"Amen to that!...And being out of th' coach, we take th' fight to them!"

"That's my plan,…hope it works!"

"What about him?" He gestured at Hatcher.

"He goes, too,…can't break his arm any worse!"

"You did a job on it, that's for sure!"

"When it happens, Rod, keep your head down, his, too!...Knock his ass out if ya have to, but stay down!"

"What'll you be doin'?"

"Don't know yet, but I'll be right behind ya. Just remember what I said."

Nodding, Rodney looked out through the window. "Guess we're out of town now,…no more houses….Billy, I don't understand men like that at all, they got a know they won't get away with it, be a wanted poster on 'em by days end!"

"Maybe not,…if they can kill all of us. Be no witnesses."

"They'll still figure it out, Hicks knows who they are!"

"Won't do us any good, dead!" Sighed Billy, turning to watch the trees in passing. "I ain't plannin' on either one of us bein' dead, him, neither!... He's goin' back to Paris!"

"Amen to that!"

CHAPTER TEN

The stage continued along the wide, sometimes tree shrouded road at a steady, and most times quite bumpy clip,...keeping the six-horse team at a fast trot because of the two horses being towed behind them.

Billy was well aware that they needed to be traveling faster, but he also knew that there were many accidental dangers that could befall a horse running blind behind a fast moving coach. A quick turn, sudden stop, an unseen rut, or hole in the road could seriously cripple an animsl, especially two horses as precious to him as these were.

He was also very aware of the danger that was sure to be waiting for them at some tree-lined bend in the road ahead. All he knew for certain, was that he had to bring Wes Hatcher back to stand trial for his crimes. But he could not help but wonders at what cost he would be willing to pay to get him there? There were five lives at stake, with Rodney, the most important!

And there was the two horses trailing behind them,...it was very important that Doc get his pet horse back, things would not be back to normal otherwise. There was the black, too,...that horse was Jim Stockwell's pride and joy, his as well! Except for his own little Mustang Mare, that black horse was the best he had ever ridden.

He was also worried about the lives of the driver and guard atop the stage. They would be the first to be hit, that, or one of the team horses, which would be his choice, if he were a bounty man,...because that would surely stop them, and in most cases, render everyone helpless to put up a fight. It would also give Harold and the guard time to lump to safety. Maybe, he thought, and then shuddered inwardly from his frustration. All he could do now, is wait,...but he knew it would happen soon!

It would not be now, he thought then, having just seen the road marker that read "Whitesboro Township", one mile. Not even a bounty hunter would chance it this close to other possible law enforcement. He pulled the Sam Colt pocket watch to check the time, and marveled at how much time had elapsed. It was already past noon! He wound the watch and put it away then reaching down, took the spare Colt from his saddlebag, checked the loads and stuck the gun inside his holster-belt.

"Anything happened yet?" Yawned Rodney as he straightened up in the seat.

"Nothin' yet."

"I don't even remember closing my eyes,…That laudanum's pretty potent stuff!…You think it'll be soon now?"

"My gut says so, yeah!…But not for a while, we're comin' in to a place called Whitesboro….If I'm right, it'll be a couple miles past there, providin' we don't meet heavy traffic by then."

"That probably wouldn't stop 'em!"

"Normally, I'd agree with ya,…but it'd be hard to collect on a bounty with too many eyewitnesses to report what happened….Nope,…th' road will have to be clear, and far enough from a town to keep th' shooting from bein' heard!

"I hope you're right!…How long did I sleep anyway?"

"Goin' on three hours."

"Some nap!…We gonna stop in Whitesboro?"

"Cordin' to Harold, we are,…but only to eat and take a piss….When we get back on board, don't put th' leg irons on Hatcher,…we hear th' first shot, grab 'im and jump out a this thing!"

"You sure th' coach will stop?"

"Don't matter!…But yeah, a rough one, too!…I think they'll shoot one a th' horses up front to stop us."

"God, I hope not!" Sighed Rodney. "Makes sense, though." He nodded…. "I'll be ready, Billy."

"Just don't fall on that shoulder, push Hatcher out first, fall on him!… Coach is liable to flip, too, so move fast,…and roll."

"What about you?"

"I'll be on your ass, don't worry about that!…And don't forget that rifle."

"Comin' in to Whitesboro, Marshal!" Said the guard as he leaned down to be heard. "Ten, Twelve minutes. Be stoppin' long enough to eat!"

"We hear ya, Jim." Yelled Billy.

"Rodney leaned down and used the key to remove the leg irons from Hatcher's feet, and then sat back to watch as the first of a dozen small houses could be seen alongside the road,...and then they were turning off onto the main street of town to see the row of business establishments along both sides of the quite narrow roadway.

"Only one two storied buildin' in town, Billy." Commented Rodney. "And it looks like that's where we'll be stopping."

"Sheriff's office, jail, and courthouse." Mused Billy. "Best wake up Hatcher, Rod."

"Whoa, there!" Yelled the driver, and the coach came to a stop at the Courthouse boardwalk.

Billy leaned to open the door, letting it swing outward, and waited while Rodney ushered a cantankerous Wes Hatcher out and down to the hard ground.

"I'm comin', God damn it!" Yelled Hatcher as he stepped down. "Where th' hell are we anyhow?"

"All you need to worry about is fillin' your gut, Hatcher!" Said Rodney angrily. "Now move on inside." He pushed Hatcher through the open door to stop and wait for Billy and the driver to enter, and then followed them down a hallway and into a kitchen at the rear of the building.

"Appears they was waitin' for us, Harold." Said Billy when they were told to sit down at the long table. He sat and watched the woman at the stove as she turned several steaks over in a large frying pan, and the aroma gave him hunger pains.

"Only place, besides home, to eat here in Whitesboro, Marshal." Said Harold as the guard ambled in to sit down. "Food's good though, some a th' best around."

"Smells like it." Said Rodney.

The food was served then, and Billy looked the large, sizzling slab of meat over, and then came a large bowl of fried potatoes which she placed on the table, and then came the biscuits, and thick, white gravy of which he added to compliment the steak,...and began eating.

The woman, seeing that Hatcher had only one arm, leaned to take the knife and cut his steak up for him. Finished, she brought tin cups to each one of them, and then poured the coffee before leaving the hot room.

The meal was eaten silently, and when they were done, all made the trip out behind the building to the outhouse where thaey all waited their turn to relieve themselves.

Billy, Harold, and the Guard were waiting on the boardwalk when Rodney pushed Hatcher ahead of him to join them.

"Get 'im aboard, Rod!" Said Billy.

Nodding, he pushed Hatcher ahead of him again and boosted him up into the coach before sitting down to lean his arm on the coach's window to wait for Billy.

The driver climbed up to the seat, and as the guard placed a foot on the wheel, Billy stopped him, and got Harold's attention.

"They'll be hittin' us a mile or two away from here, if they do it at all. I don't rightly know for sure, you understand,…it's more of a gut feeling than anything else!...What's th' next town we go through?"

"That'll be Southmayd," Said the guard. "Wouldn't call it much of a town though, we don't even stop lest they flag us down!"

"Well, it'll be between here and there." He looked up at the driver then. "Will that seat fold up out a th' way?"

"Seat comes plumb off, that's where we stow our gear!"

"There enough room in th' floor for th' two a you?"

"I guess so,…Oh, I get it now!...Yeah, we can drive th' stage from there, what ya got in mind?"

"I may be wrong, Harold,…but I think they'll stop th' stage by killin' one a th' team horses. But, there's at least two men that I seen in town, and maybe one or two more. They could shoot th' horse, and try to shoot you both at th' same time,…if they can see ya?"

"That's a good idea, Marshal!"

"I hope so….Don't hunker down till we're at least a mile away from here, then get ready, and Harold,…when that horse goes down, jump for your lives, there won't be much time!"

"We'll do our best, Marshal, Thanks." The guard climbed on up then, and he climbed into the coach beside Rodney.

"Think they make it all right?" Asked Rodney as he sat down. "That's a long way down off a moving stage."

"It comes to it, they'll hurt some,...but that's better'n a bullet in th' head!"

"Like hell, they'll make it!" Argued Hatcher, grimacing from pain again. "This thing flips over, we're all goners!"

"Shut up, Hatcher!" Snapped Rodney. "It won't matter to you, either way!"

"Heeeyaaa!" Yelled the driver, and the coach lurched into motion again,...and was out of Whitesboro in only a few minutes, and back on the main road.

"Won't be long now!" Smirked Hatcher.

"I told you to shut up, man!"

"Tell ya what,...I'll shut up for another drink a that pain killer. I'd as soon be asleep when it happens anyway."

"Sounds like a bargain to me." Nodded Rodney, and gave him the bottle. "That's enough!" He snapped, and took the bottle from him.

"Might a gave 'im too much." Said Billy as they watched him fall asleep again.

"Be easier to handle when we jump." They fell silent then for several minutes, until the sound of the driver's seat being lifted got their attention.

"Best lift Hatcher up, Rod,...Sit on th' edge of th' seat beside 'im. We hear th' shots, I'll kick open th' door, and you jump! And roll clear, ya hear?"

Nodding, Rodney did as he was told, one hand gripping the front of Hatcher's shirt, the other clutching the rifle....And they waited!

Several minutes passed, and then suddenly it happened. Three rifle shots broke the silence with thunderous explosions. Billy kicked open the coach door, opposite the side of the shooting. "Now go, Rod!"

Rodney pulled the gunman off the seat, and grabbing him leaped from the lurching coach into the tall grass alongside the road.

Billy jumped as the coach tilted sideways, barely clearing the doorway before it toppled onto its side. He rolled into the grass, and got to his knees to peer at the settling dust around the downed coach. He also watched as the black, and Doc's horse both tried to break free, and failing, settled down again.

At least they're still on their feet, he thought with relief, and then waited until he saw the three horsemen spurring their horses out of the trees toward them. That's also when he heard Rodney's rifle, followed by one of the bounty men's screaming yell as he was lifted from the saddle to disappear in the brush. The other two men made it to the stage and dismounted, both with drawn pistols, and both bending low as they came slowly around the rear of the coach.

Billy stood up then and yelled, "Hey!" And as they turned toward him, fired twice, knocking both men into the rearing horses, each yelling in pain as the thunderous echoes died away,...and each was clutching their busted shoulders.

Billy looked back up the road to see Rodney standing in the waist high grass and even farther back, the driver and guard stood up, and all began walking toward him.

"You okay, Rod?" He yelled, as Rodney got help from the guard to carry Hatcher back.

"We're all okay, Billy." He yelled back.

"How about you, Harold?"

"Okay, he returned. "Not happy, but okay!...Your plan worked, Marshal!"

He watched as they, all three carried Hatcher back and drop him on the road.

Billy holstered the Colt and quickly rushed to calm the crazed horses before untying them to watch them walk.

"They okay, Billy?" Asked Rodney, somewhat worried.

"They're okay,...take 'em and hold 'em here, Rod." He walked toward the front of the coach with the driver and guard where three of the coach's horses were straining at the harness and squealing with pain from several cuts, two more were untouched, and only one was dead. The guard set about cutting the dead horse loose and once done, came to stand beside Billy and Harold and stare at the coach.

"Can't see either bottom wheel." Said Harold, and then stooped for a better look. "They may not be busted." He said, getting to his feet. "We might can upright it again."

"We got ropes." Said the guard. "We can unhitch th' team."

"A spare horse in th' grass over there." Said Billy. "I'll catch 'im up!"

"Okay,...Come on Jim, let's unhitch th' team, and pull that carcass off th' road."

A half hour later, with help from the six horses, the old stage was uprighted, and while the guard set them to harness again, Harold, and Billy inspected the carriage.

"What do ya think?" Sighed Billy as they stared at the thick wooden beam surrounding the rear axle.

"Well,...the timber is definitely cracked, axle could be bent, too!...But it will roll, I think,...if we slow it down some more. We might make it on to Sherman, they got a wagon yard there."

"Suits me." Nodded Billy. "Want a help me with th' wounded, Harold?"

"Hell no,...but I will!" They went back to where Rodney was sitting in the road, rifle in hand, next to a still sleeping Hatcher.

Grinning, Billy took the reins from his hand, and led them back to the coach where he secured them again. Once done, he stared down at the two wounded bounty hunters. "Shed your shirts, boys, both of ya!"

Once they were bare to the waist, and with Harold's help, they set about cleaning the wounds, and bandaging their shoulders tightly to stop the bleeding. They tore the shirts into strips to make slings for their arms. Both of the gunmen only stared at him through the entire process.

"Ya know," He said, sitting back on his heels. "I don't know why you old boys look at me that way,...it's almost like you hate me!...You ought a be thankful I didn't kill ya,...I could have, ya know!"

"You bushwhacked us!" Said the one nearest him.

"Werent that what you done to us?...Ain't time about, fair play?...You should a known we wouldn't give up Wes Hatcher! You ask me, all three of you were stupid to even try it, now you're goin' to jail for it!...Or worse!... Course that's up to a Judge, not me....Know what's gonna happen now?"

"I think we do!" Said the other man.

"No, no, that comes later!...Right now, we're gonna tie you up real snug, then you're gonna have a nice, hot ride on top a this here coach!" He got to his feet and looked around at their surroundings, seeing the other two saddle horses not fifty yards away and untied the black, tightened the cinches, and mounted.

"I'm gonna catch up them other two horses, Harold. Do me a favor and collect all th' guns, belts and all, put 'em all in th coach. Rodney'll need help with Hatcher and them other two men." He reined the black around the coach and was soon leading the loose animals back to tether them alongside the other two.

The guard had taken rope from the saddle of the dead man's horse, and was in the process of hog-tying the wounded men as he returned. "Best place for 'em is on top there, Marshal."

"I told 'em that already, can ya get 'em up there?"

"They ain't dead, yet, they can climb up!"

"I'll help ya, Jim." Said Harold, and they both hustled the two men up and pushed them toward the front wheels.

Billy loosened the horse's cinches for travel then pulled the rifles from the boots, saddlebags as well then grinning at Rodney, opened the coach door and put them in the floor between the seats.

"That shoulder botherin' ya, Rod?"

"Big time!" He breathed, still clutching his arm. "I fell on Hatcher all right, but th' momentum threw me over 'im, landed on my arm and shoulder."

"Well, hit th' laudanum again, son, and climb in. You have any trouble getting Hatcher in?"

"Harold and Jim put 'im in."

"Then get aboard,...take some laudanum."

"You all ready, Marshal?" Asked Jim.

"Yeah," He said,, looking at the top of the stage. "Are they?"

"Like a rich widow's fancy wardrobe." He grinned, and then walked to climb up to the driver's seat.

Billy opened the door and climbed inside beside Rodney, as he was recapping the drug bottle.

"Ought a be okay in a minute, now." He grinned, and leaned the rifle against the seat, "It worked!"

"We was lucky, Rod!...That whole thing had the elements of goin' all wrong. I barely cleared th coach as it went down!...Could a broke somethin'."

"But you didn't!" He said with a smile. "So it worked!"

They heard the driver yell at the horses then, and felt the coach shudder into motion again.

"Think we'll make it?" He asked, looking at Billy's shirt. "Ya know you're bleedin' again?"

"Feels like it might be, I'll get it checked again in Sherman."

"Don't know how he slept through that whole thing?" He said, looking at Hatcher. "Might think he's dead when he wakes up."

"Or in hell!" Nodded Billy, and reached down to inspect the weapons on the floor between them. "Hey, look at this?" He said, picking the Colt Peacemaker from the holster and working it. "This thing ain't more than a year old, good workin' gun, too,...think I'll keep it!" He pulled the spare from his belt, and put them both in his saddlebag.

"Here's another one." Said Rodney, picking that one up. "And this rifle." He picked it up as well. "Short barreled saddle gun, by Winchester arms!... Know what, I think I'll add 'em all to our arsenal,...good weapons."

"Works for me." He said, reaching to rub his shoulder and arm.

"Want some laudanum?"

"Hell no!"

"Well," He laughed then looked around at the coach's inside. "This old thing's movin' a bit eratic but seems to be okay."

"Axle housing's busted, Rod." He replied. "Be lucky to hold together till we get to Sherman."

"We'll make it!" He said with assurance. "We'll get another stage, and be on our way again. Can't wait to get home neither!"

"Makes two of us....What happened to th' man you shot, Rod, I just thought of it?"

"Top a th' stage, Billy."

"Good!...Rod, what say, after we make sure Doc's okay, and things are back to normal again. What say, we go home?...I'm damn tired a chasin' killers!"

"A big Amen to that!!...And you know what,...we don't have to anymore!...Once I give this badge to Peter, I am done!...I've only been a lawman for like, twelve years, but it seems like thirty!"

"A lot can happen in a few years." He said, looking down at the blood stain on his shirt front.

"It's not healed yet!" Said Rodney. "Forty-four slug makes a big hole, it hurtin' you any?"

"Little stiff, little sore, but no,...it's pretty much healed on the inside, I think." He nodded across at Hatcher then. "He's wakin' up!"

"About time,...Bastard'll be a dope head by th' time we get 'im home!"

"What th' hell is a dope head?" Asked Hatcher, pushing himself to a sitting position on the seat.

"Somebody hooked on drugs." Returned Rodney. "Too much laudanum will do that!"

Hatcher glared at him for a moment then looked out through the open window. "Thought th' Bounty Hunters would a hit us by now!" He gripped his arm and grunted in pain then. "Arm hurts, man, better give me another shot a that stuff....I don't want a be awake when they kill me."

"Don't think so, man!" Returned Rodney. "You've had enough for a while."

"Well, kiss my ass, I don't think so!...My arm is killin' me!"

"That just might upset th' hangman, that happens!" Said Billy.

"Yeah, well fuck you, too!...I don't want a be awake when I die, it's bad enough bein' here with you!"

"You ain't gonna die, Hatcher!" He responded, ignoring the man's profanity. "Not today, anyway."

"What about th' bounty hunters?"

"Oh, them?" He grinned. "They already hit us, Mister Hatcher,...I believe you were asleep!"

"Almost a half hour ago!" Added Rodney. "Look in th' floor here,...and if you don't recognize what all this is, I'll tell ya,..."

"I know what it is, God damn it!...What did you do, kill 'em?"

"Tied 'em up real good." Said Billy with a grin. "They're ridin' on top up there, they weren't good enough neither!...Decided they'd as soon be arrested, as to die!"

"Just who th' hell are you, man?...How th' hell did you beat me, anyway,...I'm th' best there is?"

"Was!" Said Rodney, also grinning. "That's what a dozen other would be gunfighters said after they went up against 'im....And like them, you'll never fire another gun with that arm!"

"Then let him answer me,...How'd you beat me?"

"We've had that conversation already!...As for who I am,...only a few people in th' world know that,...and you never will!"

"Couple a days ago, back in th' wagon....That thing you said, about there always being somebody better than what a man thinks he is....Is that th' truth?"

"Didn't you get beat?" Grinned Rodney.

"Yeah," Sneered Hatcher. "And that means that one day you're gonna go down, too, Mister Gunslinger!...And I'm gonna be watchin', maybe from hell, but I'll see it!...I'm gonna laugh my ass off, too!...What do ya think a that?"

"I think you're right!" Nodded Billy. "But it's gonna be a long wait, Hatcher!"

"I'll say,...you should a kept on running." Laughed Rodney. "What made you want a team up with rustlers, anyway?...That's what got you caught, ya know."

Hatcher opened his mouth, but closed it again to look out the window. "I have wondered that myself, of late!" He looked back at them. "He was gonna take this last herd to Kansas." He shrugged then. "I've never been to Kansas....Never been anywhere, but the Indian Nation, and Texas,... got chased out a New Mexico when I was twelve....Got run out a Colorado, too!"

"You shouldn't a went to Paris." Said Billy.

"Yeah,...hour late, and a dollar short." Said Hatcher. "My old man used to say that all th' time."

"Know what he meant?" This from Rodney.

Hatcher shook his head. "This, I guess!...I wondered about it for years, still don't know!" He looked at Billy then. "What did you shoot me with, a cannon?"

"Forty-four Colt."

Hatcher nodded then. "Mine was a forty-five Peacemaker."

"I know, it's in my saddlebag."

Nodding again, Hatcher grinned widely, and looked at Rodney. "Sure you won't give me another shot a that pain killer, Marshal,...arm hurts pretty bad?"

Shaking his head, Rodney opened the bottle, and gave him a swallow before putting it away again,...only to watch the gunman stretrch out again.

"Amen to that, too!" He looked at Billy then. "Wonder if he rambled that much when he had his gun on?"

"Wouldn't need it if he did,...could a talked 'em to death!" Yawned Billy, as he pulled out the pocket watch again. "Almost one o'clock." He said, and then smiled when he looked at Rodney. He was already sound asleep.

"Never seen anybody fall asleep that quick!" He said aloud. He scooted his frame down in the seat, and leaned his head against the window's opening and closed his eyes.

*   *   *

His eyes popped open when the guard leaned down to yell at him.

"Half hour, thereabouts to Sherman, Marshal!"

"Yeah, okay,...thanks, man." He pulled the watch again and looked at it blearily. "Five o'clock?" He put it away then looked at Both Rodney, and Hatcher, before reaching to wake up Rodney. "Wake up, Rod!" He said, as he shook him.

"What?...Who?" He sat up to look around, his eyes going from Hatcher's sleeping form to Billy. "What is it?"

"Not a thing." Grinned Billy. "Be in Sherman before long."

"I can't believe I went to sleep!...But I'm glad we're here,...only about sixty miles to Paris from Sherman."

"How's th' shoulder?"

"It's okay right now, only hurts when I turn th' wrong way,...but when I do, shit, man!...Takes a long while to subside....But you, ny friend, are gonna see a Doctor in Sherman,...that spot on your shirt's getting' bigger!"

"I plan on it, Rod."

"Good,...Who's Sheriff in Sherman, anyway?...I was al;seep when I came through."

"Name's Cartwright, a dapper sort a fellow."

"Well, old Cartwright's gonna have some visitors today!"

"He won't like it much!" Chuckled Billy. "Opinion I got from 'im is he don't like to work much!"

"That kind of Dapper, huh?" He retrieved a thin cigar from his vest and lit it. "Glad we're almost home, man, only got one a these left!...A dapper Dan, huh?"

"Pretty much!"

Rodney leaned to look at the weapons under-foot then. "Got a question, Billy. Didn't we put them rustler's hardware on th' coach when we left?... They sure ain't here, if we did!"

"They're under th' canvas, back a th' stage….I asked Hicks about that before we left."

"Old Hatcher really believed you had his gun in that saddlebag."

"What he don't know won't do 'im any good!"

"Ain't that a fact?" He blew bluish smoke out through the window, and they both were content to take in the surroundings for a time, until Rodney looked back at him. "Strange, ain't it,…we ain't seen not one thing on this road today!"

"Too damn hot, Rod!"

"Amen to that!"

They were watching as the slow moving coach entered the outskirts of town, and it was not long until they began to notice pedestrians stopping to point at them in passing, and laughing about it.

"You see that, Billy?…Guess they don't see a coach comin' in like this very often!"

"Guess not!" He grinned, and while Rodney continued to watch the street traffic, he lay his head back and closed his eyes again, only this time, he allowed something to enter his mind that he had blocked out before as he reseurected the slender image of a loving, beautiful Jaclyn Garnette, as she stood alone, tears trickling down her cheeks to watch him ride out of her life.

He knew that she loved him because a person's eyes do not lie! However, it was something he did not understand, having only known her for a few days. Why, he wondered?…How could she love a man like him, she did not even know him!…'I could have been a killer myself", he thought, yet she chose him!

He knew that the why of it didn't matter! His only regret was that he might never know the answers, nor see her again! One thing was certain, he thought then. He would never forget her, because she somehow managed to keep a large chunk of his heart when he left. He also felt sure that he had most of hers.

He opened his eyes as her image faded and smiled, remembering the conversation he had with Hank. He was also in love with her, and he had no doubt the man would make her a good husband,…and he wished him luck!

"Comin' into down town, Billy." Voiced Rodney, and as his last thought of Jaclyn Garnette dissolved from his mind with the interruption, he leaned his head slightly out of the window to watch the busy storefronts and boardwalks.

"They're still gawkin' at us." Continued Rodney, turning to look at Billy. "What are you lookin' at?"

"Got a fair crowd in th' street up ahead, right around th' Sheriff's office, looks like."

"Guess they heard about Hatcher, too, huh?"

"Maybe so,…best wake 'im, Rod." He continued to watch the pedestrian movement as the coach neared Cartwright's office, thinking that something else was at hand here,…everyone seemed to be walking, or hurrying toward Cartwright's office.

Rodney had Hatcher awake, and sitting on the edge of the seat as the coach came to a stop some twenty feet away from the boardwalk, and was staring out of the window at the two, dark-clothed men on the walkway. Both wore black pants and vest, both sported tied down sidearms, but onle one of them wore a coat to match, and had a star on his vest. But, it was the other one that stirred his memory.

"One of 'em's got a be th' Sheriff, Billy."

"Cartwright, yeah,…never seen the other one before." He leaned to push open the door and then stepped down to the ground, seeing Cartwright and the other man step off the boardwalk and come toward him. He moved aside to allow Rodney to usher Hatcher out of the coach, and when Cartwright approached, saw him stop to look up at the men on top.

"Mister Upshur!" He said, looking back at him. "What have you up there?" He asked, shaking Billy's hand.

"One dead man, two wounded." Said Rodney, forcing Hatcher to stand beside Billy. "Bounty Hunters, tried to take Hatcher from us by force, other side a Southmayd. They're all yours, Sheriff, I'll file th' complaint,…assault with intent to kill Federal Officers."

Nodding, Cartwright turned to a deputy, assigned to crowd control. "Dennis,…get some help, get those men down and lock them up!...Get Doc Brown, too!" And several men came forward to climb atop the stage. Sighing, he looked back at Billy and then at the four horses tied to the rear of the coach.

"I see, you got your man, Sir." He said, looking at the prisoner. "And your horse!"

"You can keep th' two saddle horses, Sheriff,...Th' black, and th' gray are mine."

You got room in jail for Hatcher, overnight?" Asked Rodney.

"Yes sir, I surely do, but that, I'm afraid, won't be necessary." He said, taking the other man's arm and moving him forward. "This is United States Marshall, Norman Stogner, gentlemen. Came all the way from Kansas City to escort Mister Hatcher back!"

"By whose authority?" Asked Rodney.

"Judge Issac Parker!" Said Stogner. "I'm to take him straight back to Fort Smith, Arkansas."

"It's only been a couple a days." Said Billy. "How'd you get here so fast?"

"Train." Replied Stogner, a little fidgety.

"I'll need to see your paperwork,...Marshal!" Said Rodney, a half grin on his face. "You do have a warrant to bring 'im back, don't ya?"

"Don't need one, I'm just followin' orders!"

"I see,...well I work for Issac Parker, too, have for th' last six years, and I do not recall th' Judge ever sending anybody after a prisoner without a warrant....And that being said, I'll need to see your badge and identification, too!...Know why?...Because it'll be a cold day in hell before I turn Hatcher over to you!"

"Why don't you kill th' son of a bitch, Marshal?" Laughed Hatcher. "Hell, he ain't no lawman!"

"Shut up!...I'm waiting, Stogner!"

"I have my orders!" He took a slightly bent star from his shirt and showed it to them. "Satisfied?"

"Mister Stogner," Began Rodney. "That's a Sheriff's badge." He tapped his own badge with a forefinger. "This is the official U. S. Marshal's badge!... and No, I am not satisfied....See th' men they're takin' off this coach?... Scum of this earth bounty hunters, Stogner,...they wanted Hatcher, too!... But they didn't want a work for it,...I don't think you do, either!"

"What th' hell are you sayin'?" Shouted Stogner. "You gonna hand over Hatcher, or not?" He dropped his hand to his side then. "You can lose your badge over this, Marshal."

"Tell ya what, Stogner." He said, glancing at the frustrated look on Billy's face. "You show me that warrant, I'll turn 'im over!...That's simple enough, ain't it?"

"I ain't got no fuckin' warrant!"

"Then you don't get Hatcher!...You didn't work for it either."

"Gentlemen, Gentlemen!" Interrupted Cartwright suddenly. "Let's settle this thing in a friendly manner here, we're all on the same side."

Billy, though beside himself with frustration, eased his hand down to unlatch the Colt Pistol as he listened.

"This don't concern local law enforcement, Sheriff." Said Rodney evenly. "Please step back, Sir!"

"But I don't understand!"

"It ain't that hard, Sheriff." Returned Rodney. "He's a bounty hunter just like those oth…"

Billy had been listening intently to the back and forth argument, and was as surprised as Rodney when Stogner, without warning yelled and went for his gun.

Stogner's gun was clearing the holster and coming in line, when he drew and fired, the slug striking The gunman high on the right shoulder, shattering his collar bone as he was spun around and thrown bodily onto the hard packed street.

The explosion had been tremendous in the late afternoon heat, and made even louder by the sudden yelling of men, and the screams of women as they all quickly dropped to their knees, or ran for cover elsewhere.

Breathing a sigh of relief, Billy holstered the gun and walked to where Rodney and Cartwright were standing, to numbly stare down at the sobbing gunman. Stepping in front of Cartwright then, he squatted to unbuckle Stogner's gunbelt and pull it free, and then stood to go retrieve the unfired pistol. He eased the hammer down on it, and returned it to the holster.

"I stand very much corrected, Marshal!" Said Cartwright in astonishment.

"How's that, Sheriff?" He asked, stopping to peer at him.

"I recall telling you, you didn't look like a gunfighter!"

"You were right, Sir, I'm not!" He moved to the coach and dropped the holstered gun onto the floor.

"Sheriff?" Interrupted Rodney getting his attention, and still gripping Hatcher's good arm. "Could I trouble you to lock Hatcher up for the night?"

"Oh,…yes sir, Marshal, you surely can!...What about this man?"

"Man's got a poster out on 'im, Sheriff, I'll leave that up to you!...Assault on a Federal Officer is th' new charge,...poster says he's wanted for fraud, extortion, and murder. You might want a check into that."

Nodding, Cartwright called to another of his deputies to take Hatcher inside, and then as Dennis returned, had him escort the wounded Stogner in behind them. They both watched them as they entered the office. Cartwright nodded, and as he turned back, grinned as he looked over at Billy.

"Bill, there said he wasn't a gunfighter!" He chuckled then, and slapped Rodney's good arm. "Pigs can fly, too!...Know what I mean?" He laughed then, and followed the deputy into his office.

"Yeah, Mister Cartwright." He smiled as he watched him walk to his office. "I do know what ya mean!" He turned then to see Billy talking with the driver and guard, and went to join him, seeing Billy turn toward him as he approached.

"Harold here said they'd have a coach ready in th' mornin', Rod."

"Man, that's good news!" He looked at the driver then. "You been here before, where can we get a nice, juicy, thick steak?"

Harold laughed. "Norma's,...on th' corner yonder."

"That'll work!...Billy, that sawbones is gonna be busy for a while, let's go eat, man, come back later."

"We'll grain your horses for ya, Marshal." Said the guard. "Have 'em ready for ya in th' mornin'." He grinned then from ear to ear. "That was the fastest draw I ever did see, Marshal." He said, reaching to shake Billy's hand. "My friends will never believe me when I tell 'em!"

"What about that small arsenal in th' coach there, Marshal?" Asked Harold. "What do you want done?"

"Load 'em in th' other coach." Said Billy. "And about th' horses. Th' black, and that gray belong to us, best one a the other three, too. Th' one in your team, and one a them there goes to th' Sheriff."

"Good enough, I'll have all three ready by morning." He replied, and they both climbed back up to the seat and drove the coach away.

"Know what, Billy?...This has been one crazy couple a days."

"That it has!...Let's go get that steak."

*   *   *

"Sheriff," Said Billy, as deputy Meeker went into the cellblock to retrieve Hatcher. "Whatever reward you might collect on this bunch,…I'd appreciate you bein' generous with an Indian friend of ours. Name's Toby, works on th' J. and M. Ranch, Garnette spread at Decatur.…Wouldn't a caught Hatcher without 'im."

"I'll see about it, Marshal." He shook Billy's hand, then Rodney's as the deputy shoved the gunman into the room.

"Let go a me, you horse's ass!" Yelled Hatcher, and jerked out of the deputy's grasp.

"I'll take 'im from here, deputy!" Said Rodney, and grabbed the gunman's good arm. He then shoved him toward the open doorway and onto the boardwalk.

"All right, God damn it!" Snapped Hatcher, trying to dislodge himself from Rodney's firm grip. "Quit shovin' me, Asshole!"

"I will if you'll keep movin', asshole!" Said Rodney angrily. "Get on th' fuckin' coach, man!" He pushed him in front of him and then up into the stage where he replaced the leg irons.

Shaking his head and laughing, Billy turned to the Sheriff. "Mister Cartwright, you won't mind if I say, I hope I never see you again. Will ya?"

"Not at all, Marshal." He laughed then, too. "Have a safe trip th' rest of th' way."

Billy nodded and walked out to the coach, with Cartwright on his heels, only to stop when they got there and watch Rodney seat himself.

"Come on, man!" Said Rodney impatiently. "Shut your sorry ass up, will ya?"

"You can kiss my sorry ass, too!" He snapped. "Ain't got but one arm, or I'd beat hell out a you, God damn it!"

As Rodney settled in across from him, he saw Hatcher eying the arsenal of guns on the floor of the coach. "Tempting, ain't they?" He bent down and picked up one of the pistols. "Got a good feel to it, too."

"Kiss my ass!"

"No, thanks.…Anyway, th' driver unloaded all of 'em last night.…Now, do yourself a favor, and shut up!"

"You two settled in?" Grinned Billy as he climbed inside and seated him self.

"Hell no!" Grumbled Hatcher. "That asshole threw me in here, hurt my arm real bad,…don't one a your fuckin' laws cover that kind a treatment?"

"No," Said Rodney. "And you've caused enough trouble!" His obvious anger was causing Hatcher to grin. "Enjoyin' this, ain't ya?"

"Why not, you should be so popular!...Only reason these bounty hunters are comin' after me is cause they know I can't fight back!" He looked at Billy then.

"You should a killed that fucker yesterday, too!...I would have!"

Billy stared at him for a minute, and then sighed. "Few years ago, I would have!"

"What's th' difference, man, he would a killed you?"

"I ain't a killer!...Not anymore." Just then the coach shuddered and groaned into motion as the driver gave out a yell, followed by the crack of a whip. He quickly leaned out of the window and called to Harold. "Don't run 'em, Harold, do it like before!"

"You got it, Marshal!"

Nodding, Billy looked back at Cartwright and waved, and then to several other pedestrians along the way before sitting back again.

"Hey," Continued Hatcher. "If you ain't a killer, why'd you kill before?"

"I was young, thought I had to!"

"That's a bad idea, man....You don't kill a man, he might kill you someday, maybe hire somebody to do it for 'im!"

"Maybe." He nodded.

"That don't scare you?...That's crazy, man!...Okay then, what changed you?"

Billy sighed again. "I realized I was good enough, not to!"

"More like lucky enough!" Scoffed Hatcher. "I was still half asleep when you shot me, man!...We had it to do over, I'd kill ya!"

"Wouldn't a changed what happened, Hatcher!" Said Rodney.

"Now just how would you know that?"

"You went up against th' best there is, that's how I know!...Besides, you're here ain't ya? Now shut up, man!...Here." He reached the bottle from his shirt pocket and gave it to him. "One swallow!" He retrieved the bottle and put it away as the gunman leaned back grimacing with pain, causing him to grin and wink at Billy.

"Man, you look tired!...What did th' Doctor tell you about that wound, you went to sleep last night before I could ask ya?"

"Said it would take a few days to heal proper, is all….It's okay, Rod! You were right though,…don't think I ever been this tired."

"Well, we'll be home tomorrow."

"If we don't run into another U. S. Marshal!...How'd you know he was a fake, I missed some a that?"

"He didn't have a warrant,…can't bring a man in without one, it ain't legal!"

"I got that part, Rod,…what else?"

"I got a wanted poster on 'im in my desk at home!...Looked at it a dozen times. He cut his hair, shaved off a goatee, but I still recognized him!...Might not have, but he forgot to change his name!...Worth a thousand dollars, too!"

"Norman Stogner!" Mused Billy. "Don't think I ever heard of 'im."

"You never heard of any of 'em, Billy!...I sure didn't think he would try to draw on us with Cartwright next to 'im….Fooled me good!"

"He had no choice, Rod, he was caught and he knew it!"

"Took us off guard!" Chuckled Rodney. "And you damn near drew too late!"

"Why hell," Smirked Hatcher drowsily. "That ain't no big thing!...Stogner was second rate, at his very best!"

"I told you to shut up, Hatcher!" Threatened Rodney.

"Yeah, yeah, Marshal,…but you two make me sick! I knew what was gonna happen from th' start!"

"Hatcher, I'm warnin' you!" He said hatefully. "You talk too much."

"Got nothin' to lose, do I?"

"Man's got a point, Rod." Grinned Billy. "Besides, gettin' justice anymore presents a hard row to hoe for a man!...Man has to work hard at it sometimes."

Rodney stared at Hatcher for a minute and then at Billy. "Hard Justice,…last month or so would damn sure qualify, wouldn't it?" He nodded then. "That's a good one, Billy, I like that!...Hard Justice!...That's just what you're gonna get, Mister Hatcher!"

"Fuck you, Marshal, asshole!"

"Never th' less, Rod, it's all justice." Said Billy. "And we sometimes get hurt pullin' it off!"

"Amen to that!"

"What th' hell is all this Amen shit?" Blurted Hatcher. "You must a said that a hundred times, th' last three days."

"It's a good thing, Hatcher, you ought a try it sometime!...You had, you might not a wound up in a hangman's noose!"

"Kiss my ass!" He turned his face away from them then, and closed his eyes.

Still a little angry, Rodney plucked his last cigar from his vest and lit it, purposely blowing the strong, bluish smoke in the direction of the, now snoring gunman.

"Never knew you to let a prisoner get to you like that, Rod."

"Never had one do it before!...I swear, that bastard could intimidate a fence post!"

"He does have a knack for it!...I'm glad we could stop 'im now, though, instead of a year from now!...His old man must a been a real son of a bitch, for him to turn out this way!"

"Yeah, maybe,...he could a just left home, Billy, instead a bein' forced to run. He didn't have to kill his old man!"

"Maybe, he thought he did!...Could be, his mother was in danger."

"Well, he should a just left, be done with it!...Hell, even if he did kill him for that reason, the law would a been on his side if he had stayed? Would a been a lot better than bein' a fugitive."

"I agree,...but I doubt a twelve year old boy would give that much thought!"

"Guess somethin' like that would scare a kid!"

"No doubt!"

Rodney blew blue smoke out of the window before looking back at the gunman. "But that's no excuse for what he is now, Billy."

"No doubt about that, neither!"

"What th' hell are we doin', Billy?" He asked in disbelief. "We keep this up, we'll wind up feelin' sorry for 'im!"

"No doubt!"

Rodney frowned at him, and then they both burst out laughing. "Okay,...I'm done with this shit!...Besides, we still got a decision to make, and we have not talked about it yet."

"What would that be?"

"Our gold mine."

"Man,...I ain't thought a that since we left Shreveport!...And I still don't know what to do about it?"

"If we file a claim, like th' law says,...what's gonna happen, Billy?... What's th' downside to it all?"

"Damn if I know!...Problem we might have, would be with th' Choctaw."

"How,...they sold us th' mountain, they'll have nothin' to do with it!"

"They could say they sold it under false pretenses....We lied to 'em!"

"We didn't lie to 'em,...we just didn't tell 'em about th' gold mine!...And they didn't ask us where it came from!"

"That's true,...but it could tie us up in court for a long time!...I like things th' way they are, Rod, smooth and easy going."

"Me, too, Billy,...but the only place that happens is at th' mountain."

"It could change, if we file that claim!"

"Okay, I know you're right!...Why don't we just leave it alone for now, gold will still be legal tender, far as I know?...We just use gold dust instead a money to buy with!"

"Guess that's what we'll do, Rod,...and it might work, for a while." He sighed then. "But, sooner or later we'll have to file that claim!"

"Okay, Billy....As long as we're in Paris anyway, why don't we confide in Judge Bonner, get his opinion?"

"Damn, Rod,...I don't know!...We do that, our well kept secret'll be out!"

"I don't know about that, Bonner would know then how our gold helped rebuild th' town,...I don't believe he'd do a thing about it!"

"He's tough when it comes to law, Rod, you know that!"

"Yeah, I know it!...But it's somethin' to think about, Billy....He just might be our best, last hope!"

"Tell ya what I thought about....Us takin' what we want out a that treasure cave, and turnin' what's left over to th' Government."

"What,...tell 'em about it?"

"Why not, it bein' a part a history, not countin' all that wealth and artifacts....Keepin' our mine would be a done deal!"

"My, God, Billy!" He shook his head then. "What about that other thing, you know, th' time tunnel?"

"They wouldn't need to know about that! They'd move all the treasure out a th' cave,...take it to Washington or somewhere....That'd be th' end of it!"

"You really believe that, Billy?...Hell, they would make that whole mountain a historical site, be uppity people diggin' around in that valley for years, all in th' name of antiquity!...And I have another senario,...What if there is th' slightest remote possibility that the sale of Devil Mountain was not a legal transaction?...I mean,...maybe th' Choctaw didn't really own it!... We could a bought it under those same false pretenses!"

"Damn, Rod!" He breathed deeply of the sultry air. "Then maybe Bonner would be our best bet....Right now, though, I think we oughta get paperwork together,...th' deed to th' mountain, for when we see th' Judge. If we do see Bonner about this, we'll have to give 'im th' whole story!...He's gonna want a know how we came up with that first fifty thousand dollars to buy it with?"

"We tell 'im th' truth, Billy,...the mine!...He'll also know how to go about dealin' with that Aztec treasure th' right way!"

"Let's give it a rest for now, Rod, I'm getting' a headache!"

"Yeah, naybe we'd better." He clamped the half smoked cigar in his teeth, and looked out through the open window.

*   *   *

Jaclyn Garnette, once again went to the hutch for clean bed clothes and also, once again looked over her shoulder at the bed where Billy had recouperated,...and for the dozenth time dropped the linen back into the drawer unable to to force herself to wash the bedding, because his scent would be lost to her forever.

She knew it was crazy, but as tears flooded her eyes again, she didn't care. She was in love with the man she had nurtured back to health, knew it was wrong to lust after a married man! But, as hard as she tried, she could not control the way she felt. She was lost in his memory, and the depressing idea that she might never see him again.

She was also quite upset that Hank had not told her everything that Toby had surely told him about the capture of Wes Hatcher,...or how Billy was? She had gotten the idea that he had purposely withheld any information on him! She knew, too, that he was in love with her himself.... But that was a union that would never come about! Because whatever the reasons were that had brought Billy Upshur into her life, good or bad, it had to be the way it was meant to be!...And she would wait for as long as it might take, fot she believed that Billy was meant to be with her.

She dried her eyes with a kerchief and closed the drawer before running to throw herself onto the bed, and the lasting smell of the man she loved. But as soon as she pulled the pillow to her face, she remembered that Toby had been left at the ranch today to repair a fence.

Excited, she got up, grabbed her sunbonnet and hurried across the sitting room floor and out the door. She stood on the porch to look around the yard, and then toward the bunkhouse and barn before seeing him as he was hammering a board in place. She went down the steps, put on the bonnet and hurried toward the barn.

"Toby?" She smiled, coming to stand at the fence. "Good morning!"

"Good morning, Ms. Garnette!" He smiled and removed his hat. "What can I do for you on such a hot day?"

"When you get the time, Toby, please come to the house, I'd like to talk with you about something?"

"Of course, Ms. Garnette. "When I finish with this board."

"Great,...I'll have some cool tea waiting for you on the porch."

"Yes ma'am!" He smiled, and watched her walk away.

She climbed the steps and hurried into the house for the crock jar of tea she had cooling in the cistern-well, came back through to the kitchen for two glasses then continued on out to the porch. She put the jar and glasses on the table there, and quite nervously sat down in one of the chairs to wait.

'Why do I need to know what happened', she thought?...It wouldn't bring him back to her!...But she had to know that he was all right!...That would be the only way, she knew, that she could go on living. Besides, she thought then. 'I still have a large ranch to run', and that would be very hard to do without some sort of closure, and that closure would be in knowing that he was safe.

'Damn Hank, anyway,' she thought, and then wondered if he might know what she felt for Billy?...'Yes', she thought then, he was jealous enough to know!...It was the same way he acted when any man came around her!... But it would not do him any good, she vowed! Because he would never be the man she knew that Billy was! It was just something she felt in her heart....Billy Upshur was the only man for her, and she would wait ever how long it takes to be with him again.

She was shaken from her thoughts then when she saw the sweat-soaked Indian come around the porch and climb the steps. "Come, Toby." She smiled. "Do sit down, please?" She poured the cool tea in a glass and gave it to him before pouring hers.

"I need to talk with you, to ask you some questions, Toby, and please answer them truthfully for me?"

He frowned at her for a moment, as if trying to grasp the point of the question. "Always, Ms. Garnette!"

"I know you must think you've done something wrong, but believe me, nothing is wrong, Toby. You are one of my most trusted wranglers,...okay?"

"Yes, Maam, it is okay."

"Toby,...Hank pretty well told me what happened at Rush Creek the other day,...but he seemed very close-mouthed when I ask him about the rest of it....You did tell him what happened when those men were captured, didn't you?"

"Oh, yes, Maam, everything!"

"Would you tell me what happened?...And please, this is strictly between you and I,...there's no need for Hank to even know we talked!...Do you agree?"

"Yes, maam!"

"Good!...Then tell me everything, from the moment you left Rush Creek!...How was Billy's wound when you left?"

"The wound was not bleeding,...but he did have me release his arm, the other Marshal, too. Said it was too,...confining! Mister Hank, and the other men came home, the Sheriff, too,...that's when we began tracking those men."

"There was, what, twelve men there, Toby?"

"Yes, Maam,...counting the gunslinger....I found a shallow grave in back of the saloon, it was fresh."

Go on with your story now, please?" She listened intently as he gave her a day by day version of the chase, and of the encounter with the two outlaws,...only stopping when he told her that he went for help.

"You didn't actually see what happened, when they found those men?"

"No, Maam, me and twenty ranch hands arrived when it was over. The Marshal, both of them, had all of them in custody already.

"And the man that shot Billy, was he there?"

"Yes, Maam, Billy, Mister Upshur beat him to the draw, his arm was busted real bad, I put splints on it myself!...This Mister Upshur is some fast with a pistola, Ms. Garnette."

"What about his injury, Toby,...was he all right?"

"I think so, it was bleeding a little, but he was all right, they were,... Ms. Garnette, why is this so important to you?" He looked at her moist, reddish eyes for a moment and then smiled. "I understand, Ms. Garnette." He nodded. "This Billy is a fine man,...and I am sorry!" He got up then, and drained the cool glass of tea before placing the glass down.

"Do not worry, Ms. Garnette, my first loyalty is for you....No one will ever know of our conversation."

"Thank you, Toby." She sniffed. "Did you see him when he left?"

"I am sorry, but no, I left before that!...I go back to work now, Mister Hank wants the fence done by tonight." He donned his sweat soaked hat and smiled at her.

"Your Marshal Upshur is a good man!...He wounded this pistoleero, when he could have killed him....He uses a pistola like nothing I have ever seen!...No man can match him, I think....Do not worry!" He bowed slightly then left the porch, leaving her to fold her arms on the table, and lay her head on them,...and the way her body was shaking when he looked back, he knew she was crying.

* * *

"Aproachin' Dodd City, Marshal!" Yelled the guard, as he leaned down close to the window. "You got a piss, we'll be stoppin' to water th' team."

"Thanks, Jim!" He yelled back then looked at Rodney as he opened his eyes.

"Where are we, Billy?"

"Dodd City, we're stoppin' for water."

"Good, I got a go!" They were both looking through the coach windows as they entered the community.

A couple of false-fronted stores were on the left side of the wide street, along with a Post Office and bank. On the other, stood a saloon, hardware, and a feed and grain. A few more buildings were farther on, but the coach stopped in front of the Sheriff's office. The guard climbed down with a bucket and dipped it in the watering trough,…and began quenching the six-horse team's thirst.

Billy leaned over to open the door then stepped down to go check on the horses. Patting each of them on their sweaty necks, he checked to make sure they were secured then followed Rodney down the alleyway to the outhouse.

"Think we ought a wake, Mister Pain-in-the-ass?" Asked Rodney as they came back to the coach.

"What?…Are you a glutton for punishment?…Let 'im sleep!"

"You're right,…what was I thinkin'?"

"Get on board, Rod." He laughed. "I'm gonna water th' horses." And as Rodney climbed in, Jim came back with the bucket. He took it and carried water back to the three animals.

He was letting the black drink while he looked over the weathered buildings, and as he looked back, he saw movement from the corner of his eye, and looked as he took the bucket from the black's nose. As he put the bucket over the gray's nose, he peered at the lean, well-groomed man that was watching him from a storefront a few steps away. As Doc's horse drank, he studied the man, and his attire, lingering on the low-slung, tied down pistol on his hip.

His thought, when he saw the man, was that he was someone else wanting to cash in on Hatcher, and as he watched him, moved the bucket to the spare horse's nose. As the horse drank, he turned his body slightly then reached slowly down to unlatch the Colt.

Removing the bucket from the animal's nose with his injured left arm, he let it dangle and turned toward the man. "You just watchin', friend?…Or do you have somethin' in mind?" And when the man didn't answer. "Okay,…just so you'll know, friend….I'm a U. S. Marshal, and I'm transporting a prisoner back to Paris,…and if you're of a mind to try somethin' stupid, I got a tell ya,…I already shot three so-called gunslingers these past two days,…you don't want a make it four!"

"Mister," Said the man in a low voice. "If I was of a mind to do somethin', you'd already know about it!" Without changing his expression, the man turned and disappeared back inside the store.

"I guess so." Muttered Billy, and shaking his head went forward to toss the bucket up to Jim,…and with a last look at the empty doorway, climbed inside.

"He-yaaaa!" Yelled Harold, and the coach jerked into life again.

"Next stop is Honey Grove, Billy." Said Rodney. "If we stop there?...I ain't seen old Charlie Daniels since we took down that Mormon renegade."

"I saw 'im briefly on my way through."

"We're sure takin' a long time getting' home, too, with them horses in back."

"That, we are." He said, leaning forward to look back at the empty doorway again.

"Thought I heard you talkin' to somebody back there?"

"Just calmin' th' horses, Rod,...they don't like it much back there."

"I can believe that....Wonder if Doc's home yet?"

"Be a load off my mind, if he is!...I never missed my family this much before."

"Amen to that!...Hope they got th' wire I sent, they'll want a know we're comin' home?"

"I'm sure they did." He removed the bandana from his neck then to wipe his face and neck. "What's to do when we get there?"

"We'll have to fill Jim in on what happened,...write a report about th' whole thing, and sign it.... Give th' Judge somethin' to work with! Gonna be a lot a legal formalities to work out, I'm sure! Got several places around that wants to hang Hatcher themselves, especially those that put up th' reward for 'im....Could be a fight! We can't leave nothin' out a that report, that's for sure."

"Bonner'll figure it out....I want Doc to see this bird hang, Rod,...think Bonner'll be able to keep him here?"

"It all comes down to jurisdiction, Billy and truthfully, don't be surprised if jurisdiction goes in another direction....It's been known to happen."

"Then, maybe I should a killed 'im!"

"Maybe you should have,...but I'm glad you didn't!...Because I want to slam that cell door in that asshole's face!"

"Job ain't over till we do!"

"Job?" He laughed then and shook his head. "Just thought about this, Billy!...We brought charges against old Stogner for impersonating a Federal Officer, and we're doin' th' same exact thing!...We're criminals!"

"Guess they could make a case of it!"

"Well, Let's hope they don't,…I've had my fill a this thing!…I just want a go back to runnin' th' store,…listening to the Junebugs on a still summer day."

"And don't forget that cool summer breeze that's always blowin'."

"Yeah,…and no more gunfights for a while!" He looked at Billy then. "What do you think about Willy wanting to wear a gun already?…He seems pretty determined to me."

"I can't blame nobody but myself, Rod,…he's been around it too much!"

"That's true,…but he's got a good head on his shoulders, he'll know th' right and wrongs of it."

"I hope he will." He grinned then. "I'm proud th' way he tried to take up for th' folks….Glad he didn't get hurt, too!"

"Th' boy's feisty all right!…Wants to be a lawman, he tell ya that?"

"No,…he didn't. He tell you?"

"Sure did,…sort a made me proud, too!"

"Guess they'll grow up to be what they want a be….I was hopin' he would do it without wearin' a gun, though."

"I don't agree with ya, Billy….Times have not changed all that much, it's still dangerous!…It's good that a man's able and willing to take care of his own. You have to admit that!…And from what I've seen, my Nephew fits that description all th' way.….Anyway,…all we can do is try and steer them in th' right direction."

"He can be anything he wants," Said Billy, and nodded at Hatcher. "Long as he don't grow up like him."

"Like Hatcher?…Not a chance, Billy, that boy comes from great stock!"

"Thanks, Rod….But I still ain't been much of an influence!"

"He knows th' difference in fighting for a good cause, and fighting for th' bad one. He's a great kid!"

"Just th' same, I think I'll have 'im sit in on Hatcher's trial, let 'im see what bad decisions can lead to."

"Great idea, if they hold th' trial right away….They could set it for July, or even August, ya know."

"Got company comin, Marshal!" Yelled down the guard. "They're gonna stop us, looks like!"

The stage rolled to a stop, and they both looked out through the windows for a look ahead.

"Could be a posse, Billy."

"What can ya see?" He reached down to unlatch the Colt.

"Just a group a men ridin' up in front of us."

Billy leaned to open the door, and then to step down to the ground as the riders approached. Rodney stepped down beside him then. "That looks like Charlie Daniels." They both moved up to stop at the coach's front wheel and raise their hand to Daniels in greeting.

"What's goin' on, Charlie?" Asked Rodney as all the riders stopped around them.

"Oh, hey, Marshal!...I wouldn't a stopped ya, I knowed it was you!...Hi ya, Bill, you get your man, did ya?

"In th' coach there,...you got trouble, Charlie?"

"Sure do,...bank holdup, two men....They rode off down this road. Don't guess you seen anybody?"

"Hell,...we ain't seen any traffic at all since leavin' Sherman!"

"Damn," He blurted. "I didn't feel like they'd stay on th' road....Tell me, Marshal, you was me, what would you do?...I mean, where would you start lookin' for two bank robbers?"

"Damn if I know, Charlie." Said Rodney. "Would depend on how far ahead a me, they was."

"I'd send a couple a men back th' way you came," Said Billy. "One on each side a th' road, they had to turn off it somewhere!...If they did, they left tracks!...Might try it this way, too."

"That's pretty good advice, Bill." Said Daniels with a smile then turned to his men. "I need two men that knows how to track. You'll go back toward town, one on each side a th' road,...slow. Look for tracks leavin' th' road, you see 'em, fire off a couple a shots!...Go ahead now." He watched them leave then looked over the rest of th' posse. "I need two more men now, we'll do that same thing between here and Dodd City. Any questions?...Get goin'!" He turned back to them then.

"Sorry for th' delay, Marshal." He tipped his hat. "Be a seein' ya."

They watched him lead the remainder of posse down the center of the road at a walk, and then climbed back into the coach.

"We won't get home till sometime tonight, Billy." He said, seating himself again,...and that's when he saw Hatcher open his eyes. "Look who decided to join us?"

Billy sat down as the coach began moving again and looked at Hatcher.

"What are you lookin' at?" He growled, pushing himself upright on the seat.

'I don't know,…ain't figured it out yet!"

"Am I that complicated?"

"Nope!" Said Rodney. "You're a killer!"

"I ain't no different than you are!…Him neither!" He said angrily. "You kill when somebody tries to kill you!"

"But you like it, I don't!"

"Yeah, whatever!…Know what I'd really like right now?"

"I wouldn't even start to guess, Hatcher!"

"Well, I'd really like to get you both in my rifle sights!"

"Too bad that won't happen."

Hatcher smiled then. "You're right about that, Marshal,…so I guess you'll just have to kiss my ass!"

"Shut up, Hatcher, I'm tired a your whinin'!"

"Then why don't you just shoot me in th' head, be done with it?"

"We can't cheat th' hangman, man,…just wouldn't be right!"

"Fuck th' hangman, you, too!" He leaned back on the seat then.

"You'll sing a different tune on the gallows." Said Rodney. "A whole crowd a folks will be there, just to watch you piss your pants!"

"You'll sing a different tune on th' gallows!" Said Rodney. "A whole crowd of folks will be there, just to watch you piss your pants!"

He ignored the remark. "When we gonna stop again, man's got a piss ya know?"

"We already did that,…you slept through it!"

"And what am I supposed to do, piss in th' floor?...That's what I'll do, ya know, all over them guns, rust hell out of 'em!...Man can't even move his feet for 'em!"

"It ain't them guns, keepin' you from movin your feet."

"Yeah, whatever!...But I still got a piss."

Billy reached a hand through the window and slapped the side of the coach to get their attention. "Stop th' coach!" He yelled. "Prisoner's got a piss."

*   *   *

Sheriff, John Gose closed and locked his new office door then walked to the edge of the boardwalk to watch a wagon load of carpenters cross the square on their way home then stepped down and walked across to the Courthouse.

"Hi, ya, John!" Said Jim Stockwell as he opened the door and came in. "Grab a seat for a minute,…I was waitin' on Ben to get here, so I could go to th' Telegraph office."

"You haven't heard anything else?"

"No,…not from Rodney, or Billy since that one yesterday mornin', you seen that one.!" He took the folded papers from his shirt pocket then. "But I got this one." He said, and unfolded them. "Yesterday afternoon, from a Sheriff Hicks, in Gainsville, Texas,…I'll read it!..." Marshals Taylor and Upshur left here this morning with prisoner, Hatcher……Were followed by two or more bounty men when leaving…..possible trouble in making…… would like hear from you if arrived in one piece." He put that wire away.

"I got worried then, so I wired th' Sheriff in Sherman last night, to see if they showed up?...He wired me back about noon today…." Marshals Taylor and Upshur arrived Sherman late in day with three wounded men one dead man…..Left here seven a m by stage with prisoner today"….Signed, Sheriff Cartwright, Sherman, Texas!"

"Well that's good news, Jim, they're on their way!" Said Gose as he leaned back in his chair. "You tell the family about that?"

"Oh, no!...They're worried enough as it is. Besides, accordin' To Sheriff Cartwright, they're all right....But, if they're comin' by stage, shouldn't they be here? That's what I was goin' to the telegraph office for, to find out?"

"I don't know, Jim." Mused Gose. "Sherman,...that's got a be a good sixty, seventy miles from here, could be ten, eleven o'clock to night getting here......If anything happened between here and there, we wouldn't hear about it, not till we started an inquirie and then it would take some time....I wouldn't worry too much about 'em, they're plenty tough, both of 'em!"

"I know that's right!" He sat down on the edge of his desk then. "This last seven or eight days have been a son of a bitch, John!"

"Tell me about it!...Ever since we got word they were bringing Hatcher in, the Judge has been to my office every hour, on the hour lookin' for news about 'em....Did you know that he's already ordered the gallows to be built,...be starting on it in the morning?"

"You're kiddin' me!...Well," He sighed. "Him and Doc go back a long ways, John. Hatcher ain't gonna have a chance in his courtroom!...Don't deserve one, neither, I guess....As mad and upset as Billy was when he left, I'm sort a surprised they ain't bringin' 'im back dead!"

"It was me, he would be!" Replied Gose,...Doc Bailey is Paris, Texas, been here from the start!. Ain't a soul in this town, Doc ain't touched in one way or another."

"You sound like you're worried about somethin', John?"

"Yeah,...a little, I guess!...I've heard a few men talking, mostly them at the saloon,...anyway there's some talk about lynching Wes Hatcher, Jim!... If they get enough backers in this thing, Hatcher may not go to trial!...That being th' case, what are you going to do about it?...Only reason I'm asking, is that I'll stand with you if need be!"

"Jesus, John!...That talk from people we know?"

"You bet it is!"

"I won't have any choice but to stop 'em, John,...or try to!"

"That's what I thought!...Well, here's Ben, Jim." He said getting up. "I'm goin' home to supper, be back in a couple hours, I want a be here when they arrive."

*   *   *

"Honey Grove, comin' up, Marshal!" Yelled down the guard. "Be about a hour, maybe less, you want a get a bite?...We're changin' horses!"

"Thanks, Jim." Returned Rodney, and then looked at Hatcher, who had just taken another swallow of the pain medicine. "Can you stay awake long enough to eat?"

"Yeah, sure,...I could use a steak!"

"How about you, Billy,...I know I could?"

"Yeah, okay!" He said, taking out his watch. "Five o'clock, Rod, we ain't makin' very good time, be midnight getting' home at this rate."

"Naww, it's only twenty odd miles now, we'll be there around ten, or so."

"What's th' fuckin' hurry, anyway?" Asked Hatcher with a sneer.

"Well,...I don't know, Mister Hatcher." Returned Billy, just as nasty. "I didn't murder my father, I'm sort a anxious to get home!"

"Well, fuckin' good for him, man!...Old fart ought a be dead!"

Billy looked at him for a minute then suddenly leaned out over the arsenal on the floor, and hit him with his fist. It was so sudden and unexpected that Hatcher's head was snapped back with the blow, striking the metal frame around the seatback with enough force to render him unconscious. "He ought a be dead?...You ought a be dead,...you shit faced son of a bitch!" He drew his fist back to hit him again, when Rodney grabbed his arm to stop him.

"He's got a hang, Billy, don't beat 'im to death!...Settle down, man."

Billy released the air in his lungs, and breathing hard nodded and pushed himself back into his seat.

"Calm down, Billy,...I've wanted to do that fifty times already, but we can't!"

"I had it to do over, I'd kill th' fucker!" He snapped. "No man talks about my family like that!"

"I know, man, I feel th' same way."

He looked at Rodney then and nodded. "I'm okay now,...he just hit a sore spot!"

"I never seen you lose your temper like that before, you're always th' calm one, ya scared me, man!"

"Hurt my hand, too!" He grinned, flexing his fingers a few times.

"Felt good though, didn't it?"

"Felt damn good!" He looked back at Hatcher then. "Ya think I might a broke his jaw?"

"If ya did, it might shut his ass up!...But, naw, beard was too thick, cushioned th' blow. He knocked his own self out." He looked out at the houses then. "Comin' in to town."

They both watched the few pedestrians along the boardwalks in passing, and commenting on the fact that there were very few horses or wagons along the hitchrails. But then the coach came to a stop in front of the local hotel and he leaned to open the door and step down to the street. Rodney stepped down beside him then turned to look back in at Hatcher.

"You gonna wake 'im?" Asked Billy.

"Don't know,...what do ya think,...be okay here alone?" He looked up then as the guard climbed down, and then Harold. "Somebody gonna stay with th' coach, Harold?"

"I am, Marshal. We're gonna unhitch th' team, and Jim's gonna drive 'em around th' corner there and harness up fresh horses....What ya got in mind?"

"Hatcher's dead to th' world in there, gonna leave 'im that way....And we don't want any curiosity seekers."

"I'll watch 'im. He can't get out, can he?"

"He's chained to th' floor."

"Good enough."

"Come on, Billy, let's go inside."

"What do we do about feedin' 'im, Rod?" He asked as they crossed the lobby to the dining room.

"I'll take 'im a couple biscuits, piece a meat, that'll hold 'im."

"Suits me,...you notice th' bank across th' street?...Closed up tight. Must a got away with a lot a money."

"No doubt did." He replied, sitting down at a window table. "May not a been much there to start with, either....Here comes th' waitress, let's order."

*   *   *

"Well," Commented Rodney as they came back out to the boardwalk. "Ain't a hell of a lot a cook can do to fry up a bad steak, Billy,...but that one sure qualified!"

"You're getting' picky in your old age, Rod." He said, nodding at the driver. "Any problems, Harold?"

"Old boy's still asleep, no problem at all."

"Good!" he replied,…and then movement at the corner of his eye caused him to look at the street, seeing the lone horse and rider approaching and watched him.

"What's wrong, Billy?" Asked Rodney, also turning to watch the man rein his horse in to the hitchrail and dismount in front of the saloon. He tied up, and then turned to look at them for several long seconds before going inside. "You know that man, Billy?"

"No,…but he was in Dodd City when we was."

"What was he doin'?"

"Watchin' us."

"Well he ain't no cowhand, fella moves like a cat!"

"We both know what he is, Rod,…he just challenged me, too!"

"Challenged you, how?…I didn't see anything!"

"You're not a gunslinger!"

Rodney turned to look at him, plainly frustrated. "Well what now, you gonna accommodate 'im?"

"No,…I'm gonna get on th' stage."

Rodney frowned at him then looked back at the saloon. "Okay, then…. Jim ain't back yet, so I'm gonna go wire Jim Stockwell. Here,…if Hatcher wakes up, give 'im his supper." He gave him the covered plate of steak and potatoes and walked off to the telegraph office.

"You gonna go eat, Harold?" He asked, opening the stage door.

"Already did, Marshal. We bring our own."

Nodding, he climbed inside and sat down, placing the plate of food on the seat next to Hatcher, watched him for a moment then leaned to look out of the window at the saloon across the street. He was unable to tell if the man was watching him, it was too dark inside the building,…but he felt sure he was. Sighing, he leaned back in the seat, searching his memory for anyone he might have seen before, anything that would identify the man, somebody he might have come into contact with,…but there was nobody….The man was a stranger to him!

But, what was his agenda, he wondered?…He definitely did not fit the role of Bounty Hunter, he was too dapper! Rodney was right, too, he moved with the slow, almost gliding grace of a cat,…a stalking cat! He was a gunman, that was for sure, and he definitely sent him an unspoken challenge, felt it in every nerve in his body….'So why didn't he call me out'?"

At that moment, Rodney opened the door and climbed inside. "Jim's back with th' team a horses, be on our way soon now….Hatcher still asleep?"

"Hope he stays that way!...Say, Rod,…did you get a good look at that man a while ago?" He asked, looking back at the saloon.

"Not his face, no,…why?"

"He's a gunny!"

"I know that, Billy,…but why do you ask?"

"He's a dangerous man, that's why!"

"You're serious, ain't ya?...Think he's after Hatcher?"

"I don't think he even knows Hatcher!...I saw him in Dodd City while waterin' th' horses, asked 'im what he had in mind?...He turned and left!... He's up to somethin', though, I just don't know what?...He ain't afraid neither!"

"We're all hitched up, Marshal, be on our way in a few minutes." Said Harold as he secured the door.

"Wait, Harold!" Said Billy, stopping him. "We could be followed again, you see anything, let us know."

"How many this time?"

"Just one,…and maybe none at all….I don't know."

"We'll watch for 'im, long as we got light to see by." He climbed up to the seat, and when the guard joined him. "Heeyaaaa!" He shouted, the coach shuddered once and began to move again.

*   *   *

Jim Stockwell took a sip of the hot coffee and put the cup down quickly. "Jesus, Cyrus, you put th' fire it's self in there, it's hot, man!" He looked toward the door then as John Gose came in.

"Hi, ya, Sheriff!" Welcomed Cyrus, and waved at him.

"Cyrus, Jim." He nodded, and came on into the room.

"Pour yourself a cup, John." Said Stockwell. "Be careful, it's hot!"

"Heard anything yet?" He asked, grabbing a cup and pouring his coffee.

"Don't really expect to, John. I'm here just in case."

Gose looked at the clock on the wall. "It's well after six o'clock, they'll roll in here in a couple a hours."

"I hope you're right!...You see th' Judge?"

"Earlier, yeah,...told 'im when I expected 'em in....Don't worry, he'll be here!"

"Listen up, fellas!" Said Cyrus. "One comin' in here." He began writing down the message and when done, sent his verification of receipt then turned around to give Stockwell the paper.

"They're in Honey Grove right now changing horses. Says all okay, to look for them soon."

"That's good news!" Said Gose. "Ought a be here by ten or so."

"That long, it's only twenty one miles?"

"Didn't you tell me they was bringin' horses back with 'em?"

"Yeah, two of 'em."

"Can't run that team a horses while towing horses behind it, Jim... Could injure 'em!...Takes time to trot a team a horses twenty miles."

"Yeah, your right, forgot about that, John.,,,I'm just too anxious!"

"You gonna let th' folks know?"

"I don't think so,...if it was bad news, I would."

"I agree." Nodded Gose. "Judge will want a full report from 'em tonight."

"I know, and that might not set too well with 'em!"

"He might want more'n that!" Said Curus.

"What do ya mean?" Asked Stockwell.

"Judge got four telegrams today,...one from Fort Stockton in New Mexico, another from Phoenix, Arizona, and one from Golden, Colorado!... They all want Hatcher turned over to them!"

"That was only three, Cyrus."

"Two was from New Mexico!...They want 'im for three murders, one was his own daddy when he was twelve years old."

"What's th' difference, he's gonna hang anyway?" Voiced Stockwell.

"Seems they put up most of the reward money, least that's what they're a saying."

"Well, If I know Bonner, they won't get 'im!" Said Gose.

"You're right about that!" Added Stockwell. "Let's go back to my office and wait, John!" He turned to Curus then. "Thanks, Cyrus, for stickin' with us on this thing.... You're a good man."

"My pleasure, Jim,…Doc's my friend, too!"

*   *   *

Connie was sitting in Doc's rocking chair on the front porch, where she had spent the last two late afternoons watching the Bonham Road. Willy sat on the floor at her feet, also watching between the road and his siblings as they played with Angela's jacks on the top steps of the old porch.

She looked up then, as Doc and his walking cane pushed open the screened door and came out, quickly getting up to help him sit down in the chair before moving to sit atop the porch railing and smile at him.

"Daughter," He said, placing the cane between his legs. "You are going to be sick in bed by the time William gets home pining like you are,…it ain't healthy!…Them boys,…at this very moment are no more than twenty or thirty miles from home, and they are headed this way!…I do wish you would accept that."

"Oh, Doc, I do, I know that!…I'm just anxious, that's all."

"Course you are, we all are!" He reached a hand out to ruffle up Willy's full head of hair then. "You're not worried, are ya, son?"

"Nope,…my daddy is the fastest gun in the whole world, I ain't worried at all!"

"Not worried, William!" Reprimanded Connie. "Ain't is not a word. Not a good one anyway."

"Sorry, mama….But he is, mama, nobody can hurt him!"

"It's okay, Daughter," Replied Doc. "At least William is his son's hero, that's better than it being someone else….And you know what else?…I think so, too!"

"All right, Gramps!" Laughed Willy.

"We do, too!" Voiced angela.

"Yeah," Chimed Christopher. "Me, too!"

"All right!" Said Connie, throwing up her hands in defeat.

"I'm serious, daughter,…those boys would be here already, but they happen to be bringing my horse home, too! Therefore, they will have to take it slow in that coach while leading Freckles behind it. It's dangerous for a horse to be pulled along too fast, because, being behind that coach, like that, he can't see the road in front of him,…it could cripple him."

"Okay, Doc, you win!" She laughed.

"I always do!...They'll be here before morning, you have my word on it."

"Well, I declare, Walter,...there you are!" Fussed Mattie as she came out. "You sneaked out on us, old man."

"I won't go far, old Darlin', I'd have to walk back, and right now, that's out of the question!"

She came on out to sit in the other rocker. "Whooo!" She complained. "There's hardly any breeze at all out here."

"If you think it's hot now, old Darlin',...just wait for July, and August!"

"Well I don't recall it being this hot last summer."

"I do!" He replied. "It's hot every summer,...just not this early....Going to be a cold winter, too,...wet, and cold!"

"Now, just how would you know that, you old coot?"

"I pay attention to the seasons!...Last hot summer we had this early on was back in sixty-nine, and you know what a winter that was....In more ways than one!" He reached to run his hand in Willy's hair again.

"Lord, I hope not!" She said, also looking at Willy. "We could hardly get out of the house."

"Can I bring you all a pitcher of cool lemonade?" Asked Mary Beth at the screened door. "It's already made."

Yeaaaa!" Yelled Christopher, and his response was in tune with Angela's.

"Guess that means yes!" Said Connie, getting up. "I'll come help you, Mary Beth." She hurried into the house.

"Think I'll go for my towel." Said Mattie, and also got up. "I'm sweating like a hog!" She moved in front of Willy and went into the house behind them.

"You really think Daddy's coming home tonight, Gramps?" Inquired Willy.

"Yes, I do....Jim Stockwell brought that telegraph wire to us two mornings ago, and they were just leaving Gainsville. That's only a hundred miles from here!...Yes, sir, they'll be home tonight, you mark my words."

"I'll sure be glad of that, Gramps!"

"I know you will, son!...What's this, I hear about you wanting to be a lawman, William?"

"Yes, sir!...I want to be just like my Uncle Rodney and Uncle Peter!...Bringing bad men to justice!...I want to be the fastest gun there is, too, just like my daddy!"

"I see!...Well, don't be disappointed if you're not ever as fast as your Father is, William....Because he is exceptional, there is nobody else quite like him anywhere, none that I have heard of anyway....No, if you learn as much as you can, be the best you can be, and be satisfied with that!...Then you'll make a good lawman some day. Just don't set a goal so high that you can't reach it, like trying to compete with your father when it comes to using a gun,...because you can't, son, nobody can!...You do understand all I'm telling you,...don't you?"

"I guess so, Gramps,...a little!"

"Well, you will, as you grow older!...Just listen to what your Father teaches you, and pay attention to what Rodney teaches, because he is an experienced lawman....Learn right from wrong when using a gun. Know when, and when not to use it!...Because it's not a pleasant thing to kill a man, William,...but for the right reasons, you can live with it!" He looked toward the screened door then.

"Okay, here come the women,...keep all this between us men, okay?"

"You got it, Gramps."

*   *   *

"Be dark in a bit, Mister Hatcher." Said Billy, watching him pick at his food. "Might ought a eat up, while you can see what you're doin."

Hatcher stared at him hatefully, and then angrily threw the plate of half-eaten food through the stagecoach window. "Guess you feel like a big tough man, hittin' me like that, don't ya?...There's laws against abusin' helpless prisoners!"

"Did I abuse you?" He looked at Rodney then. "Did I abuse this man, Rod?"

"I never saw it, if you did!" He looked at Hatcher. "What did he do, man?"

Hatcher glared at them for several seconds. "Fuck you both!...Fuckin' animals!"

"Now, just wait a minute, Hatcher!" Began Rodney. "Does using such vulgar language make you feel like a tough guy?...Does it somehow make it not your fault that you're headed for th' gallows?...Tell me, man, I'd like to know!"

"You kiss my ass! He glared at them hatefully for a time and then grinned slightly. "Think you could roll me a smoke, Marshal,...got th' makin's right here in my shirt?"

They both laughed. "you're unbelievable, man!" Laughed Rodney. "You got more gall than anybody I ever saw."

"Well,...can ya?"

"No," Said Billy. "Smokin' could ruin your health." They laughed again.

"You're a funny man, too,...ain't ya?" He blurted and then reached up to rub his jaw. "You nearly broke my jaw, you bastard!"

"You should watch what you say." Returned Rodney. "Now, shut up for a while,...give it a rest!...Ain't a language you can use that'll get you out a this!"

"Then give me some more pain medicine, my arm hurts?"

"I don't think so, I want you awake when we get there!"

He continued to stare at them for a minute and then shrugged. "I'm wanted in New Mexico, ya know,...you'll have to send me back!"

"We'll send your body back if they want?" Said Billy. "But you're gonna die in Paris, Texas!"

"I don't recall askin' you, asshole!" He sneered.

"Then don't talk at all, man!" Said Rodney angrily. "You don't, I'm gonna gag your ass!...Now shut the fuck up,...Jesus!" He watched as the gunman stared out through the window then looked at Billy. "We ought a be half way home by now,...want us to drop you off at Docs?"

"No,...I'm gonna see this thing through....We'll go home then!"

"Amen to that!"

"Amen to that!" Repeated Hatcher. "Shit fire, man!"

"Shut your ass up, man!" Yelled Rodney. "Next word out a your fuckin' mouth, I'm gonna put a gag in it!...Damn,...I'll be glad to get home!"

"Keep your calm, Rod." Grinned Billy. "You'll bust a gut!"

"Ain't doin' my arm any good neither!" He took the vial from his shirt pocket, and took a swallow.

"How about me, Marshal?" Asked the gunman.

"Hatcher, I told you t..."

"Okay, man, I'll shut up!" He said quickly then reached to grip his upper arm.

Rodney leaned his head back then and closed his eyes, while Billy sat and met Hatcher's cold, stare,...and when he heard Rodney snoreing.

"Can you hold a conversation, Wes,...without all that cussin'?"

Hatcher glared at him a while longer before nodding. "I guess so,...if I thought it would do me any good?"

"It won't,...but I'd like to know why you killed your old man?"

He stared out the window for a time then looked back as his bottom lip began to tremble then finally. "My old man was a filthy drunk, drunk every day,...and every day he'd beat my mother, me, too, when he could catch me!...Th' day I shot 'im, he broke her arm, and was choking her to death!...I shot 'im with his own gun,...six times!"

"Why didn't you go to th' Sheriff, Wes, Law would a been on your side?"

"I did go to 'im, couple a times. Told 'im what was happening!...He said he couldn't interfere in family squabbles!...He was th' second man I killed!"

"What about your mother?"

"I shot th' bastard too late, he had already crushed her windpipe....She died, too!"

"Thanks, for tellin' me, Wes....Now why did you shoot my Father?"

"Wasn't goin' to!...He hit me with a piece a wood, I shot 'im on instinct!...You got any more questions?"

"I guess not."

"Then, tell me who you are?"

Billy stared out of the window then. "I'm just a storekeeper, Wes, and before that, a farmer!...I just happen to be good with a gun."

"And you ain't no Marshal, are ya?"

"No,...Rod there deputizes me when he needs my help."

Hatcher shook his head in disbelief. "A God damn farmer beat me!... Why didn't you kill me, man?"

"I gave you my reasons!...." You'll just have to pay for what you done, now!"

"And I'm here right now, all because I shot your old man, Right?"

"That's why you're here!" He nodded. "You mean nothin' to me, otherwise!"

"I don't want a talk anymore, Man!" He leaned back and closed his eyes.

'I don't blame ya', he thought, still watching him. He knew how easy it must have been for him to go wrong, alone at twelve, scared, angry, with no thought of anything but running, getting as far away from there as fast as he could! He had been there once himself, torn between heartache, and hate! But he had never purposely goaded a man into a fight just to kill him. That is, except that one time, he thought, remembering Snake Mallory, and Jason Ryker. But that had ben strictly revenge on his part!...He was never like Wes Hatcher, but, he thought with regret, he had come close. Sighing, he stared out at the growing darkness and thought of the man that had followed them from Dodd City....What was he up to?

Maybe he would find out if he showed up in Paris. Maybe that would be where he would call him out?...In front of his friends, the people that knew him? One thing he knew, or thought he knew, was that the man had put on an air of confidence, both in Dodd City, and Honey Grove...He was a man that was sure of himself,...his attire reflected it!

'Well', he thought, leaning his head against the inside of the coach. 'What will be, will be', there was nothing to do but cross that bridge when he got to it!

"Eight miles to Paris, Marshal!" Yelled down the guard.

"Thank's Jim!...What time you make it to be?"

"Round nine o'clock, Marshal,...be there in a hour!"

"You awake, Rod?"

"I am now, yeah!" He sat up to look around, and then out of the window, seeing the pale, yellow light thrown off by the lanterns on either side of the coach, and then at the horizon. "See some lightening off there to th' south of us." He looked across at the dark form of Hatcher.

"He asleep?"

"Don't know!"

"Don't think I ever had a prisoner in custody like that man!..."

"Don't think I ever been in custody with anybody like you, neither!" Said the gunman in response.

"Good, you're awake!" Said Rodney. "We'll be at your new hotel in an hour or so, I want you to make a good appearance,...be on your best behavior and all that!"

"Anything for you, Marshal asshole!,...Sir!"

Billy reached over and patted Rodney on the leg. "Be over soon!"

"God, I hope so!"

"Come on, Marshal, I want to hear another, Amen to that!"

"Look, shit for brains!...You're about an inch and a half away from an ass kickin',...and you won't just have a knot on your head when I finish!...Now shut up! I'm damn tired of listenin' to your aimless babblin'!"

No one said much of anything for the next thirty, or forty-five minutes until Billy looked out at the lighted windows in Doc's house. "He's home, Rod, lights are all on....That house familiar to you, Wes?"

"You know it is!"

*   *   *

Judge Bonner pulled his pocket watch from his vest and stared at it before looking up at them. "It is going on ten o'clock, John, you sure about that arrival time?"

Gose looked at him and nodded. "It was just an estimate, Judge,...but I'm still fairly sure they'll be here at any time now."

"They might a stopped at Doc's on th' way in, too!" Said Stockwell.

"No,...they know how important this is!" Replied Bonner. "They would not do that!"

"What are you doin' about them four states that want Hatcher back, Judge?" Asked Gose, going to pour himself more coffee. "They got a leg to stand on?"

"Hell, no!...Mister Hatcher shot poor Sheriff Nooney down in the streets of Clarksville.....He tried to murder this town's most loved citizen. And from what those telegraph wires said, murdered two more men, maybe more before Billy Upshur caught up to him!...His crimes were committed in Texas, and he will be tried for those crimes in Texas! Therefore, he will be hung in Texas!

"We're all for that, Judge!" Agreed Stockwell.

"There's also been some talk about lynching, Judge." Continued Gose. "Have you heard anything?"

"No,...but I wouldn't!...But it will be up to the two of you, to see they don't get him!"

"We're aware of that, Judge!"

"Where you puttin' th' gallows, Judge?" Asked Stockwell.

"Where else, right in the middle of the square, boys. The people of Paris have a right to see justice done for Doc Bailey!...Question is, which one of you will serve as the hangman?"

"Why not both of us?" Chuckled Gose.

"That is up to you." He looked at his watch again and at that moment, they heard the audible, "WHOAA Horse, Whoaaa!"

"That's got a be them!" Said Gose, putting his cup down and hurrying down the corridor to the street door.

"You comin', Judge?" Asked Stockwell.

"I'll wait here!"

*   *   *

The stage rolled to a stop a few feet from the boardwalk, and when Harold set the brake, they both climbed down, Harold to open coach door, allowing Billy to step out and down, The guard to got to the rear of the coach and untie the horses.

"Harold," Said Billy. "Ain't enough words to thank you two, man,...I do appreciate what you did for us."

"It was our pleasure, Marshal. We did it as much for Doc, as we did for you." They moved aside then as Rodney got Hatcher to the door and as Gose came out, he quickly moved to take Hatcher's good arm just as he stepped down to the ground, forcing him up onto the boardwalk.

"Watch th' fuckin' arm, you asshole!" Blurted the gunman.

"He's all yours, John!" Said Rodney with relief.

Gose stared at him. "I can't thank you enough, Mister Taylor....Hey Jim!" He said, as Stockwell came out. "Escort your prisoner inside, if you will."

"You're so good to me, John!" He said, taking Hatcher's arm and pulling him through the door and then down the hallway.

"Good to see you both." Said Gose, shaking their hands.

Billy looked to see the guard leading the three horses to the hitchrail and tying them there. "Thanks, Jim!" He said, and waved at him.

"You got Doc's horse back, I see."

"Horse was a lot tougher than I thought, John, asshole rode 'im hard!" He turned back to get Harold's attention, and Rodney's. "We're gonna need a tarp, blanket, or somethin' to wrap them rifles in! Any ideas?"

"Got a small tarp in th' boot, Marshal." Said Harold, and went to open the heavy leather cover. "Got four, no, five holstered handguns back here, too!...Guess there weren't room enough on the floor for all of 'em."

"Bring 'em out, Harold,...and spread th' tarp on th' boardwalk here!" He opened the coach door and began bringing the confiscated weapons out to lay them on the boardwalk.

"Where did you come by such an arsenal, Billy?"

"Eleven rustlers, four bounty hunters, and Wes Hatcher!" Said Rodney. "I'll tell you about it later, John!...Billy, while you take care of this, I'll go get started on that report for the Judge."

"Good idea, Rod."

"Eleven rustlers, and four bounty hunters?" Asked Gose. "That's incredible!"

"Yeah, It weren't a very fun trip, John!" He placed all the holstered handguns to one side, and then placed the rifles on the tarp and rolled them up in it. By this time, Stockwell had come back to stand and watch them with an open mouth.

"Don't ask, Jim." Said Gose, "I'll explain later."

"Jim!" Said Billy, and reached to shake Stockwell's hand. "I appreciate th' loan of your horse, man, it's one a th' best horses I ever rode."

"Oh, that's not my horse, Billy, it's yours,...and you're welcome to it!"

"Say what?"

"It's your horse, I give 'im to ya!...I can't ride 'im! Tell you th' truth, I'm scared of 'im!...I tried to ride 'im several times, he let me saddle 'im okay, but he wouldn't let me mount 'im."

Billy looked at him in disbelief. "It's been three years, Jim, why didn't you say somethin'?"

"I didn't want to let on."

"Well, Jim, I appreciate it,...you don't know how much!"

"Believe me, you're welcome." He watched as Billy picked up the tarp and carried it to the black to tie it down behind the cantle.

"Rodney tells me you beat Wes Hatcher's draw, Billy, sure wish I could a seen it."

"Weren't too much, Jim." He grinned. "He was just overconfident, that's what happens when a man thinks he's th best there is at somethin'!...No man's ever th' best at anything, includin' me!"

"Somehow, I don't believe that!"

"Makes two of us!" Grinned Gose.

Billy had bent down to pick up a couple of the holstered pistols, but left them, and stood up to respond to their comments, and as he started to turn around and face them, he quickly scanned the empty square, and had a brief glimpse of a horse and rider beneath one of the pole lamps, and quickly had to look again,…but he was gone! He shook his head, not believing his eyes, and thinking that he was seeing things.

"What is it, Billy?"

"What?...Oh, nothin', Jim…. I thought I just saw a man on a horse at that street corner yonder."

"Grand street?" Stockwell and Gose both looked the square over before also shaking their heads.

"Guess it was nothin'…John, give me a hand with these gunbelts?" He bent and picked up four of the holstered guns, as did Gose, and started toward the horses. "Hang 'em on th' saddle horn, John, on Doc's horse, okay?" He carried his and hung them on the black's saddle, and they both went back for more of them. "Grab th' rest for me, Jim, put 'em on that spare horse."

When they were done, they all went back to join Harold and Jim on the boardwalk.

"You need us anymore, Marshal?"

"No, sir, but I want a thank you again." He shook their hands then watched as they climbed up to the seat and drove the stage away.

"Let's go inside, Billy." Said Stockwell. "Got coffee on."

"Be right in, Jim. I want a move th' horses up closer to your office here."

"I'll help ya, Billy." Said Gose.

"Say, John." He said as he took the black's reins, and then Freckles'. "You ever hear of a gunslinger that dresses fancy?...Maybe on your wanted posters, anything?" He looked back at the place where he was sure he saw the rider.

"Can't say I have, Billy, not right off hand….Why?"

"Man like that followed us,…I first saw 'im in Dodd City, and again in Honey Grove!...And I just thought I saw 'im again a minute ago!"

"I'll be damn!...Well, Billy, I'll sure check my wanted bills for 'im….Did he do anything?"

"No, nothin' like that!...But he sure gave th' impression that he could."

"What did he look like?"

"Close to six feet tall, black boots and pants, black vest and hat, a dark blue shirt, I think!...He was clean shaven, short black hair and mustach, gunbelt was black, too, and tied down."

"That's quite a description, Billy."

"Yeah, well he was ten feet away from me when I saw 'im watchin' me." He tied the horses' reins to the rail, as did Gose.

"I'll have my deputies keep their eyes open for 'im, might tell Jim, too."

"Well, it could be nothin', John. But if it is, it could have somethin' to do with our Mister Hatcher!...Let's go get that coffee, I need to get home pretty quick."

"Yeah, you got several people worried sick about you."

"Doc is home, ain't he?"

"Yes he is, getting around real good, too!" He walked ahead of Billy down the hallway, and into Jim's office.

"Billy Upshur!" Said Bonner, quickly coming to shake his hand. "My boy, my boy!...You pulled off a miracle again, the both of you!"

"How are ya, Judge?" Grinned Billy.

"I am great, now!" He laughed. "Most had a seizure waiting for you boys to get here!"

"He gonna have a trial?"

"Why, of course!...he's guilty as sin!...I'll arraign him tomorrow, have a hearing on Friday, to make it legal,...then I'll hang him on Monday!"

"Doc will want a be there, Judge,...and I want 'im to."

"I wouldn't want it any other way, my boy!"

"I appreciate it!...Uh,...Judge, when you get th' time, me and Rodney need to talk with you about somethin', if that's okay?"

"Fine, fine, dear boy, come see me any time next week!"

"We'll be goin' home after th' hangin', Judge, can we make it sooner?" He saw Rodney look up from the report then, and nod his agreement.

"That sounds important, William,...you boys in any trouble?"

"No, sir, Judge." Said Rodney, turning around in his chair. "It has to do with Business,...and th' law, I guess. But it is important!"

"All right then,...I will be in my office this Saturday morning, say,...ten o'clock, is that good for you?"

"Yes, sir, it is." Said Rodney, seeing Billy nod.

"Ten o'clock, it is then."

"Come on, Billy." Said Rodney. "Do your report, so we can get to Doc's, I can't wait to see my girls."

"Uh, Rodney, your wife is at th' ranch." Said Stockwell. "Went out there a couple days ago."

"Thanks, Jim,...I'll need a horse, then."

"Take th' spare horse, Rod!" Said Billy, pulling a chair up to the desk.

"Yeah, forgot about that one. I will,...now, let's get this done!"

"I will need a day by day account of it, William." Said Bonner. "Leave nothing out, my boy."

It was near midnight when they finished the reports to Bonner's satisfaction, and walking out to the horses, Rodney stopped him at the hitchrail.

"When did you decide to talk to th' Judge, Billy?"

"At that minute, I guess,...I don't know, it just came out!"

"Well, I think it's th' best thing to do!" He said, pulling the reins free.

"Tighten them cinches, Rod, you ain't gonna make it far?" He lifted the black's stirrup to do the same, and then Doc's horse as Rodney mounted.

"Keep your eyes open, Rod." He said, going to pull himself into the saddle. "I think our Mister Dapper followed us in."

"Man from Honey Grove?...How do ya know?"

"I'm almost sure I saw 'im tonight, right under that street lamp off yonder. I got a glimpse of 'im when I was loading these guns,...but when I looked again, he was gone!"

"Sure thing!...I'll put these guns in th' wagon tonight."

"Good,...Put 'em in th' gold bin. I'll bring these when we start home,... tell th' folks hello."

"You got it!" He reined the horse around, and galloped away.

He looked once more at the place where he saw the rider, and then mounted to lead Freckles back the way they had come in.

                    *   *   *

Judge Bonner was at his desk when they knocked and looking up, saw them through the glasss-panelled door, and waved them in.

"Right on time, boys!" He laughed, getting up to come around the desk and shake their hands. "What did you think of the hearing yesterday?" He asked, going to move an extra chair up beside his desk.

"Okay, I guess." Replied Billy as he sat down. "Doc seemed satisfied."

"Who was the man arguing jurisdiction, Judge? Inquired Rodney.

"That," He said, sitting down. "Was the honorable, Kenneth J. Brazeal, attorney at law!...Seems he was hired, by mail, to represent Fort Stockton, New Mexico's rights to Wes Hatcher!" He looked at them and smiled.

"Of course," He continued. "They don't have any rights, where that killer is concerned....But of course, they will try again come Monday morning of which, afterward, I will hang Mister Hatcher until he is dead!... What did you think of the gallows out there,...Befitting for such as Mister Hatcher, wouldn't you say?"

"Works for me." Nodded Billy.

"Okay then," He said, still smiling at them. "What can I do for you?"

"Well, Judge," Began Rodney. "Do you recall when Billy and me bought our mountain from the Choctaw?"

"Seems I do, I believe it was back in seventy-one?"

"Seventy-two,...anyway, what nobody knew at the time, and still don't,...is that we have a gold mine in that mountain,...the mountain is full of it!"

"Good Lord, boys!" He reached up to rub his chin. "Well, isn't that a good thing,...the stuff men dream about?...how did you find it?"

"We didn't, th' Spaniards did!"

"I'll be damned!..., Would I be right to assume that,...that's where a great deal of our rebuilding fund originated from?"

"Yes, sir, it is!" Returned Rodney. "Anyway, this past May, I had orders to transport escaped prisoners back to Fort Smith, Arkansas, so we took some of that gold with us to Shreveport to trade for cash money....And that was the first we heard about th' new Government tax! The Banker there said we'd have to file a claim if we had a mine, so that the Government could get their share of taxes from it....We didn't tell 'im we had a mine, we told 'im it was a years worth of panning creeks."

"Then why not file a claim,...it's on your property, it's your mine?"

"Point is this, Judge," Said Billy. "When th' Choctaw sold us th' mountain and property, we didn't tell th' Chief we was usin' Choctaw gold to pay 'im with, or that it came from th' mountain!...We file a claim on it now, and they find out about it, there just might be a problem!"

"In other words, you bought the property under false pretenses!" He looked at them for a minute. "Do you have the deed with you, or a bill of sale?"

"It's all at th' mountain, Judge." Shrugged Rodney.

"Then why don't you bring it to me on your next visit to Paris,...I'll look it over, and If I find any discrepancies, we can go from there?...But by law, once you buy a property, and you have a clear deed to such property, and a bill of sale for that property, false pretense or not, it is still binding!...But, since the Federal Government, and the Choctaw Nation are both involved here, and since we do not know the particulars of that relationship, it will take some looking into before we do anything rash."

"We will bring you th' Paperwork, Judge." Said Billy. "But, if you do find a big problem,...there's somethin' else you should know about?" He looked at Rodney for approval and saw him nod. "Nobody else knows about this neither"

Bonner smiled at them. "This is sounding more and more intriguing as we go along!...What might that be, William?"

"Judge," Said Rodney. "Have you ever read anything, or seen anything, any evidence at all that the Aztec Indians were ever anywhere near this part of th' country?"

"All the history I've read, says no!...Are you saying that history is wrong?"

"That's exactly what we're sayin'." He nodded. "History is very wrong!"

"And your evidence of this, is what?"

"Judge," Said Billy. "We made a promise to protect that secret....So, let's just say, you'll need to see it, to believe it!"

"Wealth, you never thought to even dream about, Judge!" Said Rodney.

"Weapons, artifacts, gold, the whole thing." Said Billy. "What we was wanting to know, Judge, was,...if there is a problem with us stakin' legal claim to our mine, and if th' Government is involved....Maybe, turnin' over that Aztec treasure could persuade them to rule in our favor,...if it came down to it!"

"My God, boys!" He exclaimed, shaking his head. "I just don't know!"

"We don't want a bunch a bureaucrats bringin' in a hundred historians and soldiers to screw up our mountain, either!" Said Billy. "It has to stay like it is."

"In other words, the mountain is not what it seems from the outside?"

"No, sir, it ain't!" Said Billy.

Bonner leaned back in his spring-loaded chair. "Boys,...I have been a lawman for nearly thirty years. I would not break my oath to defend, and uphold the constitution of these United States for all the treasure in the world!...But,...I would give anything just to see that evidence up close!...If it is what you say it is, and I do believe you!...It would rock history's foundation, for one thing,...and for another, it would have to be handled delicately where the Government is concerned."

"So, let us do this!...You bring me all your transaction papers, and I'll go through them in depth....If I find a discrepancy, then we will discuss that other option you mentioned....If I find none at all, then I see no reason on earth why anybody should ever know that the Aztec was here!"

"Comes down to it," He continued, "I can't see any reason for anybody to know about your gold mine. Gold is a legal tender, as it stands right now!...You can spend it anywhere just like money. Just know what you are doing when using it in lieu of cash money. Spend it a little at a time!" He got up and went to the hutch and opened the glass doors.

"This is an assayer's gold scale, boys,...it is yours!" He took a black valise from a corner and brought it to them, placing the scale inside. "Weigh the gold before you spend it, otherwise you could be cheated."

"Thank you, Judge." Said Rodney.

"You have to promise me something, boys." He said. "After all this is settled to your satisfaction, you will allow me to see this Aztec evidence?"

"You have a deal, Judge!" Said Billy, reaching across to shake his hand,... and that's when they heard the knock at the door, causing all three to look.

"Are we done here, boys?" And when they nodded, he waved Stockwell in.

"Sorry to butt in, Judge, but I saw them ride in." He looked down at Billy then. "That man you asked about th' other night, he's in th' City Saloon right now!"

"You see 'im?"

Yeah, Ben spotted 'im, and came for me. Don't know if it's th' same one, but he's a stranger to Paris, and he's dressed all in black, like you said."

"Thanks, Jim?...Think you could spare Ben to keep an eye on 'im, least till after th' hangin'?"

"I can do that, Billy.'"" He nodded. "Sorry for th' intrusion, Judge." He left then, leaving Bonner to rub his chin again.

"Who is this man, William?"

"Never saw 'im before, till a few days ago, Judge. First time was in Dodd City, then in Honey Grove, and here Thursday night again....It could have somethin' to do with Hatcher, but I don't know!"

"What do you plan to do?"

"I can't do anything, Judge, the man ain't done nothing,' that I know of!...And it's Jim's problem if he does....But, if he tries to free Hatcher, he'll become my problem!"

"Our problem!" Said Rodney, getting to his feet. "Thanks for your time, Judge, I hope we did the right thing?"

"You did!...Bring me that paperwork!"

"Be a couple a weeks, Judge." Said Billy.

"That'll be fine!...And not to worry, boys. It's against the law for a Judge to violate the Attorney-Client priviledge, too."

"Thanks!" They shook hands again, and left.

Once on the boardwalk, they stopped to look at the hot, bustling square.

"You feel better about this, Billy?"

"I don't know, Rod, it's been a kept secret for so long!...Th' Judge ain't never gave me reason to doubt his honesty,...but gold has a way of drivin' some men to do anything!...But I guess we'll go along with 'im, see what happens."

"I think so, too!...What about this mysterious stranger now, we gonna wait till he starts somethin', maybe kills somebody?"

"Rod, I don't know!" He sighed heavily then. "I'm tired, I know that!...But I would like to know what he's up to! I'm ready for all this business to be done with."

"Wouldn't do any harm, just askin' th' man his business?...He'll either tell us, or he won't?"

"He could shoot us, too!...You think about that?"

"I promised you, I wouldn't, remember?...I'm not anxious for him to start shootin' at that hanging, neither, our folks will be there!"

"Makes two of us,...let's go!" He stepped off the boardwalk into the dirt of the square, and as Rodney stepped down, walked with him across the bustling square to look up at the brand new gallows in passing, and speaking to the many who knew them both.

"Guess we're right popular these days." Commented Billy, after thanking the few that stopped and congratulated them.

"We do seem to be!" Reflected Rodney…. "Wish they knew what we had to go through, they wouldn't be so happy about it!"

"Here we go!" Said Billy as they stepped up to the boardwalk, and moved to look over the swinging doors.

"Dark in there, you see 'im, Billy?" The saloon was semi-crowded, with several men standing at the bar. About half of the tables accommodated from one, to as many as four men as they played cards. "I can barely see anybody in all that smoke and darkness."

"He's at th' far end of th' bar!" Said Billy. "All by his lonesome."

"Well, let's do it!" Said Rodney, and pushed inside to stop and once again look over the room as Billy passed him.

"Hey, Marshal!" Yelled a loud voice from somewhere in the room. "Come on over, I'll buy you a drink!" He waved a hand at the voice and followed Billy along the bar to nod at Stockwell's deputy in passing.

Billy's eyes never left the face of the strange man, but he knew that the man had been watching them from the time they entered. He came to within a few feet of him and leaned on the bar, with Rodney doing the same.

"What can I get you, Marshal?" Asked the burly bartender, wiping the counter with a wet rag.

"Cool beer!" Nodded Rodney.

"And for you, Mister Upshur?"

"Th' same!" Said Billy, turning to meet the dark eyes of the stranger. "What's on your mind, friend?…Why did you follow us in the other night?"

"Did I follow you?" He asked.

"Seein' as you're here, I'd say so!"…What's your business here?"

"My own, mostly!" He returned.

"What's Wes Hatcher to you?"

"Never heard of the man."

"Okay, do you know me?"

"I know what you are!"

"That why you followed us?"

The man smiled at him then, and tossed off the shot-glass of whiskey. "Maybe!" He said, placing the glass on the bar. "Guess I wanted to see what you were made of?...Guess I wanted to see someplace I've never been."

"What's your intention, man?"

"I'll leave that up to you."

"You do, you'll leave town unhappy!...What's your name, anyway?"

"What's yours?"

"Names, Bill Upshur!...Now, who are you?"

"I think I'll keep that to myself for a while."

"Then you'd best leave town!" Said Rodney, leaning over the bar to look at him. "We run a peaceful town here, we don't need any gunslingers!"

"Does that include Mister Bill Upshur here?"

"Billy's a lawman, he keeps th' peace here."

"But that is not all he is." Returned the man. "But of course, you know that already!"

"I know somethin' else, too,...you call 'im out, he'll kill you!...Now do yourself a favor and get out a Paris!...You don't, you start anything at all, I'll arrest ya!"

"Don't get your unions in a knot, Marshal,...I don't plan on starting anything."

"Then what are your plans?" Asked Billy.

"No plans,...I just have a question, or two that I need answered....And I have to admit, sometimes I have to kill a man to get them answered....But I do get them!"

"Then I think you'd better leave, right now!" Said Rodney, pushing away from the bar.

"Let it go, Rod!" He said, moving in front of him. "He's goading you, calm down." They heard chairs scraping back as men moved out of a possible line of fire. Those men at the bar all quickly moved farther out into the room, all except Ben, he left the saloon at a run.

"Mister!" Said Rodney thinly. "You'd better be damn sure you're fast enough to get us both, you don't, I'll blow your damn head off!"

"He gets mad, don't he?" Grinned the gunman, shaking his head. "Do you get mad, Bill Upshur?"

"No, sir,...and if you go for that gun, I'll kill ya!"

"That happens to be one of my questions, Bill, how did you know that?"

"I've got your answer, too!" Said Billy, slowly reaching down to unlatch the Colt Pistol. "Better unlatch yours, you might not get your answer!"

The man slowly reached down, and with his thumb, pushed the loop from the gun's hammer, and in the same instant, made his draw, only to freeze before the gun was in line to fire, finding himself staring down the muzzle of Billy's Pistol. He smiled then, and slowly returned his gun to the holster.

"That th' answer you wanted?" Asked Billy.

"That's it!" He said, and reached his hat from the counter top. "I'll be leaving your fair city now." He said, and then looked at Rodney. "Unless you have other ideas, Marshal?"

"Just keep goin', and don't come back!"

He looked back at Billy then, and then at the unwavering muzzle of the gun in his hand. "Don't believe I have ever seen anybody quite that fast, Bill,...but I had to know!"

"Why?"

"You challenged me back when you was watering your horses, remember?...If you hadn't beat me, Bill, I would have killed you both!,,,So why didn't you?"

"I ain't no killer, till I have to be!...You weren't no threat!"

"Ohhh, that hurts!...You sure know how to damage a man's pride, Bill!"

"Don't come back to Paris!" Warned Billy.

"Don't believe I will, Bill Upshur!" He smiled, and then moved past him to stop and nod at Rodney. "Marshal,...adios!" He walked to the door and left.

Rodney pulled his gun and followed him to the swinging doors, watching as he mounted his horse and galloped down the Bonham Road. Then cursing came back down the bar amid whistles, and yells of congratulations as the men all converged on them with backslaps, and hoorahs.

"What in holy hell was this all about, Billy?"

"I ain't got a clue, Rod,...beats hell out a me!" He holstered the pistol then, just as Stockwell and Ben burst through the doors with drawn guns.

"You two okay?" He blurted. "Where's th' gunman?"

"He's gone, Jim." Said Rodney. "He drew on Billy, or tried to!"

"You let 'im walk away?"

"He didn't do anything, Jim. Billy beat 'im badly....He quit and left town." Rodney grinned then. "Come on, Jim, I'll buy you two a drink, everything's okay."

"Okay,…but who th' hell was he, anyway?"

"John Wesley Hardin." Said the bartender loudly. "Seen 'im pull that same trick on several would be gunslingers before!…Drinks are on me, Marshal!…Hardin ain't never been beat before, and it was a sight to behold!"

"Yeah!" Yelled one of the men at the bar. "He never met Bill Upshur before!" That brought a roar of laughter from everyone in the large room, and caused Billy to shake his head in disgust.

"Let's get out a here, Rod!" He said, and they elbowed their way to the door, and out onto the boardwalk.

"You okay, Billy?"

He nodded. "I didn't aim for that to happen, is all!…I ain't no gunfighter,…all this is gonna do, is bring more guns to Paris, once that crowd in there gets through braggin' on me!"

"We'll be long gone if that happens, Billy,…besides, Hardin won't be spreading th' word, that's for sure!"

"Ya know, Rod,…I've heard a Wes Hardin a hundred times th' last few years, like he was some kind a legend!…Well,…I guess he got his answer, hell of a way to get it though."

"Well, if that was him, I'd a thought he'd a been a lot faster!…Hell, I think I could a beat 'im!"

"Oh, no, Rod….Never start thinkin' like that!…It'll get ya killed."

"Yeah, I know that!…But if you hadn't beat 'im, we'd both be dead now!…How'd you know he'd pull when he did?"

"First off, he is faster than that, Rod,…he just didn't think he had to be any faster to beat me! Besides,…a gunfighter don't forget to unlatch his gun, especially in a saloon. It was on purpose to throw me off,…his way a playin' his game, I guess."

"To give 'im an edge?"

"Naw,…I don't think he needed one….He just underestimated me."

"Ya got that right!…At any rate, I guess Mister Wes Hardin just got a taste a that Hard Justice, you talked about!"

"Getting justice is sometimes always hard, Rod, you know that!" He adjusted his hat and stepped down into the heat of the sun.

"Amen to that!" Grunted Rodney, and stepped down beside him.

CHAPTER ELEVEN

"Ohh, Billy!" Winced Connie as Doc pulled the bandage away from the red, puffy wound. "That looks awfully bad to me!"

"It looks worse than it is, daughter." Continued Doc as he did his prodding and mashing on the wound.

"Well, just how bad is it, Doc, because it feels fine?" He looked from Connie's frowning face to Doc's stern-faced gaze. "Doc,...you see somethin' wrong?"

"Well, William,...aside from the fact, that you went too long, too often with dirty bandages, it's not that bad!...Like I told daughter, it looks worse than it is. How does it feel when I mash on it?"

"Feels all right,...it only hurts some when I move my arm too quick!"

"Figured as much." Nodded Doc as he sat down again at the breakfast table. "It could hurt for a while yet before it heals proper, and it could hurt some from now on, too,...it's hard to tell."

"Well, if it's okay, Walter, let him put his shirt on, breakfast table is not the place for that, it looks terrible!"

"Sorry, Mama." Said Billy and reached for his shirt.

"Are you sure it's all right, Doc?" Asked Connie again.

"Oh, yeah, daughter,...wound's healed completely. Puffiness is due to proud flesh buildup, caused by using that arm too soon after being shot, he's all right!" He reached to help Billy pull the shirt back on.

"You're not going to bandage it?" Asked Connie.

"No need, daughter,...it's all healed."

"Thanks, Doc." Grinned Billy as he buttoned his shirt.

"Well, it's nigh on to nine oclock!" Reminded Mattie as she poured more coffee around.

"Mrs. Bailey!" Fussed Mary Beth. "That's my job, dear lady, you sit down with family, I'll pour your coffee."

"Oh, fiddlesticks, Mary Beth!" She argued, but then sat down to allow the younger woman to cater to her. "You'll make an invalid out of me yet."

"Oh no, You have earned your rest, dear lady,…enjoy."

"What time do we have to leave, William?"

"Pretty close to right now, Doc.…Finish your coffee, we got time."

"Walter, are you sure you're up to this?" Asked Mattie with concern. "I worry about you."

"I have seen a few dozen hangings in my time, old darlin',…pronounced them dead, too,…as you well know!…I'm fine, my dear. Although, I admit, I'm not as full of hate for Mister Hatcher as I was. In fact, I feel a mite sorry for him now, him being so young and all!…Such a waste!"

"I'll keep an eye on 'im, Mama." Said Billy, grinning at them both. "But I am glad you and Copnnie decided not to go, that's no place for a lady, and especially not for kids!"

"According to Jim, there's a lot a strangers in town." Said Doc, placing his cup down, "Think there could be any trouble, son?"

"There's always a chance for that, Doc.…Jim and John Gose have enough men between them to stop any trouble."

"Well, what if that,…Wes Hardin gunman comes back, Billy,…you don't even know for sure that he left town?"

"He's gone, honey." He soothed, pulling her down for a kiss.

"Well, how do you know?" She argued, pulling away from him.

"I know the kind a man he is, honey.…He's gone!"

"Well,…okay.…But I don't think our oldest son should be a witness to this hanging!…I don't want him to go!"

"I agree, honey, I've already told 'im he's not going."

"Thank you."

He smiled at her then looked at Doc. "You ready, Willy ought a have th' buggy hitched up by now?"

"I am!" He replied, getting to his feet and moving around the table to hug Mattie against him.

Grinning, Billy got up and pulled Connie to him in a hug. "We ought a be back by noon, or after." He said, and kissed her on the mouth. "We'll be goin' to pick up Rod, and Melissa first thing tomorrow, and we still got a load th' wagon when we get there, so ma,......"

"I know, I know, this isn't my first trip, you know!"

"I know, guess I'm a mite anxious, honey, we been gone a while."

"I'm anxious too." She smiled and walked with him through the house and out onto the porch where he kissed her again, and then went down the steps and across the yard to help Doc climb into the buggy.

*   *   *

They waved at the women and kids, and Billy slapped the lines on the backs of the horses, urging them to a trot along the road into town, almost a half mile away. He watched the older man's wrinkled profile for a time before speaking.

"You okay, Doc,...you sure you're up to this?"

"Course I'm sure!...I just don't like hangings, that's all, ...never did! It's an agonizing way to die, William....If it don't break your neck right away, you spend the next several minutes choking to death,...and that's agony!...I'm okay, and Hatcher deserves to die for the things he done. It's just a shame he's so young!"

"His old man was a son of a bitch, Doc, always drunk, always beating him and his mother....He killed 'im one day while he was choking her, she died anyway.

"He tell you all that?"

"On th' way back, yeah."

"Probably why he's like he is then,...kid never knew any other way!"

That's about th' size of it!"

"I still don't like it!"

"We can turn back."

"You know I can't do that, William, and don't think I don't know why the town's doin' this, too....It's all for me, they think they owe me."

"They love ya, Doc!...You are Paris, Texas....You helped build it."

"That may be, but I still don't like hangings!"

"It appears you're the only one, though, th' town's full!" He slowed the team to a walk as they entered the business end of town, and that's when they began experiencing random slaps on the back and endearing remarks to

Doc. Billy kept the team at a walk through the milling crowd until he saw the rider rein his horse toward them.

"Rod made it in!...Mornin', Rod!" He said, as his best friend and cohort pulled his horse alongside the buggy.

"Mornin', Billy, Doc….News of th' hanging got around fast didn't it, town's full a strangers."

"We noticed that ourselves….Jim expectin' any trouble?"

"Ain't seen 'im yet, don't know….Did see Bob when I rode in, said th' Judge roped off an area around th' gallows. Got chairs set out for us."

"Now, why did that old blowhard do that?" Blurted Doc.

"You mean a lot to this town, Doc, like it, or not!" Said Billy.

"There's Bob now, Billy." Said Rodney. "Wants us to tie up here, I guess." He urged his horse ahead of them and dismounted as they stopped at the hitchrail.

"Good to see you, Doc." Laughed the deputy, coming alongside to help the older man out of the buggy…. "You, too, Billy!"

"Where'd all these people come from, Bob?" Queried Doc, as he looked up the congested boardwalk and then the crowded street.

"Don't know, Doc, just here for th' hangin', I guess. Somethin' like this always draws a crowd!"

"Where to, from here?" Asked Billy, also watching the crowd.

"Town square, come on, Judge Bonner sent me out to meet ya, we got front row seats,…he had chairs put out for us." He led the way off the boardwalk and into the street where he cleared the way through the mob of congestion to finally work their way almost to the foot of the gallows where they were met by Jim Stockwell, and three other deputies.

Stockwell shook hands with them before seating them, and sending a man to tell the Judge they were ready. He then took his seat next to Rodney as he surveyed the mob of people around the gallows.

"I recognize about one face out of every five men here, Jim." He said, turning back to look at him. "How's it feel to ya?"

"You mean th' people, noise, or what, Rodney?"

"Th' mood of th' crowd, Jim,…how's it feel to ya, any tension in th' air, any tension in you?...You expectin' any trouble?"

"Oh,…no, Rodney, I don't expect any trouble at all. We screened every man that's here on th' square, we disarmed 'em, put all their weapons in a spring-wagon, and I've got Lee guardin' 'em!...Why, you're not expectin' any trouble,...are ya?"

"With a crowd like this, in all this heat,...ya never know, Jim....You may have disarmed th' men on th' square here, but what about those not on th' square?" He looked at Jim again.

"If anything happens here, Jim, it won't come from a handgun!...I was you, I'd place deputies up high somewhere, rooftops maybe, a place where they can keep an eye on things."

Stockwell reached and scratched his jaw, which was his way of facing indecision, and stared back out over the crowd while he thought about it.

"You don't have to do a thing, Jim." Said Rodney. "You're th' Marshal, not me,...but somethin' don't feel right about all this! Maybe it's nothing, I don't know."

"You've taught me a lot over th' years, Rodney." He looked back at him as he spoke. "Guess I'm still learnin'" He got up to hurry across the way and converse with Bob, sending him and three other deputies back through the crowd again.

"Well," He said, coming back to sit down. "That's done, Rodney, thanks."

"My pleasure, Jim." He said, looking past him at the welldressed man seated across the way from them. "Who's that man over there, Jim, never seen 'im before?"

"Name's Riggs, U. S. Marshal out of Arkansas. Here to report th' proceedings, I guess, witness th' hanging....He was here a time or two, two, three years ago. Nice enough guy."

"Well, maybe Hatcher's a lot worse than we thought he was!" Chuckled Doc, as he had been listening in on their conversation. "Can't hang him more than once, though."

"Might be here to arrest th' Judge, too!" Grinned Billy.

"What??" Laughed Stockwell. "Don't go sayin' things like that, Billy,... what makes you say that, anyway?"

"Couple of other states wanted Hatcher turned over to them, claiming priority....Th' Judge told 'em to go to hell!"

"I remember that now!...But,...they couldn't arrest a Federal Judge,... could they?"

"Federal Judge ain't above th' law, Jim." Said Rodney. "But I doubt that's why he's here. Likely makin' sure it's carried out legally."

"Yeah, that's got a be it!" Grinned Stockwell. "But I never heard of anything like that before."

"Makes two of us,...never had occasion to." He looked around at the throng of onlookers again, seeing them begin to move aside, with many hecklers cursing Hatcher's name in the background. "Bringing Mister Hatcher now, I reckon."

Stockwell got to his feet to watch as a lane opened up through the crowd, allowing the heavily armed deputies to lead the way to the gallows steps, and standing guard there until John Gose and his deputy escorted the shaggy, yellow haired Wesley Hatcher across the roped-off area of ground and up the gallows steps to the platform above, with Judge Bonner climbing the steps behind them.

Billy watched Hatcher's face as he was turned to face forward, and as their eyes met, he was sure he would see the immature side of the condemned teen break through the tough outer shell of the killer. But Hatcher never broke, never changed his expression, only stared back at him with the same hostility he had shown before.

"You all right, William?" Asked Doc, placing a hand on his arm.

"I'm okay, Doc." He nodded then looked at the old man's tired features and grinned. "I was just watchin' Hatcher's face up there. Guess I was hopin' to see a little remorse, a little fear, maybe, somethin',...I don't know!"

"He's a little too far gone for that, son....Probably lived with fear all those years, right up to the point of killing his father!...Come on, son, help me up, old windbag's about to speak!" He waited for Billy to get up, and then Rodney before allowing them to help him to his feet.

"Here comes th' Parson." Said Rodney, and they all four watched him climb the steps and take his place beside Hatcher.

Until now, the noise in the square had almost been constant, but when Judge Bonner took the paper from his inside coat pocket and unfolded it, most everyone in the square fell silent as he read the transcript of the death sentence. When he was done, he refolded the paper and put it away, nodded at John Gose and came back down the steps to stand with Doctor Snyder, both watching as Gose placed the black, cotton hood over Hatcher's head, and then the noose,...and that act alone brought a roar of approval, hand-clapping, and rebel yells, along with several outbursts of unrepeatable cursing for dessert.

Gose moved aside to allow the Parson his moment of prayer, and as he finished and moved aside, and just as Gose reached for the release-lever, the thunderous crack of rifle fire drowned the stillness, causing women to scream, men to yell, and all to fall to the hot, hard ground of the square. The instant the rifle spoke, Wes Hatcher grunted loudly and if not for the noose around his neck, would have been bodily thrown from the gallows.

The crowd, and everyone at the gallows experienced several moments of sudden, unexpected shock before slowly regaining their feet, all looking toward the rooftops in anticipation of more gunfire.

Several long seconds passed before Judge Bonner and Snyder quickly climbed the steps to squat beside Gose, who had already removed the hood and rope from the killer's head.

"Through the heart, Judge." Said Gose, moving aside to allow Doctor Snyder to legally pronounce him dead. "He is dead, Judge." He pulled his pocket watch and looked at it. "Right on time, too!"

"All right!" Said Bonner savagely, and then stomped to the gallow's handrail to look out over the still-disbelieving crowd for several long seconds before speaking.

"My friends!" He said loudly, to be heard across the square, and stopping those people who had already started for home. "Justice was not served here today!...And I want that piss-poor excuse for a man that fired that shot,... and I want him quick! Because he not only committed murder here today, he put a lot of you in jeopardy as well....He robbed all of us of that justice. There was not a god-fearing one of us here today that did not want to put a bullet into Mister Wes Hatcher, I know I did!...But we didn't, and we know why!" He looked down at them again and nodded.

"I do not want to believe this, or even to think it,...but I believe there could be one, or more of you who might know who fired that shot. If I am right, friend or not,...if any one of you knows who did this, and you do not come forward, I will be hard put not to hang you right along with him,... right here on this very gallows!...We will find this cowardly killer, and if there is one, the person who helped him. This is a black mark on our great city!" He glared down at them for another minute then came down the steps with Gose and snyder to stop in front of Stockwell.

"Jim," He said, gripping both lawmen's arms. "I want that shooter caught and brought before me, post haste!...Nothing else matters, am I clear?" He came on to stand in front of Doc then.

"Something like this is a slap to all our faces, Doc, but to you, especially because of what you went through, and to me, because I let you down!...You as well, Rodney Taylor, and especially you Bill Upshur, for your sacrifice. You two men went through hell bringing him back so we could hang him. I am both humbled, and sorry, but I will bring closure to us all, I promise that!" He shook their hands, and as Marshal Riggs approached, joined him to watch as Hatcher's body was removed.

"I do believe old windbag is mad!" Said Doc, taking both their arms.

"How about you, Doc?" Asked Billy. "You mad?"

"Foot, no, I ain't mad, he's dead, ain't he?...I never liked hangings anyway."

"Whoever shot him was a damn good shot! Said Rodney, looking at Billy. "Where do you think it came from, one a th' north side buildings,... roof maybe?"

"That would be my guess." He said, looking toward the Courthouse. "Courthouse would make a good spot."

"Well it's not our problem, anyway, boys, take me home, I'm hungry!"

"You got it, Doc." Laughed Billy, still watching the Courthouse. "But that would add insult to injury, wouldn't it!"

Rodney saw him looking that way, and nodded. "Shooter hidin' in th' Courthouse, I'd say so."

"Hey, Billy, Rodney!" Called out Stockwell, stopping them as he came forward. "Got a question for ya,...well, for both of ya."

"Sure thing, Jim." Nodded Billy. "What is it?"

"Well, you all heard th' Judge, he wants this killer caught!...What I would like, is your thoughts on it!...Any ideas at all, I got a start somewhere?"

"I wish I did, Jim." Said Rodney. "We both believe the shot might a come from th' roof a th' Courthouse, though." He looked at Billy then. "Any ideas, Billy?"

"Maybe," He looked out at the dispersing crowd for a minute before looking back. "I been thinkin' about it, Jim. This weren't done by somebody livin' a long ways off, be too far to come just for revenge, in so short a time!... It weren't sanctioned by no other law enforcement neither, they wanted to hang 'im, too!...And to me, that leaves just plain old revenge....Most of his killings happened a long ways from here, so you can rule out somebody from those places and, far as I know,...he only killed one man that lived anywhere close to here!...And that's where I'd start lookin'!"

Stockwell stared at him, and then Rodney in obvious confusion.

"Think about it, Jim." Said Rodney. "Sheriff Nooney died from his wounds some three weeks ago."

Stockwell's eyes widened. "Nooney's own son,...you think it was him?"

"We're not thinkin' anything like that!" Said Billy. "But that's where I'd start lookin', it was me!...Like you said, got a start somewhere."

"It might, or might not be young Nooney, Jim," Added Rodney. "But Billy's right, th' answer's gonna be in Clarksville, and everybody there liked Sheriff Nooney! So, if th' boy is guilty, you'll have to prove it on your own, because nobody there's gonna give 'im up."

"Thanks, Rodney, and you're right!...I like young Nooney too." He sighed deeply then nodded. "I do appreciate it, Rodney, you too, Billy,...I might never a made th' connection with Nooney."

"Well, keep an open mind about it, Jim, and good luck to you and John." Said Rodney. "We're leaving for home in the morning, by th' way!"

"I heard ya was,...have a safe trip." He shook their hand again then hurriedly turned away to go join Gose and Judge Bonner, who were in deep conversation with Marshal Riggs near the gallows steps.

"Well," Sighed Rodney. "I guess some a that hard justice is about to be learned right here in Paris, Billy."

"What's that?...I didn't know there was but one kind of justice." Mused Doc as they walked. "What's the hard kind?"

"The kind you have to work for, Doc." Grinned Billy. "Or suffer for,...at any rate,...it's th' kind that don't come easy!"

"Amen to that!" Laughed Rodney.

END

Printed in the United States
by Baker & Taylor Publisher Services